Sweet
OBSESSION

Sweet Obsession

A Sweetbriar Romance Novel

DANIKA ROSE LYNN

Sugar, Spice, & Words that Entice

Copyright © 2024 Danika Rose Lynn.

All rights reserved. No part of this publication may be reproduced, distributed, or transmitted in any form or by any means, including photocopying, recording, or other electronic or mechanical methods, without the prior written permission of the publisher, except as permitted by U.S. copyright law.

To request permission, contact: info@danikalynnbooks.com

ISBN: 979-8-9917364-1-1 (Paperback)
ISBN: 979-8-9917364-3-5 (Hardcover)
ISBN: 979-8-9917364-5-9 (E-book)

This is a work of fiction. Names, characters, places, and incidents are either a product of the author's imagination or used fictitiously. Any resemblance to actual persons (living or deceased), events, or locales is purely coincidental.

Artwork created by Danika Rose Lynn.
Cover and interior designed by Danika Rose Lynn.

Published by: Evermore Media

EVERMORE MEDIA

*To the ones who rose from the ashes,
and to those still being forged in the fire.*

Table of Contents

CONTENT WARNING:
This story contains references to and depictions of sensitive topics that may trigger some readers. If you would like to learn what these potential triggers are and where to find them, please go to the Content Warnings section listed below.

Prologue	1
Chapter 1 My Life	15
Chapter 2 Keeper	31
Interlude 1	43
Chapter 3 Safe and Sound	45
Chapter 4 Darling	55
Chapter 5 A Memory Away	67
Chapter 6 Shadowboxer	79
Interlude 2	88
Chapter 7 Obsession	89
Chapter 8 Bad Blood	97
Chapter 9 My Mirror	107
Chapter 10 Do You Still Love Me Like You Used To?	119
Chapter 11 I Miss You, I'm Sorry	129
Chapter 12 Spellbound	143
Interlude 3	158

Chapter 13 Overwhelmed	159
Chapter 14 Intrusive Thoughts	173
Chapter 15 Crave	183
Chapter 16 Little Girl Gone	195
Chapter 17 Learn to Fly	213
Chapter 18 Birds of a Feather	227
Chapter 19 Lose Control	239
Chapter 20 Ghost in My Guitar	253
Interlude 4	266
Chapter 21 Play with Fire	267
Chapter 22 Be My Queen	281
Chapter 23 I'm With You	295
Interlude 5	314
Chapter 24 Possession	315
Chapter 25 Fix You	327
Chapter 26 Bad Dream	339
Chapter 27 Feral	357
Chapter 28 Be Your Love	369
Chapter 29 Old Days	387
Chapter 30 Take Me To Church	403
Chapter 31 Panic Room	417
Chapter 32 Burn It All Down	433
Chapter 33 Raise the Red Flag	449

Chapter 34	Six Feet Deep	467
Chapter 35	Nervous	483
Chapter 36	Playground	501
Chapter 37	In Love with a Girl	513
Epilogue		529
Author's Note		543
Content Warnings		545
What comes next?		547
About the Author		549

Prologue

Piper

Twelve years ago

My body moved on autopilot through the hospital entrance. I barely noticed the glaring lights overhead or the sharp, bitter scents of bleach and antiseptic. An unfamiliar name sounded over the loudspeaker. That loud crackle of static destroyed what tiny bits of calm still clung to me.

Emergency rooms bred chaos. Hundreds of different people swarmed the area for hundreds of different reasons. But I came for three out of those hundreds. And of those three, Simon was the one who took up all of my thoughts. If I dwelled on the other two, I might have been sick on the hospital floor. I had no time—no way—to process what happened and what Simon had told me. And right then, all my attention focused on reaching the front desk.

Frenetic energy propelled me forward until I was standing opposite the receptionist. The woman barely met my gaze before I blurted out, "Simon Brooks!"

My only response was the blank look she leveled my way.

"Sorry." I gathered what little composure I had left to try again, slower this time. "John and Sara Brooks were admitted tonight. I'm looking for their son."

The receptionist's previously bored expression softened with sympathy, and she looked down at her computer screen while typing something. After a moment, she said, "He'll be in the family waiting room for the ICU." She motioned behind her. "Through those doors, down the hall, and to your right. I'll buzz you in."

After a quick word of thanks, I waited just long enough to hear the beep of the locks before pushing through. While I rushed toward the end of the hall, my mind kept repeating the words: *Please let them be okay.*

As soon as I rounded the corner into the waiting room and spotted Simon, I stopped. His large frame looked uncharacteristically small. He sat in one of the waiting room chairs, hunched over with his head in his hands.

The sight of him stole my breath. "Simon…"

Simon looked up and locked me in place with warm hazel eyes turned dark. He looked devastated. My heart stuttered in my chest, but I forced myself to move, placing one foot in front of the other until I stood close enough to touch, even though I left my hands clenched at my sides. If I reached out now—if I felt any part of Simon—then this nightmare would no longer be a figment of my imagination.

Please be a dream. Please wake up.

But it is impossible to wake from reality. So I steeled myself to speak, to ask the question lodged in my throat. Simon spoke first.

"They're gone."

Those two tiny words sucked all the air from the room. My ears filled with the deafening roar of rushing water that blocked the words and all ambient noise. Every part of me rebelled against the truth. Shaking my head in denial, I took a half-step backward—and froze. I looked around the room in a daze.

Then I remembered Simon.

Oh, god, Simon.

Frantically, I tried to think of something to say—to comfort, inspire, *anything* but this crushing silence. But no words formed. Nothing but a strangled sob.

When reality hit, it hit *hard*. The walls that kept Simon's emotions in check crumbled, and I watched the larger-than-life man I loved shatter. That jolted me into action. My arms gathered up what I could of the pieces as I did my best to hold Simon together. He hugged me around the waist and burrowed against my stomach. Shivers wracked his body from head to toe.

"What the fuck am I going to do?" he growled, low and wounded like a wild animal.

There was no answer to that—no comfort I could give—so I closed my eyes and held him tighter.

"How will I take care of Ellery and go to school?" he asked. "I can't. There's no way. I have to drop out. God, I don't know the first thing about how to raise a kid…"

Simon's voice was quiet, and I sensed he was thinking out loud. He may not have realized he had spoken. I let his stream of consciousness continue unfettered until he ran out of steam.

But then everything shifted. His grip on me tightened. The floodgates opened. His silent sobs shook his body and my composure like a battering ram. I didn't know what to do or the right thing to say.

So I said the only thing I could.

"I'm here, Simon," I whispered into his hair. "Whatever you need."

His tremors subsided. My eyes closed against the tears I had held back. They threatened to fall, but I refused to let them. I couldn't. Simon needed me to be strong.

Be his strength.

Even as I thought those words, I felt them in my bones. I could do that. I could be strong enough for the both of us. However long it took to heal, whatever trouble came our way, we could weather it together.

✳✳✳

Vehicles were parked as far as the eye could see. So many, in fact, that people had begun piling them up in the surrounding field. Even from the street, I heard music thumping inside the house. Beyond that, the din of conversation and drunken laughter permeated the air. I tried to shut the ambient noise out. Instead, I focused on cooling the flare of anger in my chest at seeing Simon's car among the others.

I had already known that he would be here. It was why I had come, after all—to confront him. Still, my fragile heart had been clinging to the hope that he wouldn't, couldn't, do something like this.

Not *my* Simon.

Then again, as of a week ago, Simon wasn't mine anymore.

I wrapped my arms around my middle and shuffled toward the front door. A restless energy in my limbs kept me moving, even though each step forward was a step closer to the unknown. It felt like ants crawled under my skin.

This was *not* my kind of scene.

Once upon at time, Simon hated these kinds of parties, too.

Knowing how much he had gone through these past few months—how much he was *still* going through—I gave Simon a lot of grace. I tried not to take it personally, the distance between us or how he was closing himself off. Everyone said to give him time, so I did. Time, space, whatever he needed, I offered. But it wasn't enough. The more I gave, the more he took until I had given him everything in me, and then he threw it all back in my face.

Like the last four years never happened.

Like we had never promised each other forever.

I never even got to fight for us. The coward broke my heart over a text and then ghosted me. Not that it stopped him from posting on social media. Every night, he was out with a different girl. I thought his words in that text would have hurt the most, but no, it was seeing someone other than me clinging to him. Someone other than me who looked at him with stars in their eyes. Strangers that got to touch and kiss him while I watched from the sidelines.

No. He didn't get to play this game anymore. I deserved answers.

I deserved a real reason for the pain he inflicted, not the stupid cop-out excuses he sent me.

As soon as the front door opened, I was slammed with the smell of weed and cheap beer. Heavy bass pounded out a rhythm all around me, a weight that pressed in on all sides before reverberating deep in my chest. I steeled myself against the desire to turn tail and flee, instead putting all of my focus on searching for the man in question.

By the time I finally found him, I had worked myself up into a frenzy of conflicting emotions. Confusion, disbelief, heartache, and fury all coiled together into a ticking time bomb. I took in the scene. Simon lounged on a couch along the back wall, feet kicked up on the coffee table, one arm draped over the woman tucked into his side. She whispered sweet nothings while her fingers played with curly locks of his hair.

Strangely, Simon had a distant look on his face, barely listening. I could always tell when his thoughts were a million miles away. A half-empty beer bottle dangled from his fingers. Several more empty ones littered the floor at his feet. Based on the state of the rest of the place and the litter that was scattered throughout, I had no clue if they were all his.

As though he could sense my presence, Simon's gaze lifted and our eyes met across the room. He frowned, just for a second, gone so fast I could have imagined it. Then a self-satisfied smirk weaved its way across his face. The arm resting along the woman's shoulders tightened, corded muscles shifting when Simon pulled her close. She preened under the attention. When she nuzzled his jaw, his eyes never looked her way. Instead, he focused squarely on me.

Like he was daring me to go over there and make a scene.

But my feet were locked in place. I could do nothing but stare at him, fire and ice warring in my blood as I watched the man I loved act like I was nothing to him.

Finally, he broke eye contact and turned his attention to his date. He wrapped one hand around the back of her neck and pulled her in. When their lips met, I felt it like molten lava in my veins, scorching me from the inside out.

That sharp, burning stab of pain thrust me into motion. Unfortunately, I stumbled back into something solid and warm. A pair of large hands gripped my shoulders to steady me.

Then I heard an unfamiliar voice say, "Hey there, gorgeous. You okay?"

I pulled away, whirling around toward the person attached to the voice. My gaze landed on the handsome face of a stranger. Most of these people were strangers, though. College kids, primarily, but also recent high school graduates out celebrating the start of summer and the next phase of their lives.

Like I should have been doing. As a recent graduate myself, I should have been excited about the future, but I felt only hollow inside. Dread was the only emotion to come to the surface when I thought about what lay ahead.

Looking up, I noticed the stranger watching me curiously. Then I realized that I had never given him a reply. My face heated in embarrassment.

"Um, hi," I stammered awkwardly. "Yeah, all good. Thanks."

"Anytime." His dark features brightened as he smiled down at me. "I'm Darien."

"Darien," I parroted.

Silence stretched between us.

"Think maybe I could get your name, too?" He smiled wider. "Or, better yet, your number?"

I blinked in surprise, then a laugh bubbled out of me—the result of all my pent-up stress from the evening. Laughter seemed to be my default reaction to uncomfortable situations. "Sorry, sorry. I'm not laughing at you. I just..."

Damn. I tried to think of some believable excuse, some way to let him down easily, but my mind blanked out after seeing Simon. Then someone else decided to step in and do it for me.

"Alright, back the hell up, man." Simon's voice was hard, his jaw clenched into granite. He stood taller than Darien by a few inches, and much broader, and there was a dangerous glint in his eyes while he stared Darien down. I just watched both of them in a kind of detached state, through a film lens in my mind.

Darien quickly held up his hands and took a step back. His gaze darted over to mine for a second. "Hey, no disrespect. I didn't realize she was taken."

I opened my mouth to say that I was not, in fact, taken—then I immediately snapped it shut again. Because that would have been a lie. My heart was very much taken by the overbearing asshole in front of me.

Every broken and jagged piece.

When I didn't argue the point, Darien nodded and, with a small smile in my direction, turned and disappeared into the crowd. Simon tried to leave, too. He turned from me without another word and I just—snapped. Who the hell did he think he was, that he could just walk away after that little performance?

Not a chance.

I grabbed his bicep, catching the rolled-up sleeve of his henley with it, and tugged. Hard. He had no choice but to stop. I refused to let go until he looked down at me.

Then, with an angry growl I said, "Outside. Right now."

Without waiting for a reply, I turned on my heel and stormed away. There was no point in checking to see if he had followed. I could feel him behind me.

As soon as I found the back of the house, I escaped out through the French doors and onward, not stopping until I neared the fence line. Here, there were plenty of trees, shrubs, and privacy. It was quiet and secluded enough to hash this out without an audience.

As soon as Simon came within reach, I pounced. "What the hell, Simon?"

He crossed his arms over his chest and shrugged. "I know that guy. Darien," he sneered. "I don't trust him."

"Do I look like I care what you think?" I bit out. "After you sat there and made out with some random girl right in front of me? Or did you forget during your little tirade that we aren't together anymore?"

He frowned. "We broke up, Piper, but I still care about you. That includes your safety."

"Oh, you care about me, huh?" I scoffed. "That's rich."

"Well, it's the truth."

"Yeah? You could have fooled me," I argued, "considering the way you acted this week. We didn't break up, Simon. There was no mutual agreement. You didn't even have the decency to tell me to my face. No, *you* decided we were done. *You* told me over fucking text. Then *you* went radio silent."

God, it hurt having to say out loud.

"If you care about me so much, then explain that. Tell me why." My voice faltered. "You owe me that much."

Simon's mask slipped. His expression softened for a moment when his eyes filled with regret and met mine. "Piper…"

My name on his lips was the sweetest pain. Loving hands that caressed against an open, festering wound. My eyes burned from it, red-rimmed from holding back tears.

Never let them see you cry. Something my dad said to me when I was little, but I never really understood why until that moment. Because I wanted to fall apart. Every bit of me was brittle, ready to break. But who would put me back together if I did?

No one.

Crying would do nothing to wash away this pain, and I would walk over hot coals barefoot before I ever let Simon Brooks pity me. Instead, I stood my ground, waiting while time ticked by. Waiting for him to give me a reason, any reason. Seconds dragged on, each one an eternity, and Simon simply stood there.

I think that hurt worse than anything.

"Right," I whispered. Then, with a grim and resolute nod, I squared my shoulders and prepared to walk away. Only I stopped myself at the last second and turned back. "No. You know what? You may have nothing to say, but I do."

Then I unleashed everything I had been bottling up inside for seven long days.

"Life is unfair, Simon," I said. "Terrible things happen to good people every day. You didn't deserve what happened to you. None of us did. I know your world turned upside down. And I know you've been scrambling for control ever since."

My hands lifted to my hips as I drove my point home. "But trauma doesn't give you a free pass to bulldoze the people who love you. And I did. I loved you. You meant everything to me, and I wanted to be there for you. I wanted to help you shoulder the burden of taking care of Ellery and the farm. I wanted you to lean on me when you needed strength."

"Instead, you closed off, and you ran, and I deserve to know why." Then my voice broke when I asked him, "Why was my love not good enough?"

Simon stood there, stoic, except for the tight clench of his jaw. He said nothing, not one single word, in defense of his actions. Fine, then. I had plenty more to throw out.

"You showed me how to reach for my dreams. Made me believe that they could come true. But you were my dream, too," I argued.

I could no longer keep the tremble out of my voice, not that I tried to. Let him see the weight of my words. Let him see how much he hurt me.

"You were my dream," I whispered, "and you killed it."

He quietly watched me, unable to hide anymore behind an expressionless mask. For once, he looked just as wrecked as I felt. But his continued silence told me everything I needed to know, and the reality crushed what little hope I had left. Heartache became a poison that turned my insides black, filling me with its bile. The pain spread outward until, with nowhere else to go, it leeched out of me.

"Fuck you, Simon Brooks," I snapped, seething. The weight of everything came crashing down and crushed what little hope I had left. "I wish I had never met you."

With that parting shot, I whipped around and started to storm across the yard toward the house. I only made it a few steps before a large hand clamped down on my wrist. It held me in place, unyielding even as I tugged to get away.

Suddenly Simon was there in front of me, crowding my personal space. He pressed me back against the wood panels of the fence until all I could see or feel was him. The shock held me immobile for several breaths. Then, with a cry of outrage, I shoved my hands at his chest. He barely budged—though, in truth, there was little strength behind my actions.

Deep inside, I wanted this. My body craved it. As much as my head knew this was going to end badly, my heart had taken the reins—even though it was about to break even more.

It only cared that Simon was close.

Especially when he grabbed hold of my chin, tilting it up so that I had no choice but to meet his intense gaze. For a few breathless seconds, I thought he might kiss me.

Worse, I wanted him to.

He was so close that I could feel the heat of his breath on my lips. Each time he exhaled, I could smell the beer he had been drinking. Desire swirled in his eyes. He may have been able to fake everything else, but not how much he wanted me. Never that. As much as I wanted him, too, I fought the urge to close the distance.

If he was going to kiss me, he could damn well do the work.

The illusion shattered when he released me and stepped back. My traitorous body tried to follow, swaying toward him, the stubborn tether between us weak but still holding.

Then my heart shattered, just like I knew it would, when his face hardened in anger. "Fly back home, little bird," he said, his voice caustic as he threw my pet name out like a curse. "You don't belong here."

Words meant to taunt, to wound.

"Stop it," I bit out. "Never call me that again. In fact, just go ahead and forget my name completely."

He opened his mouth to say something else.

I didn't give him the chance.

Turning away without another word, I shoved through the crowd and made my way up the stairs, bent on escaping this hell. It felt like years before I finally broke out into the fresh night air. But I didn't stop. My shoes slipped on damp grass while I started to run for my car, only stopping once I wrenched open the door and collapsed onto the front seat.

My chest heaved. Physical pain gave me something to latch onto, so I focused on the way my lungs burned and the white-knuckled grip of my hands on the wheel. I dropped my head down between my shoulders. It took several slow breaths in and out for my heart to stop racing. But while my body calmed, my emotions were a whirlwind threatening to consume me. I bit back the sob that tried to escape.

No more.

I had cried my last tear over Simon Brooks.

And I was officially done.

"Fly back home, little bird."

Chapter 1
My Life

Piper

Present day

Every musician feels that shift in the air right before a song. A charged moment that hits my body like a jolt of electricity when the audience holds its collective breath. Pure adrenaline rushes through my veins.

There is no more incredible high.

I love crowds. I thrive on their energy. To survive in the music industry, you have to. But even though I love to perform, I hate when I have to perform on command like some dancing monkey. The more fame creeps into my life, the less control I have over my autonomy. Gone is the woman, replaced by a commodity. My music, time, appearance, and relationships are all ruled over by my record label—and him.

Cedric.

The man who owns me.

Signing with a label may have been the best for my career at the time, but it was the worst thing for my person. I try to convince myself that no one in my position would have done differently. Because I got everything I wished for—and much more than I bargained for. Fancy suits wooed me with fancy dinners and promised me the world. All the glitter and glamour enchanted me and pulled me under its spell.

They gave me the world, all right. But now I am stuck looking at it through a gilded cage. This life I am living has never felt more hollow.

Lately, I find myself wishing for escape.

My name, spoken over the loudspeakers, snaps me back to attention. I take a deep breath and then step onto the stage. That familiar hush falls over the crowd while I walk toward the center mark. Anticipation builds when I pull the strap of my guitar over my head, strum the first few notes with my fingers, and form the opening lyrics with my lips. Then I start to sing.

Lost girl, trapped inside this gilded cage
People say I'm blessed, but they don't see the chains

Lost girl, locked inside this ivory tower
People think I'm free, but they can't see the pain

I'm a lost girl
I am nameless

put me in a silk dress
I'm a lost girl
just a plaything
parts of me are missing
I'm a lost girl
full of pretty lies
to hide the tears I cry
I'm a lost girl
with clipped wings
but even caged birds sing

Everything else falls away in the moment, and—for the rest of my set—nothing exists but me and the music. I play to a sea of nameless faces while spotlights beat down on the stage. I wring out every ounce of emotion—my songs demand no less—until the beginnings of a migraine pulses at my temples. I am running on fumes when I finish my last song.

Still, I prefer smaller venues like this one. I'm going to miss performing in them.

I'm going to miss performing at all.

Maybe someday, in some capacity, I will be able to return to the stage.

But right now, I need a break.

Thank goodness tonight concludes the current leg of the tour. My label will likely schedule new shows and interviews starting right after the holidays. That still gives me a couple of months with space to breathe. To figure out my next steps.

Because wherever I land, it will be far from the life I live now.

✶ ✶ ✶

At the end of the night, I settle into the backseat of the car and direct my driver toward the city limits of Nashville. Once we are on our way, I take out my phone. Three rings later, I hear my older sister, Grace, as she warmly greets me over the din of children playing in the background and the television blaring some cartoon.

"Hang on a sec," she says. Seconds later, I hear the distinct click of a door shutting. The noise dies down, and I hear Grace sigh with relief. "Sorry about that. This place is a madhouse tonight."

My chest swells with affection—and I feel the tiniest prick of envy—when I picture her loud, boisterous, loving family. "Your house is always a madhouse."

"True." I can hear the smile in her voice. "Chaos except in sleep."

"You love it," I reply, smiling in return.

She sighs happily. "I do."

Silence settles in the car, and I fidget with the hem of my shirt. When the quiet stretches too long, I need noise—anything to drown all the doubts floating to the surface of my mind.

"Tell me I'm doing the right thing," I whisper.

"You're doing the right thing." Grace says the words without hesitation and with the conviction I lack.

Like this is the easiest decision in the world.

Like leaving everything behind—this life I built through years of blood, sweat, and tears—and starting over is no different than a trip to the dentist: inconvenient, uncomfortable as hell, but necessary.

Still, the unwavering certainty in her voice settles some of the restlessness in my limbs. I release a slow, shaky breath and quietly echo her words.

Before another lapse in conversation can take hold, Grace sighs. "Are you sure you don't want to come stay here for a while? You know that we have a guest room. Jake and I always love seeing you. The twins would be excited to spend time with their Auntie Piper."

Longing tugs at my chest. Part of me wants to say yes, but instead, I say, "You have enough going on without adding my mess to the mix."

Grace neither agrees nor disagrees. "Just know that the door is always open, okay?" she reminds me.

"Okay."

"I mean it." Her voice hardens. "As soon as you start to doubt or second-guess yourself, you come straight to me. At least until you've got a good therapist there, someone who can help direct you where I can't."

Grace works in child psychiatry, but she has extended her services temporarily to help me figure things out. She was the one who finally broke through to me and got me to realize just what this life is doing to me.

What Cedric turned me into.

Even thinking his name turns my stomach, fear starting to leech in, so I quickly pivot my thoughts.

"Thank you, sissy." The breath I release is shaky, but my voice is steady and full of gratitude. "Seriously. If not for you… Thank you for not giving up on me."

"Never. Besides," Grace says, trying to inject a bit of humor, "My reasons for helping were never entirely unselfish. I need someone to be indebted to me. That way, I can guilt them into taking the kids off my hands for a weekend or two whenever they drive me crazy."

My lips curve up. "I would take them in a heartbeat. You know that."

"Yeah. I know." Grace shuffles slightly. I picture her sitting there, curled into the armchair in Jack's study with a knitted blanket on her lap. I also know she is wondering what I plan to do, how I expect to untangle myself from the intricate knots of my life.

Not to worry, dear sister. I wonder the same thing.

When we finally hang up, my driver has just pulled into the car dealership. I have an appointment here, where a brand new SUV waits with my name on it. My getaway vehicle—something without any ties to Cedric, my label, or anything about that world.

Without giving myself a chance to think, I step out onto the lot. First, I walk toward the front of the car to hand the driver a generous tip. Then I head toward the showroom's large glass windows.

An hour later, I get back to my hotel room and unlock the door. I am exhausted but too wired with caffeine and frayed nerves to even consider sleep. All that will have to wait, anyway. I don't plan on staying in the city any longer than necessary.

When I enter the room, I notice my two massive guard dogs snuggled up on the foot of the bed. They lift their heads at my entrance and, seeing me, give a few enthusiastic tail thumps. Seeing them settles a bit of the agitation still coursing through me. Technically, a hotel this fancy would never allow animals, but being a minor celebrity sometimes comes with perks.

"Hi, babies," I coo.

Stepping up to the edge of the mattress, I lean down and hug them tightly around their thick necks. I bury my face into their fur and inhale the comforting doggy scent. Then I laugh and shove back when they treat both sides of my face to a slobbery tongue bath.

"Gross, you two."

I wipe at my cheeks, feeling calmer by the second. Having Ozzy and Cooper close always settles my nerves. They are registered service animals as well as fully-trained Personal Protection dogs. I spared no expense, sending them to the very best trainers.

Keeping them at the hotel while I go to the venues has been torture. Cedric put his foot down early on, however, calling them a nuisance. Truthfully, he hates anything he has no control over. I have more than enough security during my tour, according to him. He says I have no need of two "slobbering, ill-bred beasts."

Cedric also thinks my worry stems from fear. Like I am afraid of a rabid fan coming after me.

The bastard needs to take a good, hard look at himself instead.

Ozzy and Cooper are the only ones I trust to keep me safe. Other than my assistant, Rue, I have no one to rely on professionally. Every other person on this tour is loyal to Cedric—or at least faithful to the money that lines their pockets. They all act as his little spies, reporting my every move.

Rue, however, was there with me before Cedric. She has always stuck by my side, even during the worst parts. She has more than earned my trust.

As though thinking Rue's name conjured her, I hear a knock at my door. By now, everyone else is at the after-party. Rue told them that I had a migraine and would be staying in. She even stayed at the party long enough to help spread the word and ensure it reached the right ears.

Once I check the peephole, I let Rue in.

"Everything go okay at the dealership?" she asks, getting straight to the point. Without breaking her stride, she moves toward the other end of the room, stopping to give the fur babies some attention before ending up at the large windows overlooking the city.

"Yeah," I say, following a few steps behind. "Any trouble at the party?"

"Nope. I don't think anyone cared enough to question, especially not with copious amounts of liquor and—other things—flowing."

"Good," I reply, joining her at the window. Together, we silently watch the lights from the Nissan football stadium glitter and reflect off of the Cumberland River.

After a moment, Rue sighs and turns toward me. "So," she says, "What are our next steps?"

Letting the curtain fall back in front of the glass, I turn and walk across the room while I speak. "My next steps are: pack everything up, take Ozzy and Cooper, and get the hell out. Go home and find a quiet place to rent while I figure out my *real* next steps." Opening the closet door, I pull my suitcase out. Then I lug it over and onto the bed. "I need to hire a law firm, too. Someone I can trust to help me get the hell out of this contract. Everything after that can wait."

"You're sure you want to go to Sweetbriar?"

"Yeah." I sigh quietly, looking down at my empty luggage. "Grace offered me a room but—I don't know. She has Jake and the kids to worry about. I'm afraid that if Cedric retaliates—which he will—somehow they'll get caught in the crossfire."

"Okay, then." She moves to help me pack.

"Rue, you don't have to do all this," I start to say—until she sends me a death glare that shuts me right up.

"I was your friend long before I became your PA," she argues. "So hush and let me help."

Despite the heaviness in the air, I smile. "So bossy."

"You love it."

Conceding the point, I head into the bathroom to gather my toiletries. Having two people to do the work means that it takes a half the time to get everything ready. Before long, Rue and I have lugged all my stuff down to the parking lot and packed it into the back of the SUV. Ozzy and Cooper quickly work to get comfortable on the backseat.

With nothing else to keep me tethered down, I turn to the one friend who has been in my corner no matter what. We share a long hug and then I ask, "Are you going to be okay?"

"I should be asking you that," she replies with a quiet laugh.

"Rue, I'm serious."

"I'll be fine." She shakes her head, amused expression melting into fierce anger. "Seriously. I don't work for that asshole, and I have no ties to the label. What is he going to do to me?"

Exactly the thing I am afraid to find out.

"Don't worry about me," she says with a firm tone. As though I can help it. "Focus on getting yourself home in one piece. You've been on your feet for, what, eighteen hours now?"

"Give or take." I sigh and open the car door. "I plan on getting out of the city and booking the nearest hotel room. That way I can catch some sleep before making the rest of the drive. I've got a new credit card attached to an account I've been stashing money in. It should be safe to use. And I have my new phone ready to go. I turned off my old one."

Rue watches me, concern in her eyes. "Do you really think he'll try to track you? Mess with you?"

"Maybe, maybe not. But I'm not taking any chances." My heart races at the thought of Cedric trying to control me from afar. "Either way, I want to be back home and settled before he has a chance to figure out where I disappeared. I know the fallout is coming, but I need a minute to breathe first."

"Be safe." Rue hugs me one last time. "Let me know when you get to the hotel and then Sweetbriar."

"Okay, Mom." I laugh, a much-needed tension release.

After I slip behind the wheel, Rue closes the door and steps back. I look up just before I turn out of the parking lot, catching one last glimpse of my friend—and the remnants of my old life. Then they disappear, too. Feeling strangely adrift, I start to follow street signs toward Interstate 40 until I am safely cruising along on the route toward South Carolina.

During a drive filled with nothing but silence and my own thoughts, my mind slowly starts to drift. How did things go so horribly wrong in my life that I have to sneak away like a thief in the night? How did I miss so many red flags? I stuck my head in the sand for years, not wanting to see what was right in front of me.

Even my muse abandoned me in the end. I have been unable to write anything new in months. Not one note. Not one verse.

Cedric keeps insisting that I just need to push through the mental block. He thinks I can wrestle my music into submission. But no matter how many times I try, my efforts leave me with nothing but a blank page and a headache.

This problem is more than a simple mental block. My words have completely dried up. The wellspring is empty.

Still the bastard tries to force them out of me. My label blindsided me, hinting at a new album a few months prior. Now I have to fumble through every interview, dodging any questions lobbed at me that had to do with new music, new lyrics, new anything.

All that extra pressure he puts me under only compounds my problem. Every time I try to picture lyrics in my mind, I see Cedric. Every time I try to hear the beginning strains of a melody, his voice fills my ears. He drowns the music out with a litany of veiled put-downs and passive-aggressive comments.

Just force yourself to write, Piper.
How hard can it be to jot down some words on paper?
All you have to do is throw some silly lyrics together.
Is this how you repay me for all my help?
Quit procrastinating.
You're just being lazy.

Maybe Cedric is right. Maybe I have grown too pampered. Maybe I let the fame go to my head like he always tells me.

Maybe I really am a sellout.

I was staring at the comments section underneath my most recent interview. New ones popped up in rapid succession, my gaze catching on each one like a fiery wreck on the side of the road. Horrifying, yet my eyes stayed glued there, unable to look away.

─────

songbyrdgrrl231: Ahh! A new album! When do you think they'll make an official announcement?

ladybirdsings: Hopefully soon!

thisismyjam1s0n: I doubt it's true. Songbyrd hasn't even posted snippets on her socials, not for a few months at least.

user80123902: Songbyrd is a sellout. Did you see what she was wearing in that interview? Who even is she anymore? She looks like some Taylor Swift wannabe now, instead of the badass indie rocker she's supposed to be.

ladymusiclvr42: She *does* look way too mainstream now... Is she going through something?

thisismyjam1s0n: Probably some celebrity mid-life crisis.

pixelprincess: Dude. She's like 29.

thisismyjam1s0n: And you're point is...? She's either having a meltdown or she sold her soul to the music gods.

─────

I watched each new comment pop up and, with each one I read, the urge to laugh maniacally warred with the threat of tears. Maybe I would do both at the same time. Because, as harsh as the words were, there was truth in them.

Songbyrd was a sellout.

How had I let this happen?

The tears came then, and I hated them. I felt like a stranger in my own skin.

I felt like a fraud.

Someone at the front door of my condo jolted me out of my pity party. When I heard the lock turning, I quickly tossed my phone, where it landed face down behind one of the throw pillows. Then I jumped to my feet and frantically wiped my face a few seconds before Cedric appeared in the doorway.

My chest tightened at the sight of him. Once upon a time, that pressure was a pleasant one. Comforting like the feel of a heavy knitted blanket wrapped around me. Now, the pressure coiled around my heart like a vice. Because Cedric had been systematically inserting himself in almost every area of my life over the past several years. From friend and advisor to agent, then from agent to music manager. From music manager to more. Much more. I never realized just how reliant I was on him until recently. Or maybe I was just in denial. Either way, every time I tried to regain some semblance of control, he managed to weasel himself in further.

"Well, now, what do we have here?" Cedric asked, taking in the scene before him first with curiosity and then with suspicion.

"N-nothing."

"That," he said, pointing toward my splotchy face, "doesn't look like nothing. Explain."

Shrugging helplessly, I fibbed, "There was just something sad on TV."

He slowly made his way across the room and stopped right in front of me. His hand reached out and I fought to keep from flinching. But he only gripped my chin to turn my face this way and that.

Then his grip turned painful when he forced my gaze to meet his. "Now, the truth."

"What are we doing, Cedric?" I blurted out. And now that the words were out, hovering in the air between us, I let them stand. Even knowing the anger coming my way.

His eyes narrowed dangerously. "You'll need to be more specific."

My heart started to race, but I pressed on. "What are we doing? Songbyrd—I don't recognize her anymore. That music isn't mine."

"Darling girl," he said, smiling. He dropped his hand back down to his side. "Of course it is. You wrote those lyrics. You created those melodies."

Cedric thought I was just feeling self-doubt. It happened frequently enough now. But suddenly I felt the need to dig deeper.

"No," I argued. "I didn't. Not really. Not like my other albums. The version of Gilded Cage that got released feels like a white-washed, watered down version of what I started with. There isn't one note that sounds like me."

Cedric stepped back, and I noticed the way his left hand suddenly began to clench and unclench. My chest tightened. The fear was instinctual, conditioned from a thousand moments just like this.

He was getting angry.

It was my fault.

I kept pushing, anyway.

"Tell me you don't see it." I waved my arms around. "The magazine articles. Fan comments. They're calling me a sellout. And they're right."

"Watch it, Piper, dear." He gritted his teeth and warned, "You're starting to sound awfully ungrateful. Is that how you feel?" He took a menacing step closer and I froze. "Do you wish I hadn't taken you on as a client? Do you want to go back to Nashville, to singing in dive bars and tutoring spoiled little rich kids? To living with four other roommates and living paycheck to paycheck?"

My cheeks turned ruddy. "No, I—"

"Just say the word, and I'll drop you right back there." Cedric towered over me then, and I saw the dangerous glint in his eyes. "After I take everything that's mine, of course. Because all of this?" He motions around the apartment. "All your fancy clothes, your expensive things, the trips we take, and the money in your accounts? Those belong to me. And even that won't be enough to cover the massive breach of contract you'd be facing."

Cedric's cruel words socked me in the gut and stole my breath. Then my airways restricted for real when his hands clamped around my neck. He squeezed just enough to remind me how easily he could break me.

"I own you, little songbird," Cedric said with a sneer.

Only my dad called me 'little songbird.' No one else ever dared. Only one other person came close: Simon, when he started calling me 'little bird.' But that privilege died with him.

Cedric knew how much I hated when he used that nickname. He never cared. He also knew that I would bite my tongue and take it.

Cedric did own me.

I was nothing but a puppet.

Cedric spent years crafting a world of smoke and mirrors around me. That night changed everything. The smoke cleared and the veil finally lifted from my eyes. Suddenly I recognized the lies for what they were.

Suddenly I saw the monster behind the man.

Before that moment, I had no idea just how helpless I had become. Cedric held all the pieces of me in an iron grip and was choking the life out of each and every one. He spent that night making damn sure to remind me just how much power he had over me, and in how many different ways. After he finally left, I curled onto my bed and sobbed into a pillow. I cried for all the years I had lost. For all the pain I had endured.

Then, once the tears dried, I called Grace.

Together, we made the plans that, once put into motion, have led me here to this moment.

Maybe I'm making a mistake, traveling to Sweetbriar after so long away. But when I think about my reasons for returning, my resolve hardens. Am I not already past the hardest part? I've taken the first step. I can do this. Sweetbriar is the right choice—the only choice that makes sense. Out of everywhere in the world, the only place I wanted to escape to was home.

Home. What a joke. Sweetbriar has been no home of mine, not for a long time. The sad irony is, nowhere feels like home. I'm a drifter; a lost, wandering soul.

My thoughts continue to sift through moments and memories, ripping apart each one and looking for all the clues I missed. The self-recrimination lasts a couple of hours into the drive until my brain becomes fuzzy from lack of sleep. I have the wheel in a white-knuckled grip while I keep a close, drooping eye on the road signs for the next exit and the hotel it promises.

Meanwhile, Ozzy and Cooper are piled on top of one another, passed out in the back seat. I peek into the rearview mirror and smile as I watch them twitch and grumble in their sleep. They are completely unaware of how much our lives are about to change.

"We did it, babies," I whisper to them, knowing full well my words fall on deaf ears. "We actually did it. We'll be in Sweetbriar soon."

In Sweetbriar, I can work to cut out all the rot that Cedric and his pestilence spread throughout my mind.

Before I lose myself completely.

Chapter 2
Keeper

Simon

Most days, I love being a cop. I grew up idolizing my father, who served in our local police force until his death. Even if I never pictured myself as an officer of the law, I loved my dad and am proud to be his son. And even though I thought I would be off chasing my dreams in professional football, following in his footsteps is a hell of a consolation prize. So, yeah, most days, my life fulfills me and gives me a sense of contentment.

Today is not one of those days.

My partner, Nate, and I have just left the property of Mr. And Mrs. Ryder, an elderly couple who live alone with their cat. Mrs. Ryder calls so frequently about that damn ball of fluff that, years ago, the department started drawing straws to see who would be stuck rescuing Flufflestiltskin next.

Yes, that is indeed the cat's name. (I call him Demon Cat.) I have been the unlucky bastard with the short straw on more occasions than I care to admit.

Today, the call came in just after lunch. Everyone hung around the bullpen in various states of food coma and the afternoon slumps. After a slow morning with nothing but paperwork to keep my mind occupied, I jumped at the chance to get out of the station.

I regret that decision.

With a weary sigh, I slump back in the passenger seat while my mind goes over the details of the last hour—time I will never get back.

When the dispatcher hung up, my head popped up from behind my computer. "Did I hear that right?" I asked. "A call from the Ryders that has nothing to do with a furry animal?"

Lydia, who had taken the call, smirked. "Yep. Looks like they had a smash-and-grab. The only place that seems particularly trashed is the kitchen, which is weird." Then she shrugged. "Ahh, well, not my job. I suppose that's what you useless oafs are for."

"Hey! Rude." Dominic, one of our younger recruits, sat up and looked suitably affronted. The rest of us may have taken him more seriously if not for the powdered sugar dotting his upper lip from the donut he just wolfed down.

Lydia rolled her eyes. "So, who wants it?"

"We've got it." I jumped up before anyone else could. Then, without waiting for an answer, I motioned for Nate and headed toward our cruiser out back.

We had barely pulled into the driveway when Mr. Ryder came bursting through the front door like his pants were on fire. Then we were being ushered inside to 'investigate the crime scene' while an overwrought Mrs. Ryder looked on.

Break-ins around our small town were infrequent, though we did get the occasional errant teenager with too much time on their hands or the odd delinquent looking for drug money. Neither of those was the case. My initial thought that this incident wouldn't involve a furry, four-legged creature was way off the mark—because the culprit of this particular break-in was a family of raccoons.

Welcome to Sweetbriar, ladies and gentlemen.

"So, that was fun," Nate quips from the passenger seat after we start heading back to the station.

"Don't start," I grumble.

But the laughter is already starting to bubble out. "Seriously, man, raccoons? What are the odds?"

"A lot more likely than you'd think." I smile despite my best efforts. His amusement is too infectious. "I know you big city folks aren't used to dealing much with wildlife."

I peek over to see Nate roll his dark eyes. "You act like I moved here from New York City instead of Charleston."

"Still counts, man."

"Anyway," he says, "I'll take stray wildlife any day over all the big-city shit I had to deal with."

His matter-of-fact statement sobers me, and I nod. I have seen more than enough death for one lifetime, and that's only a fraction of what Nate has seen during his years as a Charleston investigator. What little he shared with me only scrapes the surface of his experiences.

We settle into silence while I drive us back toward the precinct. After a few minutes, Nate reaches out to switch on the radio. Familiar strains come through the speakers from a song that I have listened to far more times than I would ever admit out loud.

"Haunted" is the debut single written and performed by Songbyrd, an indie rock singer/songwriter who came onto the scene four years ago. When I first heard that song on the radio, it was also the first time I heard Piper Easton's voice after she disappeared from my life.

After I *shoved* her out of my life.

That day, my obsession started with the musician and her music. I may have looked insane, hoarding every album, watching every interview—but if that was the only way I could be close to Piper, nothing else mattered. Everyone else could think what they like, but I was going to take what I could.

Nate leans forward to change the channel with a quick, concerned glance in my direction. I catch his wrist with my hand.

"Leave it," I say, voice slightly strained.

"You sure?"

"Yeah."

Too many late nights working and having drinks together at the bar led Nate to learn a bit about my history with Songbyrd. He is my partner—and a good friend—so it was only a matter of time before the story came out. I would rather he hear it from me than the small-town rumor mill.

Nate levels that unnervingly perceptive gaze my way for a moment. Then he leans back and stares out the window while the arresting lyrics fill the car.

All my dreams are hollow, empty
Memories, promises, they choke me
And the ghost of you still haunts me
Taunts me
Keeps my mind so confused

I'm haunted
Haunted
Haunted
(By the ghost of you)

Shattered trust, misspoken words
No one said how bad it hurts
That the pain would just get worse
Marks me
Keeps me battered and bruised

I'm haunted
Haunted
Haunted
(By the ghost of you)

All these wounds will never heal
Scars that I try to conceal
But the ghost of you still feels
So real
But none of it is true

I'm haunted

Haunted
Haunted
(By the ghost of you)

When we pull into the back lot at the station and park, I am long past ready for a drink. Thankfully, my shift ended about twenty minutes ago. I still need to gather my things but after that, I am as free as a bird.

As I leave the cruiser and head toward the back entrance, I hear a slight sound from the shadows between the large trash receptacle and the back wall. Nate and I glance at each other. Then I turn on my heel and head toward the sound. Frowning, I kneel on the cold concrete, squinting into the darkened, shadowy space behind the receptacle. Without sunlight to penetrate, I can only see the slight outline of a shape.

"You find anything?" Nate shines his flashlight over my head.

"Not yet." But, with the extra light, a puppy comes into view. My shoulders relax, and I say gently, "Hey there, little buddy."

The puppy cowers in the corner, shivering, but the soothing sound of my voice makes its ears perk up. It whimpers. Taking that as a good sign, I slowly reach toward it with the back of my hand. The puppy flinches. I stop. My hand dangles in the air several inches away while I wait.

I don't need to wait long. The puppy sniffs the air first and then takes a few cautious steps closer, sniffing at my hand next. When my fingers reach out and brush along the scruff of its neck, its tail gives a tentative wag. After another minute of back and forth, the small bundle lets me scoop it up.

Nate chuckles while I stand.

"What?" I ask.

"Nothing." But he smiles while he clicks the flashlight off and reattaches it to his belt. Then he steps close, bending forward to consider the puppy.

When the puppy lifts its head and sniffs at the scruff of his beard, its tail starts wagging with more excitement.

"Look at you, cutie," he says in that ridiculous voice most humans get when seeing an animal or baby. He scratches the puppy behind the ears. The puppy promptly flops in my arms to beg for belly rubs, which Nate happily obliges.

"No tags," I say, running a gentle finger up and down the puppy's neck. Its eyes close happily, and it stretches its little body. "Been on its own for a while."

"Or it was neglected." Nate's face darkens in anger.

I get it. Nothing makes my blood boil hotter than those who prey on innocent victims.

Nate steps back after one last belly rub and asks, "What will you do with her?"

I look down, and—sure enough, the puppy is a female. "I'll have to drop her off at the shelter. Unless you'd like to take her home?"

"Oh. No," Nate says, looking slightly horrified. He quickly snatches his hand back. "Brit will lose her shit if I try to bring anything with fur past our threshold. You know how she is."

Boy, do I ever. Nate is one of the kindest human beings I have ever known, and his wife, Britagne —pronounced BRIT-tah-nyah, as I have been informed on multiple occasions until I got it right—is the cattiest. I often wonder how two opposites like them ended up together, what they could possibly have in common, and why in the world they have lasted so many years.

Since I have no right to judge, I keep quiet except to reply, "Yeah. I do."

We watch the puppy for a few moments while I contemplate my options. She closes her eyes in sheer joy, lolls her tongue out of her mouth, and then stretches her little limbs. My heart clenches at the sight of such a sweet little dog. While not too fond of taking her to a shelter, I have little-to-no spare time to dedicate to a pet—especially one so young.

Nate pats me on the shoulder. "I'm sure they'll take good care of her."

✳✳✳

I now have a dog.

Her name is Duchess.

Once the local animal shelter confirms that they have no vacancies, I immediately turn around and try the county shelter. But as soon as I learn it functions as a kill shelter, I walk back out.

Then, I call Ellery for help.

That is my first mistake.

My second mistake is letting her pick out a name. All of our animals at the Briar Patch have a fairy tale name. Ellery started this at a very young age with a farm goose she named Guinevere—we shortened it to Gwinnie—which began a years-long practice. One that I have upheld in honor of our parents.

So, when it came to naming Duchess, I thought to myself: who am I to neglect tradition?

Of course, my sister jumped at the chance to name her. But I should realize by now Ellery will always choose something utterly ridiculous that will haunt me for the rest of my life. The men I work with will never let me live this one down.

But Duchess is tiny and adorable, and she has the prissy personality to match the name. Plus she already responds to it. Renaming her is not an option.

Fuck. My. Life.

But Ellery looks so excited about the stupid name that I go along with it. Beckham leans over and whispered, "I get it, man."

I chuckle. If anyone knows how well Ellery can wrap someone around her little finger, Beckham does.

We continue to watch from the back porch of Beckham's cottage while the puppy and woman bond out in the yard. Then for the rest of the evening, I have to purchase—in Ellery's words—"all the necessary bells and whistles that come with owning a dog," while Ellery tags along to enjoy every second. She has laughed almost nonstop since I first called her for help.

Ellery laughed when I picked her up and brought her to the pet store. She laughed while we picked everything Duchess would need—every bit of it pink and sparkly. Now she laughs while I try again to pawn the dog off on her.

"Come on, Elle." I hold Duchess up next to my face and pout. "You've always wanted a dog. Duchess would be perfect for you."

"Yeah, but this way, I get all the love and affection of a dog without the work." She winks. "Besides, this little gal has already imprinted. You, big brother, are her human. You may as well accept your fate."

To demonstrate, she gently pulls Duchess out of my grasp and holds her against her chest like a baby. Duchess wags her tail a few times, looking up at Ellery with all the love in the world—until a few seconds later, she turns her oversized head toward me. Instantly, she whimpers and wags her little tail with excitement. She stretches out, almost falling out of Ellery's arms to get back to me.

"See? She wuvs you!"

Dammit. Ellery is right.

With a sigh, I take hold of the wiggling bundle and settle her in the seat between us, where I have set up a no-shit, car-travel dog bed. Duchess snuffles around for a minute. Then she curls up and rests her head on the side where it can press against my thigh. I have to admit that the sight melts my heart. Deep down, I know I made the right decision to keep Duchess.

I think the two of us need each other.

Ellery and I fall into a comfortable silence while I drive us home. Duchess stays curled up in the middle seat between us for the duration of the ride, although her body soon stretches out so that her head continues to touch my thigh while the tips of her back paws press against Ellery. She is snoring—the dog, not Ellery (although she does snore)—a light, airy sound that makes me chuckle.

Ellery speaks into the silence that follows. "Puppy fatherhood looks good on you," she says, a smile in her voice. I turn to look at her, ready with a sarcastic response, until I see the earnest, genuine happiness on her face. "I mean it. Fate intended you to find each other."

"Hm. Maybe."

I don't tell her I was thinking along those same lines.

But it says a lot that my baby sister can still sense my missing pieces while I always pretend that I have none. That I'm whole.

Despite my abundance of coworkers, friends, and family–I'm lonely. I come home after work to an empty house and make a meal for one. At the end of the night, I slide beneath the sheets of a massive king bed with no one to hold onto.

There have been plenty of offers over the years. Countless women have asked me on dates, but I declined every one. I have no use for relationships, so I keep my encounters strictly casual, and I have never taken a woman home with me.

Only one woman belongs there—the same woman who has always owned my heart and the only one who ever will.

Piper just needs to come home so I can return it to her.

"*Fate* intended you to find *each other.*"

INTERLUDE 1
One

- Saturday 10:43 pm -

Unknown number: Real cute, changing your number

Piper: How did you get this?!

Unknown number: Christ, you're such a stupid slut

Unknown number: You think I don't have ways?

Unknown number: I've been tracking you for years—this is a cakewalk

Missed call.

This number has been blocked.

- Sunday 12:15 am -

Unknown number: Nice try, but you aren't getting rid of me

Piper: Lose my number, Cedric

Piper: I'm not your puppet anymore

Unknown number: You NEED me, you bitch

Missed call.

This number has been blocked.

- Sunday 2:08 am -

Unknown number: Answer the fucking phone, Piper

Unknown number: So we can talk like grownups

Piper: Talk to my lawyers

Piper: STOP. TEXTING. ME.

This number has been blocked.

Chapter 3
Safe and Sound

Piper

Cedric forced me to change my number. Again. I can only pray he fails to figure it out this time. For the rest of the drive, my body cycles between anxiety, frustration, and exhaustion from lack of sleep—the latter clocking in at a total of four hours out of the past twenty-four.

When I reach Sweetbriar, the normally bustling downtown streets are quiet. I take advantage of the sleepy Sunday traffic to drive slower and linger longer at stop signs. My hometown has changed quite a bit over the years. So much new mixes with the old that my eyes have trouble figuring out where to look first—but for all its differences, Sweetbriar still feels familiar in all the ways that count. Being here blankets me with a sense of safety and comfort like a warm hug from a longtime friend, the steadfast kind you can rely on to be there whenever you need them.

But I have been gone a long time. That friend has become little more than a stranger. No amount of familiarity can erase the ache of knowing time moved on without me.

Silly, I know, thinking things would stay the same here. I changed, after all. All my years away shed the skin of that naïve young girl with stars in her eyes and a pocket full of dreams. Time turned me into something else entirely.

Of course Sweetbriar suffered the same fate.

Downtown slowly shifts into residential neighborhoods. Several minutes later, I turn onto an old, familiar street—and straight into a postcard. Rows of quaint houses, picturesque yards, and massive trees line the street. Time has frozen this peaceful small-town sanctuary firmly in the past. Here I find the sense of home that downtown lacked.

Smiling for the first time in hours, I roll down my windows to enjoy the sound of the rustling trees and birdsong—and to let Ozzy and Cooper have their first real glimpse of our new lives. They each pick a window and shove their massive heads through, tongues lolling and wind tugging at their ears and fur.

Then my childhood home comes into view. My breath stutters at the sight. As soon as I pull into the driveway, I park, shut off the ignition, and lock my gaze on the two-story house.

Growing up, I called it "the sunshine house," and my heart warms at the fresh coat of yellow paint on the wood siding. My mother's garden flourishes in brilliant colors around the front yard. Pop's rusty old truck still sits in the driveway.

Guilt settles like a rock in the pit of my stomach. I never meant for things to turn out like they did. Cedric is only partially to blame. Even before him, I shoved my family into the same box as the rest of my trauma and slapped a red, clearly marked label on the memories. It reads, "Warning! These things cause intense pain. Do not open."

Like a coward, I ran and hid.

Sure, I sent gifts on holidays and birthdays in those early years, mailed cards just because, and called my family regularly. Once I had enough money, I started to fly them in for visits as often as possible.

Then I met Cedric.

Slowly those visits vanished.

You don't have time to be entertaining people. Your family just wants to ride the coattails of your success.

After that, the gifts dwindled.

Why are you wasting your hard earned money on frivolous crap like that? Just send a card like any other sensible human being.

The cards turned into texts.

When was the last time your family came to visit you? If they cared even half as much as you do...

Then, as Cedric continued to fill me with his venom, the texts slowly shifted to silence.

My family gave me the space I continually shoved between us. I gave them no choice. Mom and Pop still reached out on occasion, refusing to give up but not wanting to push me away even more. Daisy completely wrote me off, not that I blame her.

I wrote her off first.

Grace, however, dug in her heels and refused to let me ghost her. Her tenacity paid off. Because of that stubborn streak, Grace stayed as close as I let her—and when I finally reached out, she pulled me from the quicksand.

My mind is a million miles away when the front door swings open and reveals my mother. She calls my name and pulls me back from the past. The joy on her face melts some of the frigid trepidation that built up during my trip.

Nothing compares to a mother's love when a child is sick or hurt, and mine envelops me in her warm embrace as soon as I leave the car. I sink into that comfort, needing something to cling to while the strain of the last several hours drains away. My body starts to shake.

"Oh, sweet girl." Mom squeezes me tighter. Her tears start to mingle with mine. We stay that way for a lifetime and no time at all, until we finally pull apart.

My body is wrung dry like a used rag. I croak on the words when I say, "Hi, Mom."

"Hi, baby." She smiles sadly, cupping my face in her hands while her thumbs wipe away any lingering tears. "Welcome home."

"Home," I echo. Uncertainty leeches into my voice. "Is it?"

Mom can hear the real question behind my words. "Yes, Piper. This will always be your home, no matter what. And we are both so glad to have you back."

My gaze drifts to the porch where Pop stands, watching over us. Slowly, I let Mom go and then trudge up the steps. Pop opens his arms when I step close enough. Once again, I am wrapped up in the love and security only a parent can provide. He may not be my father by blood, but Pop took that role on voluntarily, and he worked hard over the years to be a father in all the ways that count.

"Missed you, Pip," he says, voice gruff with emotion.

"I missed you too, Pop."

The laundry list of reasons I stayed away for so long seems so trivial now. I should have done more. I should have fought harder. Pop stops me when I tense and try to pull away.

"Don't you dare," he gently chides. "We all make mistakes, sweetheart. Nothing matters to your mother and me except that you're safe, and you came back to us."

I want to argue. I need Pop to yell and rail at me for abandoning my family for years. He should be as angry with me as I am with myself. Not one bit of me deserves the understanding and patience this man shows me.

But I am far too selfish not to accept it.

After another moment, Pop leads me inside before getting my things from the car. I head toward the living room, curl up on our oversized couch to wait, and get lost in all the memories surrounding me.

Mom walks into the room a few minutes later, breaking the spell when my two massive beasts follow just behind her.

"So, these gentle giants are my grandpuppies, are they?" she asks with a smile.

I grin back, opening my arms to the dogs. They lope forward and snuggle on each side of me. "Yep, these are my babies. Meet Ozzy"—I ruffle his massive head—"and Cooper." I tug him closer with an arm around his thick neck. "I found them through a rescue in New York."

Adopting Ozzy and Cooper marked a turning point for me, a precursor to the plan Grace and I made to help me escape Cedric's iron grip and untangle the web he had me trapped in. In order to do that, I needed a safety net. My security detail worked for Cedric. He paid them, therefore their loyalty lay with him, forcing me to take my protection into my own hands.

Mom stays quiet while she runs her hands along the fur on Ozzy's and Cooper's backs. But I can see the questions in her eyes, so I decide to give her the highlights.

My search for security led me to a local animal shelter. Dogs frightened Cedric—one of the only things that did—so I sought exactly that to protect me. The second Cedric went away on one of his talent-scouting expeditions, I seized my chance.

"Do you have any specific breeds in mind?" the attendant asked after my arrival.

"Not really, other than size," I said. "I'd like to see the biggest ones you have."

With a nod, she motioned for me to follow her. "I can definitely do that. Come this way, please."

She led me through a small hallway that ended in a small courtyard area. It looked like some sort of dog park or playground—somewhere the dogs could play or be paraded around to potential new owners. I sat on a nearby bench and waited while she went to retrieve the first dog.

With a sigh, I leaned back on the bench and tilted my head toward the sun, enjoying a rare moment of peace and quiet. A few moments later, I heard heavy, huffing breaths before the door opened. The massive black dog that loped out alongside the attendant had at least some Great Dane in his genetic makeup. He certainly seemed a gentle giant, calmly sniffing my hand while I held it out, tail lazily wagging side to side. His face, eye level to mine, reached forward to sniff at my nose—then he swiped his tongue across my cheek. Laughing and wiping the drool away, I melted when the dog plopped his butt on the ground and rested his massive head in my lap with a loving gaze.

"He's perfect," I cooed.

When the attendant brought out the second dog, also massive, I fell in love a second time. This dog was a German Shepherd and Rottweiler mix, menacing in looks but a total sweetheart. I immediately noticed how well the two dogs got along. Right then, I knew the three of us were meant for each other.

That day, we became a family. Ozzy, the German Shepherd/Rottweiler mix, I named after Ozzy Osbourne due to his thick, shaggy mane. Cooper I named after Alice Cooper, a perfect fit with his long black face and white freckled chest.

I immediately enrolled them in the best training facility I could afford. On the other side of the program, the trainers gifted me a pair of sweet, cuddly bodyguards—ones that will not hesitate to protect me from danger.

Bodyguards that Cedric cannot control.

I mentally veer myself away from that dark path, looking up and around the room. Mom settles into her recliner and my two turncoats leave my side to investigate their new best friend. Their betrayal would bother me, but I get it. Mom makes friends everywhere she goes and, since she loves to bake, she usually smells like cookies.

"You two are just the biggest sweethearts," she coos.

Ozzy rests his head on the armrest. He nudges her with his cold, wet nose until she laughs and scratches him behind the ears. After a moment, she looks over at me.

"They're beautiful dogs," she says. "Very intimidating."

Mom gives me that look that says she can read between the lines—and that she understands. But when she gets another look that says she wants to ask more questions, I still feel too raw and exposed to get into the gritty details, so I get up from the couch. Then, walking toward Mom, I do what I do best: deflect.

"Is it alright if I pass out for a bit?" I ask. "The drive did me in."

"Of course, sweetie. I'm sure you're exhausted. We have all the time in the world to catch up."

"Thanks, Mom." I stop and bend over her, wrapping my arms around her neck and kissing her head. "I'm sorry," I whisper—one last time for good measure.

She pats my arm. "All in the past. I'm just glad you're home."

There's that word again. *Home.* I climb the stairs toward my old room and realize that I can feel that sense of home all around me. My room proves no different. Nothing here has changed, despite Mom always threatening to turn it into a craft room after I no longer occupied the space.

Moving slowly around the space, I scan all the memories from my childhood. Posters of my favorite films and celebrities hang on the wall over my old desk. Next to the desk sits a small bookcase full of music-related books and memorabilia. But the top shelf, the place of honor, holds all of my songwriting journals. My fingers lightly dance across the worn spines—a testament to how often I used them.

When I wander to my old bed, I take in all the photographs that cover the wall space above. The pictures span my birth through high school graduation. They include photos of Grace, Daisy, and me at play, school, and special events. I wistfully smile when I see a picture of us sitting in the stands at one of the Hazelwood High football games with Ellery, our parents, and Ellery and Simon's parents. Every one of us wears the school's black and gold colors. Ellery and Daisy went as bees during that night's special event—complete with striped shirts, black leggings, and antennae headbands.

My gaze moves on only to stop on a photo from early in my childhood. My biological dad, Mom, and me all wear team colors on matching baseball caps and jerseys. My toddler self sits proudly on my biological dad's shoulders. A half-eaten hot dog is locked in my tiny fist while I giggle. Mom is laughing, too, while Dad gives his best impression of a turtle while trying to keep me from sharing my condiments all over his face.

By the time I have taken in each tiny detail and put the photo back, a smile has spread across my face. But then I notice more than a few empty spaces where pictures used to hang. My fingers hover over each spot as my mind fills in the blanks: prom photos, high school birthdays, random special memories I had wanted to cherish. Gone. Because each and every one of them include Simon Brooks.

What I once wanted to cherish, I ripped away and hid in hopes that I could forget.

But I never forgot—not one single moment.

I shut my eyes against the barrage of memories. Feeling the exhaustion more keenly now, I curl up on the mattress and tug the covers over my fully clothed body. Too many emotions fight for control, knotting me up inside until I completely shut down. When sleep finally claims me, my last thoughts are of Simon.

Simon Brooks: the only man I have ever loved. He broke my young heart and then abandoned me, leaving me to fend for myself in a world that chewed me up and spit me out. I am nowhere near ready for a trip down that memory lane.

Not now.

Maybe not ever.

"But I *never* forgot. Not *one* single *moment.*"

Chapter 4
Darling

Piper

I wake full of restless energy and no plan.

Something I am no longer used to. Every facet of my life up until now was carefully curated and laid out in front of me, with no room for anything other than abject perfection. Cedric turned me into a doll. He made me look pretty, vapid, thoughtless, and ready to be molded into whatever the world expected.

Even though it sickens me to admit, part of me is lost in a storm at sea without that structure.

My childhood bedroom disorients me when I open my eyes—at least until the grogginess wears off enough that I remember where I am and how I got here. Then, my brain slowly fills in the blanks while carefully avoiding one sensitive topic in particular.

Slightly disappointed at the lack of rest my nap provided, I sigh and slowly stretch. My gaze lands on the photograph of my biological dad and I wistfully smile.

Then a plan forms.

Suddenly, I know what I need to do next.

After shuffling through my luggage, I quickly clean up in the bathroom across the hall, put on some activewear and sneakers, and head downstairs.

Mom lifts her head from the book on her lap. She smiles when she sees me. "Hey, honey, are you hungry?"

I look down at my watch. My nap took me right through lunch, but instead of hunger, I feel twitchy. Too many thoughts swirl in my head.

"No, but thanks," I say, gentling my rejection with a smile. "I feel like taking a walk."

"Okay. Have a good time."

Mom returns to her romance novel. I call out for the Ozzy and Cooper. They race out of whatever room they have commandeered and flank me on either side as I head toward the backyard. The woods behind our house have many walking trails, but I am looking for one in particular. It takes me a surprisingly short amount of time to remember the path. Even if my mind forgot the steps, my body falls into the muscle memory from years of taking the same route almost daily.

Eventually, I hit a break in the trees and can make out the wrought-iron fence bordering the cemetery. When I get close enough, the front archway comes into view. I pass through, following the main path that weaves in and out of the rows of headstones. I pay them no mind, my thoughts firmly on one grave that rests under a large, gnarled oak tree.

One foot moves in front of the other until I stand before my dad's grave. Here, staring at that weathered tombstone, long-suppressed emotions start to bubble to the surface. I only have to wait a little bit for that familiar ache to start pulling at the center of my chest.

Ozzy and Cooper rest against either side of me, and Cooper nuzzles his head into the space under my arm. I am grateful for their presence while I think of something to say.

Finally, I settle on, "Hey, Daddy. It's been a long time, and I"— My throat closes up.

The words I practiced so many times in my head shrivel up and die, leaving me with nothing but deafening silence. Tears gather behind my eyes and spill over.

"I'm sorry I stayed away so long. I was ashamed. You told me always to stay true to myself, but I failed. I failed miserably. You wouldn't even recognize me." A sob chokes me. "I don't recognize myself. I have no clue who I am anymore."

In moments like these, I keenly feel Dad's absence. I miss hearing him call me his little songbird, and the way he would hold me and tell me how much he loved me.

Dad would know what to do. He would fix everything. But he is long gone.

"I missed you so much." My breath shakes when I exhale, and I pause to look around me. "I missed *everyone*. Even Sweetbriar, believe it or not." I press my hand against the ache in my sternum and rub. "But I finally made it home. I promise never to stay away like I did before."

After a moment of silence, I kiss my fingertips and rest them on the headstone. Then, with a whispered "I love you," I turn to start the slow trek back up the path I came down.

About halfway to the cemetery gates, I hear a feminine voice call out from across the grounds. "Piper? Is that you?"

I turn toward the sound without thought, and freeze when I see Ellery Brooks standing at her parents' gravesite with a pale, shocked expression and wide eyes. She has changed quite a bit over the years—the Ellery I knew was a newly minted teenager, still in that awkward phase of braces and bony knees—but I would still know her anywhere.

Part of me wants to weep at how much of Ellery's life I missed out on. While I vowed to keep in touch with the little sister I had adopted when I started dating Simon, it soon became too painful to do more than send her an occasional email or letter and a card on her birthday and holidays.

How could I be so selfish?

How could I let her turn into yet another stranger?

"Elle," I say hoarsely. My hand lifts in an awkward little wave.

Her face breaks out in a brilliant smile. Suddenly she is running, weaving carefully through the graves. I command the dogs to stand down. Then, at the last second, Ellery lunges forward and flings her arms around me.

She cries out in shock and relief. "It's really you!"

After my own shock wears off, I relax into her hold and wrap my arms around her, squeezing tightly. More tears flood my eyes. I feel like I have cried more today than I have in years.

"I can hardly believe that you're here." Her voice in my ear is strangled and shaky, her own tears falling. Knowing she is as affected as me has a surprisingly calming effect.

"I'm here," I say, hugging her tighter.

Then she asks, "Are you real?" and I answer with a choked laugh.

"Yes, I'm real." Then I quietly add, "I convinced myself that you hated me."

"Never." Ellery pulls back, expression darkening. "But I am beyond pissed that you didn't call or write or anything to say you were coming home! I know we don't really talk anymore, but this is a huge deal."

She shrugs helplessly. Pain darkens her hazel eyes. Guilt slams into me, and I take a step back. My arms immediately wrap around my middle—a defense mechanism—and my eyes fall to the ground.

"I'm sorry." Shaking my head, I force myself to look at her. "This was a last-minute decision. I would have said something if"—I cut off and shake my head. Because I doubt I would have said anything.

If not for my current circumstances, I would still be far away from here.

The silence stretches awkwardly until a man clears his throat nearby. Panicked, I look up with a jolt, thinking maybe Simon came with her. When my eyes fall on Beckham James—and his familiar icy-blue gaze—part of me relaxes. But only a tiny part. Beckham and I were friends once, but Beckham and Simon have been as close as brothers for most of their lives.

I have no idea where we stand, Beckham and I. But his gentle tone when he says, "Hey, Piper," tells me all I need to know. His expression shows curiosity and concern, but no censure.

My shoulders drop further, and I want to cry in relief. The smile that stretches across my face is small but genuine. "Hey, Beckham," I reply. "Long time no see."

"Bit of an understatement, I think." The humor in his voice soothes the bite of his words.

I notice that Beckham lingers well behind Ellery with a slightly wary look on his face. His gaze shifts to the dogs lying just a few feet away, and I realize why. Ozzy and Cooper watch the scene unfold with alert curiosity, wondering who these new potential friends are but still ready to come to my aid if I need them. My heart warms, and I smile bigger.

"It's okay," I tell Beckham. "They know you're a friend." Then, to Ozzy and Cooper, I whistle. "Come."

They stretch and stand to their full height. When they reach my side, I command them to sit. "These are my goofballs," I say, ruffling the fur on each of their heads as I say their names. "Ozzy and Cooper."

Ellery practically vibrates with barely contained excitement. "Can I come over and say hi?"

"Sure," I say. "They are both well-trained, and total sweethearts beneath their menacing exteriors." I giggle, thinking of just how intimidating they must look if even Beckham gives them a wide berth.

I wave Ellery up to me. "Just treat them like your horses. Hold out your hand and let them sniff first. Once they get used to your scent, you'll be best friends."

Ellery does as I instruct. Within seconds, they nuzzle her hands, drooling all over them while she laughs in delight. "Oh, aren't you the most precious sweeties!"

When she wraps an arm around each and nuzzles into their fur, they try to cover her face with doggy kisses. The three of them look like a comedy skit. While I am on the short-size of average height, Ellery is quite petite. She could probably ride them like one of her horses.

I am laughing at the ridiculous picture they make when Beckham walks over to my side. Ellery continues to love on the dogs, and the dogs lap up the attention.

Beckham chuckles while he watches the scene with me. "You know Ellery's going to try and steal them now, right?"

I grin. "She can try. They're very loyal."

Ozzy and Cooper finally head over to Beckham to sniff him out. He stands still, hands out in front of him so they can do the sniff test. He gains instant approval, and I snort when they sit at his feet, putting their weight against him and almost knocking him off balance.

Almost. Beckham's a sturdy guy.

"What are you guys even doing here?" I look from Ellery to Beckham and back. "Not that I'm not thrilled to see you. I just thought you were off, you know"—I shrug uncomfortably—"living your lives and all that."

Then I realize how contradictory I am, asking them questions I would never in a million years want to answer. They have no obligation to tell me anything.

Before I can backtrack, Beckham speaks up. "Well, I left the military a few years ago," he explains. "Figured it was time to move home after that. I wanted to put down roots."

"And I love creating art, you know that," Ellery says. "But that life isn't for me. Something drew me back here, so I came home, too."

Ellery turns her head to smile up at Beckham. At that moment, it clicks how closely together they are standing. My gaze snags on the way Beckham weaves his arm protectively around Ellery's shoulders, and the way his normally flinty gaze is soft with warmth—and love.

"Oh!" I gasp.

Ellery's gaze returns to me. Her smile has turned positively giddy and a bright red stains her cheeks. I yank her out from Beckham's side so that I can throw my arms around her.

"I'm so happy for you!" I cry out.

I start to rock her back and forth in a bit of dance until we both start laughing. Then I stop, releasing her to look up at Beckham. My smile stretches wide as I carelessly throw my arms around his middle. His rich laugh vibrates through me. He returns the hug without hesitation, adding a squeeze for good measure.

"So happy for *both* of you," I add in complete sincerity. Then, pulling back, I clap my hands in excitement while bouncing on my heels. "This is amazing!"

Ellery had an intense crush on Beckham growing up. Knowing that they found their way to each other after all this time kindles a little spark of hope deep inside me.

But the spark fizzles quickly. Whenever I think of that kind of love, the fairy tale ending kind of love, I only ever see one face.

The face of the one man I can never have.

"Holy shit," I whisper loudly, eyes flaring when Simon comes to mind. "How are you both still alive right now?"

Beckham throws his head back with a hearty laugh. Ellery tucks herself back into his side. Looking equal parts naughty and chagrined, she says, "That one is a long story."

"Why don't you come to our place for dinner?" Beckham looks from me to Ellery.

"Yes!" she says, bouncing on her heels. "You should come see the house. Beckham built it." She smiles proudly up at him.

I blink. "You built a house?"

He rubs a hand along the back of his neck. "Yeah. I own a renovation company."

"Beck, that is huge," I say, in complete awe of the man in front of me. "Congratulations."

He flushes with embarrassment. Beckham always hated getting compliments. I see that hasn't changed.

Deciding to let the poor man off the hook I turn back to Ellery and say, "I wish I could, but I just got into town. Mom will never forgive me if I don't at least spend a little time with them first."

Ellery's disappointment softens into understanding when I mention my parents. "Rain check," she says in agreement. "I've still got a lot of planning for this weekend anyway."

"What's this weekend?" I ask, curious.

Ellery gasps and grabs my hands. "Right, you don't know! Do you remember how I always wanted to build a community art center here? Well, I did."

"Wow, Elle," I reply. "That's amazing."

"Thanks," she replies, the excitement in her eyes contagious. "We opened this week, and this weekend we are throwing a charity art gala to raise funds and introduce ourselves to the community."

"Sounds fancy."

"Yeah," she agrees. Then she winks. "I get to see Beckham in a tux."

I laugh and reply, "No comment."

Beckham just shakes his head, smiling. He knows how good-looking he is, but he still gives Ellery a hard time. "I swear I'm just a piece of meat to you, shortcake."

And now I want to melt. Beckham started calling Ellery "shortcake" long before I knew either of them. It began as "strawberry shortcake" because of her red hair and petite stature, but eventually the term shortened. But now, as a pet name, I could swoon.

I have officially been reading too many romance novels.

Ellery lifts on tiptoe to kiss Beckham's cheek. "You know I love you."

"Yeah, yeah. Love you too."

I could laugh and cry in equal measure. I am so wonderfully happy for Beckham and Ellery, but witnessing them together only drives home my life's severe lack of romance.

I have *definitely* been reading too much romance.

Ellery squeezes my hands, returning my attention to her, and says, "Anyway, please tell me you'll come to the gala."

"Oh, I"—I cut off, frozen in place.

Ellery looks at me with so much hope, but I know I am nowhere near prepared to show myself at an event that will surely bring news outlets. And I am certainly not ready to see Simon in the flesh—although no amount of preparation will ready me for that moment.

The excitement on Ellery's face slowly leeches away the longer I stay silent. Guilt flares again. Against my better judgement, I blurt out, "Yes, I'll go."

Ellery immediately brightens. "Really?"

"Yeah. This gala is important to you"—I squeeze her hands once before letting them drop—"and that makes it important to me."

After we exchange numbers, and Ellery promises to text me all the important details. We part ways. I watch them for a little while, until they turn and walk out of the gates hand-in-hand. With a bittersweet ache in my heart, I slowly make my way back to my parents' house, my thoughts firmly on the art gala and *not at all* on Simon.

Despite my happiness at reconnecting with old friends, I feel like I made a huge mistake by saying yes.

"How are you *both still alive* right now?"

Chapter 5

A Memory Away

Simon

Tonight, Ellery puts on her art gala.

The chaos starts early this morning, from the moment I open my eyes. My phone blaring Chief's ringtone yanks me from sleep, and I answer only to get a request to come into work because of short staffing.

"I know your sister has her big event tonight," Chief says in apology, "and normally, I would make do, but we've got two guys out with the flu, and Meg's daughter broke her ankle playing tackle football with her brothers."

My mouth imitates a fish on land while I scramble to figure out how to make this work. I hate to say no to Chief, especially since I'm technically on-call today—but I would also like to avoid Ellery trying to skin me alive. It turns out that I don't need to worry about either.

"Oh, shoot, hang on, someone's calling in." Chief mutters something about newfangled technology and cuts off mid-sentence. About a minute later, he returns to say, "You're off the hook, son. Nate offered to take Harden's shift."

I blow out a breath. "Thank goodness for Nate. Ellery would have made my life extremely miserable if I missed even a portion of this thing tonight."

Chief chuckles. "Too true. Tell that sister of yours hello for me."

"Will do. Bye, Chief."

After we hang up, I pull up a new text.

Simon: Thanks, man

Nate: No problem *wink emoji*

Simon: You and Brit were going, too, right?

Nate: Yeah, but she'll get over it

Nate: This is your family's night, not mine

Nate will do anything for a friend in need—even risk the wrath of his wife. He probably wanted to score a few hours away from the house with this little favor. Britagne may be pretty, but her looks only carry her so far. Beneath that sugary-sweet veneer is nothing but vinegar.

✳✳✳

By late afternoon, I think Nate may have gotten the better end of the bargain. Ellery has been at the center since morning, supervising its transformation from an art co-op to an upscale event space. Beckham and I both repeatedly volunteered to help, but she assured us that she and Lena had everything well in hand.

Unfortunately, well-in-hand is turning into chaos. Ellery has kept Beckham and me in the loop all day—whether we want to or not. However, for the last few hours, she has been sending Beckham and me increasingly frantic texts.

I have complete faith my little sister can pull this thing off. Without any sense of urgency, the texts are damned amusing.

- 10:30 am -

Ellery: *photo of gallery* Everything is coming together!

Beckham: Looks good

Simon: You aren't going to do one of your play-by-plays, are you?

Simon: Pipsqueak?

Simon: Ellery?

Beckham: That's a *yes*

- 12:00 pm -

Ellery: Babe, are you still bringing lunch?

Beckham: Yep, leaving now

Simon: Your brother is stuck in this group text

Simon: So please refrain from pet names and other lovey-dovey crap

Beckham: You hear that, shortcake? He doesn't like PDA

Ellery: Aww, schmookums, do you think we should leave him alone?

Beckham: I don't know, sweet cheeks, it might be fun to rile him up

Simon: I hate both of you

- 1:15 pm -

Ellery: Do you think we have time to add some extra decorations?

Beckham: No

Ellery: *pout emoji* Fine

- 2:30 pm -

Ellery: OMG, I can't find the prizes for the silent auction! *sob emoji*

Beckham: They were near the kitchen area when I was there

- 2:35 pm -

Ellery: You're a lifesaver! xoxoxo

Simon: STILL here

Ellery: Aw, okay, you can have xoxoxo, too

- 3:45 pm -

Ellery: OK, the caterers are due to arrive here at 5:00, and the party rental place has misplaced the table where the food is going to go

Ellery: What are we going to do? They've been looking EVERYWHERE, even at their warehouse

Ellery: The gala will be ruined!

Simon: Breathe, Elle. They'll find it

Ellery: But what if they don't?!?!

Beckham: Then Simon and I will bring those folding tables from his place

Simon: Wait, I did not sign up for manual labor

Beckham: Too bad

- 4:30 pm -

Ellery: CRISIS AVERTED! Table found

Simon: Thank god. I was on pins and needles the whole time

Ellery: Sarcasm is NOT appreciated

Simon: And yet, so much fun

- 4:45 pm -

Ellery: On my way home to get ready

Five minutes after that last text, I hear a knock at my door. I'm buttoning the last button on my shirt. Duchess perks up from her dog bed and gives a halfhearted yip before standing, turning around three times, and then curling up in the same position she was in. *Damn silly dog,* I think as I head downstairs, fiddling with the cufflinks at the same time I open the door.

"Hey, man," Beckham says.

I look up and then smirk. "You look like a fucking penguin."

"Shut up. Ellery thinks I look sexy." He winks at me.

"Gross." I pretend to gag as I open the door further to let him in.

He laughs and brushes past me. Stopping in the living room, he turns around, hands in his pockets, suddenly looking anxious. "You still have the ring, right?" he asks.

"Of course, I have the ring. What would I do, use it as collateral on an impromptu gambling spree?"

"The hell if I know. Stranger things have happened."

I fight the urge to roll my eyes, knowing he doesn't need any added stress piled on top of whatever is already going through his head. Instead, I motion him to follow me back upstairs.

"Well," I say, "it's been sitting in my nightstand drawer since you asked me about it the last time. And the time before that. And the time before that." I arch an eyebrow at him. "That ring hasn't moved ever since you forced me to search for it in Mom and Dad's things."

I cross the threshold to my room, Beckham following on my heels. My voice is laced with sarcasm when I say, "You're welcome for that, by the way."

"I already thanked you for finding the ring." Beckham sits on the edge of the bed, watching me move toward the nightstand. "You only get one because you're a pain in my ass."

"You should be so lucky."

Beckham ignores me in favor of Duchess. Having heard our voices, the puppy is up and trotting across the carpet toward him, wiggling her fluffy butt in excitement. When she sits at his feet and waits patiently for his attention, I say, "good girl, Duchess."

At this rate, I will have her fully trained in no time.

Beckham leans down to give Duchess the head pat she has quickly become accustomed to. He dutifully waits while she licks his hand before pulling away. Then, with a yawn, Duchess returns to her bed.

I wonder what it must be like to be so utterly pampered.

Meanwhile, I have already opened the top drawer of my nightstand. I start sifting through the junk accumulated over the years, diligently searching for the ring box.

"Look, Beck," I say, taking advantage of the silence. "I know I give you and Ellery a hard time, but… I hope you know that I'm happy for you both. Truly."

Behind me, he clears his throat. "Yeah, I know."

When I stand back up, I'm holding the small ring box. "And I know Mom and Dad would be thrilled if they were here. They'd be calling you son or some shit, Mom would be crying, and Dad would be crying but pretending he had something stuck in his eye."

The smile on my face is wistful. Twelve years later, I still feel the sting of their absence. Time has dulled it to more of an ache, much like the phantom pain of a missing limb. Something I'm not sure will ever go away.

Something I'm not sure I ever *want* to.

Shaking my head, I hold the box to Beckham and say, "My point is that you're family. Always have been, and now, you always will be."

His eyes have a light sheen to them when our eyes meet. Then he shakes his head with a light chuckle. "She has to say yes first."

"She will."

As his fingers wrap around the ring box, Beckham deeply exhales in relief. He stares down at the black velvet covering, lost in thought for a moment, before gently lifting the lid.

A look of confusion steals over his face. "Um, Si? Are you sure this is your mom's ring?" he asks. "This isn't a diamond, first of all, or yellow gold—and the ring Sara wore doesn't have all this intricate swirly crap twisting around it. Does it?"

Shit. Fuck. Shit.

I quickly snatch the ring box from Beckham's hand and look down. He's right. This ring is definitely the wrong one. The "intricate swirly crap" covers the top half of the very noticeably *white*-gold band, and where the diamond would be is a ruby gemstone.

At the time, I wanted something unique for Piper—and it was the best I could afford.

Quickly and without a word, I shove the box back into the nightstand and move items aside until I find a second, identical ring box. Beckham takes this one much more slowly. His eyes narrow while he watches me, his mind puzzling through what he just witnessed.

He finally looks away, but only to double-check the contents of this box. When his shoulders slump in relief, so do mine. Then I turn on my heel and stride over to the door.

Beckham needs to get back before Ellery gets home, and I need to escape the slowly dawning look of understanding on my friend's face. But when I turn back, Beckham is still perched on my bed, staring hard at me.

"Ellery's going to be home any minute," I say, trying to deflect. "You should go. Otherwise, she'll wonder where you were. You know how curious she gets."

But he ignores me. "Simon." He looks back down at the nightstand again. The drawer is firmly closed, but it doesn't matter. I may as well frame the other ring box on the wall with a neon light pointing straight at it. "That ring… is that what I think it is?"

Dropping my head back to stare at the ceiling, I count to ten before I respond. Because I *really* don't want to answer that question.

"Maybe." I shrug. "Probably. Yes."

He shakes his head slowly. "That's the ring you bought for Piper. When…"

While the sentence trails off into heavy silence, my mind picks up the thread of his thought and finishes for him: *when you planned to propose.*

Before Mom and Dad got hit.

Before my life went up in flames.

Before I pushed Piper away.

People would have said we were too young, too naive about the world. They probably would have said that asking Piper to marry me right after her high school graduation was ridiculous and short-sighted.

I never planned for us to get married right away. I only wanted my ring on her finger. I wanted the world to know that Piper Easton was mine. Marriage and family could come later. We had the rest of our lives.

But then the rest of our lives turned into never.

"Why do you still have it?" he asks. No judgment, just concern.

"I don't know." *Liar.* "Forgot it was there." *Another lie.* "Honestly, I rarely go through that nightstand."

That much is true. The rest of it, though… Beckham is my closest friend. He can probably see right through my bullshit. But, like a good friend, he doesn't call me on my bluff.

"Makes sense," he says slowly, not believing a word. Still, he lets it go, pocketing Mom's ring before standing.

Duchess starts to wriggle her little body in excitement at the movement. She yips, hoping Beckham will see her and lavish her once again with the attention she feels she rightly deserves. Beckham chuckles, bends down, and quickly ruffles her fur behind the ears.

"You keep this one straight," he says to her, throwing a look over his shoulder. "He's shifty."

"Yeah, yeah." My phone chimes, and—after I see the preview—my face twists into a wicked smile. "You'd better start worrying about yourself. Ellery just got home and is wondering where you are."

His eyes widen as I start to wiggle my phone at him. "Fuck," he exclaims. "Gotta go."

Without another word, he disappears out my bedroom door. I hear his heavy footballs down the stairs before the front door opens and closes. When I hear his engine start and peel out of the driveway, I double over laughing. Duchess watches me with her head tilted, looking at me like she thinks I'm nuts.

Hell, maybe I am.

Keeping an engagement ring from a failed relationship for twelve years certainly qualifies as insanity.

So does the shit job I did at deflecting—but Beckham's question threw me off. It is a question I could never answer it, because my reason sounds pathetic out loud.

Why do I still have the ring?

Simple. Because it belongs to someone else.

That ring always has and always will belong to Piper.

The truth is, I kept it while hoping that someday, Piper would let me try and fix what I broke. I hoped that she would forgive me. And I prayed—I *still* pray—that we can finally be what we were always meant to be:

Together.

"I wanted *the world* to know that *Piper Easton* was mine."

Chapter 6
Shadowboxer

Piper

When it comes to the Brooks family, I have zero defenses. Their charm has as much of a hold on me now as in high school. I regret accepting Ellery's invitation to this gala, but her excitement and the hope in her eyes that I would say yes made it impossible for me to do anything else.

Despite all our baggage, Ellery is family, and I have spent far too much time keeping family at a distance. I could blame life for my absence: fame, crazy expectations of the music industry, my insane work schedule, and spending most of the year living out of a tour bus.

Sure, I could blame those things, but I don't. I have nothing and no one to blame but myself. My absence happened because of pain. It happened because being back in Sweetbriar *hurts*. The wounds of my old life never healed properly.

Coming home has ripped them wide open again.

Like any other well-adjusted adult, I ran from my problems when I turned eighteen. I ran straight into the glittering lights of Nashville. Then, when my career started to take off, I put even more distance between myself and my past and immersed myself in the New York City music scene.

Nothing has changed. I have been hiding ever since I left home, and all I have wanted to do since returning is hide more. Anything to avoid the memories that haunt this place and the people I tried to forget.

Still, here I am. I fulfilled my promise to Ellery, made an appearance, and now I am just biding my time. Hopefully, I will be able to escape without causing a disturbance. The only saving grace of being out tonight is that the good people of Sweetbriar are loyal to their own. No resident will reveal me to some outside reporter or paparazzi. At least for now, my whereabouts are safe from the outside world.

What I am *not* safe from is idle conversation.

Everyone and their brother wants to talk to me. Within thirty minutes, I have heard more town gossip than I know what to do with.

After an hour, I have to search for a stiff drink.

Two hours in, I have spent more time deflecting on new music I may or may not be working on, celebrity gossip, and my own life than I have in ages.

Honestly, small towns are worse than a gossip rag or talk show.

By hour three, my dress has turned into a tourniquet. The bodice presses so tightly against my chest that I have trouble catching my breath. I need to get some fresh air before I pass out. As soon as I can extricate myself without being noticed, I slip away from the crowd and disappear out the nearest open doorway. It deposits me somewhere on the large porch that wraps around the front of the estate. Now that night has fallen, a chill replaces the comfortable temperature and bites at my exposed skin. I rub my arms to get the blood flowing a bit.

At least now I can hear myself think.

Small mercies.

I used to thrive on crowds. I loved being the center of attention. But Cedric stole all of that from me.

Sudden, loud chatter from inside catches my attention. I peek curiously through the window, worried that I missed an important speech or something, but I have trouble seeing anything through the crowd. While contemplating if I need to find a better spot, a few people move to the sides.

Then I see it.

Beckham rests on one knee before Ellery. My hands fly to my mouth just as a delighted gasp of surprise escapes. Because Beckham is proposing, and I get to witness the happy event.

He must have only just finished asking. Tears run down Ellery's face while he slides the ring on her finger, and I watch the scene, utterly enthralled. It feels like I am watching a real-life romantic comedy.

Just as Beckham stands, Ellery throws her arms around his neck, sobbing and laughing. She almost knocks the poor man over in her enthusiasm. I giggle in relief when he rights himself and wraps his arms around her with a laugh.

People start to cheer and applaud all around them. They break apart, Beckham reaching up to wipe the tears from Ellery's cheeks, which honestly makes me sigh dreamily.

Damn him.

Then Ellery catches sight of someone off to the side, and she dashes away. Beckham follows a few steps behind at a much slower pace, chuckling and shaking his head. Meanwhile, my stomach roils with a tumultuous storm of emotions.

I am genuinely happy for Ellery and Beckham—after all, Ellery gets her prince. But my joy has a bittersweet aftertaste, followed by a slight twinge of envy that has no place here but that I can't avoid.

Part of me wants to laugh. The other part wants to cry.

Ellery deserves her happily ever after.

But will I ever get mine?

Pinching my eyes closed against a headache starting to form does nothing to lessen the pain, so I turn away from the window and step back up to the railing. There, I lean forward and take several slow, soothing breaths. When I open my eyes again, I feel a little more centered.

My headache and heartache are still present, but at least I can ignore them now.

Just until I get home.

Someone opens the door behind me and steps outside, sending a swell of music and lively chatter rushing out into the night before shutting it in again. Silence settles over the porch. Soon, all I hear is the sound of heavy footsteps creaking on the wood. Only seconds later, an imposing figure fills my peripheral vision. Not wanting to get sucked into another round of polite chitchat, I slip into the shadows and pray the darkness keeps me hidden from view.

Until dim lamplight illuminates the stranger. When I see his face, I gasp in surprise.

Simon. Fucking. Brooks.

No one could have prepared me to see him in the flesh. I never expected Simon, not out of all the people who could be standing here now. I can hardly be surprised. His own sister coordinated the whole event and has been running it all evening. The proceeds even benefit her charity.

Of course, Simon is here. He will always do anything to support Ellery. Despite my blind hope that our paths would never cross, it was unrealistic to expect anything different.

Sweetbriar is a small town. Logically, this little reunion was inevitable, even if I had hoped to have more time. Not that my heart would ever be ready. Simon is the one person in this town I have been trying my hardest to avoid, yet the one person I have wanted to see more than anything. Now here he is, standing only a few scant feet away and looking like he just stepped off the set of a James Bond film. A tailored tux clings to his form while he holds a glass tumbler of something (maybe whiskey, but probably bourbon) in his hand.

As soon as Simon hears my sharp intake of breath, he turns toward the sound. "Who's there?" he barks.

Every limb locks into place at the sound of his command. My heart races, and the heavy pulse in my throat tightens my airways until my lungs fight for breath. Despite the adrenaline that rushes through me, urging me to run, I stay rooted to the spot.

Simon's rich voice ignites a familiar ache deep within me, but the steel threading through his words and the edge of authority in his tone are both new. Every nerve ending tingles with awareness as if waking from a hundred-year sleep. My entire body comes alive and yearns to get closer—so, gathering every ounce of courage, I slowly step out under the dim overhead light.

The motion pulls Simon's attention toward me. His soft lips are pressed together in a firm line while he searches me out in that little dark corner. Meanwhile, my gaze is glued to his face, watching the play of emotions while my eyes map out every tiny detail and commit them to memory. Everything from the deep crease between his furrowed brows to the slight crook in his nose from a break in tenth grade, courtesy of a stray football to the face.

I catch the moment when Simon sees my face. His eyes flare in surprise, and my sudden appearance has stunned him into silence. I guess I need to be the one to break it.

"Hello, Simon." His name feels strange on my tongue.

The sound of my voice breaks whatever spell he is under. "Piper?" He blinks rapidly, like his eyes are playing tricks on him. "You're... here. In Sweetbriar."

I nod.

"When did you...?"

"Just a few days ago."

"You look..." His words trail off on a slow exhale while he thinks of the right word to use. Then, after another slow perusal of my figure, he finally settles on "beautiful."

"Thank you," I say, my cheeks flushing under the admiration in his gaze. A small smile blooms on my face while I look him over in the light. "You clean up well, too."

Any awkwardness I felt between us dissipates, slowly replaced with something much more dangerous. I am helpless, caught in Simon's snare, while an invisible wire wraps around me and tugs me forward. I am barely aware that I have moved until the scent of sweet tobacco and sandalwood wraps around me.

One corner of Simon's mouth curves up at the sound of my shaky breath. He takes a step forward, eating away at the rest of the space between us, his close proximity making my heart race.

Having Simon's gaze locked on me like this feels good. Too good. It makes me bold and reckless, and I reach up without thinking to lightly run my fingers down the silk sleeve of his dinner jacket. He tenses in surprise, a tiny reaction that only lasts seconds yet hits me like a slap to the cheek. I hastily drop my hand back down to my side. Then I retreat a step.

Simon is poised as if to follow. Then he shakes his head and, clearing his throat, breaks the awkward silence around us. "I, uh, try to avoid them as a rule."

I blink in confusion. "Clothes?"

"Only the formal kind." He chuckles, and the sound of it trickles over me, soothing more of my frayed nerves.

We both have goofy grins on our faces. I can't help but think how good Simon looks when his lips curve into that same boyish smile I remember.

"Pity," I reply, quickly slipping into our old banter. My eyes flare in surprise at how easy it is to joke with Simon. How quickly I forget everything but being in the moment.

Simon's gaze heats. "I think I could make an exception for you."

"Tempting, but"—I tilt my head toward the large picture windows and the crowded room within—"I doubt everyone is looking to see a nude display tonight." Then I giggle. "Well, other than the ones already available."

We are at an art center, after all.

"I don't know," he says, stepping forward again, drawing nearer. "It might help raise more funds."

"You seem terribly confident."

"Oh, I am, little bird."

Hearing my pet name after all these years jolts me right out of this little fantasy. It feels like he dumped a bucket of ice water over my head. My face burns in contrast with the shiver that runs down my spine.

Fool.

I should never have fallen so quickly into these old patterns. I should have known better. This sense of safety and familiarity surrounding Simon is a lie. Simon is far from safe. Minutes in his presence, and my walls start to crumble.

I need those walls intact.

"Piper..." Simon cringes at his mistake, too late.

"I have to go," I gasp, fighting for air.

Gathering my skirt in one hand to keep from tripping, I turn toward the stairs. I only make it one step before Simon places a hand on my wrist. He gently tugs me to a stop.

"Wait," he pleads.

My heart twists at the sadness in his voice, but I can't bring myself to look at him. "What do you want, Simon?"

One breath. Two. "Nothing." Simon's hand drops from my skin, though his heat lingers there like a brand. I hear the defeat in his voice when he says, "I'm sorry."

I risk a glance in his direction. His face already wears that polite mask, but his eyes flicker with emotion—guilt, sadness, and frustration—forcing me to look away again.

Simon keeps collecting things to apologize for, and I'm not sure which apology this one refers to. Honestly, no verbal regrets will help. No words will get rid of the pain he caused years ago–or that deep-rooted sorrow carved into my bones.

So I say two words of my own, and I hope he gets the message behind them:

"Goodbye, Simon."

INTERLUDE 2

Two

- Sunday 3:30 am -

Unknown number: Do you think you make a fool of me?

Unknown number: After I cleaned up after your little disappearing act at the last tour stop?

Unknown number: I was willing to overlook that, but then I find out you're whoring yourself out in that podunk hometown of yours

Unknown number: Dressing up, attending fucking galas?

Unknown number: I never approved that

Unknown number: I never approved any of this, you bitch

Missed call.

Unknown number: This is bullshit, Piper. PICK. UP. THE. DAMN. PHONE!

Missed call.

This number has been blocked.

Chapter 7
Obsession

Simon

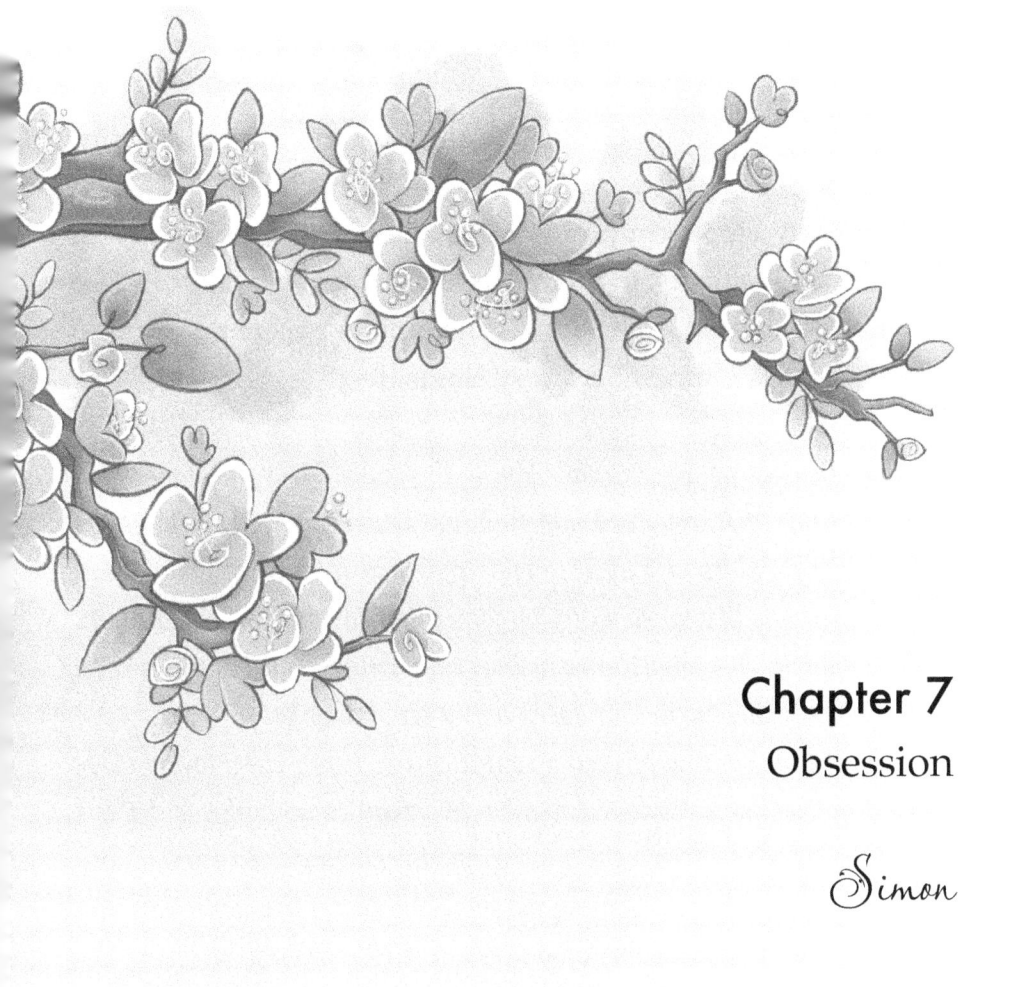

Piper and I were acquainted before meeting face-to-face because we grew up in such a small town. Our families were involved in some of the same activities; we attended the same church, and I often saw her around town.

Sweetbriar has always been progressive, especially when it comes to the arts. The local café, Jelly Beans, always puts on live events for local artists. One night in particular, they held a singer/songwriter competition, so my friends and I decided to go check it out. (It was a Friday, and we were bored teenagers with nothing better to do.)

That night, I fell hard for Piper Easton.

She was the second-to-last act to perform. Everyone prior had been good—some even exceptionally talented—but when Piper slowly stepped up onto the stage, quiet and purposeful with her movements, everything else fell away. None of those other acts mattered. All I saw was her and her acoustic guitar.

To this day, I remember every single detail.

Jelly Beans was filled to the brim with people. Near the stage stood a large group of starry-eyed hopefuls just waiting for their chance to shine. Café regulars and local townspeople had taken over every other surface—people like me looking for something to do on a Friday night. Since small towns aren't exactly bursting with social activities on a nightly basis, this particular event was a bit of a novelty.

My friends commandeered a round corner booth close to the stage while I got in line to order us drinks. Beckham came with me. I think he needed a breather from the other guys. Beckham played football, but the sport was far from a lifelong passion. Not like it was with me. And our crew could be a lot for anyone, especially a broody introvert like Beck.

Unlike my best friend, I lived and breathed football. Someday I would play for the NFL. I dreamed of winning the Heisman trophy and becoming a household name. I had the talent and the drive. I made the varsity team as a freshman—which, for Hazelwood High, was extremely difficult to do—and scouts were already taking notice.

I was on top of the damn world. Mostly.

Beckham pulled me from my thoughts with a shoulder nudge. When I looked at him, he nodded toward the girl behind the counter, who watched us with a bored expression while she waited to take our order.

After, we quickly paid for and gathered the drinks, and then returned to our booth—just in time for first performer. He dressed like a character out of that old western show, Bonanza. His cover of Wagon Wheel, while not bad, was nothing to write home about.

The next performer—a middle-school Broadway star wannabe— fared only slightly better.

After that, there was a heavy-metal singer, two rappers, three country singers, a folksy, Simon-and-Garfunkel-style singer with a pan flute, and at least half a dozen budding pop stars.

We stayed for them all, but I could feel my interest dropping in time with my energy. Our group had been there from the beginning. I could tell Beckham's fun meter was pegged, and mine followed close behind.

Just as I opened my mouth to suggest leaving, the evening's master of ceremonies introduced the newest act. As soon as I heard the name "Piper Easton," I straightened with interest and my mouth snapped shut. The young woman walking onto the stage was someone who— until now—I only ever saw in passing. We never spoke one word to each other. We ran in different social circles. Even then, I could never forget Piper.

Not in a million years.

Piper had the kind of beauty that snuck up on a person. Her long, white-blonde hair hung down her back in a simple braid, while several loose pieces escaped their confines and framed her heart-shaped face. Black eyeliner gave her otherwise natural face a dramatic look. She wore her signature style: knee-high black cowboy boots, a cropped and ripped band shirt paired with denim jeans, and a makeshift bandana headband. Rock and roll mixed with a touch of country.

My breath stalled while she approached the microphone. I knew that Piper loved music, but I had never heard her play before. Suddenly, I needed to know everything: how her voice sounded. what kind of music she played.

After a few seconds spent fiddling with her guitar, a rich and slightly haunting melody drifted through the room. The song she played brought to mind late-night bonfires, intimacy, and sharing secrets in the dark.

Then she started to sing.

Her voice had a smoky, husky quality, like one of those old-time jazz singers. The song started soft, but her voice held a restrained power behind every word, and when it needed to, she turned into a vocal powerhouse. Her sound weaved itself in and around me. The lyrics cast a spell that lasted until the very last note faded into silence.

When the room erupted into cheers and applause, Piper jolted out of her own musical trance. Flustered, her cheeks flushed a pretty shade of pink. She stood and backed away from the microphone after an awkward little bow.

I kept her in sight, tracked her while she headed offstage and neared our table. Just as she moved past, our gazes locked. Time slowed to a crawl. Those pale green eyes flared in recognition. A small smile curved her lips. Even though we were in a crowded room, that smile felt like a secret meant just for me. My own lips curled up in response.

We held like that for an eternity, silently saying everything and nothing all at once. When she finally moved past, the sweet aroma of peaches and cream wafted by with her. I breathed in deeply, trying to memorize the scent, but time snapped back into place as soon as she passed by. Everything connected to her slipped away.

Beside me, Beckham whistled low. "Damn," he breathed.

"Yeah."

Beckham knew all about my infatuation. Nudging my shoulder with his own, Beckham nodded toward the front counter when I *glanced his way. Then he raised an eyebrow and asked, "What the hell are you still doing here?"*

Fuck. He was right. This was the first chance I had to hold an actual conversation with Piper, and I would not squander it.

Time to make my move.

- 9:15 am -

Simon: You awake yet?

Ellery: No

Simon: I'm downstairs

Ellery: No

Simon: I brought coffee

Ellery: …. from Jelly Beans?

Simon: Obviously.

Ellery: On my way

I'm not above bribery to get my way. Besides, I need coffee as much as my sister. Maybe more. I barely got any sleep last night.

After the gala, I headed home in a haze of confusion and other conflicting emotions: surprise, delight, concern, worry, excitement—and a healthy dose of lust. I stripped down, crawled under the covers, and stared at the ceiling for the next hour. Then I gave up and went downstairs until I started to feel sleepy. I went back to bed and stared at the ceiling.

Lather.

Rinse.

Repeat.

When Ellery finally answers the door, I see what she meant about not being awake. She leans heavily against the doorjamb.

That rat's nest of strawberry-blonde curls on her head bounces chaotically around her face. Her hazel eyes are drooping, threatening to flutter closed at any moment.

Then Ellery's gaze zeroes in on the cardboard cups in my grip. I silently hold out the one with her name scrawled in loopy script, and she snatches it from my hand. Greedy goblin. Then she absently motions me inside.

I follow Ellery through the house and onto the back porch. Both of us settle into rustic Adirondack chairs that face the water.

"Where's Beck?" I ask.

"Still sleeping." She lifts the cup to her lips.

I mirror the action, letting the warmth of the coffee seep into my bones and loosen some of the tension lingering since last night. The bitter taste jolts my sluggish system.

The coffee also gives me enough liquid strength to demand, "Why didn't you tell me Piper came back home?"

Ellery slumps her shoulders. "I guess we're already done with the small-talk portion of the morning."

"Come on, Elle, you had to know I would come beating down your door about this. You"—I shake my head and rephrase—"no, *Piper* completely blindsided me." Frustrated, I run a hand through my hair. "Would it have been so bad to warn me? I felt like an idiot."

Ellery sets her drink down. She takes one of my hands in hers. "I'm sorry, Si. Truly. I ran into her just a couple of days ago myself. The invitation tumbled out while we were talking, and then I was afraid to say anything because I thought you wouldn't attend the gala if you knew she would be there."

"That gala was a huge deal for you and the art center," I argue, hurt that she could think so little of me. "I never would have missed that, pipsqueak. Not for anything."

Ellery nods, looking down without responding. Not that she needs to. My sister knows exactly how it feels to have a tangled up love life. A little over a year ago, she and Beckham came face-to-face after a decade long estrangement. She had always been in love with my best friend (news to me; I was oblivious to the whole thing). When Beckham started developing feelings for her, the timing was all wrong, and he used his military career to distance himself.

They had some twists and turns in their relationship—including ones I caused out of a misplaced sense of responsibility—but they are finally getting their happily-ever-after. After I got my head removed from my ass, I could see how good they are together.

I just wish that my own situation held that kind of promise.

"Did Piper say what she came home for?" My voice stays neutral even though my insides burn with curiosity.

"No. Just that she planned to stay for a while—I think for at least a few months. Something about needing a break."

"From?"

Ellery shrugs. Then, after a moment, she peeks over at me. "Piper looks good, don't you think?"

Piper looks like a goddess.

"I didn't notice," I lie.

Because I did notice. I noticed everything that night, from the curves that filled out her skin-tight dress to the toned leg peeking out from the thigh-high slit. I noticed every strand of white-blonde hair as it cascaded like silk over one shoulder, her cherry red lips, and those familiar, pale green eyes.

I also caught her haunted expression and the tension in her limbs—despite doing her best to act flirty and unaffected. And those mental walls she built were solid, welded steel. No one could possibly break through. It hurt like hell, being something she wanted to keep out, but I only have myself to blame.

Ellery and I finish our coffee in silence, staring out at the water. The natural symphony all around us makes the lack of conversation slightly less awkward. But my muscles are twitchy, still reacting to the news that Piper is home.

In the light of day, our every interaction from the gala takes on a different meaning. Each word spoken, a different nuance. I dissect the entire encounter like one of my cases, looking for clues and trying to fit bits of information together like puzzle pieces.

Suddenly I need to move. Figure out my next steps. Something. Anything. So I say my goodbyes to Ellery with the a promise not to "do something stupid."

I wave her off, barely listening while I head to my truck and climb inside.

The entire ride home, I can only think of one thing:

Piper came home.

Everything else can be managed. I just need to get her to talk to me—really talk to me—without all the fake platitudes and flirty overtures. That's the first step.

It will be far from easy, but when is anything of worth easy? And when have I ever shied away from a challenge?

Chapter 8
Bad Blood

Piper

- Sun, Nov 3 at 5:00 pm -

Piper: Hey, lil sis. I'm in Sweetbriar! Staying with Mom and Pop

Piper: Do you want to come over for dinner? I'd love to see you

Read 5:15 pm

- Sun, Nov 3 at 5:30 pm -

Piper: Mom said you can't make it. Maybe another time?

Read 6:50 pm

- Wednesday 11:30 am -

Piper: Could we meet for lunch?

Daisy: Busy with work

Piper: Oh, OK - rain check?

Read 11:45 am

Forgiveness is difficult—hard to give and even harder to earn. My new therapist, Delaney Abbott—a good friend of Grace who specializes in different types of mental and physical abuse—uses our time together to focus on rebuilding bridges that I burned during the last few years. We talk a lot about forgiveness during those hours. I still struggle with the concept.

How can I hope for others to forgive me when I can't even forgive myself?

Delaney thinks I get closer with each session. I still have a long way to go before I am near self-redemption. But she is right: I need to start rebuilding bridges.

That starts with my little sister, Daisy.

Out of everything I ruined, all the relationships that burned to the ground, ours took the worst hit.

Mom and Pop are my parents, so they love me unconditionally. They loved me through all the hard years and trauma. That never changed, no matter how I behaved or how much distance I created. Grace loves me like only a big sister can: one with the added benefit of professional insight. It allowed her to see through the fog, and she used her stubborn nature to stay as close as possible.

Daisy loves like the sun: big, bright, and all-encompassing.

Her love is also fragile.

When I severed our ties, Daisy internalized the hurt and left it to rot. Years of bitterness and resentment have created a wall to keep me out. Now, I have to try to find a way back in.

Reaching out that first day proved futile. Daisy has been frustratingly unreceptive. She has somehow managed to dodge every invitation from Mom to come for dinner, which is a feat in and of itself. (Mom has perfected the art of guilt-tripping manipulation.) Pop even tried a few times and had just as much luck. My only successful interaction with Daisy comes from the single text she sent me last week. Everyone can see how well that turned out.

While I walk down Main Street at lunchtime, my mind whirls with thoughts of Daisy and my current predicament—frustrating since I came into town to *escape* everything for a bit. Unfortunately, my brain insists on hyper-fixating on the problem. Admittedly, the walk helps with that. By the time I come up to the entrance of Beauty & Bliss—Sweetbriar's local hair salon and beauty bar—I have the beginnings of a plan.

Daisy appreciates honesty and genuine emotion above all else. I love that about her and always have. She says what she means and means what she says. We used to share that personality trait until I let Cedric reprogram me into a mindless robot. Daisy never would have fallen for the manipulations and mind games Cedric likes to play.

Her inner strength far outweighs mine.

Daisy also has no tolerance for bullshit and petty drama. But that no-nonsense attitude means I need to take a more direct approach. A more direct approach means bulldozing myself straight into her path. Once I get there, I have faith that everything else will fall into place, but the getting there part gives me severe heartburn.

Just as I pass the doorway to Beauty & Bliss, I hear someone call my name. Confused, I retreat a few steps and peek through the doorway.

Speak of the devil...

Daisy hurries toward me from the back of the salon, and my body instantly braces for a confrontation. There has been too much discord since I returned home. The stress I had hoped to release by coming home has only piled on top of the strain of the past several years, and I am beginning to buckle under the weight.

But when Daisy stops before me, her face is contrite instead of condemning. Sadness colors each feature. Fidgeting, visibly uncomfortable, she asks, "Do you have a second to talk?"

I am beyond grateful that she sweeps straight past fake pleasantries.

"Well, I'm headed to Jelly Beans to grab lunch." I motion vaguely in the direction of the coffee shop. "Would you like to come with me?"

Daisy smiles at my invitation. I am taken by surprise to see a genuine smile on her face. My hope flares brighter at the sight, and a tightness in my chest starts to loosen.

"Yeah," she says. "Let me just grab my stuff."

Seconds later, she reappears with a large tote bag slung over one shoulder and a chunky scarf wrapped around her neck. She slips a pair of adorably ostentatious sunglasses onto her nose and motions me forward.

We walk silently for a few blocks to Jelly Beans. The quaint artisan café is in an old duplex that the owners—Faith Doherty and her partner, Anna Thompson—bought and renovated. The right side is now Jelly Beans, a coffee shop and cafe, and the left side is the Quill, a restaurant and grille. Both establishments have a literary theme.

Soon our destination appears at the end of the street. When we get close enough, I can see through their tinted windows—and right into the packed interior. Unfortunately, it seems like everyone in town decided to eat lunch out.

Daisy opens the door. Bustling midday activity greets us, and the tantalizing aroma of coffee grounds and freshly baked pastries wafts out onto the sidewalk. Once we step inside, I notice that only a few people stand in line, which means that we get to the front in record time. Anna works the register, greeting everyone with a warm and friendly demeanor. Her graying brown hair is wrapped up in a bun, and she wears a punchy pink "Jelly Beans" apron.

When we step up to the counter, she lifts her gaze and smiles. "Well," she says, "hello to two of my favorite customers!"

"Hi, Anna." Daisy shakes her head at the older woman, laughing. "I know for a fact you say that to almost everyone who walks in here."

"What can I say?" she says with a wink. "I have lots of favorites."

She can hardly mean me. Before now, the last time I stepped foot in Jelly Beans was over a decade ago—much like everything else in this town. My disbelief must show on my face, because Anna's expression softens and she reaches out to grasp my hands.

"I'm so happy to see you, Piper." Her chocolate brown eyes sparkle with warmth and understanding. "Congratulations on all your accomplishments. We're all very proud of you."

"You are?" My voice holds a note of uncertainty.

Anna nods, her smile brightening. "You left home to chase your dreams. Who in their right mind would begrudge you for going after the life you were made for? Not one person I can think of feels bitter about your success. We celebrate it."

My chest has held onto a knotted ball of anxiety since I stepped foot in town two weeks ago, fearing—what, exactly? I have no clue. Maybe small-town gossips who believe everything they read in trashy magazines. Maybe censure or blatant hatred. I have spent so much time believing Cedric's lies that they blur together with the truth. Now I jump at shadows, unsure of who or what to believe.

But I want to believe Anna. No. I *do* believe her. For the first time, that ball of anxiety feels much smaller and more manageable.

"Thank you, Anna," I say with a grateful grin. "It's good to be back home."

And I mean it.

We quickly give our food and drink orders, starting with Daisy. Anna shocks me when she remembers the exact drink I used to get every time I came in.

"One large Butterbrew Latte," she recites, "with oat milk, whipped cream, and an extra drizzle of butterscotch."

"Y-yeah," I say, impressed. "Exactly that."

Daisy insists on paying. "My treat," she says with a small, hopeful smile on her face. I let her, not wanting to risk causing any more bad blood.

Too much has been spilled already.

Daisy looks around the room for seats while I grab our drinks and the number for our food. When I join her, I notice that the room has only gotten more crowded.

"Do you want to sit outside?" Daisy asks.

"Can we?" I ask.

Anna and Faith used to keep the courtyard reserved for outdoor events and private parties. Closed to the general public means that Daisy and I will have plenty of privacy to talk. I love this town but not how everybody seems to be tied up in everybody else's business.

"Leave it to me," Daisy answers, winking before she saunters back over to the counter. After a few words spoken to Anna, the older woman nods, smiles, and hands over a small key. Daisy waves and then returns to my side.

"Shall we?" she asks, dangling the key from her fingers.

I motion for her to lead the way.

Afternoon sunlight keeps the outdoor space warm and pleasant wherever it touches. We sit down across from each other, sinking into two plush outdoor seats. Needing something to keep me occupied, I wrap my hands around and hold tightly to the ceramic mug, studying the speckled glaze and the Jelly Beans logo stamped on the side. The heat gives me something else to focus on other than wondering who will speak first. Steam wafts under my nose. I close my eyes to breath in the aromas of fresh coffee, butterscotch, and toffee mingling together. Then I take a tentative sip. Familiar flavors burst on my tongue just as Daisy speaks, turning them to ash in my mouth.

"Mom told me."

I gasp and swallow at the same time, choking on the coffee yet somehow managing not to devolve into a coughing fit. Slowly, calmly, I set the mug down. Then I turn toward my sister. Her face looks wary like she expects me to react badly.

But I have no reaction at all.

I just feel numb from the shock.

Daisy rushes to fill the silence. "Not every detail," she explains, nervously talking a mile a minute, "but enough. Please don't be mad at her. It was my fault. We fought, and she just kept saying that it was your story to tell, that she refused to betray your trust—but I kept pushing, and I finally hit the right buttons, and it just sort of came out."

In the silent aftermath of her admission, I mull over the words. Should I feel angry that Mom took the choice away from me? Maybe I should worry more about what Daisy must think of me. But I just feel relief.

Daisy knows the truth.

Right now, nothing else matters.

"I'm so sorry." I reach out and take her hands in mine. "Sorry for the distance, the way I treated you…"

"Piper, you really don't need"—Daisy stops when I squeeze her fingers.

"Yes, I do. As much as I wish I could blame everything on"—I stop, shaking my head. It feels wrong to say his name right now. "Not all of it was *him*. I could have reached out if I really wanted to, but I felt too ashamed, too embarrassed. I was sure everyone here hated me, and I didn't blame them one bit. So many bridges burned. Over time the rifts grew too big to cross"—I shrug and look away—"so I never tried."

Daisy watches me in silence, contemplating my words. I notice how young she looks. Like this, she reminds me of the little girl who chased me around our backyard with pigtails in her hair.

Life back then felt so much simpler—less painful and messy.

But time only lets us move forward.

"I wish you had trusted me enough to tell me," she adds, "but I understand why you chose not to."

"It was never about trust, Daisy. I promise." I look down at our joined hands. "Not a day went by without all of you taking up space in my thoughts. My love has always been there. I just let fear overshadow it."

Daisy nods and pulls me into a hug. When we separate, she whispers, "I'm sorry, too."

"For what?" I ask, surprised.

Of all the things to say, I never expected that. Daisy laughs, a sound full of bitterness and sharp edges. Then her chin starts to quiver.

"Take your pick," she says bitingly, wiping at the tears in her eyes. "I'm sorry for not realizing something was wrong. I'm sorry I turned away when you tried to reach out."

"Don't." I look away, shaking my head at her apology. Despite my best efforts to hold them back, the tears that have been threatening to fall now spill over and down my face. "You have nothing to be sorry for"—my words cut off when Daisy interjects.

"Yes, I do!" she cries. Then, something between a sob and a caterwaul comes out of her tiny body. Her next words are a garbled mess, and it takes me a minute to decipher their meaning. "I was an ugly, raging bitch."

Daisy says the word "bitch" with such disgust that it smacks me right in the chest, knocking the breath from my lungs. I stare at her, wide eyed, and she stares back.

Something in her red, blotchy face—identical to the tantrums she threw as a little girl—sets me off. A watery giggle bubbles out of my chest. Daisy's expression turns wounded and petulant, tears and snot running down her face, which only makes me giggle harder.

Then her lips wobble, and her nose twitches, and she pouts, "Not funny!" while suddenly fighting off her own fits of laughter.

We feed off of each other—crying and laughing, and looking for all the world like we just broke out of an asylum. But the laughter is as cathartic as the tears, one final release of guilt and blame so that we can move forward. I feel much lighter by the time we both taper off into silence.

Hopefully Daisy does, too.

We take a few moments to put ourselves back together. Then Daisy turns back to me. She has an uncharacteristically solemn expression on her face.

"I really am sorry," she quietly states.

"Me, too," I reply, equally quiet.

"Sisters forever?" Daisy holds a pinky in the air between us.

Her words echo our childhood. We spoke the same mantra then, whenever we needed a reminder that no matter what, we would always be there for each other. Hearing the phrase again brings another smile to my face, one so big that it hurts.

"Sisters forever."

Chapter 9
My Mirror

Piper

I need my own space.

As much as I love Mom and Pop, living in my childhood home has done nothing to help my creative block. Living there may even be making it worse. Daisy offers to let me stay with her, but I want nothing to risk our truce and newfound relationship.

When I bring the issue up with my therapist, Delaney suggests I find a place to rent. It just so happens that her parents recently moved into a retirement home. They put their small cottage on the market but have had no luck finding a decent renter.

Honestly, the whole thing feels like fate.

They take me on a tour of the fully furnished house, which feels like a warm hug when I walk inside for the first time. Everything has a cute, kitschy vibe. While not my usual style, I can see it growing on me.

But the thing I love most of all is that this house feels like a *home*.

I jump at the offer.

Within forty-eight hours, I sign the paperwork, get the keys, and sit curled up in a rocking chair on my new back porch. I stare out over the woods that line the edge of the property, a sense of peace seeping into my bones.

I love everything about my new rental except one tiny detail: the back property line butts up to the Briar Patch, which means that Simon's house is within walking distance. While sitting on the back porch, I can even see the roof through a break in the trees.

Which had absolutely no bearing on my decision to rent.

None at all.

Ozzy and Cooper lay sprawled out on the sunlit part of the porch, snoring loudly. I chuckle while I watch them, finding comfort in how well they have adapted to small-town life.

They are both thriving.

So am I.

Nothing has changed since coming home—not really. So many things still hover in the air, waiting to drop. I have so many thoughts and feelings left to sift through and wounds to heal, but I have made great strides. I now know, without a doubt, that my family will never abandon me, no matter how much I think I deserve it.

That's what makes them family.

And not just any family. Mine.

Forever and always.

That knowledge settles into my bones, a truth I will never forget again. But those relationships include more than just flesh and blood relatives. I look up and peek through the trees at the Brooks' farmhouse. Sunlight glances off the roof like a beacon, tugging my heart in that direction.

Ellery will always be a sister to me.

And, Simon, well—maybe someday Simon and I can be friends.

Friends.

My chest burns at the word, a sharp jab like a hot poker running me straight through. I reach up to rub my sternum.

It sounds so wrong.

Friends.

How can Simon and I ever be friends? Just hearing his name sends my pulse fluttering like a hundred butterflies. Every time I recall that night at the gala, I feel the ghost of desire take hold. I remember the feel of his heat and the smell of his cologne. I remember wondering if he tastes as good as he looks.

I have no desire for his friendship.

But I may have to settle for it.

What I truly want from Simon is something I can never have.

Enough, Piper. Shift that train of thought.

For once, I listen to myself.

Tonight is my first Easton family dinner since returning home. I focus on that. Now that Daisy and I have reconciled, Pop has declared the dinners back on. It may be silly, but I'm looking forward to this—a little taste of simpler times in the middle of the mess that is my life.

I need those little bits of normalcy like I need air.

Sighing, I look down at my phone. When the time lights up on the screen, I jolt to my feet and hustle toward my bedroom. Unfortunately, my wandering thoughts pushed me past the "politely early" arrival time and much closer to the "more than fashionably late" arrival time.

Whoops.

See what a distraction Simon is? You don't need that in your life right now—or ever.

I hate how right my inner thoughts can be.

"Cooper, Ozzy," I say, then follow their names with a short whistle. They scramble to their feet and follow me in.

I shower in record time, throwing my hair up in a messy bun instead of going through all the trouble of shampooing, conditioning, and styling (there is a lot of hair to deal with). Besides, I washed it yesterday. It's fine. No problem. Who am I trying to impress, anyway?

Just my family—and I did say they love me no matter what.

With that thought, I also skip makeup. My bare face will pair nicely with my last-minute outfit choice: a slouchy, oversized Led Zeppelin sweatshirt and black leggings. I quickly throw the clothes on before shoving my feet into simple flats.

Honestly, it feels good not to get dressed up. Cathartic. I hold onto the feeling while I walk across the room.

It almost works.

Right before I step outside the bedroom, I catch myself in the full-length mirror by the door. I come to a dead stop in front of it. My gaze locks on my reflection while I give myself a thorough once-over.

I missed this.

That single thought is fleeting, shoved aside when Cedric's cruel voice takes up all the space in my mind.

You're not going out in public wearing that, are you? Doll, you're a celebrity now. People expect a certain flair, but not whatever the hell that is.

Your little punk, rock-a-billy look was cute when you played dive bars in Nashville, but come on. You're playing in the big leagues now.

God, you're such an embarrassment. Put something on that won't have the TV audience laughing you off the set.

Well, I suppose you could look worse.

Is that really how you're wearing your hair?

Why can't you act like you care about your appearance?

Pinching my eyes closed and covering my ears, I try to block him out. I take several slow, deep breaths to exorcise his ghost. When my gaze snaps back up to my face, I see how even the echo of him sinks its claws into me. Embarrassment flushes my face and neck a mottled red, the same red as the rim of my eyes where tears start to form.

My reflection frowns at me from behind the glass. Then a sudden rush of anger floods my body. Cedric is hundreds of miles away. He has no control over me. Not anymore.

I look fine—no, *better* than fine.

I look like *me*.

But I still feel this intense urge to change, to put on something *more appropriate*. I have to fight it back with everything in me. I will no longer change who I am for another human being.

Never again.

"Come on, babies," I call out to Ozzy and Cooper, heading toward the front door. My steps are heavy with purpose. "It's time for Mama to reclaim her identity."

✳✳✳

As I pull up to my Mom and Pop's house, Daisy peeks out and waves excitedly. I am barely out of the car, letting Ozzy and Cooper out of the backseat when she squeals and comes racing down the front sidewalk.

"Let me meet my furry nephews!" she cries out.

I roll my eyes. Daisy ignores me in favor of dive-bombing between the two massive dogs. When she looks up at me, she has a big smile, and I feel it spread through me, telling me that things are genuinely okay between us. Daisy is quick to forgive, a fact that I am grateful for.

"Piper, is that you, honey?" My mom calls out, voice muffled from somewhere inside the house.

I look at Daisy, who waves me on. "I'll take care of these cuddle bugs," she says, standing. Then she bends over them and asks, "Do you want to play in the backyard? I bet you do, you precious noodles," before leading them in that direction.

Meanwhile, I head into the house through the front door. I find Mom in the kitchen, working on some last-minute dinner preparation.

"There you are." Mom smiles warmly and wraps me in a hug. "I miss having you here, believe it or not. The house is too quiet now. I feel like an empty nester all over again."

"You don't miss me," I say with a grin, "You miss having Ozzy and Cooper here to spoil."

"True."

I laugh and hug Mom tighter. After a minute, she pulls back. Her gaze turns toward the kitchen counter and lands on the items I set down when I arrived. She notices the bottle of wine peeking out of my bag.

"Oh, sweetie, you didn't have to bring anything," she chides even as she reaches for the bottle like a kid grabbing candy.

"Please," I say, voice teasing, "like I would ever step past the threshold for family dinner without a bottle of wine in hand."

I learned long ago that my dear mother's love language is wine. Her eyebrows shoot almost to her hairline when she reads the brand printed on the label.

"Oh, my." She peeks up at me and then back down at the label.

"I, uh, hope that's okay." Nervously, I fidget with the ends of my sleeves. Maybe I should have asked what to bring instead of assuming she would like this one. "It's one of my favorites."

"Of course, it's okay, honey, but…" Mom trails off, turning the bottle over slowly in her hands. "This is an expensive bottle."

My cheeks flush. "Yeah, a little."

"No, not a little. More like a lot." Mom shakes her head slowly, staring at the bottle like it might disappear if she looks away. "A whole lot," she murmurs absently.

I swear that if Mom calls that bottle of wine her precious, I will leave. But she hugs it to her chest momentarily like she fears someone will swipe it from her. Then, her expression transforms into one of childlike glee when she looks my way.

"This is just perfect, sweetie," Mom says, grinning ear-to-ear. "Thank you."

She flits around the kitchen without waiting for a response, opening the bottle before pouring herself a generous glass. I bite my lip to keep from laughing.

"Can I help with anything?" I ask, looking around.

Mom follows my gaze and answers almost absently, reciting the list of tasks in her head. "Well, dinner is all taken care of. I've got dessert warming in the oven. Once I set the table, I'll need to run upstairs to freshen up and then—"

"Go." I gently push her toward the stairs. "Freshen up. I'll set the table." Mom hesitates until I sternly say, "Stop micromanaging and shoo."

"My children," she gripes, "always so much sass."

"Yeah? Who do you think we got that from?" I deadpan.

She shoots me a halfhearted glare. "You see? Sass."

I laugh and wave her away. But, before she disappears onto the top landing, I ask, "Hey, where's Pop?"

"Fiddling with the grill, of course." Her voice trails behind her after she slips from view. "Set the table. Then you can say hi."

"Yes, Mom." I throw a little extra sass into my voice just for her. Then, smiling, I head into the dining room to get started.

My mind wanders while I set out the plates, silverware, and wine glasses. Our weekly family dinners started with my biological father, but they were nightly family dinners back then. Dad always made sure we sat down as a family every night, no matter how busy life got. After he died, Mom wanted to honor him by keeping the tradition alive. Then the tradition carried over into our new life with Pop.

Getting lost in thought means I finish setting the table in record time. Once I finish folding the last napkin, I head onto the back patio to find Pop. He stands in front of the grill with a spatula in hand, arranging the finished steaks onto a serving platter while keeping an eye on the others. Daisy likes hers well done. We like to joke that she is a changeling, because no one else in our family would ever defile a steak like that.

"Hi, Pop," I say as I sidle up to him.

"Well, hey there, Pip." He pulls me into a sideways hug. I lean into it, siphoning the warmth and security that only a father can bring.

Pop has never been anything less than an actual father to me, despite starting as my stepfather. He even legally adopted me when he married Mom. Pop wanted me to have his last name and to legally be as much his daughter as Grace (and Daisy, when she came two years later).

"Mom driving you crazy yet?" I ask, smirking up at him.

Releasing me to slide the spatula under Daisy's steak, Pop winks and says, "Why do you think I'm out here?"

"I heard that, Foster." Mom appears after her voice, crossing her arms over her chest to level Pop with a mock glare.

Pop bends and kisses her on the lips. "Crazy with love, my dearest. So crazy that sometimes I have to escape for a while so it doesn't consume me."

"You and that silver tongue of yours," she mutters, a reluctant smile blooming.

Pop sets his spatula aside and pulls her closer. "But you like my silver tongue. Especially all the ways it can—"

"Ugh, Dad! Stop." Daisy trails toward us with the dogs in tow. "I do not want to hear what you do to Mom with your tongue." She grabs the tray of steaks and brushes past us. "I'm too hungry to lose my appetite, and it'd be a shame for this amazing food to go to waste."

"Oh, like that hockey puck that you plan on eating?" Pop asks.

Daisy shoots him the middle finger over one shoulder just as she disappears behind the sliding glass door. We burst into laughter and follow her. Mom has the dogs at her side, lapping up the attention she showers them with while Pop hangs back and matches step with me.

"How you holding up, kiddo?" he asks.

"Holding steady, I guess." I shrug. Then a sigh escapes, and I add, "It's hard being back, you know?"

Pop stops at the open doorway and waits for me to continue. I scuff my shoe against the patio's wood. Maybe I should have kept my mouth shut and left it alone, but my internal conflict has been eating away at me, and I feel like if I keep it inside—if I fail to get it off my chest—it may very well eat me alive.

"Everything here feels the same, you know? But I've changed. I'm not sure where I belong anymore." I swallow thickly. "How do I make myself fit back into place here?"

"You don't."

I look up at him in confusion. "What do you mean?"

"Like you said, you changed," Pop explains. "You've grown out of your shell, left the nest, and seen the world. Hell, you made the world see you." He shakes his head, smiling gently. "Of course, the Piper in front of me is nothing like the Piper from back then. How could she be?"

I shake my head and start to pull back. He catches me by the shoulders, squeezing them gently in his grip once. Then he dips his head so we are eye-to-eye. His gaze is fierce.

"The Piper in front of me is someone I am very proud of," he says gruffly. "Someone I love very much. Never forget that. Because who you are at your core—kind, fierce, full of love and life? That part hasn't changed a bit."

Pop could always see more than anyone else. I can hardly be surprised that he sees how I struggle to find my way back to that person. But what if he is wrong? Maybe that Piper is lost for good. Still, despite my inner turmoil, his words take hold. They burrow into my heart, taking root and sprouting into a tiny seed of hope.

"We all change." Pop's voice pulls me back into the conversation. "None of us is immune. We change, little by little, day by day. Even old curmudgeons like me."

A relieved laugh escapes and, with it, the tension that has bunched up my shoulders. "So, what?" I ask. "I'll never fit in again?"

"Sweetheart, you were never meant to fit in. You were always meant to stand out and shine." Raising an eyebrow in challenge, he adds, "You just need to go out there and carve out a new place for yourself."

My heart swells for this big, gruff, bear-of-a-man. For the surrogate father and unlikely friend. I throw my arms around him and kiss him on the cheek. My voice cracks when I whisper, "Thanks, Pop."

He chuckles in my ear. "Anytime, Pip."

"You were *always* meant to *stand out* and *shine.*"

Chapter 10
Do You Still Love Me Like You Used To?

Piper

Family dinner transports me straight back to high school.

After our little heart-to-heart, Pop and I walk into the house and find the table laden with food. As soon as we all sit and dig in, we easily slip into our old roles. I eat my fill and laugh until my sides hurt. Daisy and I quickly devolve into our old sisterly banter while Pop throws conversational curveballs to keep us on our toes. Mom looks on with maternal pride, a wistful smile on her face.

Only one thing would make this night perfect. I can see it in Mom's eyes each time they glance at the space on Pop's left where Grace always sits. I make a mental note to call Grace soon.

Maybe they could come down for Christmas or New Year's. I know that would be a better surprise than any present I could think of.

While I make plans in my head, the front doorbell chimes. Mom hops out of her seat. The sudden motion yanks me from my thoughts and pulls my attention straight to her.

"Oh, good," Mom exclaims, cheeks rosy with excitement. She bustles out of the room with a few parting words. "I was hoping he would be able to stop by."

He? He, who? I look over at Pop and Daisy, but they busily clear the table of our empty plates and serving dishes. They quickly disappear into the kitchen while studiously avoiding my questioning gaze.

My entire family has lost its marbles, I decide.

I stand—curiosity piqued despite my best efforts—and wonder if I should sneak into the living room and eavesdrop. Before I take a step, I hear Mom from the hallway. Her voice grows louder the closer she gets, mingling with another voice—this one, a rich baritone.

My heart stutters.

I *know* that voice.

Seconds later, Mom rounds the corner, smiling. But my eyes lock on the figure directly behind her. Simon's sudden appearance sucks all the air from my lungs. His gaze sweeps the room, stopping when it lands on me.

Time freezes. I want to ask him why he came. I want to ask him so many things, but my tongue sticks like glue to the roof of my mouth.

I notice much more under the bright fluorescent lights than I could at the gala. Part of me wishes shadows still hid Simon because lust—pure, potent passion—and a long-dormant ache of longing shoot through my veins now that I see him in high definition.

Every new detail etches into my memory, trying to reconcile the Simon I remember with the Simon before me. Some things look the same—that familiar warmth in his hazel eyes and the russet gold of his hair. But other things—new things—require further study. His curls are longer and more artfully chaotic than he kept them in high school. He wears a short, trimmed beard and mustache that I itch to feel under my fingers.

Every night since the gala, Simon wearing a tux plays a starring role in my dreams. As good as he looked then, nothing could have prepared me for seeing him now in his police uniform. I memorize the tailored cut of the dark blue fabric on his tall frame and how it hugs his broad shoulders, then follow it down to where the shirt tucks into the waistband of his pants. My gaze locks there, and I am unable to look away.

"Piper," Mom says pointedly when my silence stretches too long. My gaze snaps up to hers, face flushing in embarrassment. Mom gives me a pointed smile and raises her eyebrows. "Look who stopped by on his way home from the station. So thoughtful of him, don't you think?"

Simon gives me a small, tentative smile. By the look of chagrin on his face, he knew that coming here would blindside me.

Yet he came anyway.

Wordlessly, I watch Simon run nervous fingers through his hair. His gaze returns to Mom when he explains, "I didn't think I could make it, to be honest. But paperwork got done a little earlier than expected."

Mom affectionately pats his arm. "You are welcome any time, dear, you know that. But you're lucky—you made it just in time for dessert."

Have I unwittingly entered an alternate dimension? My ex, the failed love of my life, stands in the middle of my childhood home while my mother acts like she expected him—like he does this all the time. Mom is oblivious to the bomb she lobbed at me, or she knows but feigns ignorance.

Either way, Mom notices my lack of manners. "Piper," she hisses, "don't be rude. Say hello to our guest."

My lips curl in a brittle smile. "Simon. What a surprise to see you. Here. With me. In my parents' home."

Yes. Simon knows how angry I am. He shifts slightly from one foot to the other—something he used to do whenever he felt uncomfortable. I feel a slight twinge of guilt. Maybe Simon deserves better than my cold welcome, but my entire body has switched to fight-or-flight mode.

This room has grown too stifling, and I have trouble breathing.

I need to go somewhere private to scream.

Simon wrecked my composure. I need to build it back up.

Twin menacing growls shred through the awkward silence right before Ozzy and Cooper appear. They must have felt my rising tension. Both dogs stand tall and flank me on either side, watching Simon with deadly focus and wary gazes. Simon immediately holds out his hands in a placating gesture.

"Sorry about that, fellas," he says, his voice gentle and slow. "I apologize if I startled you. I mean no harm."

By his relaxed posture and soft gaze, I can tell this is far from his first experience with fully trained guard dogs. Part of me wonders if he works with any police dogs.

Not important right now, Piper.

Right.

While I am grateful for how quickly Ozzy and Cooper picked up on the energy shift, Simon will never be a threat to me, and this standoff has gone on long enough. Resting my hands on their heads, I take a deep, calming breath to show them I am okay. Once I feel the tension leave Ozzy and then Cooper, I gesture and command them to "lay down." They retreat to the couch. While their keen eyes stay trained on us, they no longer look seconds away from killing a police officer.

Once the situation is under control, Pop and Daisy quietly slip back into the room. I notice that they also avoid my gaze.

Daisy says, "Hey, Simon," when she walks past and sits back at the table.

Pop claps him on the shoulder in a silent greeting before he joins Daisy.

I must be the only one who knew nothing about Simon stopping for a visit.

Mom, bless her heart, gives me the perfect opening to escape. "Here," she says, trying to clear the air, "why don't you two have a seat, and I'll grab the pie from the oven."

"I'll help." I move before she has a chance to protest.

"Oh, honey, you don't have to"—I cut her off with a glare and a curt, "I insist."

Mom quickly backs down. "Okay." To the family—and Simon—she adds, "We will be right back." Then she turns to enter the kitchen while I follow fast on her heels.

"I can't believe you invited Simon," I hiss, whirling on my mother as soon as the door closes behind us. "To family dinner, Mom? Really?"

Frowning slightly at my tone, she replies, "Well, he comes every week when he can manage it. That boy works entirely too much." Her voice warms with fondness. "Though, I suppose that's the sacrifice you make when you join the police force."

"Mom. Focus." I throw my hands out to the sides. "Do you have any idea how this makes me feel? You completely blindsided me."

Hurt seeps into Mom's voice, and she moves around the kitchen, gathering dessert plates and other utensils to avoid my gaze. "If you came home more often," she says quietly, "or even called during the holidays, you would never have felt blindsided tonight."

All my righteous indignation withers and dies. Guilt and shame take over; I burn with it while I watch Mom finish her task. She still refuses to look at me when she sets the utensils on the countertop.

"Mom," I softly say. The waver in my voice finally grants me her full attention. "You know why I—I thought you understood—I wanted to, but…"

My disjointed words somehow make sense to Mom. She takes my hands, her features softening in concern. "I know, baby. Now. But for years, I thought we had lost you. After you left, it felt like you had left all of us behind—not just Simon."

"I'm so sorry," I whisper. "More than I can say."

"Me, too." Her face blooms with a small, wistful smile. "Simon and I were both dealing with loss back then," she says, "and it was nice to talk about you with someone who missed you as much as I did."

I highly doubt Simon missed me, not with his string of females to keep him company—though I keep that thought to myself.

"Your Pop has never been a great conversationalist," she continues, "but Simon… That boy could talk with me for hours about you, even when it hurt. I think he was more afraid of forgetting than of the pain."

Her words carve new wounds into my chest, and I lash out. "Simon was why I left and never returned," I sneer. "He broke me. How can you stand there and act like he's the victim?"

"Piper Marie Easton," she scolds, "now I know I raised you with more empathy and understanding than this."

Pulling away, Mom points toward the other side of the house, where Simon sits at the table with the rest of my family. My gaze follows the path of her finger. I picture them all in the dining room, chatting and laughing at one of Pop's corny jokes.

"That young man made a mistake that he has regretted for years," she says, cutting into my thoughts. "I know how much he hurt you, but your pain does not white-wash the fact that Simon had just lost both of his parents and all of his dreams in one fell swoop. Dreams that included you, young lady, despite how things ended. Despite his hand in ending them." Her voice softens into sadness. "Simon needed someone in his corner."

"He had someone!" Hot tears fill my eyes until they start to burn. "Simon had me, Mom. *I* was in his corner. I would have done anything for him. Anything."

"I know, baby." Mom lets out a shaky breath. "Even so, Simon needed family. Ellery, too. And I needed to feel like my family was still whole."

Her admission hangs heavy between us for several breaths. As much as I try to fight—clinging to my hurt and trauma where I feel safe—the words still penetrate my armor and cool some of the fiery anger in my blood. Sighing with resignation, I reach for the peach cobbler cooling on a rack.

Before I exit the room, however, I turn back. "Hey, Mom?"

"Yes?" she asks, moving toward me while she cradles the dessert plates.

After a moment to sort my thoughts, I admit, "You're right about Simon. And"—I inhale, filling my lungs, and then releasing before I continue—"I'm glad he had you in his corner. I'm glad you had each other."

I smile at her, small but genuine, before quietly slipping through the door. When I return to the table, boisterous laughter teeters off at the end of one of Pop's jokes. I set the dessert down in between everybody. Pop and Daisy let loose rowdy cheers when Mom appears with the serving utensils. Simon stays silent through the familial chaos, but I feel his gaze on my skin like a warm caress. I settle back into my seat while Pop dishes out pie onto every plate.

After a beat, I risk a look in Simon's direction. His eyes shine with concern, making my heart skip a beat. I had forgotten that heady feeling that comes with being the sole recipient of Simon's focus.

When he mouths the question, *Everything okay?* I nod in response and give him a tentative smile.

Because, for once, everything does feel okay.

Since Simon came through that door this evening, I have been clinging to my anger like a lifeline—only that lifeline has turned into an albatross around my neck that threatens to pull me under. I have no desire to drown in bitter feelings any more than I want to be crushed by the weight of my guilt. Right now, I want to focus on family and forgiveness. The very least I can do is to show Simon the same grace my family has shown me these past few weeks.

Just for tonight, I decide to let go of all the baggage. I vow to live in the moment. All my old and new hurts will still be there in the morning.

"Simon had me, Mom. I was in his corner."

Chapter 11
I Miss You, I'm Sorry

Simon

I owe Piper an apology.

What I did the other night was underhanded—worse, I knew it was wrong even before I arrived at Stella and Foster's home. Not that it stopped me from showing up.

Call it a moment of weakness. I needed to see Piper and talk to her—even for a moment—enough to prove that she was real and not a hallucination from my mind. It was a stupid idea, and of course, it spectacularly backfired.

Piper showed me more grace that night than I deserved.

"Dude, where's your head at today?"

Nate's voice pulls me out of my thoughts and back into the middle of the park where I stand. I look down, brows knitting together in confusion. Am I meant to be doing something? I slowly turn around in a circle—and then notice the football resting several feet behind me and to my right.

Ah. Yes. Football.

"Sorry," I mutter, reaching down to grab the offending object. Then I arc my arm and toss the ball back toward the other makeshift team.

Whenever our schedules align, we all get together to play some casual football. Our teams often include some combination of Nate, myself, other officers, firefighters, an EMT, and Beckham. Hawk comes when he can, but he is visiting family up north this week.

Usually, we open up our homes—each one of us taking turns to host. It gives us more privacy, plus easy access to food and drinks. Today is supposed to be Nate's turn to host. Imagine our surprise when his wife gets a horrible migraine when we are due to arrive at the house.

Shocking, I know.

Luckily, Nate lives just a few blocks from Meadowbrook Park. After a quick course correction, we meet up there, which leads us to my current predicament.

"Simon, do you need a nap or something?" Beckham comes up beside me and slings a sweaty arm around my shoulders. "You're playing like shit, man. You keep zoning out, and honestly, you look cranky."

"I don't need a nap, asshole." Shrugging his arm off of me and giving him a friendly shove to the side, I make my way over to the picnic table laden with all of our things.

"See?" He follows behind me. "Cranky."

"Seriously. What's with you today?" Nate asks, joining us for a quick water break. "Still having girl trouble?"

I answer with a glare. Nate already knows way too much about my "girl trouble." Neither of them needs any more fodder for their lame-ass jokes.

"Too much bird watching," Beckham replies, shooting a smirk my way. *Here we go.* "Old man here has been looking for the elusive sandpiper. Didn't you know, Nate?"

"Bird watching, huh?" Nate chuckles. "Is that what the kids call it these days?"

"Screw you both," I mutter.

They laugh while I grab my water and drain a good portion. Then, while I stare down at the plastic bottle in my hands, Beckham and Nate continue to enjoy making me the butt of a thousand bird jokes; many include the naughtiest bird names possible. I hear "swallow," quickly followed by "woodpecker."

I'm only half listening while a plan forms in my head.

In the next few seconds, Beckham has just enough time to say my name and "boobies" before a stream of water hits him square in the face. He stands there in shock, sputtering. I tilt the bottle down across his chest before shifting to Nate. I drench them both from the chest up before the bottle empties. I grin at them like an idiot—they *look* like idiots, though, which feels like a fair trade-off.

Nate's face slowly morphs from disbelief to downright wickedness. His grin turns sly, and he says, "Fucker, you are going down."

Shit. I run. Beckham and Nate both give chase, and we all barrel through the other guys milling around. They scatter across the grass like bowling pins. Unfortunately, they also slow me down enough that Nate lunges forward and tackles me at the waist. I manage to keep my footing, but barely. Beckham yanks me in a headlock. I put Nate in a headlock. We knot together in a flurry of tangled limbs.

Right then, distinctly feminine laughter cuts through our cacophony of grunts and expletives—and we freeze in place. I look up to see Ellery and Piper standing side by side, wearing twin expressions of amusement while watching the scene before them. How long have they been standing there? We must look ridiculous, latched onto each other like spider monkeys.

What a great way to make an impression.

"I swear," Ellery whisper-shouts to Piper, "get them all together, and the collective age drops below ten."

Piper snickers. Some of our guys watching the show laugh and elbow each other in the ribs, and—yep, we will be catching shit about this for years to come.

"Hey, shortcake." Beckham's greeting sounds slightly sheepish as he loosens his hold around my neck. I release his hair so he can stand. Nate then drops his arms from around my waist. Finally, the three of us slowly stand up and try to look nothing like the epic man-children we turned into while wrestling on the ground.

Ellery's eyes twinkle when Beckham makes his way over to her. They share a quick kiss. Then Beckham tucks her against his side. "Hey, Piper," he adds as an afterthought.

Piper just shakes her head, smiling, and mutters something about "lovesick fools."

It may just be my imagination, but her eyes seem to flick in my direction while she says it. Her cheeks are flushed with a pretty shade of pink, too. Then again, I *do* stare at Piper like a lovesick fool. Even now, my eyes soak in every detail of her outfit. She wears those little high-waisted drawstring shorts and a cropped sweatshirt. They leave me with very tantalizing glimpses of sun-kissed skin.

"So this is the infamous Piper Easton," Nate says quietly.

Tearing my gaze away from the woman in question, I turn to see Nate shoot me a knowing look. Glaring at him, I mouth the words "no bird puns" while slicing my finger across my neck in a threatening gesture. Nate chuckles at me and walks in their direction.

Following a few steps behind, I wonder if I should warn him about her hell-hound protectors. Then again, animals fucking love Nate—and these two are no exception. When he gets close, Ozzy and Cooper start wriggling their massive, furry bodies. He tries to ruffle their fur, but they're too busy slobbering all over his hands to let him. He just stands there giggling like a damn schoolgirl.

Show off.

I approach much slower, unsure if their reaction will be as *welcoming* as last time, especially since they almost tore my head off during our initial meeting. Of course, Piper seems much more relaxed this time—happy, even. That may explain why the dogs greet me with equal enthusiasm to Nate.

When I open my mouth to greet Piper, only a croaked "hi" comes out. I had planned on sounding a little more eloquent. But when her peaches and cream scent fills my lungs, I feel fortunate that I can string any words together.

Nate saves me from thinking of something better to say by holding his hand out to Piper, saying, "Hi, I'm Nate Walker."

After they shake hands, he hooks a thumb over his shoulder at me. "This SOB and I are partners on the force."

"Nice to meet you." She smiles at Nate, and his bronzed skin flushes slightly. He clears his throat and smiles back, although he looks somewhat dumbstruck. *Interesting.* Even big, bad Nathaniel Walker isn't immune to Piper's charm.

Not that I can blame him.

My obsession started when we were young. Twelve years later? *Holy. Fucking. Hell.* Like a fine wine, Piper has only improved with age—her beauty, style, and even how she carries herself.

Just one look from her could bring a person to their knees.

"I must say, I'm a huge fan of Songbyrd." Nate rubs the back of his neck, grinning boyishly. "I think *Simon Says* might be my favorite song, though *F.O.O.L.* is a close second."

"Oh. Well, thank you, Nate. That's so sweet of you to say." Piper's face flushes beet red. She peeks over at me again, and I swear I see her cringe before her gaze flits back to him.

I bite my lip to keep from smiling in amusement.

Simon Says and *F.O.O.L.* both show up on Songbyrd's sophomore album. The tracks feel punchier than her previous songs about me, and the whole album has more sass and much less anger. At the time of its release, Piper still very much considered me public enemy number one. But a sick part of me loves that she had me on her mind, even then.

"I'll let you in on a little secret." Leaning forward, I smirk at Nate, but my eyes shift to capture Piper's attention. I let her see the heat in my gaze when I admit, "*Simon Says* is my favorite, too."

The pink blush staining her cheeks darkens further. After a quick wink, I turn my attention to my sister. "What are you two doing out here, anyway?"

Ellery shrugs. "I stopped by to visit with Piper, and she was getting ready to take the dogs for a walk. So, I offered to come with her." Her expression turns to pure impish glee when she continues, "I suggested we go to the park. Imagine my surprise when I see all of you playing football here instead of at Nate's house."

Nate flushes slightly and explains, "Brit had a migraine."

"Oh." Ellery's eyebrows scrunch in confusion. "She gets those an awful lot. Has she been to a doctor? I could recommend some"—Beckham pinches her side and quickly cuts Ellery off.

After she spears Beckham with a halfhearted glare, Ellery smooths her expression into a gentle smile. She looks at Nate and says, "Never mind. It's none of my business. I hope Britagne feels better soon!"

"Thanks." Nate smiles, but it feels a little strained. I can tell what Ellery just said embarrasses him. He looks at his watch. "Speaking of Brit, I should probably get home and check on her."

We watch while he jogs over to grab his things. With a wave goodbye, he trots off the field and toward the sidewalk that leads toward his house on the outskirts of town.

Once he disappears, I arch an eyebrow. "Really, pipsqueak?"

"Ugh, I know. Me and my big mouth," Ellery huffs, growing embarrassed under my gaze. Her cheeks turn red. "But Britagne is just so *difficult*. How can someone so amazing be married to that, that…" and waves her hand around when she can't think of something appropriate to call Britagne Walker in mixed company.

Piper's eyes flare while she watches the exchange. "So, we are not Britagne Walker fan club members," she says. "Got it. Remind me not to get on your bad side, Elle."

Ellery laughs and pulls Piper into a hug against her free side. "Not possible, sister from another mister."

Beckham groans and slides his arm off her shoulders to take her hand. "Alright, come on, you. Let's grab my stuff and head home." He looks over at Piper. "You need a ride back to your parents' place?"

"Oh." She glances at me for just a second. Then she shakes her head. "I think I'll walk. These boys need the exercise—don't you, you giant, tubby babies? Grandma is sneaking you too many treats; yes, she is," she coos, kissing at the top of both heads. The two *giant, tubby babies* in question wiggle happily at their mama's attention and lean into her on each side.

"Simon?" Beckham asks me next since we rode down here together.

But I am still itching to talk to Piper alone—or as alone as we can in a public place. Before I can think better of it, I turn toward the woman in question and ask, "Would you like some company? I feel like a walk, myself."

I hold my breath. Half of me expects Piper to decline outright or make excuses. Imagine my surprise when she nods.

"That would be nice," she says slowly and with caution. No matter. I will happily take whatever she gives me.

Beckham and Ellery both say their goodbyes. But when they turn to leave, Beckham reaches around her waist and slips a hand into her back pocket. I watch him squeeze a handful and shudder.

"Dammit, Beck!" I bark. "I can still *see you*."

Ellery's shoulders shake with laughter. Instead of removing his hand like a gentleman, Beckham holds his position (literally) while lifting the other hand to flip me off.

Beside me, Piper giggles. "Holidays must be so weird for you now," she says.

"You have no idea." I huff in mock frustration, and she giggles again—just a tiny sound, yet it spreads warmth down my spine.

After the two of them disappear, I turn to Piper and motion toward the direction they came from. "Shall we?" I ask.

"Sure. Ozzy! Cooper! Come," Piper calls out. They immediately stop chasing whatever animal or bug has their attention and bound over to us. Both dogs impress me when they immediately fall in line, one on either side of Piper.

"They're very well trained," I comment.

"Thanks," she says proudly. "These two are the best boys. Aren't you?"

Ozzy and Cooper wag their tails and pant in response.

We lapse into silence after that—not quite uncomfortable but not relaxed, either. Whenever I look over at Piper, I notice her carefully blank expression. Annoyance burns in my chest at how little I can read Piper's moods. I used to be a pro, deciphering every look no matter how she tried to hide.

Now, things are a lot more complicated.

Even while time and distance dulled my skills, some muscle memory remains. When I feel Piper's eyes on mine, I sense curiosity behind her deceptively disinterested expression. What

I have trouble figuring out is what has piqued that curiosity. Still, knowing I have any effect on her warms my insides. My fingers twitch with the desire to pull her closer. I wonder if her skin feels as soft as I remember. She still smells as good. Her beauty still takes my breath away.

After a moment, I realize Piper has started to speak.

"Does that—?" Piper stops and shakes her head. Then she tries again. "Beckham and Ellery, I mean. I imagine that hasn't been easy for you."

"You know how I am. I love to give Beckham and Ellery a hard time," I explain, eyes twinkling when I look down at her. "But, yeah. It may have taken me a bit to come around."

"Yeah?"

"Honestly, I was an asshole."

"No!" she exclaims, face morphing into an exaggerated look of shock. "Were you?"

My eyes narrow at her sarcasm. "In my defense, I may have accidentally walked in on them…"

Trailing off, I wave my hands around instead, hoping to get the point across. I have no desire to finish that sentence. Thankfully, Piper fills in the gaps. Her eyes widen in shock, and a strangled sound escapes just before she slaps her hands over her mouth.

Piper says through closed fingers, "You're *kidding*."

"Do I look like I'm kidding?"

I can laugh about it now. Sort of. But damn, that whole scene has permanently seared itself onto the back of my retinas.

I will never, ever, *ever* get it out again.

When I say as much, Piper nods in emphatic agreement. "Yeah, I could see that causing some tension."

Snorting, I reply, "*That* is putting it mildly."

"So, what made you change your mind?"

"Honestly?" I look straight ahead as I give her question some serious thought. "The whole time, Beckham never thought he deserved Ellery. And after I calmed down and took a step back, I realized that Beckham is precisely the type of man I have always wanted for her. Who will take better care of her, do you think? Someone who loves her, or someone who loves her and spends every waking moment knowing what a precious gift she has given him?" I shake my head. "Beck will never take Ellery's heart for granted. He will protect her better than I ever could. The truth is, they deserve each other."

Piper falls silent. When I look over, I notice a slightly broken look on her face, and I wonder what I may have done or said to cause it. Then her expression shutters. Part of me wants to shake her, demanding she stop hiding from me.

But I have no right.

Instead, I clear my throat and try to lighten the mood. "Besides," I tease, "Beck knows if he ever does hurt her, I'll be there, and no one will ever find his body."

That does the trick.

Piper rolls her eyes, a smile stretching across her face as she says, "There's the Simon I remember."

Chuckling, I face forward again as we exit the park and turn onto the sidewalk. It leads us to the residential area where her parents live. "The one thing I still haven't quite wrapped my head around is that Ellery had a crush on Beckham all those years—right under my very nose."

"Oh, yeah," she says. "That girl was totally gone for Beckham. I knew it from the moment I first met her. Remember?

We went to the Blossom Festival for the first time and met up with your family."

"Yeah, I remember, but"—I shake my head in disbelief—"how could you have known? Neither Beckham nor I had a damn clue."

Piper glances at me sideways. "Because you and Beckham are men, and men are completely oblivious to matters of the heart."

"You could have said something," I mutter grumpily.

"Please." Piper giggles and shakes her head. "What would that have done other than cause bad blood between you and Beckham? He couldn't control her feelings any more than she could."

Then, after a slight hesitation, Piper pats me on the shoulder. I swallow thickly, praying silently to the heavens that she keeps it there. When she moves it—much to my disappointment—the spot tingles with warmth for a long time afterward.

"Anyway," Piper continues, "it was glaringly obvious when Ellery lost first place in the Blossom Belle pageant, and Beckham was the only person who could make her feel better. She clung to him for the entire rest of the day."

"Ellery was ten."

Piper rolls her eyes. "Ten or not, she looked at Beckham like he hung all the stars in the sky. I recognized it then because I"—her sentence cuts off abruptly.

But I know what words come next:

Because I looked at you the same way.

All the tension from the other night rushes back, filling the air between us with awkward silence. Even the dogs pick up on the suddenly tense atmosphere, ears perked, tails straight, everything on high alert. Suddenly I am so damn tired of it all. I wish that we could wipe the slate clean and start over.

There is no better time than the present to try.

Staring straight ahead, I shove down my pride and say, "Look, Piper. Can I—?" I clear my throat from the nerves tightening around it. "What I mean is, I'd like to apologize for dinner the other night if you'll allow me."

When Piper says nothing to shut me down, I take that as permission to continue. "When your mom first invited me to those dinners years ago, after—well, after everything—I never went. It felt wrong. But she kept asking, and eventually, I gave in. I needed it more than I realized. Ellery, too."

"Mom told me," Piper admits. "She admitted as much when I followed her to the kitchen that night."

Okay, then. Good. I can work with that.

"This time, I tried convincing Stella that it should be family only. You can guess how well that went." I peek at Piper and catch the briefest smile on her face. Yeah. She knows how stubborn her mother can be.

"If you knew I was coming, you would have stayed away, and your mom would have been heartbroken. So I made no promises—only to try, but work may make it impossible."

Frustrated, I shake my head and kick at a stone beneath my shoe. "I could have made an excuse to stay away. Hell, the comment about work would have been perfect. But after the gala, I was dying to see you again."

Christ.

Who knew an apology could be so tricky?

"You deserve better," I finally say, "and I am truly sorry for surprising you the way I did." After a deep breath to center myself, I take a risk and admit one final truth. "I'm not sorry I went, though. I would be a liar if I said otherwise because seeing you that night was worth whatever price I would pay." I brace myself for anger, rejection, or any other adverse reactions.

Then I turn my head—and stop in my tracks.

Piper watches me silently, and I can see past those impenetrable walls for once. Her eyes shimmer with pleasure at my words. Her flushed cheeks could be from the walk, but not how her lips slowly curve up in a smile. That one is all for me.

"Well," Piper says, trying to reestablish her air of casual disinterest, "thank you for being honest."

The breath I have been holding rushes out. While far from forgiveness, Piper's words at least take us a step in the right direction. I motion for us to continue. We start moving again, falling back into silence as we turn up one street and down another before coming to the small neighborhood where her parents live. Their house is just a few streets away now. It butts up to the woods along the farthest northern street.

As we make our way in that direction, Piper clears her throat. "Apology accepted, by the way," she says quietly. When she peeks up at me, I let her see my relief. "Next time, though, maybe less subterfuge?"

My smile is bright as it stretches across my face. "I can do that."

Then, excitement thrums through my veins for the rest of the walk. I feel a new sense of purpose. My steps are confident, my mind is determined, and my heart is full of hope.

Because Piper said, *next time.*

Chapter 12
Spellbound

Simon

Every year on Halloween, The Apothecary hosts an epic costume bash. My work schedule often keeps me from attending, but this party is different. The owner—Jude Warren—hired B&H Solutions (Beckham and Hawk's company) last year to renovate the existing bar. The results excited her so much that she hired them to build an entirely new addition this year. Since Jude has quite a dramatic flair, she uses the Halloween party to do a big reveal.

So, in support of my friends, I am making an extra effort to attend—not because I hope to catch a glimpse of a certain blonde dominating my thoughts day and night. My ears may have perked up when Ellery mentioned Piper would be here, but nothing more.

My dear sister Ellery has taken it upon herself to play matchmaker between Piper and me. She loves doing things like that, and she usually drives me crazy. I am happy for her assistance, possibly for the first time, because our goals (for once) are aligned.

When Nate and I finally arrive at the bar, we are more than fashionably late, and our clothes are decidedly unfashionable. We got stuck doing paperwork at the station later than usual, so neither of us had time to race home and change into costume—another thing I would usually never participate in. This time, I liked the idea of being a 1920s gangster for the evening.

Jude will sadly have to deal with us in civilian clothes.

Nate whistles when he sees the line of hopeful attendees without tickets purchased in advance. We get to walk past them to show the bouncer our VIP invitations. I guess there are some perks to being friends with both the owner and the guests of honor.

After the bouncer waves us through, we step inside—and into another world. Jude has taken the speakeasy theme of the bar and amplified it tenfold. Tonight, several of the waitstaff have transformed into gangsters and showgirls. Any staff who chose not to dress in costume wear pinstriped pants (or skirts) with suspenders and shirts printed with the Apothecary logo. I also see a lot of fedoras and headbands with elaborate feathers and bits sticking out of them. Halloween-themed music fills the air, and each breath I take is filled with cigar smoke and incense. The atmosphere feels classy and intimate, even with this many people pressing in from all sides.

When Jude said she wanted a big party, she meant it.

Speaking of Jude, I notice she has taken full advantage of the dress code and is in full costume: a short purple flapper dress paired with high heels and long fingerless gloves. Her chin-length hair is dyed lavender gray and pinned back with one of those elaborate mini hats. Smoky eyes and dark red lips complete the look.

When I say that Jude is a character, I mean that she bleeds theatrics. There is nothing she loves more than putting on a show. Most everybody in town adores her. Half the men and women at the police station are in love with her. And she enjoys every second of the attention.

Right now, she plays her hostess role by flitting around all the tables, greeting guests, and turning the charm to eleven.

"Well, hello, boys," she says when she gets to our booth.

Beckham gives her a lazy salute while Hawk lifts his beer bottle in greeting. The rest of us say hello in various ways.

"You look pretty as a picture, Jude," Harden comments, smiling charmingly. The younger officer screams unrepentant playboy.

"Why thank you, hun." Jude gets a mischievous twinkle in her eye.

I watch with amusement as Jude leans forward, resting her forearms on the table— a deceptively casual pose, but it gives Harden an up-close and personal view of her ample cleavage. He coughs, quickly looking up over Jude's left shoulder while his face turns fire-engine red. I smother a hearty laugh with my fist, quickly turning it into a cough. Jude looks my way and winks.

"I see you got the memo," she says to Harden, pointing to his costume. "Most of you did a great job. Even you, Beck."

"Rude," Beckham comments, pretending to be insulted.

Hawk snorts into his beer. "Woman, I love your sass. You give out backhanded compliments like candy to children."

Beckham glares at Hawk. "Why am I friends with you again?"

"For my never-ending wit and effortless charm."

"Be honest," Jude interjects, grinning. "You would have showed up in jeans and a black t-shirt if Ellery hadn't forced you to dress up."

He grumbles something unintelligible as the table erupts with laughs and good-natured ribbing.

"And you two." Jude turns her attention to Nate and me. She wedges herself in between our chairs, pouting. "What happened? Don't you love me? Are you boycotting costumes this year? Ooh, or are you doing undercover work? If so, I hate to tell you, boys, but you're sticking out like a sore thumb."

"Cut us a little slack, Jude." I look down at my dark jeans and the jade green button down shirt I threw on this morning. Then, shrugging, I say, "We had to race here straight from the station. No time to go home and get into costume."

"Pity you fine specimens didn't come in your police uniforms," she laments—quite dramatically. "You'd have had every single person in this place drooling over you. Could probably triple my sales for the night."

Nate smiles bashfully and shakes his head, looking embarrassed.

I roll my eyes.

"What?" Hawk leans forward, smirking. "People around here don't call you Sexy Cop for nothing, Simon."

"Oh, for fuck's sake." I pinch my eyes shut. "That is not a thing people do."

Jude barrels over, laughing. When she stands back up, she has to wipe her eyes free of tears. "Oh, Simon, you sweet summer child. How many traffic violations do you write a week?"

Nate starts to grin. "More than anyone else in the station, that's for sure."

Harden jumps in next, asking, "And how many calls do we get in the station needing help where they specifically request Officer Brooks?"

"Aw, shit!" Another officer, Dominic, laughs from the table behind me and turns to grab onto my shoulder with a friendly shake. "Are we talking about Sexy Cop over here? I swear he could have anyone in this town. Any gender, any sexuality, married or single."

"You are seriously exaggerating this," I mutter, slumping in my seat and crossing my arms in a huff.

Beckham grins at me from across the table. "What's the matter, Si? Can't take the heat?"

Jude giggles. Then she gives me a side hug and quickly kisses my cheek. "You know we love you, big guy. As for the costumes—I've got you covered."

With that cryptic statement, Jude holds her fingers up to one ear and speaks into a small earpiece I didn't notice until now. When she sees me watching curiously, she grins.

"Wait for it," she says. A few seconds later, one of her servers comes rushing over with two fedoras in hand. "There you are, fellas. Now you look like you belong."

Shaking my head with a smirk, I take one of the preferred hats—black with vertical pinstripes—and plunk it on my head.

"Better?" I ask.

"Much!" She reaches up and adjusts the brim slightly. "Very Marlon Brando. Well," she adds with a giggle, "if he had red hair. And was several inches taller." Jude then does the same with Nate's charcoal gray hat, setting it just so on his head.

"Now," she adds, clapping her hands and stepping back, ready to move to the following table. "Y'all had better stay put because I've got a special surprise for everyone in just a few minutes."

I look at Beckham, curious, but he shrugs and shakes his head. I sip my draft beer and look over the sea of faces. Maybe Piper is swimming around out there.

With luck, maybe our paths will cross tonight.

I may even get to talk to her again—or dance.

The desire to be in her orbit strengthens every time we cross paths.

"This is so much fun!"

I hear Ellery's voice before I see her when she comes bounding up to the table a few minutes later, smiling ear to ear. "Isn't this great?" she asks, her face flushed with excitement. Then she claps her hands together and bounces up and down, the silver sparkles of her flapper dress catching the light. The tassels move in time with her bounces, mesmerizing a few of the officers—at least until Beckham and I hit them with death glares.

Ellery, being Ellery, is oblivious to her charm and effect on the opposite sex—not that it matters. Her focus never strays from Beckham long enough to notice anything else.

"Where have you been flitting around to?" I ask, finally prying her attention off of her fiancé.

Ellery's smile shifts and turns mischievous. "Helping Jude out with her special surprise." When she glances meaningfully at me, I shake my head and chuckle. "Don't you want to know what it is?" she asks, pouting.

I shrug. "Not really. I mean, that would ruin the surprise."

Ellery huffs. Just then, the overhead lights fade to black and cause a hush to fall over the crowd. Ellery quickly hops up onto Beckham's lap. His eyes are searching the room, assessing, but he still wraps his arms protectively around her as soon as he feels her against him. Even when his focus seems to be on something else, his every thought and action centers around Ellery and keeping her safe and happy.

That fact alone makes him the only man who could ever deserve her. I watch them for another moment, tamping down a twinge of envy when Ellery whispers something in Beckham's ear, and they kiss.

I'm glad they found each other, but having Piper home has strengthened my longing for things out of reach.

Before my thoughts can turn even more melancholy, Jude's voice comes over the loudspeaker, cutting them off. "Welcome to the 30th Annual Apothecary Halloween Bash! My parents started this tradition when I was too small to enjoy any of the perks of owning a bar."

A titter of laughter flits through the darkened space.

"But I always knew that one day this place would be mine," Jude continues, "and I had all these crazy ideas of how to revamp the place, make my mark. With the help of B&H Solutions"—at the name of Beckham and Hawk's business, our table erupts into loud cheers—"I am ready to kick off this hot new space with some live entertainment."

After a dramatic pause, she says, "So let's give it up for Sweetbriar's own, Piper Easton—also known as Songbyrd!"

At first, the only light in the room comes from candle centerpieces. But then, a spotlight turns on as the room explodes with excited cheers and whistles. Just as quickly, everything falls silent—so silent that you can hear a pin drop. The light illuminates the small, raised platform against the wall. At its center, a lone woman stands perfectly still. Her head is bowed over a retro-style microphone stand in front of her.

My heart lodges in my throat when I first catch sight of Piper in her costume. Her dress is long and fitted from the bodice to about mid-thigh, where it widens into a flared skirt. An intricate black lace design covers the entire length of the dress. Only one thought comes to my mind:

Holy shit, is Piper naked underneath?

Have I fallen asleep? Am I in a random erotic dream right now? I blink several times to make sure.

Definitely awake.

Then the spotlight on the stage brightens as the show official starts. Now I can see that the lace layer actually covers a nude-colored silk underlay. The erratic flutter of my pulse slows.

It takes another minute to will my dick back down.

Not an easy feat, considering the visual feast in front of me. Piper has always known how to make an entrance—one of the many reasons she was born to be a star. Right now, she perfectly embodies an early 20th-century lounge singer. Like Ellery and Jude, Piper has pulled her long, straight hair away from her face in an elaborate style. Those tantalizing blonde tresses, almost white under the stage lights, are held in place by a glittering headpiece. The plunging neckline of her dress pulls my gaze from her slender neck, past thin straps that precariously hold the bodice up and down to a tantalizing view of cleavage.

Even years later, I crave Piper in a way that can never be sated. I can still picture how she looked, swathed only in moonlight. I have often traced all that smooth, exposed skin with my eyes, fingers, and mouth. I worshipped every inch of Piper, then.

I worship every inch of her now—just at a distance.

When the pianist accompanying Piper starts a sultry jazz tune, her gloves wrap around the microphone stand, and she lifts her face and begins to sing. The spotlight overhead brightens and catches on the sequins of her dress, causing a gentle shimmer to ripple like moonlit water along her curves and valleys.

Her voice holds me captive from the very first note. Piper sings the lyrics to *I Put a Spell on You*, but like everything else, she makes the song her own. Her voice is haunting, mingling with the soft strains of piano music. Every word, every note, weaves a spell over the audience.

She makes me fall in love with her all over again. I am obsessed, so lost in the music and the narrative she has brought to life that I barely notice when the musical strains of the first song fade into silence and a new song begins. Only when she launches into the first verse do I recognize the words for

Witchcraft by Frank Sinatra. After that, she sings two more songs: her spin on *Superstition* and *Black Magic Woman*.

She studiously avoids any of her own music. I wonder why.

No. Fuck that.

I want to know every thought going through her head. I want to know why she looks almost sad standing up there. Performing used to be like a drug to her. I want to know if any part of that sadness is because of me.

And I want to know how to fix it.

By the time she ends her set, the entire place jumps to its feet, clapping, whistling, and making catcalls. The overhead lights turn back on, and Piper motions for the piano player to join her. They take a bow together and then disappear behind the stage curtain. The speakers turn on again to go back to Jude's eclectic playlist of Halloween-themed music.

Finishing the last of my beer, I stand and make excuses before slipping away into the crowd. After only a minute or two, my gaze lands on Piper while she walks across the makeshift dance floor. When she sees me, she slows to a stop. Even under the mood lighting, I see the blush coloring her cheeks.

Right then, a slow, sultry tune starts to play.

Perfect timing.

Slowly making my way up to her, I stop just a few feet away and reach out. "Dance with me?"

Piper stares at my outstretched hand, desire warring with uncertainty. "I don't think that's a good idea," she says, slowly shaking her head.

But her eyes tell me a different story.

Dancing with me may be a bad idea, but she wants to.

"Just one dance?" I ask, deciding to try my luck. "For old time's sake, as friends."

"As friends," she echoes, biting her lip.

Seconds later, her hand slips into mine, and my fingers wrap around hers to gently tug her to me—not giving her a chance to change her mind. Her hands lift to rest on my shoulders for balance, and it brands me, even through the fabric of my shirt.

Piper feels like heaven.

She feels like home.

We start a slow rhythm on the dance floor. Our bodies quickly fall back into old patterns while the magnetic pull between us shifts from tension to desire. Piper finally gives in and rests her head on my chest. I spend the next few minutes savoring how she feels in my arms.

Too wrapped up in one another to notice, our dance moves us away from the stage area and new addition and into a secluded section of the old bar. I can still hear the music and chatter, but only faintly. I look around the room and realize we are the only ones here.

Then, as the song fades into silence, I notice we have also stopped moving.

My arms have a mind of their own, tightening around Piper until we are chest to chest, heart to racing heart. Peaches and cream and the faintest hint of cinnamon cling to her skin. Lamplight flickers in her eyes, and they dance and swirl with unmasked desire. She tilts her head toward mine.

I feel her breath on my lips.

Then Piper whispers my name—a prayer and a plea.

At that moment, I feel the tenuous threads of my control snap. I kiss Piper and coax her lips open until our tongues tangle together. As soon as I taste her, a groan rips from my throat.

I am lost to sensation. Feral. Every sound Piper makes shoots adrenaline straight into my veins. We can't seem to get close enough. Piper leans in. I gather her in my arms, and she burrows into my heat, her arms sliding up to grip my open collar. I curl my fingers around her neck to guide her where needed.

Even through silk gloves, I feel Piper's manicured fingernails digging into the skin beneath my collar. That slight bite shoots straight to my cock. The pain also clears away the lust clouding my judgment. Because, like it or not, we are still very exposed—still standing in a very public place. No matter how secluded the area, anyone could walk in at any moment.

I slowly gentle the kiss, loathe to stop but knowing I must. When I finally pull back, I nip at Piper's plush lower lip one last time. Then, cradling her face in my hands, I memorize every detail.

Just in case.

Even in the darkness, I can see the flush staining her cheeks red. Her eyes open with a flutter of long lashes. Pale green eyes peer up at me, the haze of pleasure slowly fading from their depths. Piper is off-kilter, disheveled, and more beautiful than ever.

"Wow," Piper says, breathing heavily.

"Wow," I echo.

After a few seconds, her expression starts to clear, smoothing back into the unreadable mask she uses to hide from the world. I hate that mask. It takes every ounce of willpower for me not to grab her by the shoulders and kiss it gone again.

Because I crave all of Piper—every thought, dream, wish, and all her doubts and fears. I want to tell her not to hide from me. Unfortunately, it takes me a beat too long to form the words. The moment passes, lost when Piper slips out of my arms—and I must let her go.

Every bit of her focus turns inward. Every deliberate action gives her an excuse to avoid looking my way. She painstakingly straightens her dress. Then she smoothes down each hair mussed up by my wandering hands. If I try to talk to Piper now, whatever I say will fall on deaf ears.

Her walls have gone right back up.

"I have to go," Piper says, peeking over my shoulder toward the exit. Still avoiding my gaze.

"Yeah. Okay," is my lame reply.

Clearing my throat, I step aside to let her pass. Before she gets too far out of reach, I grasp her wrist. Gentle but firm, so she has no choice but to stop.

Fuck. What am I doing? I need to let Piper go.

But I want her to stay. I want to ask her if she can feel that tether between us getting stronger every time we touch. And I want to tell her everything I locked away in my heart, waiting for her return.

"Piper."—the only word I can manage.

Piper shudders at the sound. Slowly, she peeks over her shoulder at me. I see the question in her eyes—but behind it, when I look deeper, I see things she never intended.

Worry.

Distrust.

Caution.

Fear.

My mind blanks and something deep down inside of me shatters.

"Simon?" she asks. "Did you need something?"

My hand slips down her hand before falling uselessly by my side. Slowly, I shake my head. "Nothing important," I lie. "I wanted to say thank you. For the dance, and…"

She gives me a small smile. "You're welcome."

Then she is gone.

While I stand here, suddenly untethered, I realize what I felt break.

Hope.

Piper feels like *heaven.* She feels like *home.*

INTERLUDE 3

Three

- Saturday 4:29 am -

Unknown number: Go ahead, keep blocking me

Unknown number: I'll just keep coming back

Unknown number: If you change your number again, I'll figure out the new one, too

Missed call.

- Saturday 6:15 am -

Unknown number: You'd better be back by Jan 2

Unknown number: Or you'll be in breach of contract

Missed call.

- Saturday 6:47 am -

Unknown number: This little rebellion of yours is getting old

Unknown number: You should be ON YOUR KNEES thanking me

This number has been blocked.

Chapter 13
Overwhelmed

Piper

My nights following the Halloween party have been filled with dreams of slow dancing in the dark, a toe-curling kiss—and the defeated look on Simon's face when I ran.

His expression still haunts me.

Simon saw more than I meant him to. My mask slipped. Our dance—and the kiss that followed—battered my defenses until alarms blared and every thought screamed *run, run, run*.

I needed to escape.

Catch my breath.

Process the litany of emotions flooding my body.

But then Simon said my name—just my name, the way he used to. Stupidly, I turned back to him. Then, like a coward, I fled.

My reaction makes sick to my stomach. I want to explain but have no earthly idea what to say. Worse, I have seen nothing of Simon around town or at family dinner this week. Maybe he decided to give me space—or to avoid me altogether.

I should feel grateful.

Instead, I feel lost.

This morning, Ellery decides enough is enough and texts me while I am curled up and reading on my back porch. When I hear the text alert on my phone, I immediately tense for more harassing texts from Cedric—until I see Ellery's name flash on the screen. My shoulders drop down in relief.

When I read what she sends me, a smile pulls at my lips.

- 8:35 am -

Ellery: *waving emoji*

Ellery: Piper!!!

Piper: Ellery!

Ellery: Oh! Hi

Ellery: I didn't expect you to answer that quickly. I had a whole backlog of GIFs ready to send :(

Piper: Sorry?

Ellery: Never mind. But, hey! Come to Boozy Brunch tomorrow

Piper: Boozy Brunch?

Ellery: My girls and I do brunch at the Quill every Sunday. They have *bottomless mimosas*

Ellery: Daisy is coming, too

Piper: You sure I won't be intruding?

Ellery: Pfft no, you're family

Piper: OK

Ellery: Wait, really? I didn't think you'd say yes *crying emoji* *celebrate emoji*

Piper: *lmao emoji*

Piper: Give me the details. I'll be there

Now, because of that conversation, I stand in front of the Quill Restaurant & Grille on a pleasant Sunday morning while anxiously wringing my hands together. My brain tries to convince my feet to move, to go inside. Stepping past the threshold should be easy. Mom and the owners—Anna and Faith—grew up together and are close friends, so I spent more of my childhood in the Quill and Jelly Beans than anywhere else in town. Maybe that familiarity is the problem. Inside holds too many memories, including some I am far from ready to face.

Regardless of my conflicted feelings, I have to stop blocking the entrance. So, with a deep breath to center myself, I push open the door. Nostalgia hits me, along with the comforting scents of syrup, freshly baked bread, and coffee. As I continue to move forward, my body soaks in the warmth and comfort that always surrounds this place—a testament to the kind souls who run both establishments.

Bookshelves cover the walls on either side of the hostess stand, and around the archway behind it that leads to the main dining room. So many more than in the past. Quiet chatter floats in the air around me as I continue toward the stand where Faith,

Ellery, and a vaguely familiar woman are in the middle of a lively conversation.

As soon as I come into view, Ellery squeaks in excitement. The other two women watch on, amused, while she rushes forward and throws her arms around me. The force of it takes me by surprise, jolting a surprised laugh out of me.

"Hello to you too," I say when she pulls away.

Grinning, Ellery grabs my hand and tugs me toward the stranger, who decided to hang back during Ellery's boisterous greeting. I take in the woman's crisp jeans and tailored shirt, a pale rose color that contrasts nicely with her dusky brown skin. Dark lashes frame round, amber eyes, while her cheeks and lips have a naturally rosy tint. She styled her thick mane of black hair into a long, intricate braid.

My hand absently reaches up to pat the low ponytail I hastily threw my hair into before leaving. Maybe I should have put in more effort.

No. Stop second guessing yourself. That voice is Cedric's, not yours.

"Hi, Piper," the woman says, pulling me back from my thoughts. "I'm Ellery's friend, Priya Kumari."

Priya Kumari. Hearing her name sparks my memory. Priya and Ellery grew up and went to school together.

"I remember. Nice to see you again, Priya," I reply. We exchange smiles before I turn to the matronly woman buzzing with excitement beside her. I smile warmly. "Good morning, Faith."

"My sweet Piper," she replies with a sniff. Then she gathers me into a hug. "Your mother told us you were in town, and

Anna said she saw you the other day. Oh, it's so good to see you home again. How long are you staying?"

"I'm not sure yet, to be honest," I reply, stepping back. "At least through the holidays."

"That sounds lovely. Your family must be thrilled."

"Yeah…" I lapse into an awkward silence, unsure what else to say.

Thankfully, Faith picks up on it and claps her hands together. "Shall I get you seated?"

Priya waves her away. "You don't need to do that, Faith. We know the way and you have more important things to do."

"Like getting you ladies a pitcher of my famous mimosas, I'm sure. Knowing you all, I should go make sure we have enough bottles of the *good* champagne." With a wink and a laugh, Faith heads toward the back.

"That woman is my hero," Ellery giggles.

Priya just smiles and shakes her head. Ellery steps between us and threads her arms through ours, leading us away from the entrance toward the far back of the restaurant that Faith and Anna long ago blocked off into a semi-private indoor-outdoor space. During the milder temperatures, they close up the French doors and open the floor to ceiling glass windows—just as they are today.

Ellery and Priya both slip into seats on opposite ends of a round table. I pause before sitting down, my gaze catching on a familiar view of the town square. My fingers absently trace fabric on the white linen tablecloth while I take a seat, my mind slipping into the past.

Several members of Hazelwood's high school football team came here after home games, a long-standing tradition since the restaurant opened. Little snapshots flicker across my memory of moments when I joined them. All the girlfriends came, wanting to celebrate the team's victories. On nights when they lost, we did our best to distract them.

Until now, I had conveniently forgotten those memories—either by time or pure stubbornness. But the longer I stay in Sweetbriar, the more I remember. The longer I stay, the more Simon invades every facet of my life. I have no escape from him.

Even worse, a large part of me has no desire to escape. That part of me grows larger every day. I miss Simon. For all the years we spent apart, for as long as I have claimed to hate him—I have *missed* him.

"Piper?"

"Hmm?" My gaze snaps to Ellery, who watches me with concern. I flush and try to laugh it off. "Sorry. I was lost in my own world for a second."

Ellery looks like she wants to say more, but something catches her attention over my shoulder.

"Hey, babes!" Daisy's voice comes from behind. I turn—and laugh when she dives in to hug me. Then she turns and hugs the other two before sliding into the seat on my right. "Glad to see you, sis," she says, nudging my shoulder.

I smile. "Glad to be here."

Shortly after Daisy's arrival, a petite and curvy woman bounds up to the table. Her brown eyes light up when she sees us. Her tone is bright and sassy when she exclaims, "I have arrived, *amigas*! Boozy Brunch may now begin." She smiles when she notices me staring. "Luz Ortega," she says, reaching a hand out across the table to grip mine briefly before letting go. I remember her as the third musketeer in Ellery's childhood friend group. Luz, like her hair, bounces in excitement. "You and me, Piper. I can already tell that we are going to be the best of friends."

Surprised laughter bubbles out of me as I watch Luz hop onto one of the last remaining chairs. Everything about the woman—even her outfit—is loud, chaotic, and maybe even a little wild. Even her thick, mahogany hair has a life of its own, bouncing around her before finally settling over her shoulders.

Luz oozes life and vitality out of her pours. Her energy captivates me. I remember a time when had that same zest for life.

Maybe Luz can show me the way back.

"You know what?" I smile brightly. "I think so, too."

Luz shimmies in excitement as she says, to no one in particular, "Now, how about those mimosas?"

"Lena still needs to get here," Ellery comments, looking apologetic.

Luz pouts. "Oh, boo."

"Don't worry, Luz, I'm right here," a voice says behind us.

When I shift to look over my shoulder, I see a woman standing there. She looks strangely familiar, though I know we have never met before. Everything about her screams poised and elegant. From the way she wears her dark hair in a simple, sleek ponytail down to her designer clothes, she looks like she just stepped off the cover of a magazine.

Her dark eyes twinkle when they meet mine. "Piper Easton," she says, greeting me warmly. "It's a pleasure to finally meet you. Ellery here has told me so much about you, although I admit I had some insider knowledge through my family."

My hackles raise, wondering what she means. Still, I remember my manners and stand. When she reaches out, I politely shake her hand while trying to put a name to her face.

"Nice to meet you…" I let the sentence hang in the air.

"Oh! Silly me. Helena," she says, chuckling. "Helena Morgan, but my friends just call me Lena."

As soon as she says her last name, it clicks. Her father is Rhys Morgan. Her family owns the conglomerate, Evermore Media, which in turn owns Dreamscape Music.

Her family knows Cedric.

Fear, irrational but potent, slithers underneath my skin and freezes my blood. Suddenly lightheaded, I grip the edge of the table and slowly sit back down. Lena watches me, concerned, until I give her as bright a smile as I can muster. Even though she sits down in the last remaining scene, she still looks like she wants to say something. Thankfully Ellery saves me, grabbing Lena by the arm and pulling her into a conversation with the rest of the group.

I close my eyes and let the smallest sigh of relief escape. Beneath the table, my fingers slowly tap a rhythm onto my thighs—a trick my therapist recently taught me to stave off anxiety attacks.

When a server stops to fills my champagne glass, I watch and stare at the peach color as it settles into the glass, champagne bubbles fluttering wildly within the liquid. The drink and the finger taps slowly pull me back from the edge.

Thankfully, Lena seems blissfully unaware of my strange demeanor. I hope it stays that way. None of this is her fault.

I am the one who naïvely put my trust and faith in the wrong person. I locked myself into the gilded cage I am trapped in, bound and gagged and led by shackles of pretty lies and false promises.

Then I gave Cedric the only key.

He owns me.

Not for long, though. No matter what I have to do, I will break free of Cedric. I am done being that man's plaything.

"Piper?"

My attention snaps toward the women surrounding the table. Daisy, the one who called my name, watches me with worry. "Are you okay?" she mouths.

When I notice the server standing nearby, waiting to take my order, I flush with embarrassment. Whoops. I quickly grab the menu and order the first thing I see—anything to get the attention off of me so I can compose myself. It takes a minute or two after the server leaves, but soon I slip into the conversation and act like a semi-functioning human being. I say the right things and smile at the right times. The mimosas help.

"So, Ellery…" Priya leans forward with interest gleaming in her eyes. "Your engagement party is in, what, two weeks?"

Ellery flushes with equal parts pleasure and embarrassment. "Ugh, I know. So short notice. But we have to work around the holidays, especially since we have such a short timetable." She looks at me. "Beckham and I decided we want to get married on Mom and Dad's wedding anniversary, which is on—"

"March 2nd," I interject with a sad smile. "I remember."

"Right." Ellery's face matches the melancholy I feel at the mention of her parents, until she shakes her head and shrugs. "Anyway, I don't want to wait an entire extra year to get married, so here we are."

We chat a little bit more about party prep—thankfully avoiding the topic of the wedding itself—until the food arrives. Then the conversation naturally wanes while we eat.

Once everyone has cleared their plates and refilled our champagne glasses, Luz turns to me with a mischievous grin. "So, Piper. Word on the street is you have some history with Sexy Cop."

"Sexy Cop?" I echo, bewildered.

Ellery snickers. "Simon's unofficial nickname. Everyone in town calls him Sexy Cop."

"This is news to me," I admit. But the thought makes me giggle. That nickname certainly fits Simon, though he must hate it.

Lena leans forward and stage-whispers, "One day, I watched Mrs. McAllister jaywalk right in front of him. They locked eyes and everything. I mean, she was begging him to arrest her." Then she sighs dramatically. "But Simon was off-duty, so he just shook his head and chuckled before continuing on his merry way."

"My great aunt calls the station at least once a week for a wellness check at the nursing home." Priya's eyes twinkle with mischief. "In fact, she told me they all take turns so it doesn't look so suspicious—even though it totally is. You can bet when Simon gets there, they are all huddling around to enjoy the show."

My chuckles have turned into a full belly laugh. Poor Simon.

"Does anyone here blame them?" Daisy winks at me, the little shit-stirrer. "I mean, Simon is damn fine. Don't you think so, sis?" She looks pointedly in my direction.

"No comment." I take a long, drawn-out sip of my mimosa and avoid their eyes. Not that what I say matters, not with a flushed face that tells on me.

Priya leans forward. "Good segue, Daisy. Now, as Luz was asking: Piper. You. Simon. History?"

With a sigh, I say, "Ellery has surely told you plenty."

Even though I am joking, Ellery quickly jumps in and says, "I would never! Scout's honor. They only know that you two dated in high school."

My breath releases, one that I had no clue I was holding until now. But I know the interrogation is far from over. *Please don't ask why we broke up.*

"So," Luz says, leaning forward and steeping her fingers. "Inquiring minds want to know: how big are we talking?"

Surprise lights my features, and I blink. That question is not at all what I expected. But honestly, I should know better.

"Oh, ew!" Ellery throws her hands over her ears and pretends to gag. "Warn a girl before you ask about my brother's—anything. Just. No."

"What?" Luz looks entirely too innocent as she meets Ellery's skeptical gaze. "Simon is sexy as hell, looking like he could lift me with one hand and not break a sweat. Why would I not want to know?" She taps a finger against her chin. "I wonder if he ever uses his handcuffs in bed."

"Oh my god, you guys!" Ellery glares daggers at the other four women.

"Sorry." Luz clears her throat, looking not at all sorry.

Lena pipes up next to her. "Come on, Elle. Objectively speaking, your brother is one gorgeous piece of eye candy—utterly delectable."

"Scrumptious," Luz adds, not at all helpful.

They continue barely whispering while Ellery's cheeks get redder and more flushed with each word. Not that I am faring much better. My gaze ping-pongs between them at their sudden rapid-fire conversation.

Priya: "All that ginger hair…"

Luz: "That sexy beard."

Lena: "And those bedroom eyes."

Daisy: "He's a total snack."

Lena, again: "Yes! Snack is right. I'd like to lick his"—Ellery clamps her hand over Lena's mouth to cut her off.

"Okay," she says, sounding slightly hysterical. "I get it. The world gets it. Thank you."

Then Ellery stares at me with a mortified expression on her face, eyes as round as saucers. I war with the desire to laugh hysterically or hide. I am feeling all sorts of mortified myself.

Worse, they have made me *curious*.

My memories of Simon are from high school. Thirty-one-year-old Simon is an entirely different beast. Figuratively. Okay, okay, figuratively *and* literally. The man truly looks like he could lift any one of us single-handed. I thought high school Simon had an amazing physique, but his training regimen for the police force has undoubtedly improved on perfection. The itch to see him without clothes has become almost obsessive.

Simon Brooks, not even physically present and he throws my entire world into chaos.

At that thought, I feel thoughts and emotions starting to overwhelm me again—even more than before. I am going to need a minute if I have any hope of putting some of the chaos back in order.

"Excuse me," I interject.

My abrupt tone halts some of the conversation. Ignoring their curious looks, I stand and rush out in search of the restrooms. As soon as I see the familiar little symbol on one of the doors, I shove it open and lock myself inside. The tile wainscoting on the wall is cold against my back when I lean my weight against it. Then, bending forward, I rest my hands against my knees, taking three slow, deep breaths.

By the time I open my eyes again, my jackhammering heartbeat has settled. I step up to the sink. My reflection stares back in silent judgment, and I take in her unremarkable features: peach skin with an unnaturally pale undertone, lips pressed in a thin line, and lackluster hair. Designer clothes hug every curve. Each garment is crisp and custom-tailored to a perfect fit, with beautiful coordinating fabrics and colors. But, these clothes belong to a stranger.

The longer I stand and stare, the more I hate every tiny detail. I feel unhinged enough that if I had access to scissors, I would be chopping up my hair by now. In a far less intrusive train of thought, my fingers trace the empty holes of my old piercings. They drift down to my nose, where the tiniest bit of red marks the stud I once had there. I wonder if a tattoo parlor can salvage any of them.

Then I wonder if someone can salvage any of *me*.

Someone knocks at the door before I can even begin to think of an answer. I straighten and sigh. The existential crisis will have to wait.

Bracing myself, I call out, "Just a minute."

When I open the door, Lena standing on the other side takes me by surprise. For a long moment, I stay silent, staring up at her in quiet confusion.

"Hi," she says.

"Hi?" I respond more slowly, trailing off into a question while I wait for her to reveal why she came.

"Sorry. I promise I'm not here for nefarious reasons." She smiles, gentle and disarming, and it works to loosen a little of the unease bunching up my shoulders. "I just wanted to check on you. Before, out there, you seemed…"

"Paranoid?" I offer. My weak attempt at a joke. "Chaotic?"

"Lost."

Oh. Well, that hits the nail on the head.

Immediately I want to close myself off in self-preservation. Then I get annoyed at the thought. Forcing myself to square my shoulders, I meet Lena's gaze head-on and wait for her to continue. She looks like she has more to say.

"Do you have a minute?" she asks, confirming my theory. She motions toward the courtyard where Daisy and I had our heart-to-heart. That memory already feels like a lifetime ago.

"Yeah, I do."

"Okay," she says, smiling a little more brightly. "Let's go talk."

My therapist wants me to start building bridges again.

Those bridges may as well start here.

Chapter 14
Intrusive Thoughts

Piper

"You seemed uncomfortable back there."

Lena and I sit perched on a stone bench, similar to the one Daisy and I sat on during our heart-to-heart. I wonder if this conversation will go anything like that one, still unsure what Lena wants to talk about other than my intense awkwardness during our entire interaction at lunch.

At least this spot has a lot more privacy.

"I hope we weren't too much for you," Lena continues, cracking a smile to diffuse some of the tension. I wish I could say it works, but somehow, my tension only mounts. "The girls and I are a crazy bunch, but we mean well."

"Not at all," I say quickly, peeking over at her. "I already knew going in that Ellery and Daisy are a handful. Comparatively speaking, you, Luz, and Priya are perfectly normal."

Lena snorts. *"Touché."*

Just a tiny bit of silliness, but even that fizzles out the longer we sit there in silence, simply staring at each other. Lena's dark brown eyes glint in the midmorning sun while she watches me. That same sunlight feels unnaturally warm on my clammy skin.

My therapist often uses the senses in our sessions to help ground me, so I focus now on that sensation of heat. I hear the rustle of wind through the courtyard trees. The aroma of freshly ground coffee beans hits my nose, and I take an involuntary breath to hold it in my lungs for a moment. They work together to center me and anchor me in the moment.

Unfortunately, my efforts do nothing to erase the feeling of being stripped bare. Lena can see right through my armor, it seems. Here I am, trying my hardest to act casual and look unaffected—something I perfected over the years—and still she sees much more than I want her to.

Maybe Lena thinks I might bolt if given half a chance. (I will.) Maybe she thinks I might be seconds away from a meltdown. (I am.)

Or, maybe she hears my heart just as loudly as I do, jackhammering like a rabbit caught in a snare, or smell the desperation seeping out of my pores.

Because Lena's next words rip off the bandaid and get right to the heart of the conversation. "Look," she says, "I'm just going to come right out and ask." I bristle at her blunt delivery.

"Do you have some problem with me? Or with my father's company?"

"I—wait, what?" I ask. I am about two sentences behind in my cognitive reasoning, and I am still stuck on Lena's question about whether they are a handful.

She huffs lightly. "When I introduced myself and mentioned my father, your walls went sky-high. Like, Fort Knox level self-preservation."

"Oh." I rub a palm down my face, stopping to pinch the spot between my brows while hoping to ease some of the building pressure. "I didn't think people noticed."

Lena shrugs. "Most probably don't. But I grew up surrounded by wealthy, extremely fake people daily. I had to learn at a young age to pick up on subtle cues to know which ones to trust and which ones to steer clear of."

My heart clenches at the thought of a little girl trying to navigate the shark-infested waters of that world. Quickly, I clarify. "None of this is on you, Lena, I swear. Or even Evermore Media. Things are…"

I trail off, unsure what to say or even how to begin.

Then I settle on, "Things are complicated."

"Life is complicated, babe," Lena says, smiling gently. "We should still let things out so they don't fester."

Let things out. What a simple concept. I twist my fingers together, a familiar bite of anxiety rushing through my veins while I sort out my mind and figure out what is safe enough to share.

I still fear saying too much.

"There is—was—someone in my life," I start, choosing my words carefully. "Someone who broke my trust."

Lena frowns. "Trust in what? The media? The music industry? Or you?"

I shrug. "All of it. Everything. He broke my whole sense of self, my confidence—you name it." It takes me another second to form the words I need to say to explain. My tongue is sandpaper, stuck to the roof of my mouth like glue, and I have to pry them apart. "My record label falls under Evermore Media. He owns the record label and my contract. Hearing your name triggered me."

Silence hangs over us. The air feels heavy, like rain clouds before a downpour. After a few moments, my skin starts to itch when Lena fails to respond, but when I look up to ask her thoughts, her darkened expression has turned away while she frowns at the courtyard.

My lungs seize. I close my eyes. My mind starts a downward spiral of unwelcome thoughts at her reaction.

Lena blames me. She thinks I'm weak. She is going to tell everyone what a fraud I am.

"Piper..."

My eyes snap open at the sound of my name. Lena watches me. She opens her mouth, then closes it. Then she shakes her head.

"I don't know what to say." Her anger quickly turns to disgust. "That is seriously messed up."

I wince before I can hide it. Of course, Lena sees. She quickly takes my hands in hers.

"Not you, sweetie. The *situation* is messed up." Her face flushes red-hot with fury. "Someone in a position of power took advantage of you. Someone *associated with my father's company* took advantage of you. Who is he?"

"I—what?"

"Who is he?" she repeats, gently squeezing the hands still in her grip. "Give me his name and the name of his record label. That rat bastard will regret ever coming after you. He'll pay for what he did."

Lena's words are so full of conviction that I almost believe them.

Almost.

Because they fail to erase all the reasons I ran in the first place. I remember why I had to leave. I remember why I blocked Cedric's number and am working with independent lawyers who have never even heard his name.

I remember why I am still hiding.

Because Cedric is evil, conniving—and extremely cunning. His silver tongue knows exactly how to weave a story and cast a spell over anyone who listens.

For years, Cedric conditioned me, grooming me into the perfect little marionette. Then he became the puppet master. He pulled my strings from the shadows and did things with such subtlety that I have no proof.

Lena has it all wrong. Only *I* have regrets. Only *I* will pay for all that Cedric did. He will paint himself as the victim so fast that I will lose any chance of pleading my case.

Worse, Cedric can convince the world's biggest skeptic he is more saintly than Mother Theresa. They would see nothing but what he portrays: a successful businessman who goes out of his way to help young up-and-coming artists break into the business. They would see him as someone who, to all the world, has a sterling reputation and can do no wrong.

No. I shake my head, gently pulling my hands from Lena's grip, and repeat the word out loud. "No."

"No? No, what?" Lena asks.

"I'm not going to give you his name," I say more forcefully.

Her brow furrows in confusion. "But, surely you want to put him away. Don't you want to make sure he can never hurt anyone else?"

"Of course I do." I stand up and start to pace, needing an outlet for the frustration coursing through me. "But Cedric will never get punished. I doubt he would get even a slap on the wrist."

Everything in me—all the pent-up emotion, stress, and uncertainty—has finally reached a boiling point. Those emotions spent weeks and months stewing together, the pressure building until just the slightest press of the release valve caused everything to explode. With nothing else to hold them back, the words pour out

"I have no proof, Lena," I continue. "None. My word will go against his—and who in the world would go against a powerful man like him? Not for one poor little musician in a sea of millions.

"Everything will get twisted in his favor. Because that's what he does—tells lies, distorts reality to suit him, and then makes you believe in that fucked up reality."

My voice falters until I can barely get the last words out. By now, I am perilously close to tears. Still, I grit my teeth, and I give voice to my greatest fear: "No one is going to believe me."

"I believe you." There is sadness in her voice, but also conviction.

"How?" I ask. One word, so brittle that it breaks in half. Then, more assertive and almost angry the second time, I repeat the question. "How? I barely believe myself. His voice in my head always tells me I'm not good enough, pretty enough, or sane enough. He broke me down so he could dress me up, make me up, pose me like some damned doll, and put me on display."

My eyes burn, and my voice shakes. "I was so stupid to fall for his tricks. That's what everyone will say. Because I tell myself the same thing every day when I look in the mirror."

Lena abruptly stands and walks up to me. "People will believe you—*I believe you*—because you are telling the truth."

"What is the truth?" I scoff. "Because even I have no idea."

"Then let us help you figure it out."

Those words come from someone else. Ellery. My eyes pinch closed at hearing the sound of her voice. When I finally muster up the courage to look, guilt and sorrow are cutting harsh lines into her face.

"Sorry," she says quietly, stepping closer. "I didn't mean to eavesdrop. You took a long time, and the girls and I started to worry. But I only heard the very last bit. Barely anything at all."

Something about what she says and how she fidgets—clasping and unclasping her hands, threading and unthreading her fingers—has a genuine, albeit small, smile weaving its way onto my face. Ellery has always had this uncanny ability to pull me out of myself and into the moment. I have always envied her childlike wonder and curiosity.

And right now, that easygoing personality is precisely what I need.

Lena watches me silently. I can feel her gaze burning along my cheek. When my eyes lift to hers, she mouths the words, Tell her.

I take a deep breath. Then, I turn back to my sister, in all but blood. Ellery still considers me family even after all these years.

She deserves to know.

"You don't have to say anything," Ellery says before I can speak. "Not unless you want to. Whatever happened will never change how much I love you. You're my family. Nothing will make me think less of you."

"Elle, you have no way of knowing"—Ellery quickly cuts me off.

"Piper," she says, gently chiding. "I know you. No matter how much time has gone by, no matter how much distance came between us, you were the only sister figure I ever had. That makes you my sister forever."

My eyes glisten. I have no words, not after that declaration. Even if I did, the lump in my throat will never let them escape.

Ellery has more to say, regardless. "You're different from before. Not just the 'I'm famous and worldly now' different or the 'I've grown so much as a person' different."

"Then what kind of different am I?" I ask hesitantly.

Biting her lip, Ellery contemplates how much to reveal before finally meeting my gaze. "This deep melancholy surrounds you. When you think no one is paying attention, when you let your guard down, I can sense it take hold. You're quieter. You hold yourself back in conversations, like you fear saying the wrong thing."

The smile on my face has long since fallen away, and my chest burns with pressure from the weight of her words.

Lena is right. I need to tell her.

I *want* to tell her.

So I do.

By the end, tears are streaming down both our faces, and we are holding on to each other for dear life. I am physically exhausted and mentally hanging by a thread. But I also feel lighter than I have in a very long time.

At some point, Daisy finds us and watches from the sidelines until I lift my head from Ellery's shoulder and notice her. I lift one arm, and Daisy slips under it, pulling us into a group hug. Lena joins a second later.

Despite the seriousness of the moment, I start to laugh. Soon, all four of us double over, giggling like children. If anyone were to walk in right now, they would consider us insane.

Ask me if I care.

Ellery pulls me into one last hug. "Don't worry," she whispers. "This stays between us. I won't say a word to anyone else." Even without asking, I know she means Simon.

"Thank you," I whisper back.

"Love you, sis."

"Love you, too."

Feeling emotionally wrung out, I say goodbye to the three of them, ready to fall into bed and sleep for the next hundred years. Unfortunately, as soon as I click the button to unlock the doors and start the engine, I hear my name from down the street.

Simon.

Shit. My shoulders tense slightly, but I pretend to not hear him. I have no energy to deal with another person.

Not even Simon.

Not now, while I am still raw and exposed. Because Simon, like Lena, sees much more than he should. And I can only tackle one insurmountable dilemma at a time.

Chapter 15
Crave

Simon

The annoyingly incessant chime from my phone pulls me out of a delicious dream. One where I slowly unwrap Piper from that lounge singer costume piece by piece using my teeth. I have just reached her lace-thong panties when my eyes fly open.

Whoever is texting this goddamn early better be dying.

With a heavy sigh, I ignore my raging hard-on, grab my phone, and lift it to my face. Then, I groan. Ellery. Of course. My sister loves to be a nuisance, even during the sleeping hours.

I unlock the screen and start to scroll through the texts.

- 6:25 am -

Ellery: Simon, wake up

Ellery: Simon!

Ellery: Hellooooooo?

Ellery: Oh, come on, Mr. Light Sleeper

Ellery: Siiiiiiimon

Ellery: Will

Ellery: You

Ellery: Please

Ellery: Wake

Ellery: UP!

Ellery: SIMON, SOS!

That last text has me bolting upright in bed. My fingers frantically fly across the screen.

Simon: What's wrong? Are you okay? Is Beck okay?

Ellery: Whoops *halo emoji* Nothing's wrong

Ellery: I just have a huge favor

Simon: FFS *swearing emoji*

Ellery: *cringe emoji*

Simon: What favor requires me up at the ass-crack of dawn?

Ellery: Can you watch Ozzy & Cooper?

Simon: ...

Simon: Why?

Ellery: Because Stella and Foster are going into the city today with Daisy; Beckham and Hawk are on a job site; Lena is visiting with family; Luz is working; and Priya doesn't do dogs, so we have no one else

Simon: Gee, glad to be so high up on your list of choices

Ellery: Oh, hush

Ellery: So will you?

Simon: ...

Simon: Fine

Ellery: YAY! Be there in 20

It is way too early for me to unpack that deluge of information. Yawning and blinking the sleep out of my eyes, I set my phone back on the nightstand. Then I slip out of bed and stretch before pulling on a pair of sweats. Duchess stirs and does her own stretch before she follows me into the bathroom. Once I am cleaned up enough to pass basic human hygiene, I focus on the fluffy bundle obediently sitting at my feet.

"Morning, pretty girl," I murmur, gathering her into my arms. She licks my cheek before I have a chance to block it. I chuckle and shake my head. "Come on, let's head downstairs."

It's time for bathroom breaks (for Duchess) and coffee (for me).

Once I hit the kitchen, I set Duchess on the floor. She takes off before me, turning to yip at me to hurry up. Yet another brat in my life. She jumps up and down on her stubby little legs until I open the sliding glass door. Then she takes off like a shot out into the middle of the yard. I leave her to do her business while I make myself an extra large cup of my most robust coffee.

Then I join her outside.

The morning air has a bite, cutting through the remaining haze of lust that still clings to me. I breathe it into my lungs and hold it until it burns. Then, I release it slowly before taking a long sip from the mug.

Duchess trots back to me and right on past, heading back into the warmth of the house without bothering to see if I'm behind her. So spoiled. I chuckle to myself and follow her in. At least she knows the routine.

Sure enough, when I head over to the kitchen island, she has already sprawled out on the floor by my usual stool, gnawing on one of the squeak toys Ellery bribes her with whenever she comes over. I watch Duchess play for a minute while I drink my coffee. Soon, though, my thoughts turn inward, conjuring the face of the woman who is never far from my mind.

Fuck. I palm my face in frustration. Piper has me all twisted in knots, and I am no longer used to feeling this way.

I prefer control. In fact, I crave it. Need it.

Over the years, I have considered every possible scenario that might bring Piper back into my life. I tried to plan for all the things I may need to do to earn her forgiveness. I never dared to hope for much after that.

Then the moment finally came.

Piper is home—and every one of my plans have flown right out the window. She came in like a whirlwind and knocked my world completely off of its axis. I have been fighting for control ever since. I lost that fight once at the art gala, then again on Halloween.

Our kiss that night felt like a turning point, but in which direction?

We kissed. Everything imploded. Piper ran. After that, I gave us both some much needed space to think.

But during all that time, not once have we ever talked.

We need to talk.

This wall between us gets taller—and stronger—every day. Not insurmountable, but I do have a lot of work cut out to scale it. And to do that, I have to be honest about my feelings for Piper.

Among other things.

Eventually.

One step at a time, Simon.

The front doorbell chime cuts into my headspace. I jolt to my feet in surprise. Then, glancing at my watch, I confirm my fears that I just wasted the twenty minutes Ellery allotted to me.

"Fuck me." I sigh and look around for Duchess. She has begun circling my feet, yipping loudly at the door even though we are nowhere near the same room. "Come here, you."

Lifting her once again and settling her into the crook of my arm, I stride through the living room. At the second doorbell chime, I grumble, then call out, "I'm coming, Ellery, hold your damn horses."

Four pairs of eyes stare up at me when I open the door. Quickly, I scan them. Ellery watches me, fighting back laughter. Ozzy and Cooper shake with restrained excitement as soon as they both lock eyes with Duchess.

But, Piper—as soon as I set eyes on her, my attention locks in place. Her eyes flare while they trace along my bare chest and torso. The longer she stares, the more blush stains her cheeks. Her eyes darken with desire when they reach the low-slung waist of my grey sweats. I look down, then up again, and meet her gaze when it catches on the movement.

"Um." She clears her throat. Even then, she still trips over her words. "Thank you. For watching them, I mean. The dogs." She absently motions toward them, still laser-focused on my chest.

Ellery moves in my peripheral vision, and when I glance in her direction, I see her watching Piper with a pleased expression.

Playing matchmaker again.

I glare at my sister. She holds up her hands, declaring innocence—like I believe that for a second. Then she decides to press her luck by turning to Piper and saying, "I'll just get these two dapper pups settled inside, okay?"

"Mm-hmm," Piper says absently.

"Come, Ozzy, Cooper," Ellery says, and they quickly follow her through the open doorway.

Duchess lets out a tiny bark at the lack of attention, informing me and all in the vicinity of her displeasure. That sound pulls Piper from her daze. Turning her focus to Duchess, Piper smiles.

"Who is this little angel?" she coos, reaching out to let Duchess sniff her. Once her Royal Highness grants permission, Piper scratches the top of her head and says nonsensical things that keep the dog's tail wagging happily.

"Duchess," I say. "Her name is Duchess."

She snorts at that. "You do look like a Duchess," she says to the dog. "I bet your daddy spoils you rotten, huh?"

Innocently meant or not, my body has all sorts of inappropriate reactions to hearing Piper call me "daddy." I have to bite my lip so hard that I taste blood, but it does the trick.

"Ozzy and Cooper," I say carefully. "They're well trained, but do they do okay with other dogs?" I lift Duchess slightly.

"Oh yeah, they love other dogs," she assures me. "Smaller ones especially. She could climb all over them, and they would happily let her."

With that new knowledge, I set Duchess down on the ground. She scampers back inside without a backward glance. We both watch her disappear.

"She's adorable." Piper looks up at me. "Did you get her somewhere, or…?"

I shake my head. "Nah, found her behind the dumpster at the station. Poor thing was half-starved. The only shelter that could take her was the county one."

She frowns and asks, "They're a kill-shelter, aren't they?"

"Yeah. I refused to leave the poor furball there."

Piper smiles at me, and I swear she thaws by a thousand degrees. Her face is practically beaming. "You always were a big softy."

"Hey." I fake a scowl. "I am in no way soft."

"Hmm." She looks me slowly up and down, and her smile turns wicked. "No, I think you're right about that."

I step closer. Piper's breath hitches, and her pupils dilate. Fuck. I want to take action—lower my head and recapture the lips that have starred in all my erotic dreams. But I tamp the desire down.

"Listen," I say, running a hand through my hair while I struggle to find words. I take a deep breath and try again. "Can we start over? Pretend the other night never happened? These past couple of weeks have been nice, getting to know you again, spending time with you, and I"—pausing, I pinch my eyes closed. "I don't want to fuck that up."

When I open them again, Piper watches me in silence. I see a flicker of hurt for just a second before her face smooths and falls back on that placid, polite expression I see her use with everyone she meets.

The mask that I absolutely loathe.

"Yeah, okay." She says the words, but her tone has turned wooden. "We can just chalk it up to a mistake and move on."

"Piper."

"No, I get it. You don't have to spare my feelings. You haven't wounded my pride."

"Piper—"

"I thought there might have been a spark, but I know I freaked out on you. Anyone would want to erase that crazy—"

My control snaps. Piper is done twisting my words. She gasps when my hand grips her by the back of her neck so I can tug her toward me. Then, I dip my head so that we are eye-to-eye. Our lips hover only an inch apart, and I can feel her rapid breaths puff against my skin.

"Do you really think that kiss had no effect on me?" My words drip with barely restrained anger. "Do you really think I had no desire to slam you against the nearest wall and take you right then and there, no matter who may have seen us?" I tilt her head back, giving myself access to the soft hollow of her neck. Unable to help myself, I run my nose along her petal soft skin. Then my lips brush against her ear. "Do you think I don't have to fuck my hand till I'm raw every single time I remember the way you taste? The sounds you made?"

I feel her pulse fluttering wildly under my thumb.

"Dammit, Piper," I bite out, fighting the urge to taste her again. "There is nothing else on this god-forsaken planet I want to do more than kiss you again. But next time, it will be when both of us are good and ready, and there will be no running away. No regrets. I won't touch you again—until you ask. Understand?"

I feel her nod. Not good enough. With a gentle squeeze to the back of her neck, I ensure I get her full attention. "Need the words, sweetheart."

"I understand," she says. Barely a whisper, but I can accept that.

"Good girl."

I step back when I hear Ellery's footsteps. A few seconds later, she appears, giggling and oblivious to the tension between us, and says, "I think he's in love."

Frozen in place, I carefully, nonchalantly ask, "Who's that?"

Shit. Maybe Ellery did notice.

"Ozzy." Ellery smiles, shaking her head. "He has been hovering over Duchess since she shuffled into the room a few minutes ago and refuses to let her out of his sight. He even brought her a toy out of her basket. That sweet boy is down hard."

I sneak a glance at Piper. Her eyes are on Ellery but they look slightly glazed over, and I can tell where her mind is stuck. She may be listening, but her thoughts are a million miles away.

My lips twitch, and I relax into a chuckle. "She does seem to have that effect on men."

Piper does, too.

"Funny thing is, she's completely oblivious." Ellery shakes her head, smiling.

"Hmm." My eyes drift back to Piper. This time, she looks right at me. I let my lips curl fully into a grin and say, purely for her benefit, "Yeah, but I think she'll figure out soon enough just how gone he is for her."

Piper clears her throat, and the red receding from her face floods her cheeks again. That same flush goes straight to my groin. I have to bite my lip again to keep from groaning out loud.

Not the time or the place, buddy.

But fuck. All Piper has to do is look at me, and my cock turns harder than granite.

Thankfully, Ellery misses the sexual undercurrent between Piper and me. She grabs Piper's hand, tugging her down the porch steps and breaking our connection.

"We'll be back in a few hours!" she chirps.

"Take your time," I call out. "I've got things well in hand."

Piper's head swivels back over her shoulder, wide-eyed. Good. She caught my meaning.

Anytime Piper needs a reminder of just how much I crave her—like an addict craves drugs—I will happily give it to her—any time, any place. In fact, I will give her as many demonstrations as she needs until it sinks in.

But I still need to tread carefully where Piper is concerned.

Someone else hurt her and made her doubt herself. At first, I thought I was the cause, but I am beginning to realize that most of it stems from something darker. Her distrust has deeper roots than one idiotic (albeit colossal) mistake I made over a decade ago.

If it takes the rest of my life, I will weed out every doubt that has taken seed. I will spend every waking moment planting reminders of how goddamn gorgeous Piper is—not just her body, but also her mind, her spirit, and her compassion. All of her, every inch, can bring a person to their knees in worship. And I will continue to prove it to Piper—over and over—until that truth etches deep into the marrow of her bones.

Whoever did this to her better watch their back. I will figure out the motherfucker's name, address, whatever it takes.

Then I'm coming for them.

And I will destroy them.

"I won't *touch you* again —until *you ask.*"

Chapter 16
Little Girl Gone

Piper

My eyes stare blankly out the passenger side window, thoughts continually straying even while I try to stay present in the moment.

I should focus on Ellery.

I should be excited about whatever surprises she has in store today.

Instead, I am one giant, knotted mess of emotions. My mind remains stuck about ten miles back the way we came, trapped on Simon's front porch.

Simon.

That sexy bastard took me by complete surprise. He appeared barefoot and shirtless while his tall, broad frame filled the doorway. Suddenly, all I could see was miles of skin and a gorgeous male. My fingers itched to run through his sleep-tousled curls. He still oozed that boy-next-door charm but with a sinful smile. Then, he had the nerve to be holding the world's most adorable puppy to his naked chest.

I was *not* prepared.

Worse, I was spellbound.

I am *still* spellbound, helpless as my mind replays our heated conversation in a never-ending loop. Each time, Simon's warm breath caresses my neck. We are so close that I can feel the sun's heat on his bare skin. I still hear those wicked words he whispered in my ear. With every instant replay, Simon threatens to split me apart at the seams and stitch me back together again. And I *want* him to.

Or maybe not. I honestly have no clue what I want where Simon is concerned. I am throwing out all sorts of mixed signals, but only because my *emotions* are all mixed up.

Then Simon had to go and say he wanted to forget our kiss. I panicked when I should have been relieved. Simon regretted kissing me, yet there I stood, devastated because the same kiss that rocked my world right off its axis left his world upright.

But boy did he set the record straight. Simon left me no doubt about his feelings—both from his words and from the heat of his gaze when he told me all those dirty thoughts. They burned me up inside.

Sweet merciful heavens.

"Earth to Piper," Ellery says. Her voice, combined with the gentle nudge of her hand on my shoulder, yanks me out of my spiraling thoughts.

I jolt in my seat and look over at her, wide-eyed. "Did I fall asleep?"

"No," she says with a laugh, "but you were so lost up here"—she taps a finger to her temple—"that I was worried I'd need to find a hypnotist or something to pull you back out."

"Sorry." My cheeks flush in embarrassment. "Up here"—I mimic her motion against my temple—"is kind of a mess right now."

"Oh, yeah?" Her lips tip up in a smile. "Thinking about a certain big brother of mine, perhaps?"

"Ellery…"

"Piper," she says right back. "Come on. You, of all people, deserve some good in your life right now."

"I do have good in my life," I argue. "A lot of good. My family. You and the other girls. As for Simon, I'm glad that we can be friends."

Liar.

"Only friends?" Ellery's expression falls, her voice tinged with disappointment.

"With Simon, things are just so…" I wave my hands around helplessly, searching for the right word.

"Things with Simon are complicated," Ellery answers for me. She sighs heavily and then peeks over. "I get it. I do. But you were so good for each other once. Perfect, even. You could be again."

I bite my lip and look back out the window. "I don't know, Elle."

"That's not a no."

Her sing-song voice pulls a chuckle out of me. "You are just as tenacious as you were back then, do you know that?"

"So I'm told. Often." Ellery adds happily, "I drive Beckham crazy."

Our laughter dispels any lingering tension. Then I peer over at her and ask, "So, are you ever going to tell me where we're going?"

"No need." She smirks. The car slows to a stop moments later. "We're already here."

I realize she has just pulled up beside an open parking spot along the curb. While she maneuvers the car into place, I peek out and notice the familiar boutique shop we sit in front of. The words "Beauty & Bliss" are painted on the shop window in a delicate script, with flourishes curling around a rose and a butterfly. Beneath the logo is written "Salon & Beauty Bar." Behind the glass, I can barely make out rows of hair and makeup stations.

We both step out onto the curb, and when Ellery turns to me, she notes my surprise and smiles with a giddy little hop. "We're getting you a makeover!"

I blink slowly. "A makeover."

"Boozy brunch got me thinking, and I wanted to surprise you. After what you admitted, well." She flushes slightly. "Maybe it would help if you felt more like your old self. Your true self, you know?"

"Ellery," I breathe, unsure what to say in the face of such a thoughtful gift. My eyes stray back to the window.

Beside me, Ellery quietly continues. "You said you don't know who you are anymore. Maybe we can figure it out together."

I know I should respond, but the words stick in my throat. They are knotted up with emotion, sucking up all the air. The longer I stay silent, the more Ellery's enthusiasm deflates.

"I overstepped, didn't I?" Her voice quivers slightly.

That uncertainty yanks me right out of my stupor. "What? No!" I exclaim, stepping forward to pull her into a hug. "I'm sorry," I mumble into her hair. "I'm just overwhelmed in the very best way. This is amazing. Thank you."

When we pull apart, I have to blink away tears. Ellery does, too.

"Come on," she says, returning to her early enthusiasm.

She throws the doors open and tugs me behind her and up to the front to sign in. A young woman is staffing the counter. She looks no more than seventeen, with dark hair that falls in thick waves just past her shoulders. Her bangs are held back on either side by a cute butterfly clip, and she has freckles across her nose and cheeks. A smile tugs at her full lips when she looks up. Her dark gaze, hiding behind a pair of trendy red glasses, catches on Ellery for a split second before returning to the computer.

I realize that I am familiar with her features. She must be a relative of Luz—and since Luz owns this establishment, that makes sense.

"Hi, Elle," the girl says, speaking to the monitor.

"Hi, Mila," Ellery replies with a warm smile. "This is my good friend, Piper. She and I have a nine o'clock with Luz and Vivi."

Mila looks up again at my name, curiosity coloring her tan features. "Piper. That name sounds familiar—holy shizballs, you're Songbyrd!" She slaps both hands over her mouth, dark eyes widening in mortification. "Sorry. Oh my god, I am so sorry. I'm not usually like this. But you. You're you, and I'm me, and you're here, and my friends are so not going to believe me when I tell them, and—"

"Mila, just breathe," Ellery says, laughing lightly.

I smile at the starry-eyed teenager. "Believe it or not, I've had more than my fair share of fan encounters. This one is nowhere near the most embarrassing. Trust me," I add when Mila looks skeptical. "You're fine."

Her shoulders slump in relief. "Okay, good. Luz would never let me live it down if I ran her clients off because of my 'over-exuberance.'" She frames the last word with air quotes, rolling her eyes.

"I heard that, *bebé*." Luz comes strolling out of the back. "Hey, you two!" She smiles at us and waves her hands around in the air. "Piper, *chica*, what do you think of my salon?"

"It's lovely," I say and mean it. The colors are neutral and warm, with splashes of color from fashion photography sprinkled throughout. Each station looks a little different, highlighting the personalities of the stylists who occupy them. Plants pull in a little bit of nature. The music overhead feels bright yet soothing.

I've been to some lovely places over the years, but this eclectic mixture of high fashion and Southern comfort makes me feel like I could hang out here forever.

"Thanks! Now," Luz says, clapping her hands excitedly. "Let's go get you made up, beautiful."

Ellery tugs me along while she and Luz chat animatedly at the front. I hang back a bit, content to look around and quietly take everything in. Walking by the washing stations, the air is thick with typical salon smells: scented candles, hair dye, and various aromas of shampoo and styling products.

Luz and Ellery keep moving, finally leading me to a fancy station near the back. Ellery moves to the next station, greeted by a slightly older woman with dark blonde hair cut in a cute, chaotic pixie cut.

"Hi, Piper," the woman says, smiling warmly. "My name is Vivian, but you can call me Vivi. Luz here told me you're getting the full gambit today."

"Um…" I look between Luz and Ellery, eyes wide. "This is all a big surprise organized by Ellery, so I know nothing about anything. Elle?"

"You are getting completely pampered—shampoo, color, cut, and style," Ellery explains. "Whatever you want, Luz and Vivi here will make it happen. They are miracle workers." Her grin widens, eyes twinkling with childlike glee as she starts to tick off her fingers. "Then a facial, followed by a full-face makeup application. Manicure and pedicure with massages included."

My eyebrows inch up incrementally with each item she mentions. By the end, I can only say, "Please tell me you're doing this with me, at least."

"Like I would miss the chance to get pampered." Ellery winks.

I relax a bit at that. At least Ellery will enjoy herself, too. I also make a mental note to waylay Luz before we leave to ensure she sends the bill my way. Even if Ellery insists that this day is her treat, I refuse to let her foot an astronomical bill.

Thankfully, Luz is a mind reader. Either that or something in my expression gives me away because—while Ellery is occupied, talking something over with Vivi—Luz leans over the chair and whispers, "Don't worry about a thing, chica. Everything today is on the house. We take care of our own here."

Her expression gentles at my bright smile of thanks. Without a word, she wraps her arms around me in a brief hug. Once she lets me go, she turns the chair toward the mirror and runs her fingers through my hair.

"So, Miss Piper Easton," Luz says into the mirror. "Are you ready to let the new you fly free?"

This is the first step I need to take to reclaim my life and everything I have lost. A rush of adrenaline floods my system at the realization. The anticipation lights up every nerve ending, waking long-dormant feelings—so many that I could never begin to name them all.

My excitement makes me feel light as a feather. I really can fly if I want to.

And I want to.

The grin on Luz's reflection brightens a little of the uneasiness attempting to derail me, and I find my smile mirroring hers.

"I am," I say in answer to her question. "Let's do this."

✳✳✳

I would have been ecstatic if we had stopped only for the salon visit. But Ellery has much more planned.

First, we head into the city and enjoy a leisurely lunch. Second, Ellery takes me to one of those artist collectives that repurpose old buildings and give them new life. (This one started out of an old naval shipyard.) Finally, Ellery explains that Jude—quick to volunteer her help when Ellery told her the plan—booked me an appointment at the "best tattoo parlor in South Carolina." Jude also made sure that I would be with her favorite artist, Xander.

When we arrive, we are greeted by a tall man with dark, artfully mussed hair and rich brown eyes. His tight black t-shirt shows a mural of beautiful tattoos all up his arms, peeking out under the hemline along his collarbone and neck. The tattoos enhance the warm caramel tones of his skin. His smile is also warm, showcasing a row of straight white teeth. And when he speaks, even his voice sounds rich and warm.

"Ellery," he says, shaking first her hand, then mine, "and Piper. I'm Xander Scott."

"Pleasure to meet you," Ellery replies.

"Believe me when I say the pleasure is all mine." He winks. "It's not every day I get to play host to someone as talented or well-loved as Songbyrd."

I flush under his admiring gaze. Even Ellery seems a little flustered in Xander's presence, to be honest. A man this beautiful should be gracing magazine covers, and it feels like a crime against humanity that he stays hidden away in a studio. But Xander seems happy and in his element.

He is also extremely talented. While he leads us back to his workstation, the floor-to-ceiling art gallery collage draws my eye and holds my attention. When he helps me get comfortable on the chair in the center, I ask, "Is all of that art yours?"

"Hmm?" He looks up and around the space. "Most of it, yeah. My business partner designed the rest."

"Impressive."

His lips quirk in a lopsided smile. "Thank you." Then, stepping back and crossing his arms, Xander gives me a quick once over. "So, Jude told me that we're doing piercings today?"

I peek over at Ellery. "How did you two know?" I ask. I never mentioned the piercings to anyone.

Ellery smiles and reaches over to squeeze my hand. "I remember how much you always loved your piercings. Frankly, I was jealous." With a chuckle, she adds, "I begged Simon a ridiculous number of times to let me get a nose ring."

I laugh at that. "And his answer was no."

She snorts. "His answer was hell no."

Xander smirks and then turns to me with a raised eyebrow. "So, how many are we talking?"

"Well, if there's no scar tissue, I'd love them all back: three lobe piercings on each side, two cartilage on the left, a rook on the right, and a daith piercing in each. Oh, and, of course, the nose piercing." I grin at Ellery. "You want one?"

Biting her lip, she thinks for a moment before nodding. "You know what? Yeah, I do." She peeks up at Xander. "Can you squeeze me in?"

"For a beauty like you? Absolutely. My business partner, Riley, is free right now. Let me grab him for an assist."

He steps out and disappears down a hallway. I release a giddy laugh. "Oh my god, Elle, remind me to thank Jude when we see her again."

Ellery's gaze stays locked on the door. "Girl, you and me both. I see why Xander is her favorite."

When Xander returns, his complete opposite follows him into the room. Riley is the light to Xander's dark. He has blonde hair, blue eyes, fair skin, and, unlike Xander, truly looks like the kind of man you would see in a tattoo parlor. He is rougher around the edges, with more of a biker build—but just as gorgeous as Xander, in his own way.

Do they breed them differently in the city?

Because, *damn*.

"Looks like it's my lucky day," Riley says with a cheeky grin. "Xander usually keeps the special clients to himself."

Xander rolls his eyes. "Just get prep started, asshole."

Riley snorts and shoots us a wink before heading toward the sink to wash up.

"So, how long have you known Jude?" Ellery asks, watching Xander closely while he, too, cleans up and starts to prep everything in front of me. He pulls out an album of studs for me to choose from, and I take my time picking them out while they talk.

"Oh, we've known each other our whole lives." Xander chuckles when we shoot him twin looks of confusion. "Jude is my cousin."

"Huh." Ellery cocks her head to the side. "Yeah, okay. I can see it. The eyes, especially. That and you're both gorgeous."

Her eyes bulge out when she realizes what she said, but Xander, bless him, simply chuckles and turns his attention back to me. He must be used to that kind of thing.

After I point out the studs I want for each hole, Xander turns his focus to readying all his tools and walking me through his process. He checks both ears and the spot on my nose, commenting, "You're lucky. Many of these only partially closed up, so they'll be easy. The nose did close fully, but I don't see or feel any scar tissue." Then he winks. "Ready to dazzle, superstar?"

Xander, you have no idea.

The process takes less time than I expected—mainly because Xander and Riley are hilarious. They keep us both thoroughly entertained until the end when they hand Ellery and me a mirror to see the finished product.

My eyes start to burn while I stare at my reflection, and I have to blink rapidly to keep from crying in relief because I see *myself*, all the pieces of me that Cedric stole stitched back together.

Slowly, my head turns left and right while I take in the final transformation. Luz cut and styled my white-blonde hair into long, shaggy layers with bangs that frame my face. I kept my platinum blonde color on top and had Luz dye the layers underneath a vibrant red and orange for a flame effect. She also threaded the orange color through as a lighter peach for highlights.

Vivi is a miracle worker with a makeup brush. The look she gave me is natural but bold—and something I can wear day to day. My pale green eyes pop with shimmery nude shadow, heavy black liner on top, and rose gold shimmer along the lower lid. She painted my cheeks a rosy pink, and my lips shine with a simple gloss.

The piercings are perfect. My fingers reach up and gently run along the studs. Dazzle, indeed. Each one I picked has a simple diamond design so that it would sparkle when the light hits. The completed effect is stunning.

"Xander, this looks amazing. Thank you."

He smiles, pleased with my answer, and takes the mirror when I hand it back to him. "You think that's good? You should stop by for a tattoo sometime. Then I can really show you what I can do."

Riley snorts. "So modest."

"No need to be modest when you have the talent to back it up." His eyes twinkle when he meets my gaze for a moment before putting the mirror down and cleaning up.

My gaze wanders again over all the tattoo art and client photos he has displayed on the walls. Slowly, an idea forms—an entirely irrational, impulsive idea.

Precisely the kind of idea I need.

"Hey, Xander?" I say, catching his attention. My eyes light up with excitement. "If you're offering, there is one thing…"

***

Ellery begs me to let her drop me off first before picking Ozzy and Cooper up and driving them to my place.

"That seems unnecessarily complicated," I argue.

"Yeah, but you have a whole new, sexy-as-hell look, and I think that you should reveal it tomorrow night." She glances over at me. "Which means no one should see you until then."

I shake my head. "Elle, tomorrow night is your engagement party. I'm not about to try and steal your spotlight."

"Not if I give it freely—and I do, promise," she says. "Like you would be stealing anything, anyway. The whole night is about Beckham and me. I can spare a few minutes for my big sis."

My expression softens at her words. "Fine. We'll do it your way."

I turn my head and look out the passenger side window, smiling to myself. Ellery may think she is being clever, but I can read between the lines. She wants me to wait until tomorrow night so *Simon* gets the full effect of a big reveal.

To be honest, I love the thought of surprising him and seeing the look on his face when I walk in. Simon will see me wearing a killer dress and looking like myself for the first time since I came home.

But will he like the new me?

Maybe his tastes have changed over the years. Maybe he likes the white-washed version of me—the pampered, prissy pop-princess look that Cedric curated.

No. Don't go there.

I take a deep breath and let it out slowly. If my changes are too much for Simon, if he prefers the fake me, then he isn't worth any more of my time. No man is—not unless they can accept me as I am now. I refuse to turn myself inside out to fit some arbitrary mold.

My new tattoo burns slightly, reminding me of its existence and why I got one. I look down, eyes tracing the intricate design that decorates my skin. Even though a large bandage covers it, I can still picture it with stunning clarity.

A thin ring of fire wraps around my wrist and curls upward toward the center of my forearm. Within the flames is the black silhouette of a sandpiper. A colorful phoenix rises from the sandpiper's charred ashes directly above and surrounding the silhouette. Xander, Ellery, and I all contributed to the design, which turned out better than I could have imagined.

I owe Xander more than words can ever express. He stayed late for me, took three extra hours out of his day to make this impromptu vision of mine come to life. While I continue to stare at the image, mesmerized, Ellery notices my distraction.

"So," she says, peeking over at my wrist, "any particular meaning to the design? You never said."

"Nothing overly profound." I shrug and smile. "I just wanted something to remind me of this moment. Like a rebirth of sorts. And I want to remember that I'm strong enough to rise from the ashes, no matter what life throws at me."

"That's perfect." Ellery's voice rings with fierce pride. "You are so much stronger than you know."

"Yeah." I flush slightly with equal parts pleasure and embarrassment. "I'm beginning to figure that out."

After that, we fall into a comfortable silence. My hands are restless, unable to stay in one place for long. They clench and unclench in my lap while my fingertips tap an unknown melody on my thigh. I hesitate before blurting out, "I also think that the phoenix is going to be the theme of my new album."

Ellery's head whips around, and she gapes at me. "Are you serious? You haven't written anything new in ages!"

The excitement in her voice brings another smile to my face. "Yeah, I'm serious." I look out over the neighborhood houses we pass on our way back home. "I feel inspired for the first time in a long time."

Sunlight casts its glow on everything it touches. Outside the car, I can see families playing outside their homes. Some are grilling in their backyards. Birds flit within the trees, and I see an occasional squirrel or other small woodland creature dart in and out of sight.

All around us is activity.

But that is life—messy, chaotic, and so full of possibility. We only need to stop and look around. "I'm not quite there yet," I admit. "But soon."

Ellery squeals in excitement and smacks the steering wheel. "You just needed to find your way back, that's all."

"Because of you." I reach over and squeeze her shoulder.

"No way." Her curly hair bounces when she shakes her head. "Because of you. I just helped nudge you along a bit."

When I pull back, I hold up my phone and wiggle it in the palm of my hand. "I think I should post my new look. What do you think?"

Ellery gasps in excitement. "Yes!"

"Great," I say, smiling. "Let's get back to my place then where we can have some privacy."

"You don't have to tell me twice." With those words, she presses down on the gas. While we zip down the road, the sound of the engine mutes my loud laughter.

The thought of posting on my socials fills me with both excitement and trepidation. While I have been down here in Sweetbriar, Rue has been hard at work in New York, keeping my social media accounts active. I plan to only reveal enough to satiate my fans and pique their curiosity. Rue already put out the message that I am taking time for myself and being with family (all the usual generic updates). Somehow, she also worked her magic and removed Cedric's access.

I worry, though.

His radio silence this whole time may mean Cedric is plotting something.

Regardless, I am done hiding—from him, and from the world. My fans deserve to know that I am still here. They deserve to know that I am okay.

No. I am better than okay.

Songbyrd has been reborn from the ashes.

"But that is life— messy, chaotic, and so full of possibility."

Chapter 17
Learn to Fly

Piper

By the next afternoon, it feels like much of my newfound bravado has fizzled out. It could also just be nerves. Ellery and Beckham's engagement party starts in a few hours, and I am already close to a meltdown.

All the clothing in my closet has been pulled out and discarded, and I am still no closer to the perfect outfit—not even near a mediocre one. Cedric handpicked every outfit now on the floor, and I want nothing more to do with them.

This week, I plan to rid myself of this wardrobe and treat myself to an entirely different one—something to honor this new version of myself. Unfortunately, knowing that has no bearing on the fact that tonight, I have next to nothing.

Luckily, Daisy is due here any minute. She mentioned bringing some things with her so we can get ready together. Maybe she will have something I can borrow. We wear pretty close to the same size.

While I fret, frantically pacing the floor, the doorbell rings. "Coming!" I shout, racing out of my bedroom.

Behind me, Ozzy & Cooper have already popped their heads out from under the piles of clothes where they have been dozing. They easily beat me to the front, their excited barks bouncing off the walls.

I swing the door inward. Daisy smiles at me from behind several bags. At a glance, I notice they consist of clothing, accessories, makeup, jewelry, hair products, styling tools, and shoes.

Daisy gasps when she takes me in and almost drops her bundles. "Pip, you look even better than Ellery described." Her chin wobbles dangerously. I am alarmed to see tears welling up in her eyes.

"Hey, crying is *not* allowed," I admonish gently.

"You're right. Tonight is a happy occasion. New beginnings and all that."

I smile in agreement. Then, I take some items from Daisy's tight grip and motion inside. "Let's head to my room. I want to see what outfits you brought."

"Thought you'd steal something?" she asks with an arch look.

"I'm your big sister," I say, winking. "Of course I did."

Between the two of us, my bed looks as messy as my floor in a matter of minutes. Everything Daisy brought is laid out in piles on my mattress, pulled from bags enchanted with magic because *how the hell did she fit all of this stuff in them otherwise?*

"Okay," she says, clapping her hands together. "Hair and makeup first, and then we'll tackle the clothes."

Grabbing the hair products without another word, she disappears into the bathroom. I follow behind with the makeup. Once I have deposited everything on the sink, I look at her. "I'll make you up, and you'll return the favor?" I ask, eyes twinkling. "Just like old times?"

"Ooh, yes!" A smile stretches across her face. "But no pranks this time, okay?"

"Pinky promise." I hold out my hand. She wraps her pinky around mine for a second, repeating the words.

Solemn oaths given, I motion for Daisy to sit on the vanity stool next to the sink before I rummage through her collection. Once I find the items I am looking for, I turn toward her and get to work. We are silent for several minutes, no sound except for the rustle of brushes and clicking of opening lids or caps while I work.

I gather her hair in a reverse French braid that trails down one side. It was one of the first hairstyles I learned to do, and Daisy was my guinea pig when she was little. If anyone will appreciate this little bit of nostalgia, she will. Once I finish, I switch to makeup—nothing much, just something to make Daisy's eyes pop and accent her peaches and cream skin. It helps that we have similar coloring from Mom, because I would have no idea where to start otherwise. Pop is our polar opposite, with tan skin and salt-and-pepper hair. Daisy inherited his beautiful grey-blue eyes and tall stature.

My baby sister could have easily been a model. I am supremely grateful she never had that desire, though. Daisy may be stronger than me, but I never wish for anyone I love to endure that cutthroat world.

"Know what, sis?" Daisy asks, careful not to move while I work on her face. Her eyes are firmly closed while I dab on shimmery gold eye shadow.

"What?" I finish with her eyes before stepping back.

Daisy's fingers fidget in her lap, toying with the hem of her shirt. I watch and wait for her to open her eyes. Quietly, she admits, "I'm glad you're home."

I smile gently. "Me, too."

With those words, I turn Daisy around. As soon as she looks in the mirror, she gasps in delight. "This is perfect," she gushes.

Together, we admire the finished look. Daisy turns her head this way and that, taking in the braid with the sparkly butterfly clips I added at the last minute. As soon I spotted them, I knew they would be perfect for her.

"Okay, your turn!" Daisy hops off the stool and motions for me to sit. She starts pulling random items out of the cosmetic bags. Every so often, she peeks over and scrutinizes my hair. "I don't think we need to do anything with that gorgeous new mane. Luz outdid herself."

I am watching Daisy from the mirror. Warmth blooms in my chest at her words, and my gaze slides over to my reflection in the large mirror. "Yeah, she did," I agree.

Daisy works quickly and efficiently until she is satisfied that I look "smoking hot," and then she drags me back into the bedroom. She starts to rummage through clothes on the edge of the bed. "And I think I have the absolute perfect dress for you." As soon as she locates whatever she's looking for, she motions for me to turn around. "Close your eyes," she adds.

I do, but not before rolling them. "Is this necessary?"

"Yes. Now stand still." I hear her rustle around before feeling her hands on my shoulders. She then maneuvers me in front of the full-length mirror—or so I assume.

After I hear Daisy chuckle, she disappears for a few breaths. A soft, almost buttery fabric rests against my front when she returns. "Okay, now open."

My gaze lands on a dusty, rose-colored mini-dress that reminds me of my high school outfits. I often mixed Southern style with bohemian and punk rock. Unique dresses like this one usually hide in thrift or consignment shops, which I frequented back then. I trace the delicate lace covering the bodice and run my fingers down the length of the gathered, tiered skirt. I play with the ruffled hems, swishing the dress side-to-side to watch how it moves. The hemline hits just above mid-thigh and is the perfect length for the new boots I bought during an impulsive online shopping spree.

Thank goodness for overnight shipping.

"Well?" Daisy asks, biting her lip to temper her excited smile. "Try it on!"

There's no need to tell me twice. I shed my old outfit and then slip the dress over my head. After one last look in the mirror, I slowly rotate toward Daisy to show off all angles.

Once I stand fully in front of her, I notice she has also changed. Daisy swapped the cotton shorts and t-shirt she arrived in for a long maxi dress in gray blue, paired with a cut-off denim jacket. Currently, she fiddles with a vibrant pair of dangle earrings.

"What do you think?" I ask, waiting for her to look up.

Daisy raises her head and lets out an excited little squeal. "I love that for you!" Then she does a little fist pump and adds, "Go me for picking it out."

I snort. "Alright, I concede that you did good, baby sis."

"So glad I have your approval," she deadpans. Then we fall silent, working quickly to put on the rest of our outfits.

After a few more additions, I stand in the dress, black leather combat boots that lace up to almost mid-thigh, plus a black motorcycle jacket. I layer a few necklaces and chunky bracelets to complete the look.

I am in front of the mirror again, biting my lip in thought, when Daisy walks up behind my reflection. She hugs me from behind for a moment. Then, peeking around my shoulder, she asks, "Why so introspective all of a sudden?"

"Are you sure it looks good?" My brow crinkles while I turn this way and that. "That it looks like me?"

"Of course I do. You know I wouldn't lie to you."

So true. Relief courses through me, and I grin.

"Where's this coming from?" She hugs me again, squeezing tightly around my middle. "You were excited a minute ago."

"I still am." Looking down at myself, I add, "It really is perfect. I don't know. I'm a mess. What if Si—what if the others don't like what they see?"

Understanding dawns on her face, along with a slow, slightly wicked smile. "Well, if I were to hazard a guess—and we know I am rarely wrong—the 'others'"—she punctuates the word with air quotes—"won't be able to keep his—sorry, their hands off of you. So, stop worrying. Let's get our cute little behinds to the party while we are still only fashionably late."

She lets go and calls for Ozzy and Cooper. They slip by me, nuzzling my hand, and follow her out of the room. I take a deep breath. My reflection stands tall and, while I watch, she throws back her shoulders.

Daisy is right. I need to stop worrying and start living again. No regrets. No second-guessing.

Starting tonight.

※※※

"Hey, Elle?"

"Hmm?" Ellery turns toward me, sipping her cocktail.

We sit together on the oversized porch swing Beckham built for Ellery, watching the bustling activity before us. About ten minutes after I arrived, Ellery declared a temporary break from hosting duties, landed a smacking kiss on Beckham's lips, and ended with a quick squeeze to his behind. Then she yanked me aside for some sister talk.

Roughly translated, "sister talk" means Ellery raving over my outfit and swooning over Beckham while I gush over the house and the magical party space they set up out back.

Our conversation naturally wanes after a bit, and as we slip into a comfortable silence, I begin to people-watch. A few guests are still trickling in, and I notice Simon has yet to arrive.

No way am I going to voluntarily bring him up, however.

I notice an unfamiliar man step through the back door with Beckham. While I watch, Beckham and the stranger share a brief conversation before Beckham breaks away to check the grill.

Now, the stranger is strolling toward the gazebo currently occupied by Ellery and me.

At first glance, he looks intimidating: tall and broad—almost as sturdily built as Simon—with the face and body of a Norse god. His light blond hair falls past his shoulders, pulled back at the nape. Tattoos cover almost every inch of exposed skin—a mural of colored and black ink—from hands and wrists up to his collarbone.

Combined with the leather biker jacket and boots, he looks like he belongs to a motorcycle club. But when he reaches us and smiles, his harsh features transform into boyish charm.

"Well, hey there, beautiful," he says to Ellery, opening his arms.

Ellery hops off the swing and curls into him, laughing when he wraps her in a bear hug that lifts her off the ground. He slowly swings her side to side, and I suddenly want to laugh at this imposing man holding Ellery like she is five years old.

When he lowers her to the ground, she hops back and says, "Hey, Theo. Glad you could make it."

"You know I wouldn't miss this for the world." His gray eyes are twinkling when they land on me. His grin widens. "And you must be the infamous Piper I've heard so much about."

I blush slightly and wonder what exactly he has heard. Then I shake my head, dislodging the intrusive thought. He likely learned whatever he knows from Ellery and Beckham, not gossip around town or tabloids.

Call it a hunch, but he strikes me as someone who prefers literature and real news to trashy magazines.

"That's me," I say. "Nice to meet you—Theo, was it?"

He nods, then takes a tiny bow. "Theodore Hawkins. You can call me Theo or Hawk. Most of my friends call me Hawk, but Ellery here likes to be different."

She shakes her head, grinning. "That's because I know the truth. You want everyone to think of you as this big, scary biker, but you're just a huge teddy bear."

He growls mockingly. "Don't go spreading that around, you hear?" Then, with a wink, he takes my hand and lifts the back of it to his lips.

Oh, my, I think. *Chivalry isn't dead.*

"Pleasure's all mine, by the way," he says. "I'm a big fan of Songbyrd."

Picturing this man jamming to one of my songs makes me want to giggle uncontrollably. My music has an edge, sure, but he seems the type to enjoy hard rock or heavy metal. Then again, I know better than to buy into stereotypes, especially since I have spent the last several weeks trying to escape from the one thrust upon me.

"I'm honored," I say, my smile brightening.

He grins back, then turns back to Ellery. "I'd better go check on Beck and Jenson, make sure they're not ruining the food. Piper, I look forward to seeing you again soon." With those words, he turns and heads toward the grill on the other side of the yard.

"That little shit," she says, snickering.

"What?" I look around, confused.

She nods toward the men assembled at the grill. "Theo. He's a shameless flirt, and he loves to cause trouble. I wouldn't be surprised if he lays it on even thicker when Simon is around."

I ask why he would do such a thing, then shake my head—stupid question. Instead, I point vaguely in their direction with my drink.

"What's his deal, anyway?" I ask.

"Who, Theo?" She frowns. "No deal. Not that I know of, at least, other than the Hawk versus Theo debate."

I grin. Honestly, I prefer Theo to Hawk as well, although the nickname does fit him.

"He served with Beckham in the Navy," Ellery continues. "Things went sideways on their last mission together, and he got injured badly enough to be medically discharged. Beckham was, too, for PTSD and other injuries, so he moved in with Hawk to help him with his recovery. The other surviving team members got out when their contracts were up."

Ellery pauses momentarily, watching Beckham with a deep sadness darkening her expression. I feel like an intruder to a private moment, so I look away until she speaks again. "Um, anyway," she continues, "after some drama in his hometown, he decided to move here with Beck. Why do you ask?"

Because like calls to like.

Hawk would be downright intimidating if not for his charming, goofy personality. But I get the sense that he magnifies that persona to shield his true self from the world. He has that tell-tale haunted look in his eyes that says: here is a man with real, deep-rooted pain in his past. Those darker emotions barely skim the surface and are easy to miss—unless you know what to look for.

But I keep all that to myself. To Ellery, I state something simple. "He looks sad."

"Yeah. He does."

"You see it, too?"

She nods without looking at me. "I think you have to be part of the club to notice."

"The club?" I ask, tilting my head in confusion.

Ellery does look my way this time, a sad smile gracing her lips. "Yeah. You know, the one that says, 'This person has lost something or someone. This is another person who knows the kind of pain that gets etched into your soul and never goes away.'"

"Oh." I swallow around the lump in my throat. "*That* club."

She leans against my side and rests her head on my shoulder. "You and I are longtime members because of my parents and your dad. Plus, everything you've gone through in the last couple of years…" With a sigh, she murmurs, "What a shit club to belong to. Still, I'm glad I'm not alone."

"Me, too." I wrap an arm around her shoulders. We stay like that for a few minutes, just soaking up each other's strength and comfort, until I notice Daisy coming my way. Ever the social butterfly, she has been flitting from person to person since we arrived.

I sit up when I notice the wicked grin on her face.

"What is it?" I ask cautiously.

"Somebody's gorgeous older brother just got here," she sing-songs, eyes sliding over to Ellery before falling on me with an excited twinkle.

"Oh, yay!" Ellery leaps to her feet. "Simon called me an hour before the party started because he was stuck at the station and would be over as soon as he could get away."

With that, she hops off the gazebo and starts across the yard. Daisy follows, grabbing my arm and yanking me forward with her. I am helpless to do anything other than take her lead.

We reach where Ellery has stopped, and my heart stutters when I catch Simon standing there, arms crossed, casually looking out over the scene in front of him. He is still in his police uniform, and all my girly bits are waking up and taking notice. That man in uniform is like catnip, and I am obsessed.

"Hey there, big bro!" Ellery calls out, and everyone around us stops and looks at her curiously. She grins with wicked intent. "It's a little early for the stripper portion of the evening, though I do appreciate your dedication to the job."

Everyone around us erupts into laughter and good-natured heckles. Simon rolls his eyes like he's heard this little joke a million times. But a smile still tugs at his lips.

"You want me to strip down? I'll strip down. But it'll cost you." He winks, reaches for the top button of his shirt, and starts slowly toying with it. Ellery shrieks and bounds up to him, slamming her hands over his to still them.

"Absolutely not!" She gives an exaggerated shudder and pretends to vomit.

Beckham is off to the side, shaking his head and chuckling at the siblings. We share an amused smile. How easy it was for me to forget simple joys like this when I worked so hard, and so long, to distance myself.

It feels right to be back here and have the four of us together again. Like it always should have been.

When I peek over at Simon, I catch him laughing and trying to duck out of Ellery's slapping hands. Beckham comes up behind Ellery and wraps his arms around her, locking them to her sides. She glares up at him. He smiles in response and presses a kiss to her forehead. Of course, Ellery goes all sappy at that.

To be honest, so do I.

Then I feel that familiar pang in my chest whenever I think of Simon and all the what-ifs surrounding our relationship. Because not everything is as it should have been.

My eyes stray back to Simon at the thought, and he finally notices I'm standing here. The look of surprise that steals over his face would be adorable, and I would thoroughly enjoy it if not for the cold sweat stealing over me. My pulse thunders in my ears while I wait, feeling like I may pass out before he processes all the changes I have made.

Years go by—but only a handful of seconds in reality—before Simon's intent gaze stops its trajectory. My lungs burn, but when I try to take a breath, they stall. Until his eyes finally lift to mine, and then I can finally breathe in. Their hazel color melts into liquid amber and heats me to my core.

Slowly—oh, so slowly—a roguish smile stretches across Simon's face.

My breath leaves me in a rush. So does the tension I have been clinging to. I meet Simon's gaze head-on, and I level a smile at him that I hope is much more confident than I feel at the moment.

Simon's undivided attention is such a heady feeling, one I have quickly come to crave. He looks at me like I am the only one in his orbit. He looks at me like he is picturing all the wicked things he wants to do to me if only we were alone. Like I am the most beautiful creature he has ever seen.

Right now, with him, I *feel* like the most beautiful creature.

My newfound confidence allows me to take the initiative and close the distance between us. "Simon," I say in greeting, my voice as soft as the smile on my face.

"Little bird," he replies.

For the first time, hearing him call me that comforts instead of hurts. Being home and near Simon has allowed those old wounds he inflicted to start healing. Now, only phantom pain remains.

Simon's eyes flare like he can sense the shifting tide between us. Once more, he caresses me slowly with his gaze. His eyes lift back to mine, and his smile brightens.

Then he says, "You found your wings."

Chapter 18
Birds of a Feather

Simon

Piper could have a shaved head and be wearing clown shoes and a paper bag dress. I would still think she is the most beautiful woman in the room. I would probably roast her a bit for her fashion choices, but it could never detract from how much I crave her.

She is the most beautiful woman in the world to me.

Period.

But I am feeling a hell of a lot at the sight of Piper as she is now. She looks like she stepped off the cover of a Joan Jett album, giving me thoughts. Lots and lots of thoughts. Unfortunately, ninety percent of them should never be spoken out loud in mixed company.

She damn near brought me to my knees when I first set eyes on her. That deceptively innocent-looking dress of hers flirting with the tops of her thighs makes my hands itch to slip underneath the fabric. Those damned combat boots—I would love to see her laying in my bed wearing nothing but those fuck-me boots and a smile when I finally get my mouth in between those gorgeous thighs.

And I will get my mouth on her.

Hopefully soon.

Piper is blushing—pleased that I called her "little bird" again. Honestly, it felt right this time, unlike the night of the art gala. That was a slip of the tongue. Tonight was deliberate.

I also meant what I said.

When she first came home, Piper was different. She acted subdued. As happy as I was to have her near, I hated that she seemed like a shadow of her former self. However, Piper has been restitching, little by little, all the pieces of herself that have been ripped away, torn, or faded over time. Tonight is the first time I feel like she's the Piper I remember. The Piper I fell in love with.

The Piper I am still in love with.

So when I said that she "found her wings," I meant it. Now, she just needs to remember how to fly.

"Thank you," she murmurs.

"No need to thank me. I'm just speaking the truth."

"Either way." Then, with a soft chuckle, she adds, "I admit I was nervous to see you tonight."

When she speaks, I notice the slight rigidity of her posture. I see the way her fingers tap absently against her thighs and how her gaze lands on mine for only a split second before flitting away again.

"Why's that?" My movements are slow to avoid spooking her, but I need to touch her right now. As soon as I am close enough, I reach out to tuck a stray lock of hair behind her ear, my fingers lingering on the brilliant red, orange, and yellow ends. Then, after a second, I drop my hands back down to my sides.

"I don't know." She shrugs, looking slightly uncomfortable—as if she revealed more than she meant to. "Things are so different now, I guess, and I don't know where we stand. Maybe you prefer the old, more docile me over this." She gestures at her outfit.

"Sweetheart, I may have strong personal preferences," I argue, "but when it comes to you, I'll take any flavor of you I can get."

Her eyes flutter closed at my admission, a bright blush stealing over her cheeks. Unable to help myself, I gently pinch her chin between my thumb and forefinger, tugging her face back up from where it dipped when she lowered her gaze. Her eyes snap open in surprise.

"Uh-uh." My voice gently chides her. "A queen never bows her head in deference to anyone."

That pretty blush glows brighter, but a smile has wiped away any traces of her earlier anxiety. Reluctantly, I let my hand drop from her soft skin. I have no desire to. I would much rather pull Piper closer and show her just how much I like this new version of her. But yesterday morning, I laid all my cards on the table and meant every word. Pulling back was challenging, yet necessary. The next time we get physical in any capacity, she needs to be one hundred percent ready, and she will initiate it.

Then Piper goes and surprises the hell out of me.

"Simon." She licks her lips nervously. But when her eyes meet mine, they are crystal clear, no doubts casting shadows. "Do you think we could go somewhere private to talk?"

I look up at that. My eyes remind me that we are standing outside, surrounded by a massive group of people. Thankfully, no one has been paying us any mind. Well, except maybe our sisters, who are huddled together in a corner nearby, watching us as if we are stars in a damn Hallmark movie. When I catch Daisy's eye, she whispers something at Ellery. They start giggling and I narrow my eyes at them.

Siblings.

"Yeah," I say, running a hand through my hair. I look back toward Beckham and Ellery's house. "I'm sure we could find a quiet place inside—"

"Hey, y'all!" Daisy pops up in between us.

I jump back slightly. *Christ.* That woman is quieter than a damn cat on the prowl.

"Simon, Ellery asked me to tell you that your services are no longer required for the evening and to—in her words—get the hell out of here and take Piper back to your place. She will be keeping Duchess here for some Auntie Ellery time. Hi, sis," she says, smiling big and waving. "Ozzy and Cooper are my charges for the rest of the night."

"I, what?" Piper asks, bemused. "But, what about—?"

"Don't worry your pretty head," Daisy continues. "I'm going to take them back to Mom and Dad's after the party, and they will have so much fun playing with their grandma and grandpa.

You can pick them up there later." She pokes Piper's side with her elbow and sashays away. Before she gets too far, she calls out over her shoulder in a sing-song voice, "Or, you know, in the morning! Whatever."

"Fuck me," I mutter under my breath.

Piper snorts, looking about as mortified as I feel. After a moment, she glances up at me. "I think they just kicked us out."

"So they did," I say with a wink. "I guess the only question is your place or mine?"

***

My place is closer, of course, so we go there. The silence between us is heavy and palpable. We are both clearly in our heads, contemplating how this night will unfold.

At least, that thought is what sticks at the forefront of *my* mind.

Piper has taken the initiative, but a large part of me worries that something will trigger her again and cause her to bolt. One rejection was terrible enough. Twice will fucking hurt. Taking things slow is preferable to the constant risk of getting shut out.

I may be confident, but even my confidence has its weak spots.

Piper Easton is a definite weak spot.

What if coming to my place is a bad idea? Over the years, I have made minor changes, trying to make the house feel more mine and erase some more painful memories. Still, many things inside are just as they were back then. Hopefully, being here won't stir up bad memories for her. At the very least, I hope that the good memories outweigh the bad.

When I pull into my spot in the driveway and shut off the engine, I decide to stop overthinking things. Instead, I should be enjoying the opportunity that has fallen into my lap.

Piper is here. We can finally talk, maybe clear the air. Anything more than that is just a bonus.

I hop out of the cab and quickly round the hood, half expecting Piper to open the door herself and try to hop down on her own. She surprises me, sitting there while patiently waiting for me to open the door.

When she catches my look of bewilderment, she grins. "Simon, I remember how pissed you used to get when I wouldn't wait for you to help me. Things may change over time, but chivalry isn't usually one of them."

"Good to know." I smirk and hold a hand out for her to grab onto. "My lady," I say with a slight bow.

"My lord." She giggles and slips her palm into mine.

After helping her down, I keep her hand in mine and turn toward the front door. Piper's hand remains where it is, which is a huge relief. Even better, she sticks close to my side while I fumble with the key, then again when we cross the threshold. I toss my keys onto the fancy pottery dish Ellery made years ago. Then, I hang my jacket on one of the wall hooks before turning toward Piper.

"Would you like to hang that up?" I ask, motioning to her bag and leather jacket.

She nods while absently handing the former to me, too busy taking everything in to do more. I slip my fingers beneath the heavy collar of her jacket. I linger momentarily before sliding the garment off her shoulders and down her arms. Once she is free of it, I hook it next to mine. Then I set her bag strap over it.

"Wow," she breathes, strolling past the front entryway and into the living room. I am content to follow behind. She deserves as much time as she needs. There is a lot to process.

After a moment, Piper picks up a small framed photograph from one of the couch's side tables. Her mouth lifts in a wistful smile. "I remember this," she says softly, fingertips lightly tracing the frame.

When I peek over her shoulder, I recognize the picture. Beckham, Piper, and I—along with a few mutual friends—had gone camping in the woods near Lily Pond to celebrate the day Beckham and I (and some of the others) graduated. We spent the day swimming, horseback riding, and enjoying one last moment of adolescent innocence before our paths irrevocably shifted into adulthood.

Late that afternoon, Piper took a selfie of her, me, and Beckham while we sat around a large bonfire roasting hot dogs.

Piper and I have our arms around each other. Beckham is on the other side of Piper. I thought it would be funny to shove my hot dog in front of his face as the picture went off. Unfortunately, Beckham knew me too well, and he anticipated the prank. He took a giant bite of the thing right when the flash went off. The camera captured Beckham with puffy chipmunk cheeks, a satisfied smirk on his face, while I am peering around Piper at him wearing an appalled look on my face. Piper, of course, is laughing hysterically.

We had so many unforgettable memories that I had difficulty picking which ones to display. This one was an easy decision, though. The memory of that weekend has always been a favorite of mine.

Piper shakes her head slowly from side to side, and tears glisten in her eyes when she looks up at me. "I never thought I would see all this again. I never thought I'd see Sweetbriar at all, to be honest. Or you."

"You planned to stay away forever?"

"Yes."

I blink in confusion. "Because of me?"

Piper has no response for that. Not that she needs one. I can see it written all over her face. My shoulders droop, and the quiet sigh that escapes sounds much louder in the stillness.

"Right." I start to step away.

Piper follows. Her hands lift tentatively—waiting for me to flinch away, I suppose. When I continue to stand here watching her, she finally rests them on my pecs.

"I don't want to get lost in memories anymore," she admits. "I don't want to dig for more regrets, failed wishes, and broken dreams. I have experienced a lifetime of that already. Right now, I want you. Please kiss me. Touch me. Make me forget my name." Her eyes shine with naked desire. "I need you to break me apart and put me back together, piece by piece."

Throughout her monologue, her hands inch farther up my body until they tangle in the hair at the nape of my neck. My eyes fall closed when she lightly scratches my scalp—something she used to do often.

Fuck. That tiny bite of pleasure-pain shoots straight to my cock. I can't help the quiet moan that slips out.

Piper moves in closer. She pulls my head down, stretching up on tiptoes to meet me halfway while I slide my hands to her waist to hold her steady. Our breaths mingle in the scant space left between us. I can smell her shampoo and see her light green eyes sparkle. More than anything, I want to bridge the gap and taste those pouty lips.

"No running away," she murmurs, repeating my words from yesterday back to me. "No regrets." Then, angling her head, she presses the barest of kisses to the corner of my mouth.

"You said we both need to be good and ready, right?" Her intense gaze locks with mine. "Well, I'm good and ready. Are you?"

My answer is to grab her face in my hands and bring her lips back to mine. I am unsure who guides who, but somehow, we end up at the foot of the stairs. We collapse against the wall, and our bodies slot together like two matching puzzle pieces.

Perfection.

Our lips move in sync, breaths mingling and tongues twining together until I lose track of where I end, and she begins. Every inch of our connection is pure fire. All it takes is that tiny spark to catch on the kindling deep inside of me—all those memories and emotions I buried because they were too detrimental to keep and painful to erase.

Just *one* tiny spark—then those memories explode to the surface in an inferno.

I pull away first, needing air. My forehead rests against hers while I try to catch my breath. I also need time to gather my thoughts. When I finally lift my head, Piper watches me with questions in her eyes.

Good, because I have some things I need to make crystal clear.

Taking her face in my hands, I tilt her chin up. I want to ensure her gaze is locked on mine. Then, I tell her exactly what has been on my mind these past several days, leaving no room for misinterpretations.

"I want this, more than anything." My thumb traces along her bottom lip. "But that means very little if we're not on the same page. So, I need to ask: are you absolutely sure this is what you want?"

"Yes," she says, but her voice betrays a tiny thread of trepidation.

"Your tone says otherwise." I shake my head. "I need you to be sure."

Her expression shifts, showing me more of the old Piper: fierce, determined, and ready to fight for what she wants. "I *am* sure."

Much better. "I also need you to trust me," I say.

"T-trust you?"

"This will never work without trust, little bird," I explain. My hands slip from Piper's face to cradle her neck. One thumb rests against her pulse point. "So, do you trust me?"

The question surprises her, and her heartbeat races while she contemplates my meaning. She closes her eyes. I patiently wait her out, giving her all the time she needs. I know I am asking a lot. But I meant what I said.

We will never work without trust.

When Piper speaks next, her voice has grown steady. "I do trust you."

Her eyes open, clear and bright when they stare into mine. As she says everything I want to hear, I feel her pulse slow beneath my thumb. But she is holding something back. Her words say one thing, but walls still exist to keep me out.

I can read between the lines.

Piper trusts me with her body. She trusts me not to hurt her physically. She may even trust me to protect her.

But her heart is off limits.

I can live with that for now. I waited twelve years for a second chance. I will earn that trust back—all of it, with interest. I am not about to fail now, not when I am closer than ever. But I quickly shove those thoughts to the back of my mind.

One thing at a time, Simon.

"Prove it," I say, pushing further, needing more than words.

At my challenge, Piper's eyes flash.

There's my girl.

"Okay," she agrees. "How?"

My lips curve into a wicked smirk. My hands slowly slip along the slope of Piper's neck. They continue along her shoulders, and I enjoy the shiver skating across her skin before I drop them down at my sides. Then I take a step back.

"Kneel."

"*Sweetheart,* I may have **strong** *personal* preferences — but when it comes to *you,* I'll take **any** *flavor* of you I can *get.*"

Chapter 19
Lose Control

Piper

"W-what?"

"On your knees, Piper. Kneel. I won't say it again."

My pulse jumps at the steel in Simon's voice, but I refuse to shy away. Because his hands stay firmly at his sides. He makes no attempt to touch me, a simple truth that settles deep into my bones.

Simon will wait for me. He wants to make sure I have zero doubts, that I am certain I want this—want *him*. He wants me to take the first step. On anyone else, that expression of unyielding authority would have me running in the other direction. Instead, that authority makes me want to submit.

Then I realize his intent.

Choice.

Simon is giving me a choice: submit to him or don't. I get to make the decision. With one tiny act, Simon offers me the control Cedric ripped away.

Slowly, never breaking eye contact, I lower myself until my knees touch the wood floor. Simon swallows thickly. I track the movement of his throat—the only sign that my action has any effect on him—until his hand tucks under my chin, and he lifts my face for inspection. His intense gaze holds me captive, and his thumb gently runs back and forth along my lower lip.

"Have you ever used a safe word?" he asks.

My eyes widen in surprise. "No."

One corner of his mouth turns up at my response. Then he drops his hand and steps back, taking his warmth. I follow, swaying toward him, trying to maintain the connection like an invisible tether runs from his body to mine.

"Do you know what a safe word is for?"

His question snaps me back into myself, and it takes a moment to cut through the haze of desire scrambling my brain. When the question registers, my face flushes. Equal parts lust, embarrassment, and annoyance—at the implication of naivety, at the fact that he isn't entirely wrong in asking—add a healthy dose of snark into my response.

"Yes, Simon. I'm not a child."

"Brat." The ghost of a smile on his face stretches into a real one. His voice is honeyed, thick with amusement, and dripping with promise when he adds, "You'll pay for that later."

I feel a pulse of desire at his words. Why do I want that? I want to push his buttons. I want to drive Simon as wild as he is making me. Every muscle on my body is tight with anticipation. My pulse thunders in my ears and is so loud that surely he can hear it.

"If this is going to happen, you need one." Simon's words pull my attention back to him. He raises an eyebrow when I stare at him in dazed confusion. "A safe word."

"Oh, um…" I bite my lip in thought.

He reaches out, frowning, and tugs it free. "Uh-uh," he says. "I'll be the only person biting those lips."

I almost bite my lip again. *Focus, Piper.* "I don't know… Meatloaf?"

"Okay, I—" Simon cuts off, blinking. "Say what now?"

"Meatloaf." I shrug.

"Why…?"

"Because," I say with a sudden grin, "I would do anything…. but I won't do that."

Simon groans loudly. My lips start to quiver. Then I giggle, the sound quickly bubbling over into full-on laughter, and within seconds I am holding my stomach and sucking in heaping gulps of air. It takes me several tries for me to regain some semblance of self-control.

"Sorry, sorry," I croak out as soon as I can say the words.

Simon has fallen silent. When I look up, he stares at me in awe, as if he cannot believe I laughed out loud. Do I laugh so little now? The sudden realization makes my face flush with a different kind of heat.

"I can't remember the last time I heard you laugh like that," Simon murmurs, almost to himself. "Fuck, that sound is beautiful…"

My breath catches at the intensity of his gaze. "I haven't had much reason to until now," I admit quietly.

Simon falls silent. I know he is taking a moment to contemplate my words and what they mean. But then he reaches toward me, gripping my arms, and my heart stutters.

"Wait!" I cry out. "Simon, what are you doing?"

But he is only pulling me back up to my feet. Once there, his hands around my biceps hold me captive. I stare at him nervously while he searches my face. He is trying to figure me out, trying to slot another puzzle piece of my life into place. The silence between us stretches.

Then I start to panic.

Did I do something wrong? Have I ruined everything? We barely started, and he already wants out. I am so bad at this. Why did I think I could jump back into the fire without getting burned?

In a sudden stream of consciousness, I blurt out, "I know the 'meatloaf' thing was silly—"

"Piper."

"—and I shouldn't have brought up the thing about laughing—"

"Piper."

"And I know I'm a lot, but please don't—"

"Little bird." Rough hands gently cradle my face, but the sharp command in those two words is what quiets me. I take a deep, shuddering breath. Simon waits until my gaze returns to his. Then, he says, "Brace yourself."

"I—what?"

"Brace yourself and hold on."

"What do you—whoa!" My words cut off when Simon hoists me up over his shoulder like I weigh nothing, one strong arm braced against my hamstrings to hold me in place. He climbs the stairs one slow step at a time. I dangle behind him, stunned. All the blood rushes to my head, fueling my confusion, and it takes way too long for me to recognize the main bedroom at the end of the hallway—the room he leads us toward.

Okay, then. I guess I failed to ruin everything after all. That sudden realization drains all my lingering tension. Soon, I am a boneless heap in Simon's arms, giddy from the head rush and still just as turned on as before, which unlocks my bratty side.

"Is this necessary?" I ask. My gaze is stuck firmly on his backside. I swivel back and forth like a pendulum. (Not that I have much to complain about. I *do* have a lovely view.) "You could have just, like, tugged on my hand. Said, 'Hey, let's go to the bedroom.' Something a normal person would do."

Simon chuckles. I huff in response, then feel a sharp sting when he smacks me hard on the ass.

I jolt in his hold. "Hey!"

"Stop talking back, little bird, or I'll have to occupy that smart mouth with something else."

Holy—"Are you threatening me with a good time, Officer?"

Another smack lands, harder this time. I whimper at the heady mixture of pleasure and pain as it shoots straight to my core. Simon is in for a surprise if he thinks this is in any way a deterrent. Suddenly, I want to see what it will take to get his control to snap.

Before I can even open my mouth, he stops. I realize we've reached his bed. He hoists me back up and tosses me over his shoulder again—this time in the opposite direction. I land in the middle of a plush mattress, bouncing once before sinking back against the pillows along his headboard.

My chest heaves in surprise. The linens smell like Simon, and his intoxicating scent surrounds me with each inhale. I fight the urge to bury my face into the soft, downy fabric.

There will be plenty of time for that later.

Meanwhile, Simon is standing at the foot of the bed, sexy and authoritative in his police uniform. He leans against the large post while his sharp gaze observes my every reaction. I had forgotten how good it feels to have that singular focus of his trained on me.

Only I need much more.

His eyes burn a fiery path up my body. Still, he makes no move to do anything more than admire from afar. Even though I love that heavy look in his gaze, the waiting makes me twitchy and anxious to feel his hands on my skin.

Then I realize he is doing it on purpose.

He knows that patience has never been my strong suit.

"You ever plan on joining me?" I ask.

One large hand wraps around my ankle. With a sharp tug, Simon lays me flat on my back and jolts a surprised yelp out of me. I am staring at the ceiling, still reeling, when I feel the bed shift and dip near my feet.

Seconds later, Simon's face fills my vision. His body is a delicious weight, pressing me into the mattress and forcing my legs open to accommodate him.

"Is this what you hoped I'd do?" He flexes his hips into mine, and I groan at the feel of him even through our clothes.

His bright hazel eyes have turned molten gold. Up close, I can see the green, blue, and brown flecks. His irises swirl in a rich kaleidoscope of color, and I could easily get lost in them.

But then he goes and breaks the spell.

Sitting up abruptly, he rests back on his haunches. While the action puts some much-needed space between us, desire continues to course freely through my veins. He shakes his head, chuckling darkly when my body tries to close the distance.

Then, when that fails work, I lift my hands to pull him back down. I grip his shirt, but his hands wrap around mine before I can do anything more. My mouth pulls into a pout.

While an amused smirk stretches across Simon's face, his eyes hold a hard glint. He warns me, "You're playing with fire."

My smirk mirrors his. "I think I like it."

Somewhere along the way, I lost my sense of adventure and love of life. Being here with him, I realize I am starting to find it again.

With little more than a noncommittal hum, Simon looks down at my right hand. For a moment, he studies the fire around my wrist. Then, slowly rotating my forearm, his focus shifts to analyzing the rest of the tattoo. When he gets to the sandpiper silhouette, his thumb barely ghosts over the top of it, gliding over the phoenix's body.

"Later," he says quietly, "you'll tell me what this means."

His words say one thing, but his eyes say another. The meaning is clear: *I want to know what broke you.* I swallow thickly.

Simon's words may not be a question, yet I answer, "Okay."

"Good." His gaze lifts back up to mine. "Now, take off your clothes."

I shiver at the command in his voice but make no move to comply.

His expression goes as hard as the rest of him. "I don't make a habit out of repeating myself, Piper. Clothes, now."

My hands shake with repressed excitement as I tug at the hem of my dress, slowly revealing a lacy, dark purple thong and matching bra. I toss the dress over the side of the bed.

Simon groans, harsh and guttural, and the sound of it fills me with a deep sense of feminine pride. But I stutter to a stop when his hands cup my breasts over the lace. Each tug of his fingers on the hardened peaks is an exquisite form of torture that makes me unable to do anything more than feel.

"What am I going to do with you, hmm?" He murmurs the question, then dips to nuzzle along the soft underside of my jaw.

I open my mouth to answer, but all I manage is a shaky sigh just as his lips and tongue start to caress my skin. He moves down my neck and along my collarbone, following the path of his hands until he reaches the curve of my breast and the lace barrier.

"Time for these to go." He reaches behind for the catch. Then, using his other hand, he hooks a finger around the center of the band and tugs.

Before I can react to the cool air hitting my skin, Simon covers one breast with the palm of his hand and the other with his mouth. My back arches off the bed when his teeth clamp down lightly, and at the same time, his fingers pinch the other nipple. I feel the tiniest amount of pain, but it jolts through me like an electric current. Simon quickly swaps to give my other breast the same attention. My nails dig into his shoulders, and I beg him for more.

Then, as quickly as he started, Simon abruptly pulls away. Somehow, I know that his torture has just begun, and I lift onto my elbows to watch what he plans to do next. As soon as his eyes lift to mine, Simon winks and grabs onto the strings holding up the tiny scrap of lace covering my mound. I start to lift my hips so that he can tug them off.

Instead, he fists his hands and rips the fabric in two.

For a moment, I gape up at him. My mouth opens and closes like a fish until my mind reengages, and, closing my legs and popping up to a seated position, I blurt out, "Dammit, Simon! I liked that set."

"Same." Simon smirks, tossing the panties over one shoulder. "I'll buy you ten more pairs. Then I'll rip them off, too."

I laugh. "You're ridiculous."

"I'm also starving." He runs his hands up my thighs, tightly clenched together. "Open up so I can taste you."

My core throbs at his words. However, before I do what he asks, I sit up and start unlacing one of my boots. Simon quickly smacks my hand away.

"Did I say you could take those off, beautiful?" He grips my neck firmly with one hand, tugging me to him when I fail to speak. "Answer me."

"N-no," I reply. "You didn't."

Simon kisses me then, sipping slowly, savoring me like a fine wine until I am mewling in the back of my throat. I try to get closer, but his grip on me tightens to hold me in place. He nips my lower lip as he pulls away.

I feel his palm like a brand against my skin. The pressure he applies is gentle enough for me to be aware of him but not so much that my air supply gets cut off. I find it a strange sensation, feeling vulnerable yet safe in equal measure.

Something I have never felt before.

Not with anyone but Simon.

His lips hover over mine while he whispers, "Remember: meatloaf."

With a shaky exhale, I nod to let him know I understand. He shoots me a small smile before sliding his body back down toward my still-bent knees. His hands land on my upper thighs, and he tugs lightly on the laces of my boots.

"These stay on," he says, his voice that flinty steel I am quickly coming to crave. Then he nudges my knees, groaning low when I finally open myself to him. "I have a fantasy I need to make real."

Before I can ask what he means, his mouth is on me. I cry out in surprise and pleasure. The feel of his tongue, the heat of his breath, the way his teeth scrape lightly over my clit—all the sensations blur together until I am nothing more than a mindless bundle of nerves. He palms my backside, sliding his hands up to my waist for purchase. My legs hook over his shoulders. My shaking thighs cradle his head.

Each touch is too much and not enough. Simon is relentless with his tongue, brutally worshipping every single inch of me, sending me spiraling higher and higher—

But then he pulls away. I have to bite back the scream of frustration threatening to explode out of me. Quickly lifting on one elbow, I watch Simon sit back, chest heaving, wiping my juices away with the back of his hand.

I want to be pissed. But Simon is too damn sexy. That uniform still clings to his sinful body, his smile is full of wicked promise, and he has me so turned on that I need him to do something. Anything.

Right now, I would happily beg.

Simon must see every emotion flit across my face because he says, "Never said you could come, little bird."

My nostrils flare. I blurt out, "Gee, sorry, I didn't realize we were playing a round of adult Simon Says tonight."

Simon grins and shakes his head. "Such a fucking brat."

Then he crawls up my body, settling his hips in between my legs and applying just enough pressure, just enough movement, to tease me. I whimper. He captures the sound with his lips, kissing me hard before pulling back.

"There are consequences to every action, sweetheart," he explains. "That was one of them. Now I need to figure out what to do about your sassy mouth."

My pulse jumps at the implication.

"You did mention that thing," I say, toying with the top button of his shirt, "about keeping my mouth busy." I try to sound calm about it—disinterested—but I fail. My cheeks are flushed, and my voice has dipped and turned husky at the idea.

As soon as Simon catches my meaning, his hands are on my waist. He deftly flips our positions so that I end up sprawled out on top of him. We are hip-to-hip, chest-to-heaving-chest, while my hands bracket his head.

His grin turns brash and arrogant. "Well? I'm all yours."

Yes. Yes, you are.

My hands move to the buttons of Simon's uniform shirt, and although fumbling slightly, I manage to undo them. He sits up so I can slip the shirt down his shoulders. Then I toss the garment over by my dress. While I move to undo the buckle of his belt, Simon reaches up with one hand and yanks his undershirt over his head.

Now that I am eye-level with his bare chest, I can't resist scraping my fingernails lightly through the spattering of strawberry-blond hair. Simon lunges forward and captures my lips while yanking me by the waist to straddle his hips.

He says between rough kisses, "You're getting distracted, little bird."

Pulling away, he lavishes attention along the sensitive parts of my neck. I gasp when I feel a sharp bite of pain at the spot between my shoulder and neck. He nips it once more before soothing the area with his tongue.

"You aren't making it easy on me," I pant. My fingers thread through Simon's hair to lock his head in place. Then, I tilt my head to give him better access while he nibbles and licks his way up the column of my neck.

As soon as his lips are on my ear, he teases me. "That's what makes it so fun."

Before I can even blink, his hands have left my body. He falls back against the mattress, his arms slipping behind his head as a makeshift pillow. I blink, disoriented, until I feel Simon's hips buck up into mine. When I glance up at his face, I see that he has one eyebrow lifted in question.

Right. Simon's clothes. I quickly shuck off his belt and pull down the zipper of his pants, yanking his boxer briefs down with the waistband. Soon, I have thoroughly stripped him down. When I look up at him from between his legs, my mouth starts to water at the sight. He is watching me, eyes hooded, body tense with anticipation. One hand is already fisted around his cock, slowly pumping while he waits.

My, how the tables have turned.

Crawling up his body, I wrap a hand around his wrist and pry his hand away. I quickly replace it with my own, holding the base tightly in my grip while taking his length in my mouth.

"Fuck," he hisses, bucking slightly. "That mouth of yours will be the death of me."

I hum happily before taking him as deep as I can. He curses again, louder. Taking my cues from the delicious sounds he makes, I set a steady pace and, like riding a bike, I slowly start to remember all those things that used to drive him wild.

Before long, he has one hand fisting my hair to keep it out of my face. "Need to watch," he grits out. His other hand clenches the sheets.

He is so close. I can feel it. But without warning, Simon uses my hair to tug me off of him.

Brows furrowed, I ask, "Did I do something wrong?"

"Fuck no, baby, but you need a reward for that performance." He smiles at the confusion on my face. "Turn around. I'm going to finish in that pretty mouth of yours while you ride my face."

I never knew I could get so turned on by dirty talk. Simon liked to talk dirty when we were dating, but not like this. I liked it okay back then.

But now? I love it. I *crave* it.

So much that every inch of me is as tight as a bowstring. Simon reaches up to hold me as I carefully set my knees on either side of his head. My hand grips him at the base once again. As soon as my lips seal around his tip, Simon dives in with his tongue.

Together, we speed toward the finish line, so close that it takes only seconds to cross over. All the different sensations that flood my system nearly cause me to black out. The only thing keeping me tethered to reality is Simon. His sandalwood and sweet tobacco scent grounds me, and his warm, salty taste lingers on my tongue. As I come down from that high, his hands give me something to focus on while they shift me off of him and guide me up to the headboard.

Then Simon gathers me to him, wrapping me in his warmth and strength. I feel like I can finally take a full breath. Like my body was only waiting to be near his.

Simon makes me feel safe in a way no one else ever could. I feel cared for by how he runs his fingers through my hair. And I feel wanted. Desired. He holds me tightly in his arms like he needs me as much as I need him at this moment.

And his words—sweet little nothing words that he whispers in my ear—are what seep into the cracks in my soul like a healing rain. He makes no empty promises. Doesn't feed me pretty lies. He speaks his heart through memories we share and reminds me of dreams made in moments just like this. His words are seeds planted deep, taking root in all the things hidden between the lines, sprouting vines of hope for the future. While his rich, honeyed voice lulls me to sleep, I do something that has eluded me for a very long time.

I dream.

Chapter 20
Ghost in My Guitar

Piper

Sweet strains of music pluck at my consciousness like guitar strings, gently pulling me from the deepest sleep I have slept in years. I wake up tangled up in soft sheets and Simon. His woodsy scent fills my lungs. His body, the front of him curled around my back, covers me like a warm, weighted blanket. Every few breaths, his chest rumbles in a quiet snore.

Here I am, in the middle of a darkened bedroom, smiling like a loon because the man behind me is snoring. But I am unable to stop. Giddiness bubbles in my chest and threatens to burst out of me in a laugh. All because of a sudden, singular truth:

I am happy.

For the first time in a long time, I feel a lightness where I used to feel weighed down by life. Impossible expectations no longer bind me. Painful reality no longer hinders my dreams.

As Simon said, I have found my wings. My gilded cage is wide open, and I can finally stretch and test them out.

Maybe my muse was trapped, too.

As much as I want to burrow further into Simon's strong arms, I want to follow these unfinished strains more. Carefully, I slip out of bed, making a concerted effort not to wake him. My bare feet then carry me over the plush carpet to where our clothes from last night lay on the floor. I pick up his undershirt and put it on. Then, I make my way out into the hallway.

Under the cover of darkness, the house feels more somber than in the light of day. While I head downstairs, my gaze catches on the photos on the wall, lingering every time I reach a picture with Simon as a child. One in particular snags my attention near the bottom: a family photo taken at Hilton Head. As honorary family members, Beckham and I are both in the frame. John has scooped up a giggling Ellery and flipped her upside down in his arms. Simon stands in the middle between Beckham and me, and the two of them have each other in a headlock. Sara and I are the only two actually posing and looking at the camera. She stands behind me, her arms around my shoulders, her cheek resting against mine, and we both wear beaming smiles.

My present smile turns wistful, and it wobbles when I focus in on the two of us. Over the years Simon and I dated, I went on many trips with the Brooks family to their beach bungalow.

That trip was the very last.

I remember the day vividly. In the morning, Sara, Ellery, and I walked along the water while Ellery scoured the sand for seashells. We ate lunch at our favorite seaside restaurant. That afternoon, everyone relaxed in whatever way we preferred—reading, swimming, riding bikes, and even playing games down at the arcade.

Then, right around sunset, we decided to commemorate the trip with a photo like we did every trip before. Sara had been in control of the timer that time. Right before the flash went off, she hugged me tight and whispered how glad she was that I was a part of their family.

My heart twists when I remember how complete I felt at that moment and how thoroughly everything unraveled after.

Prying away from the memories, I finish my descent and head into the living room. I note the changes Simon has made. There is a new couch and chairs, but the coffee table remains unchanged. His great-grandfather handcrafted it, so that comes as no surprise.

Simon has upgraded the television to a large flat screen. He even added surround-sound speakers. I can picture him reclining in one of the chairs, watching a football game on the screen, and screaming at some idiotic decision thrown down by the referee.

The vision is so stupidly domestic that it makes me smile.

I start to search for a pen and paper so I can jot down the notes and lyrics tumbling around in my head. After a moment, I decide to just grab my bag. But then my gaze lands on the cracked door leading to John Brooks' home office.

Since John spent most of his days at the police station, the office served more as a study and family room. During particularly complicated cases, however, he would sit behind that large oak desk, working after hours to try and solve whatever puzzle piece eluded him and his partner.

John and I shared a deep love of music, so I spent a lot of time in there, as well. Once, he told me he had dreamed of being a musician throughout his childhood. In high school, he spent one summer doing every odd job imaginable. He saved every penny to buy his favorite guitar—a Martin D-18.

While he may have traded one dream for another, John still played as a hobby. He was thrilled to teach me every trick he knew, and we bonded over the music we played.

His guitar may not even be there anymore, I realize. Simon may have changed the entire study, and the guitar could be somewhere else in the house. Maybe he put it in storage. Maybe it got donated.

God, I hope Simon kept that guitar...

Unable to resist my curiosity, I set my palms on the wooden door and push it open. As soon as I step across the threshold, a wave of nostalgia hits me. Simon changed nothing in here. Dark wood shelves line the walls from floor to ceiling, still covered with leather-bound books and trinkets. I breathe deeply, letting the scent of leather and paper wash over me. Then, I move further into the room. I run my fingers along the top of the large mahogany desk—another woodworking project from Simon's great-grandfather—before letting them drop back down to my side.

I turn back with a sigh. My steps halt midway when my gaze lands on something in the corner, half hidden by shadow.

There you are, beautiful.

The guitar looks pristine, and I realize Simon must regularly clean its surface. There are no scratches, discolorations, faded colors, or blemishes. Even the strings look relatively new.

Reaching forward, I let my hand graze the neck. My fingertips gently strum the strings, and I feel their sound pool together and reverberate in the silence.

To say I have missed that sound would be an understatement.

Music used to be easy. My heart pumped it throughout my body as naturally as it pumped blood. Music has always been as vital as blood for me. When I hit that mental block, when all I could hear was silence, it felt like a part of me had died.

Because of that pain, my guitar is still at home, locked safely away in its travel case. Why bother taking it out? I have had nothing new to play in ages. Every time I try, I fail. Every time I fail, the disappointment I feel threatens to swallow me whole.

My old music is completely off limits. The songs still feel tainted, so I leave them well alone. Playing covers can be fun but unfulfilling—especially when my fingers itch to run along the wire strings with no clear path ahead. I want to experiment and play.

Like now. Without giving myself a chance to second-guess things, I grip the neck of John's Martin and pull the guitar off its stand. A sense of rightness steals over me, filling the air as soon as the instrument rests in my hands. I carry it to the oversized lounge chair a few feet away and sit, tucking my feet underneath me and settling into the worn leather cushions. Then, with the waist of the guitar resting over my thigh and my arm tucked around its wooden body, I carefully tune each string.

All the while, the melody from before hovers in the back of my mind. I feel that long-dormant part of me starting to wake as the notes grow louder, spreading through me, bubbling to the surface, and overflowing through my fingertips. I let the flood carry me away.

Haunting notes fill my mind and intermingle with a deep longing burning in my lungs. I start to strum out each note as it comes to me. They vibrate against my skin and settle into my bones. Before long, a song begins to trickle out and fill the air:

First, with its melody.

Then, with its lyrics.

I held onto this pain
Buried it down deep inside
But nothing can erase
All your memories from mine
Still, thought I'd be okay
Once all of the tears had dried

But now I'm only dead inside

So let the fire burn
Like a phoenix, I will rise
Rise up from the ashes
Pick up all the pieces
Prove that I am still alive

I am still alive

You left me here alone

Everything that's good went wrong
I made this hell my home
Echoes of the past, their song is
Etched into my bones
But I still need to move on

All our dreams are dead and gone

So let the fire burn
Like a phoenix I will rise
Rise up from the ashes
Pick up all the pieces
Prove that I am still alive

I am still alive

Nothing left to hide
But I can't even say goodbye
When every word's a lie
And I'm barely alive…

So let the fire burn
Like a phoenix I will rise
Rise up from the ashes
Pick up all the pieces
Prove that I am still alive

Am I still alive?

When the last note fades into silence, and I come out of the creative trance I often fall into while playing, I feel Simon's presence lingering in the doorway. I keep my eyes trained on the guitar. Everything I poured out has left me feeling too open and raw to look his way.

"Sorry," I say softly. "I couldn't sleep."

Silence answers me, and I risk a quick peek over my shoulder. Simon watches me with a soft gaze and a slight smile that tells me he is far from angry. Relieved, my body relaxes its stiff posture. Part of me—a large part—believed he would resent me coming in here.

Simon shakes his head as though he can hear my thoughts and sense my sudden anxiety. He quietly pads into the room. I wait and watch while he settles into the other lounge chair across from me.

"Dad loved this guitar almost as much as he loved his kids," Simon murmurs, his slight smile growing into a smirk. But then, a moment later, his expression sobers.

He leans forward and lightly runs his fingers along the guitar's body. They rise and dip along its curves and valleys, and Simon shifts his path when he reaches the crook of my arm. Then he slowly moves toward where my hand still rests on the pick guard. His touch on my skin is feather-light. When he reaches the tattoo on my wrist, Simon drops his gaze and traces the flames, careful not to put pressure on the irritated skin.

"There is no one else Dad would have trusted this guitar to." His hazel eyes flick back up to mine. "I think he would love knowing you're here, playing it."

My eyes blur, and I have to blink them clear. "Thank you."

His hand leaves mine. Motioning to the guitar, he asks, "May I?"

"Oh." I look down before passing the instrument to him. "Of course."

Once he has it in hand, Simon carefully sets it down against the bookshelves behind our chairs. Then he pats his knee. "Come here," he says.

Simon's voice is gentle, but there is no mistaking the underlying command. For once, I don't hesitate or question him before I do as he says. I stand, take a few steps, and then slip onto his lap. As soon as his arms encircle me, Simon tightens his hold, and warmth seeps into my chilled bones. Melting against him, I curl into his chest and fist the fabric of his shirt in my hands. Then I quietly let my tears fall. They work to purge the sadness my music has unearthed, a melancholy buried deep within my subconscious.

Even after the storm calms, I linger in Simon's arms and soak up his strength. I know that it will fade as soon as I pull away. And right now, I need to feel stronger than I am.

Simon breaks the silence first. I feel his voice quietly rumble beneath my ear when he says, "That song. The one you were singing before. Is it new?"

I nod.

"Thought so. Didn't sound like any of your other ones."

"Wait." I pull back to look at him. "You've listened to my songs?"

His lips quirk up in a crooked smile. "Listened to them? Baby, I'm obsessed with them. I know every single one by heart."

My chest clenches at his confession and the uncharacteristically bashful look on his face. But Simon has no reason to feel that way. The thought that he kept track of me all these years makes me want to kiss him—then I remember that kissing is allowed. So I slide my arms around his neck and tug his mouth to mine. Simon moans in the back of my throat. He deepens the kiss before reluctantly pulling away, but then he rests his forehead against mine like the idea of being separated is unbearable.

That craving to be close is one I can relate to.

"Guess that's a good thing?" he asks hoarsely.

I smile up at him and reply, "The best."

Simon slowly relaxes back against the chair. My hands slip down to rest on his pecs. I watch his chest for a moment, the slow and steady rise and fall calming me until his chin falls slightly and snags my attention. His eyes point down, brows furrowed in thought. He is puzzling something out in his head again. So I wait.

"Not just the songs, though," he finally admits.

My face scrunches in confusion. "What do you mean?"

Simon looks like he wants to stop with that confession. But I refuse to let him off that easy—not now that he piqued my curiosity. He must see the stubborn determination on my face because he sighs and relents.

"I've never missed any of your interviews or television guest appearances. Not even when work interfered. I just found them after, watched them when I had the time." Simon shrugs and looks at me with a shy smile. "I went to your live shows, too. Whenever you went through Savannah, I made the drive."

I melt a little at that. "Simon," I breathe. "Really?"

"The first time, I bought tickets as a surprise for Ellery to celebrate getting her degree. I thought Ellery would want to take her friend, Lena. Or maybe one of her friends in town." He shakes his head ruefully. "But, no, she insisted her plus-one be me. I'm so glad she did. I was addicted by the end of the night."

God, I remember that show. Vividly. How did I not know he was there? There could hardly have been more than 50 or 100 people in that entire place.

Simon must think the same thing, because he explains. "We were farther in the back. You wouldn't have been able to see us past the stage lights. But, Piper," he whispers in awe. "You were still so close, breathing the same air, and with the way you sing—the way you *perform*—it felt like you were doing it just for me. You owned that stage, little bird. You were as beautiful and bewitching as always. Even more so. I could have watched you forever."

I almost blurt out that I was singing to him. For all those years I sang to him, no matter where he may have been. The words rest on the tip of my tongue, but I swallow them back and lift a hand to his cheek instead.

"Why do you always say the right things?" I ask, only half joking.

He takes my face in his hands, kisses me—twice for good measure—and says, "I don't know about that. Just that it's the truth."

Humming in response, my head dips under Simon's chiseled jaw and nuzzles into his neck. I breathe him deeply into my lungs. My hand resting on his cheek slides down and curls around his neck. His heartbeat thrums lightly beneath my ear.

His arms anchor my body to his. Then, his hands slowly move down to my hips and around toward the back.

Simon distracts me with the way he glides those magic hands up and down my bare thighs, slipping just slightly under the hem of his bunched-up shirt I wear. He knows I am still not wearing panties underneath. By the impish glint in his eye, he also knows his effect on me—not that I am any good at hiding how Simon makes me feel. I never had that particular talent. He could always read me like a book.

But one thing I am learning about this new, older Simon: he likes to torture me. I also have *much* less control than he does. Without a single word, Simon continues the soft assault on my skin, every pass of his hands underneath the fabric teasing me, causing me to dampen with need. I have to fight the urge to squirm against him.

The entire time, Simon remains perfectly composed. Unlike my heartbeat, which flutters wildly like a hummingbird's wings, his heart beats strong and steady under my palm. It tempts me and makes me want to try something to see if I can speed it up.

Turns out, there is no need. Simon squeezes my bare cheeks just hard enough that I sit up in surprise. Then, with a wicked grin, he tilts his head toward the door. "Let's go back to bed."

Well, then.

That order is one that I will happily follow.

"I think he would *love* knowing you're here, playing it."

INTERLUDE 4

Four

- Wednesday 3:30 am -

Unknown number: Heard you're back in bed with your ex

Unknown number: How cute... do you think he ACTUALLY wants a whore like you?

Unknown number: Once he has his fill, he'll get rid of you again

Unknown number: You'll come crawling back

- Wednesday 4:45 am -

Unknown number: Does he know how rough you need it?

Unknown number: I bet he can't make you scream like I can

Unknown number: Or bring you to tears

Unknown number: You know how it turns me on when you cry

This number has been blocked.

Chapter 21
Play with Fire

Simon

Piper ends up staying through the rest of the weekend, and on Sunday morning, I wake up to her pleasuring me with her mouth. When my turn comes around, I lay her out like a feast and eat my breakfast in bed.

That moment lands the top spot for best ways to start the day.

A little while later, I cook us up a stack of pancakes from one of the recipes my dad loved. We need real food for fuel, and we have definitely both worked up an appetite by then.

Plus, I figure Piper would appreciate more memories of my parents—even something as small as a simple recipe. I have honestly enjoyed getting to share them again with someone. All these memories have been hidden away in the shadows of this house for too long, stuck with only me for company. And I can see how much Piper misses my parents. She tries to hide it, but I caught the wistful way she looked around the house when we first came in. I see her lingering looks at the family photos whenever she walks past.

And then last night, there was the melancholy tone of her voice, the anguish that poured out of each word, and the tears that glistened in her eyes the entire time she played. I don't think I took a single breath through the whole song. When I told her to climb on my lap, I needed the comfort just as much as she did.

Beckham drops Duchess off around mid-morning, as promised. I am honestly surprised to see him standing on my front porch instead of Ellery—at least until Beckham explains that she tried. She begged. But Beckham played the best friend card and put his foot down.

He knows the last thing I need right now is my well-meaning but nosy sister sniffing around. This thing with Piper is too new and too uncharted, and she is like a skittish foal. I refuse to let anyone, well meaning or otherwise, give her a reason to bolt.

The rest of Sunday ends up being a pleasant reprieve from all the previous heavy moments. After breakfast, we take coffee out onto the back porch and talk. We mostly talk about memories of my parents and all of us as kids—happy memories, maybe even memories we thought were dead and buried.

We steer clear of any topic with potential to bring the mood down.

Later in the day, Ozzy and Cooper arrive, excited and with Stella in tow. Each dog gives Piper an enthusiastic greeting, but

Ozzy quickly turns tail and disappears to wherever Duchess has made herself at home. Cooper stays dutifully by Piper's side. Stella lingers for only a minute or two—she is a much more subtle version of Ellery—asking a couple of benign questions while shooting me a wide, knowing grin. Right at the end, she hugs Piper and whispers something in her ear.

Whatever she says causes Piper to pull back, flushed and refusing to meet my gaze until Stella has gone home. I admit that I am damn curious, but ultimately decide it would be prudent to let it go. Whatever embarrassed Piper that badly is better left between the two of them.

After all that, we take the dogs out on an afternoon hike—another thing I failed to realize how much I have missed. Running and hiking alone are okay. But Piper and I push each other to work harder. We challenge each other.

The epic make-out session back home certainly helps.

So does the shower together that comes after.

The entire time, I want to pinch myself to make sure all of this is real. It feels domestic, like how I always pictured our lives would be if we had stayed together—the one topic I am careful to avoid.

Right now would be the worst time to dredge up my colossal fuck up, the one that caused Piper to fly away from Sweetbriar—and me. I know I need to broach the subject, and I will. But these things have to be handled delicately. Our relationship—if I can even call it that—is too new, and this path we are on is too uncharted. Piper needs to trust me fully before I reveal something that monumental.

Otherwise, she will never believe me when I tell her that I am not going anywhere. Not ever again. But that is the honest truth. Piper Easton has owned my heart from the first moment I saw her all those years ago.

No one else will ever come close.

Piper is my forever.

I just need to prove it to her.

***

Unfortunately, today is my first day back to work. Piper has taken to spending the night here whenever she comes over, so we have quickly established a nice little routine. And, since she has come over every night since the party, I have quickly gotten used to waking up beside her.

I love every second.

Except for the seconds that follow my realization this morning that I am alone. Because, instead of waking to Piper's soft warmth, I wake to a blaring alarm clock and cold sheets on her side of the bed.

Our new habit of sharing a shower flies right out the window. I have to get ready for the day *by myself*. The entire time, I plan how to punish my little bird for her disappearing act.

When I finally shuffle into the kitchen, fully dressed in my police uniform—and desperately seeking coffee—I find Piper sitting at the center island, scrolling mindlessly through her phone. She wears her hair pulled away from her face in a messy bun with little bits of the flame-colored highlights peeking out. Her yellow-gold shirt—one of mine that she must have pulled from the dredges of my closet—bares one delicate shoulder. Piper is so intent on her task that she fails to notice me standing here. A spiral notebook is open in front of her, and she holds a pencil in hand while she tap-tap-taps a faint rhythm on the marble with the eraser.

Now that I see her in front of me, most of my irritation melts into a deep sense of rightness. Then, having solved the mystery of Piper's whereabouts, my limited brain function shifts and tunes into the fancy coffee machine on the other end of the room—the one that cost me an arm and a leg.

Worth every penny, too.

I desperately need the life-giving nectar it provides.

With that thought, I begin to zombie-shuffle across the room with all the grace of a sleepy toddler.

Piper notices my presence at that moment. She peeks up from her phone and smiles brightly. "Good morning, Officer."

"Good morning," I mumble. At least, I think those are the words I say. Based on Piper's answering giggle, it very likely sounds like grumbly gibberish.

"We still have that charming, sunshine-y personality in the morning, I see." She quirks her head to the side. "Somehow I missed it yesterday."

Raising one eyebrow, I shoot her a look that clearly states, I didn't have to work yesterday. *We got to sleep in, and I woke up with my cock in your mouth.*

When understanding dawns in her eyes, Piper snorts and shakes her head. "Right. Silly me."

"Hmph." I hold up the mug I grabbed from the cabinet. "Coffee."

"Yeah, yeah, Lurch. Do your thing." Lips twitching in amusement, she turns back to her phone, and I return to waking myself up.

After pouring a cup big enough for three people—and liberally dousing it with sugar and vanilla creamer (sue me, I like things sweet)—I take a fortifying sip and groan.

"That good, huh?"

"Almost as good as sex," I quip, my brain fog slowly lifting. Then I smirk and raise my mug toward Piper's empty one on the counter. "Refill?"

Piper blinks, looks down at the mug like she forgot it was there, and then nods. "Yeah," she says. "I could use the extra pick-me-up."

Taking the mug, I turn my back to her and return to the machine. I ask over my shoulder, "Didn't sleep well?"

Strange. No answer.

I shake my head and focus on making the coffee the way she likes—or how she liked her coffee back in high school. Cringing slightly, I add two teaspoonfuls of sugar and a splash of creamer to the brew.

Hopefully her preferences have stayed the same.

When I set her mug down across from her, the heavy ceramic lands on the island's butcher block top with a loud thump. The noise startles Piper out of her trance. I notice that she still has her phone in hand.

Interesting.

Piper never used to be prone to distraction. Not like this. Something must be going on with her work, and a large part of me itches to find out what. I know so little about that side of her life, about those years we spent apart. Everything I do know comes from the internet and her social media accounts—things any fan would know—which, for me, is way too little. I want to relearn everything about her.

Starting with why she took this impromptu sabbatical.

The other day, a new video posted on Piper's profile. It showed off her new look, and she explained to her fans that she is taking some much needed time off. Everything else consisted of vague non-answers to the questions every fan has been asking.

At this point, I should count as much more than a fan—or even a friend. If only Piper would let me in and share her troubles with me—and dammit, let me help if I can—but I know we have to reach a certain level of trust before that happens.

For now, if she wants to tell me, she will.

But Piper only frowns down at the screen before shutting the phone completely off. Then she sets it face down, clears her expression, and turns her full attention to me. "Thanks," she says, smiling.

Taking the mug in her hands, Piper blows on the steaming liquid. After a moment, she takes a careful sip. Her beautiful face lights up when the flavors hit her tongue.

"You remember how I take my coffee." There is a note of wonder in her voice that makes me feel about ten feet tall.

"Of course I do." I smile gently. "I remember everything from back then."

Piper blushes. She looks pleased at my answer but takes another sip of coffee to mask it. Then her gaze travels over the crisp lines of my police uniform.

"When do you have to be at work?" she asks.

"In"—I peek at my watch—"Fuck. Fifteen minutes. I should have put this in a travel mug." I sigh and lean against the counter behind me, internally groaning that I have to leave at all.

"I'll do it," Piper says, hopping off the stool. Then she rounds the corner, lifting on tiptoe to give me a peck on the cheek while taking the mug from my hands.

Now that my brain synapses are firing properly, I notice exactly what Piper chose to wear this morning. Where she scrounged up my old jersey, I have no clue. She can be damned resourceful about the strangest things.

Don't get me wrong. I have exactly zero complaints. Piper in my high school football jersey is a sight I never thought I would get to see again. My mind floods with a hundred different memories of her looking just like this. Most of the thoughts are way too explicit, considering I need to be at work in—

Shit.

Fourteen minutes.

My brain gives zero fucks about the time, though. Especially when Piper saunters over to the coffee station I have set up in the corner, hips swaying seductively with every step. Then she stretches up on tiptoe to grab a travel mug from the higher cabinet shelf.

As soon as she starts to reach, I think, *I need to go help her.* But my body refuses to obey. Both feet stay glued to the floor, and both eyes stay glued to her backside.

Slowly, the hem of my jersey slides up to reveal twin peachy globes. They beg me to touch them. Bite them. I bite my lip instead, trying to maintain control.

Yeah, that works about as well as expected.

Smooth skin. Round ass. Plenty of surface area for my hands to grab hold of. No panties, since I may have shredded yet another pair last night. My cock twitches in my pants, waking up at the reminder and the tempting sight of her.

Fuck. Me.

I don't have time to fulfill any of the fantasies racing through my head. It takes ten minutes to drive to the station when traffic is light. During busy times, that time jumps to fifteen. I look at my watch.

Thirteen minutes left.

Piper pours my coffee into the travel mug, careful not to spill a single drop. Once the lid is firmly in place, she walks over and sets the coffee on the counter next to me

Then, shimmering green eyes holding me captive, Piper takes a few steps back. When she hits the island, she leans back on her elbows and slowly crosses one delicate ankle over the other. The movement highlights her toned legs and all that silky skin in front of me.

I narrow my eyes at the knowing smirk curving her lips.

What a fucking tease.

Of course, Piper is doing this on purpose.

Without giving myself a chance to think it through, I move to stand in front of her. Then I rest my hands on her waist. She immediately tilts her face up for a kiss.

Fuck that.

Using her hips as leverage, I flip Piper around and savor her surprised shriek. Then, I rest a palm between her shoulder blades, pressing down until she lies bent over the butcher block.

"Simon!" she rasps out, chest heaving. "W-what are you doing?"

"What does it feel like I'm doing?" I grit out. I reach under my old jersey with one hand, gathering the fabric up over her hips and baring her to me. Then I drag the other hand over her hip and along her pubic bone before delving between her legs, fingers slipping through the slick folds.

Now my dick is painfully hard.

"Dirty girl. You're fucking soaked. Does driving me crazy turn you on?" I challenge. "Do you want me fighting a hard-on all day at work every time I think of you in my jersey? Every time I picture this pretty little cunt waiting for me at home?"

I thrust three fingers into her warm, wet heat. Then, with aching slowness, I ease them in and out. The sounds of her breathless moans have me painfully stiff in my pants, but I have mastered restraint over the years. I can wait it out.

Piper tilts her hips back, trying to get me to give her more. I reciprocate by stilling the rhythmic motion of my fingers. When she tries to push against my hand for friction, I press my other arm down on her hips to stop them.

With a growl of frustration, she grits, "Seems like the only one teasing right now is you."

"Always such a brat," I taunt. "Payback is a bitch, isn't it?"

My free hand lifts, landing on her left cheek with a satisfying smack. She jolts, gasping in surprise and pleasure when the sudden motion rocks her back against my hand. I slip out of her channel with a dark chuckle and reach into my back pocket for a condom.

"Ready for your punishment?" I ask.

"I—wha—?" Panting heavily, Piper peers back at me over her shoulder. "You're going to be late for work," she argues.

But then she sees my hands lower to my waistband. The argument dies on her lips, and her expression is suddenly, distinctly lacking in remorse.

"Yeah, I am," I rebuke, "and you're to blame." With a wicked grin, I slip my pants and boxer briefs down my hips, not bothering to take them all the way off.

Like she said, I'm already running late.

Gripping my hard length, I press forward until the tip slots against her entrance. "Eyes on me, little bird, and hold on tight."

With a single thrust, I bury myself to the hilt. Piper throws her head back and cries out in relief. I pause for a second, taking in her tousled hair, flushed skin, glassy eyes, and heaving chest.

Piper's beauty takes my breath away. She is an angel. My angel.

And I am about to defile her.

I lock her hips in a punishing grip. Then I start to move. She presses her forearms against the counter and lifts her upper body. Wide eyes watch me, transfixed, while I take her roughly from behind.

Piper wants to move. Her eyes beg me to let her. I only offer her a devilish grin before redoubling my efforts. Her eyelashes flutter with each deep thrust, but somehow she manages to keep her eyes on me.

No way am I going to last long. Not like this. Not with how tightly her walls are gripping me, or the desperate moans each thrust wrenches out of her. As soon as I feel her release starting to ripple around my length, I let go of her hips and press my chest against her back. Our fingers intertwine on the countertop as we move together.

"Love the way you feel around me," I whisper in her ear.

"Simon," she whimpers, hips moving erratically under mine as she gets closer to falling over the edge. "So close."

"Let go, baby. Give it to me."

This time, she screams my name. She clenches around me like a damned vice grip and starts to pulse. My hips begin to lose their rhythm as I tumble after her. It feels like my soul leaves my body for a second, floating toward the ceiling while we catch our breath on the countertop below.

Eventually, I have to move—no more avoiding work—so I slip out of Piper's heat with a tortured groan. Then I quickly clean off and tuck myself back into my pants. Piper carefully slides back down to the floor. My jersey falls down to her thighs, and my eyes follow, tracing from the hem to her flushed face.

"You're *definitely* going to be late now," the little minx comments, a twinkle in her eye.

I wink. "Worth it."

After grabbing my keys, I head toward the door while Piper follows a few paces behind. She leans against the doorframe. I step out onto the porch.

When I turn to say goodbye, Piper smiles at me with a sleepy, satisfied expression. *Fuck.* Now I have to kiss her. Pressing my lips to hers for a brief moment, I wish I could savor her like she deserves.

But I am officially out of time.

Her eyes are closed when I pull back. They flutter open after a moment, sparkling with mischief as Piper's gaze lifts to meet mine. A cheeky grin slowly spreads across her face.

"You know," she quips, "your punishments are only making me want to misbehave more."

Cheeky minx. Unable to resist, I laugh. Then I lean down to kiss those sassy lips one last time.

"Good," I reply.

My hands slip under the shirt hem to squeeze Piper's soft, tempting skin. I press my lips against her ear. Then I whisper one last thing before heading out.

"I like it when you misbehave, little bird."

"I like it when you **misbehave,** little bird."

Chapter 22
Be My Queen

Simon

Ten minutes. I am ten minutes late getting to the office. Without Cap around, I slip into my seat and immediately boot up my computer. Unfortunately, the guys still noticed. They have been ribbing me ever since I walked into the bullpen.

Typically, being late irks the hell out of me. This morning I am too damn blissful. The guys have been ribbing me about that, too.

They all want to know the reason for the twinkle in my eyes or—courtesy of Harden—the lack of a stick up my ass.

That one feels a bit offensive. I'll be getting even with Harden later.

Sometime around lunch, we all feel the effects of hunger and boredom. Today has been slow, which is excellent in our line of business, but also awful because the hours drag on. After a while, we started to get on each other's nerves.

I, for one, am trying to be productive. I even fill out some neglected paperwork. But eventually, I give up and pull out my phone.

Several missed texts highlight the screen. I grin when I see they all belong to Piper. Quickly opening the app, I scroll to the oldest one and notice a couple of new photos from this morning.

- 7:30 am -

Piper: Dropping off the princess!

Below the text is a selfie of her, Duchess, and Ellery at Unity Art. That already spoiled dog has become an unofficial mascot after Ellery offered to keep her there while I work.

Now, she gets attention from a considerable group of people daily.

Smiling and shaking my head, I move on to the following text.

- 8:45 am -

Piper: Stopped back at your place to pick up O&C. Also wanted to enjoy your sheets again *smirk emoji*

My brows furrow in confusion—until I see the photo underneath and nearly drop the phone. I frantically lock the screen, peeking up to check that no one is looking over my shoulder before risking a second glance. Okay, then—not a hallucination.

Piper has decided to grace me with a lovely view of her sprawled out on my bed. She is naked except for her lacy bra, wearing a sultry smile. She strategically posed her legs to hide her most intimate parts, but I can see Piper's nipples peeking through the lace, and it's blatantly apparent that her panties are absent.

Her caption underneath the photo has me choking on a laugh that I quickly smother into a cough. I get a strange look from Nate, but otherwise, no one notices. I look down at my phone, rereading the text under the photo.

Piper: Payback is a bitch *wink emoji*

Yes, it is, little bird. You'll be paying for that one later, too.

The rest of the texts are just little notes.

- 9:30 am -

Piper: Heading out! Locked up & will give you the key the next time I see you *kiss emoji*

- 10:30 am -

Piper: Ugh, I've gotten too used to your face

Piper: This rental feels extra lonely

- 11:00 am -

Piper: You get lunch breaks, right?

Piper: Never mind, I'm sure you're busy, I'll ask Ellery

Looking at my watch, I see the time is almost noon—no wonder I've been feeling hungry.

- 11:30 am -

Piper: See you soon!

I frown. Wait. Does that mean Piper is coming here?

Dominic answers that question for me when he perks up in his seat. He looks over my right shoulder, eyes widening, and gives a low whistle.

"Holy fucking saggy ballsack," Harden whisper-shouts, reaching over to slap Nate on the chest with the back of his hand. "Dude, look!"

Nate jolts. He looks up with a glare, only for it to melt into a mischievous grin when he sees whatever the hell is going on behind me.

"Why are you three looking at me like that?"

"Like what?" Dominic asks.

I point at his face. "Like you're completely unhinged."

"Dom is unhinged. That's not news." Nate nods toward the door behind me. "But that might have something to do with it."

His words have me looking over my shoulder.

At the front desk, Piper is having a friendly-looking conversation with our clerk, Elaine. Piper smiles at her, looking more relaxed than she has since arriving in Sweetbriar. I take advantage of her distraction to admire the denim cut-offs and the Billie Eilish t-shirt she wears tied at the waist. A tantalizing sliver of skin winks at me every time she moves.

She also wore those sexy-as-fuck boots.

When Piper finally catches me watching her, she winks.

"Damn, Simon," Harden says while we watch Piper laugh at something Elaine says. "I'll never get over the fact that you dated Songbyrd."

The downside to small-town living is that everyone knows everyone's business. Half of the station grew up in Sweetbriar, and both Dominic and Harden went to Hazelwood at the same time as me. Harden was a year ahead, while Dominic was two years behind. Close enough to know all about Piper and me. Our private lives were never very private—not when I was the football team quarterback, and Piper had grown a following with her music.

"Dated? Past tense? No way, man." Dominic says incredulously. He jabs a pointer finger in my direction. "The bastard is fucking her *now*!"

"Hey. Watch it." I tense up and shift forward in my seat. My glower hits Dominic full blast, and he blanches slightly.

"No disrespect, man. But, come on. Piper could have anyone she wants, and she chooses him?"

Nate smirks. "Do you see anyone else in this precinct with the moniker Sexy Cop?"

I roll my eyes, muttering, "That is not a thing, asshole."

"It is one hundred percent a thing."

"Not a word about that when she gets over here," I growl.

Harden snorts and looks at me. "Dude, she's a woman. She knows. They band together and talk about you like you're some A-list actor, not a small-town cop. I'm pretty sure some local gift shops sell posters of you for people to pin up on their walls."

I open my mouth to demand names and addresses, then shake my head. *Not worth it.*

Dominic pivots back to his previous point. "Anyway, why didn't you tell us you snagged her again? If she belonged to me, I would be shouting it from the rooftops."

"In no universe would Piper ever date you," Nate says, laughing.

Dominic glowers at Nate. "Whatever, she absolutely would. Now, you"—Dominic points at me again—"answer the question."

"Because our business is ours alone and not up for public scrutiny." I cross my arms, eyebrow raised in challenge. "And for the record, Piper is not a commodity. She *belongs* to no one."

"Sorry." He holds his hands up in surrender. "Wrong choice of words."

"And you wonder why you can't ever make it past the second date," Harden says, shaking his head sadly.

Dominic smacks him upside the head, and Harden winces. But before either can make another smart-ass remark, Piper stops at my desk.

"Hello, officers," she says, smiling brightly in greeting. But her gaze quickly locks onto mine.

"I think I'm in love," Nate whispers, making moon eyes in her direction.

Harden nods and whispers back, "She smells so good…"

Dominic snorts, but even he fails to take his eyes off her.

Piper clears her throat, blushing as she grins. "Sorry, boys," she says, glancing at me warmly. "But I'm already spoken for."

Her words hit me right in the chest, and I suddenly feel a bit lightheaded as happiness floods my system. But I still try not to read too much into her meaning—not this early on. We still have to define this thing between us.

I know what I want it to be.

Could she be on the same page?

"Darling," Dominic says, interrupting my internal monologue. He rests his elbows on his desk and smiles.

I can admit that the man has a magnetic personality. His smile flashes a set of pearly whites so dazzling that any woman would swoon like a period-drama heroine. He is doing it on purpose, pushing my buttons for fun.

Damn him for succeeding.

"What are you doing hanging out with this dud, huh?" Dominic continues, tilting his head in my direction. "Why don't you let a real man take you out?"

"Oh, sweetie," Piper says, voice dripping with honey. Her smile is almost apologetic when she sticks the knife into poor Dominic and twists. "No. But thank you. It's adorable that you think you can handle me."

Laughter erupts throughout the bull-pen. Half of the precinct heard Piper, which tells me all I need to know about how distinctly un-private our conversation has become. Honestly, I'm not the least bit surprised. Beautiful celebrities never waltz into our humble station.

Dominic flushes bright red, and he slumps slightly in his chair. But he laughs it off, nodding at her. "*Touché*, madam."

I am suddenly itching to get out of here. Standing up, I rest my hand on Piper's lower back. "Ready for lunch?" I murmur.

She nods emphatically. Then, with a glance at the guys, she says, "It was a pleasure meeting you three. I'm sure I'll be seeing you around."

They say goodbye, all still looking a little star-struck. I shake my head, chuckling, and turn toward the door. "Elaine, I'll be back in an hour."

"You take your time, sweetie pie," the older woman says with a wink. "I'll cover for you."

Piper grins. "Thanks, Elaine."

With a wave, we head out into the sunlight. I let Piper take the lead since she seems to have a plan already. We stop at her vehicle, she opens the passenger-side door and pulls a basket out.

Holding it in front of her, Piper says, "I, uh, thought we could picnic at the park?"

"Sounds perfect," I reply.

Then she leads us in the same direction we started. While we walk, I sneak a peek under the lid. Sandwiches, fruit and veggie snacks, chips, and drinks fill the basket and make my mouth water.

I let the lid drop. Then I look at her with raised eyebrows. "Did you do all this?"

Her cheeks flush pink. "Mom, mostly. You know how she is. My fridge has been consistently packed with food, and I'm never going to be able to eat it all myself." With a bashful little grin, she adds, "I did slice up the fruit and veggies, and pick out the drinks."

Unable to resist, I throw an arm around her shoulders and tug her close. My pulse jumps when she shifts the basket to her other side and slips the empty arm around my waist. I half expected her to shrug me off. Then an entirely different part of my anatomy jumps when she slips her hand in my back pocket, squeezes my ass, and then leaves it there.

"No matter how this bounty came to be, my stomach thanks you for it. I'm starving." I give her a side-eyed glance. "Someone made me late for work and I completely missed breakfast."

Piper gasps, eyes widening comically. "No! How horrible!" After a beat of silence, she says, "That person should really be punished."

I choke on a surprised laugh. Slipping my arm up around her neck, I gently tug Piper close enough to whisper in her ear. "Oh she will be," I say. "I already have to punish her for sending me naughty pictures at work."

This time, her sharp inhale gives me a sick sense of satisfaction.

As much as I would love to play a little more with Piper, the park comes into view. We enter through the main gate and I shift my attention to finding us a place to sit and relax. This area of town is more populated, especially around lunchtime, and the park has a large children's playground directly inside the entrance, to the right. Benches and wrought iron fencing surround the space. People occupy many of the seats, chit-chatting while their children or charges play.

Since today is perfect fall weather in South Carolina, everyone wants to be outside to enjoy it. The benches around the playground are entirely covered. I would usually never notice—or be bothered by it—but I feel tingling on my neck like someone is watching me. Whenever I look in that direction, at least two chattering couples whisper in hushed tones and look over at Piper and me.

Of course, they quickly turn away once I've outed them.

Beside me, Piper's shoulders shake with quiet laughter.

"What the hell is so funny?" I grump, pinching her collarbone lightly.

"You," she replies. "And them."

"Well, I am trying to figure out if the gossip is about you, me, or both." I glare at one particularly stubborn pair of women shooting daggers at Piper.

I can only surmise why.

"Definitely both." She tosses a glance over her shoulder before turning back. "They have nothing better to do, and they're bored sitting there watching over a bunch of kids so no one gets hurt, so they gossip. It's harmless. They probably read trash mags and have seen my photo, and you"—she waves the picnic basket in my direction—"are infamous around these parts, Mr. Sexy Cop. And, shock and awe, we are walking together, arm in arm, with a picnic basket. Tongues will wag."

"Fuck me." I run a hand over my face. "You know."

"Oh, sweetie." She smirks. "I learned that little tidbit pretty early on."

"Do you ever get used to this kind of attention?" I ask a moment later, thinking out loud.

With a snort, she replies, "Never. But you do learn to tune it out." She peeks up at me with a raised eyebrow. "It's no different than high school. The gossip was always hot and juicy where we were concerned."

"True. I guess it's been so long I forgot about all that." I shake my head but let it go. We take a few more minutes to reach an excellent, secluded park section. Then I ask, "Do you want a table, or is there a blanket in that thing?"

"There is." Her lips turn up in a grin. "Mom even snuck some wine and grapes in here. She would have put candles in if it wasn't broad daylight and a safety hazard."

"Sounds like Stella." I chuckle at that. "So, then, what's your preference?"

She taps her chin in thought. "Let's do this traditional style."

"Blanket it is."

I motion for the basket. Piper slips out from under my arm and then passes it over to me. After locating the item in question, I hand the basket back and shake the blanket out. Once it settles over the grass, Piper sets the basket on one corner, plops herself down, and starts to pull everything out. I settle down next to her and rummage around. There are a few different sandwich options, and after peeking at all of them, I settle on a Reuben.

"Your mom went all out."

Piper snorts. "You know how she is. Food is her love language. That and wine. Speaking of…" She holds up a bottle in triumph.

Laughing, I pull out two red solo cups. "Dining in style, I see."

"You know it." She joins in laughing and sets the wine bottle back in the basket. "I get what she was trying to do, but I think she forgot you're on the clock."

"Well, her heart was in the right place."

She cuts her eyes over to me, raising an eyebrow. Her voice is incredulous when she says, "Pfft, no, it wasn't. She was being a typical, meddling, motherly matchmaker."

I chuckle. "Okay, fair point."

Smiling, she hands me one of the non-alcoholic beverage options. She opens her can with a loud hiss, and once I have done the same, we clink them together. "To meddling family members."

"To meddling family members."

We eat in relative silence, punctuated by short snippets of conversation between bites of food. I sneak a few peeks at Piper while she nibbles on her chicken salad on a croissant, gaze drawn to her mouth whenever she opens it to toss in a grape—or, hell, anything—mesmerized by the slope of her neck when she swallows.

Everything she does is so effortlessly sexy.

Even the most mundane acts feel almost erotic.

When the food has a big enough dent and our bellies are full, I turn to Piper. "So," I say, lifting a hand to the back of my neck. I rub it absently while I think of what I want to say. "Back there, at the station. What you said…"

She blushes and looks down, picking at a loose fabric on the blanket. A smile blooms on her face. Bashful. Beautiful.

"You mean about being spoken for?"

"Yeah." My voice lowers, and I lean closer. "Did you mean it?"

Piper leans forward slightly, sliding her hand over until it barely touches mine. Then she loops her pinky finger through mine—my entire focus is on that tiny touch. She stays silent for so long that I start to think she is never going to answer.

"I think so," Piper says slowly, not meeting my gaze. "I want to mean it. And I *want* it to be true, but…"

"But you're afraid."

She nods and then peeks up at me through dark lashes. I see the uncertainty wavering in and out of her pale green eyes. At that moment, I would do anything to remove it. My hand flips over so that I can thread our fingers together.

"So am I," I admit.

"Really?" Doubt colors her features.

"Is that so strange?" I ask, leaning close. "This is uncharted territory for both of us, little bird. I'm out of my depth. You have an entire life outside of this little town, which I know nothing about and have no part in. One that I can't compete with."

"Not true." Her voice is soft, but her tone is fierce. "That other life of mine is fake and meaningless. But you and I are real. This thing between us could be, too. I think it may just be too new to label. Don't you?"

I want to say *no*. I want to tell Piper everything, all the things I buried inside for twelve goddamned years, but I grit my teeth and hold the words back. Now is still not the right time.

"So we don't label it."

Piper looks unconvinced. "That simple, huh?"

"Sweetheart," I say with a chuckle. "Nothing about us has ever been simple."

"True." Her expression warms and a smile blooms.

Taking that as a good sign, I gently lift my hand to her face. My thumb brushes back and forth along her cheekbone. Her eyes flutter closed momentarily, and she tilts her head to nuzzle the palm.

"No labels," I say. "No overthinking this. We take it one day at a time."

"One day at a time," she echoes. "I can do that."

I tilt her face up to mine. "Good girl," I whisper before pressing my lips to hers.

"It's *adorable* that you think you can *handle* me."

Chapter 23
I'm With You

Simon

I have never been a big proponent of fate or destiny. I make plans and work hard to achieve my goals, and if something happens that derails those plans, I pivot and try again. Some mystical entity or cosmic plan does not control my successes and failures.

However, tonight has me rethinking my entire worldview.

Staring out over the rural landscape where the earth still glistens from an earlier freak rainstorm, I feel torn between laughing or crying. Maybe I should just do both. I turn back to the blown-out tire on my truck, gritting my teeth in frustration. My extremely flat spare is lying on the ground beside the broken tire. Not sure how the fuck that happened, but it seems to be on par with the rest of the evening.

Piper is hovering near the truck hood. I have felt her eyes on me this entire time, burning a path along my shoulder and back while I try to fix the most recent joke in the comedy of errors this date has become. When I informed Piper that I was taking her out on a date—a *real* date in the city—I had everything perfectly planned. Because, label or not, I want everyone to know that Piper is mine, and that I am hers.

I also really like the idea of spoiling her.

Instead, this date got spoiled.

Heaving a sigh, I roll my shoulders and then crack my neck. There is no salvaging this tire. I need to call for help. But, as I pull out the phone from my back pocket and mutter a few choice expletives, a strangled sound goes off in my ears like a bomb. I jerk my head around to look over at Piper. Her face is red, she is doubled over and holding her stomach, and her shoulders are shaking.

Shit.

My brain goes into immediate panic mode. I *really* fucking ruined this date. Piper is never going to speak to me again. A whole litany of diatribes flit through the synapses of my mind before I realize one crucial detail:

Those aren't tears.

Piper is *laughing*.

"I'm sorry," she gasps, visibly forcing herself to straighten and regain some semblance of control.

While she wipes under her eyes, still giggling, I watch her in wide-eyed silence. To be honest, I am really struggling to figure out what could be so funny about the situation. I expected her to be angry or frustrated. At the very least, I expected disappointment.

But stars twinkle in Piper's eyes, and her lips are curved up in an amused smile while she saunters to me.

"Come on, handsome," she says, reaching under my chin to close my mouth. She lingers there, thumb brushing back and forth to play with the short hairs of my beard. "Let's just get a tow truck and head home, yeah?"

"Worst date ever," I mutter.

"Oh, I don't know about that," she quips, slipping her arms around my waist.

"How do you figure?" I pull back to look down at her, an eyebrow raised in question and a skeptical look.

Because I have yet to see any positives.

Sure, everything *seemed* to be going well at first. I picked Piper up at five o'clock on the dot, and she met me out front wearing a sexy-as-fuck, off-the-shoulder sweater dress that hits just above mid-thigh. Piper paired it with knee-high leggings and a pair of sneakers covered in sparkling rhinestones. Her hair was in a braid that draped over one shoulder, a fedora sat on her head, and a leather jacket rested in the crook of her arm.

It took me a full minute to reengage my faculties. Every damn one of them shifted south. Piper tempted me to forego our trip with that outfit. I wanted to hoist her over my shoulder and march back into her house.

Looking back, I wish I had listened to myself.

When we got in the truck and I pointed us toward Savannah, Georgia, things started to go downhill. The normally 45-minute drive took nearly an hour and a half because of a pileup on the interstate. That made us late for our reservation at the highly fancy, costly restaurant I had booked us—one with a fifteen-minute grace period.

We were well past the fifteen minute mark when we arrived.

After frantically searching for a romantic place with last-minute openings and coming up empty-handed, I figured we could walk along the downtown promenade. Earlier, we drove past a trendy spot laden with food trucks. It was spontaneous and not nearly as romantic as I had planned, but we were both pretty hungry.

Then Mother Nature decided to shit on that little plan. We were about a block from the restaurant when the sky turned dark. Seconds later, the clouds burst open, and a torrential downpour hit us in full force.

Not one drop of rain had been in the forecast all week.

I stood there, frozen, while people scrambled this way and that, shrieking and trying to find cover. I told Piper to go to the nearest restaurant and wait for me. The fool woman grabbed my hand and tugged, insisting that she was already soaked.

Touché.

We raced back to the truck together, looking like drowned rats when we made it inside. Quickly turning the ignition, I blasted the heat to warm us up. Maybe the hot air would dry some of the excess water. Then again, maybe not. There was just too damn much.

Even though we are dryer now than we were, I take in the still-damp fabric of her sage green sweater dress, noting how the color is darker than when we started. Her makeup has mostly washed away, and a good chunk of her hair has slipped from its braid. She is also shivering from the chill in the air—a gift that the rain left behind. I tighten my hold on her and will some of my warmth into her body. Eventually, she melts against me, and the faint tremors subside.

I fare no better. Leftover moisture clings to my dress shirt, weighing the fabric down, and my socks have soaked through from trudging through puddles to get to the truck.

"So," Piper breathes into my neck, voice tinged with amusement. "About that tow truck…"

"Fuck. Sorry."

I let go of her to pull my phone from my jacket pocket. After a quick SOS text to Beckham to rescue us from the side of the road, I call Sweetbriar's local body shop, Revved Up—the only place I trust with my vehicles.

Once I get off the phone, I sigh heavily and slide to the ground against the side of the truck. Then I lean my head back against the cool metal and close my eyes. A moment later, Piper's sneaker nudges me. I open one eye. She glares down at me, arms crossed.

What the hell did I do now? At this point, it could be anything and everything. Nothing will surprise me.

"This date isn't over, Simon Brooks."

I look around us in confusion. "You sure about that?"

My truck is a paperweight. Nothing but a sea of wilderness surrounds us. There are no living souls for miles—as far as I can tell—and no one has been down this stretch of road since long before we broke down.

With a mutter, she crouches beside me and tweaks my nose. "Yes, I'm sure, you jerk." She gestures up to the sky. "We have a perfectly romantic opportunity that has just landed in our laps. I, for one, am not going to let it escape."

"Okay…" I drag the word out.

My eyes slowly follow Piper's line of site. It ends with the glittering stars overhead. I arch my eyebrow in question and return my gaze to hers.

"Don't you remember all the nights we would camp out in Black Betty's truck bed?" she says, referencing my first truck. "We would curl up on blankets you set up and lay there for hours, stargazing." Her fingers walk up my sternum, teasing me with the tiniest touches. "When it was cold out, like tonight, we would have to get up close and personal to keep warm…"

Damn it.

Have I misread everything about this date?

Did I try too hard?

Slowly, I get back to my feet. After helping Piper get back to hers, I pull open the door to the extended cab and start rummaging through the storage space under the seats. It takes me a few moments to find what I'm looking for. When I finally reemerge, I am holding a large duffel bag full of blankets and other comforts—things I like to keep on hand for emergencies. I added everything back when I bought the Dodge Ram and never used it again.

I never needed to, at least not until now.

"What's in there?" Piper's voice drips with curiosity.

"You wanted to stargaze," I say, smirking. I am starting to feel more like myself than I have in hours. "So we're going to stargaze."

Rounding the back, I toss the duffel bag into the truck bed before unlatching the tailgate and tugging it down. I hop up, turn, offer Piper my hand, and hoist her up with me. Then, I return to the bag and pull out a few heavy wool blankets, handing one to Piper. We shake them out, and then I lay mine down while Piper wraps hers around her shoulders. She plops down cross-legged against the side of the truck, watching me while I continue to pull things out of the bag: two pillows, one flashlight, a first aid kit, and some basic toiletries—including condoms (halle-fucking-lujah).

Then I come to the last few items and whoop in excitement.

"Jackpot," I exclaim, holding several bags of freeze-dried food in one hand and a large bottle of Jack Daniels in the other. I set them down in between us. "There are a few bottles of water, too, but I figure after the night we've had, liquor is the better choice."

"Man after my own heart," Piper says with a wink.

"Hey, I know my priorities."

Piper picks through the food bags, reading each label. "We've got strawberries and bananas, apples, peaches"—she raises an eyebrow at me and smiles, "or blueberries and yogurt. What'll it be, officer?"

"Peaches, of course." I wink.

Her cheeks flush prettily, but she laughs. "Of course." She tosses me the bag and reaches for the blueberries and yogurt.

We both rip open the bags simultaneously, too hungry to bother with decorum. Piper moans loudly when the first handful of food hits her tongue. The sound immediately hits me right in the groin.

"Why is this so good?" she asks.

"Because we haven't eaten in hours?"

"That must be it."

After we polish off the food and make a decent dent in the whiskey, I stretch out on the blanket. Then I motion for Piper to join me. With a bright smile, she scoots closer and lets the blanket around her shoulders fall to the ground. She snuggles tightly into my side, her warmth draping over me as her limbs do. Our heads tilt up to look at the stars. With her hand resting over my heart, I'm sure Piper can feel its rapid beat.

No one affects me quite like she does. Piper has me under a spell because holding this woman close after going so many years without is pure magic. I never thought my dream would come true. I hoped, prayed, and made plans just in case. But with each year that passed, that hope dwindled.

Yet Piper is here.

This moment is real.

Her scent washes over me as I breathe her in. She sighs, and I savor the pure contentment in that slight whisper of sound. When a colder breeze starts to cut through our clothes, I reach over with my free arm and drag the loose blanket over us. Piper turns her head and giggles into my shoulder.

I pinch her lightly. "What's so funny, little bird?"

"Tonight feels a lot like our first prom night," she replies.

Lifting my head from its pillow, I place one arm behind me to prop up higher. Then, my gaze rests on Piper. Those pouty lips I crave wear a sinful smile, and her eyes stare into the distance, lost in memory.

She blinks and looks at me. "That was one of the best nights of my life, you know."

"You and I have a very different recollection of that night," I scoff. "We missed prom because Black Betty broke down in the middle of nowhere, and neither of us had any signal on our phones."

That night and tonight share some eerie similarities.

"Not one single bar," she agrees. Her fingers absently trace along the fabric of my open collar. "But it was also the first night we slept underneath the stars. You were determined to make the best out of our bad luck, so you moved us to the truck bed, threw a playlist onto your phone, and told me every silly, useless factoid you knew about the constellations."

"Hey!" I shoot her a look of mock affront. "Those were supposed to be romantic."

She giggles. "They were. I promise."

"Hmph." I peek up at the stars, mentally picking through some of the factoids I thought were incredibly clever that night. Then I pull a face. "Okay, yeah, they were pretty lame."

"Well, I loved those lame facts." While she looks up at me, her expression heats. "And I also love what they led to."

"Me, too. Believe me," I say huskily.

My blood heats at the memory. Piper gave herself to me for the first time that night. I never knew what sex could be like until her—because with her, the sex is so much more.

Piper tilts her head up. Her mouth meets mine, slow and sultry like we have all the time in the world. Then again, I suppose we do—at least until Beckham and the tow truck arrive. So my hand threads through the hair behind her head, and I shift her so I can take control of the kiss.

When we break apart, I ask, "You looking for a repeat performance?"

"Well, we do need to keep warm." She flutters her eyelashes at me. Beneath the blanket, her hand slips down my body to palm my already hard length—a semi-permanent state when I'm around her.

My head falls back against the pillow, and I groan. "Woman, fuck warmth. Keep doing that, and I'll spontaneously combust."

Her tinkling laughter only fuels the fire. Especially when I feel the button on my jeans pop open and the zipper slide down, her deft fingers delving into my boxer briefs to take me in hand.

"Fuuuuck," I hiss. "Come here, you."

I grip her chin and pull her to me. Our lips connect, tongues dancing together while she pumps me slowly. Teasing me.

Two can play that game.

My free hand runs down her back until I reach the sweater's hem and slip beneath it. My skin is still cold, and Piper jolts at the contrast until I palm her ass, squeeze, and then start to play with her panties. When I feel how hot and wet she already is, I lose control.

Moving to the front, I wrench her panties to the side and cover her with my hand. The heel of my palm presses against her clit, and she moans into my mouth, hips moving, seeking more.

I break away from her mouth. "Dirty girl."

"You gonna punish me?" Her question ends in a sharp gasp when I shove two fingers as deep as they will go.

"No, sweetheart." She clenches around them when I start to slide back out. I grin. "I'm going to reward you."

Her hand stills its motion just as mine starts to move. She is clenching my cock in a vice-like grip that mirrors her tight channel, and I have to use my other hand to pry her fingers off of me.

"You're going to end this way too soon, little bird," I grit out.

Her only answer is a series of whimpers.

"Warm enough yet?" I ask.

Lips curving into a wicked smile, she shakes her head. Then she grips my shoulders for purchase, lifting to ride my hand.

"So close." Her breathy pants are erratic, matching the frantic motion of her hips. "Simon, please."

"Fuck, you beg so prettily." I capture her lips in a bruising kiss. Then I order her, "Let go, baby. I want to hear."

Piper tenses her entire body—back arching, limbs shaking—before she collapses against my chest, and a strangled cry wrenches from her throat. I slowly remove my hand once her climax has ebbed.

In the aftermath, Piper lay loose and limp over me, a dreamy smile on her face, her eyes firmly closed. When they finally flutter open, and I'm sure she is watching, I lift my hand to my lips and suck my fingers clean. Her quiet gasp of pleasure shoots straight through me. Then her taste hits my tongue, and my eyes damn near roll back in my head. That—and her tangy scent—have my cock standing at full attention.

Suddenly, I need her close.

"Come here," I demand huskily, and capture Piper's lips with mine. Then I grip her behind one knee and drag her until she straddles my thighs. She mewls when our bodies meet, bucking forward and helplessly sliding up and down my length. "Simon," she moans. "I need you."

"Go ahead, then." I buck my hips up into hers. "I'm all yours."

Breath hitching at my words, Piper leans over me, kissing me and delving her tongue into my mouth. One hand reaches for the box of condoms I slipped out of the bag earlier. Then she sits up and tears the foil packet with her teeth. With aching slowness, she rolls the condom onto my length.

I growl low in the back of my throat. "Quit teasing."

Giggling, Piper lines me up with her entrance and starts to slide down my length, inch by agonizing inch. I decide enough is enough. Reaching up, I grab the soft flesh of her hips, wrenching them down at the same time I thrust mine up.

We both cry out in relief.

I am already so close to the edge that I grit my teeth, struggling to hold back while she sets the pace. Her palms press down hard, fingernails digging into my chest while she rides me.

The way her lithe body moves over me, the way it sways back and forth in a sensual dance like the natural performer she is, has me completely under its spell. I could watch her like this for hours. Her eyes are closed, and dark lashes fan out from her cheeks. A deep flush colors her peachy skin. The braid in her hair has given up, and the strands are in beautiful disarray.

Piper is a drug, and I am unapologetically addicted. She satisfies a deep-seated hunger that has been gnawing at me for years. No one else has ever come close. Yet I feel the ache for her grow stronger, feeding the obsession that has me in its clutches.

"Simon," she breathes. My gaze focuses on her. The drunk look in her eyes tells me she's close, confirmed when she begs, "Please."

Just one word, but I know what she needs. I wrap my arms around her waist and tug her to my chest. She hides her face in the crook of my neck while I take control and piston my hips into hers. Each punishing thrust wrenches a strangled cry, stringing closer together until she is quietly keening in my ear. All at once, her entire body tenses before she lets go, hurtling over the edge and taking me with her.

I hold her close, anchoring us to the earth until her trembling subsides. Her body drapes limply over me. My heart takes a little longer to stop hammering in my chest. But the outside world returns to focus, and the adrenaline drains away.

With a breathless chuckle, I ask, "Warm now?"

"Perfectly toasty." She gently kisses my throat. "You?"

"Scorching." I grin at her.

Giggling, Piper lifts her body off of mine. As soon as we separate, cool air hits me, chilling some of the heat our bodies have generated. She briefly presses her lips to mine before sitting up. I take a moment to clean up and tuck myself back into my jeans before I do the same.

Slowly, we readjust our clothes. I lean against the back of the cab, redoing some of the buttons of my shirt that came undone and then running my fingers through my hair to try and tame the curls. Afterward, I watch Piper smooth her wayward hair and tame the strands into their original braid. Then she stands.

"Be right back," she says, heading toward the edge of the truck bed. "I have to pee."

We may be isolated right now, but that sky is pitch black. My deeply ingrained Southern manners would never let any woman go off on her own like this, let alone *my* woman. I quickly grab the toiletry bag and follow behind to keep watch. Once I hit the ground, I turn my back to let her have her privacy—because my mother raised a *gentleman*—while keeping my eyes trained on the road.

A minute later, Piper walks up to stand next to me. I silently hand her some hand sanitizer. Smiling, she takes the tiny bottle and squirts some into her hands.

"Who knew you were such a boy scout?" she teases.

Shrugging, I say, "I like to be prepared."

"Like I said." She winks and returns the bottle.

"Brat," I grumble, but I am grinning as I tug her toward me.

Piper wraps her arms around my waist, and I gather her in mine. Then she snuggles in tight while I keep vigil, eyes trained on the road to Sweetbriar, and say, "They should be here soon."

"Good," she replies. "That bag of food helped, but I seem to have worked up an appetite again."

"Gee, strange. I wonder how that could have happened," I deadpan.

Her shoulders shake with laughter. "You're incorrigible."

Smiling, I tighten my arms around her and rest my chin on her head after pressing a kiss there. Piper sighs and snuggles deeper into my warmth. We stay like that for a while, watching the highway for headlights.

"Hey, handsome?" Piper asks, her voice is soft and sleepy.

"Yeah?"

"Thank you for tonight." She tilts her head back to look at me. "It was perfect."

"Even with everything that went wrong?" I ask, sounding uncertain.

Sure, the date will end on a good note—as long as the tow truck and Beckham arrive sooner rather than later.

But, perfect?

Hardly.

"I know you had this whole elaborate, romantic evening planned," she says, playing with my shirt. "But you didn't have to."

"Didn't I?"

"No!" She pauses for a breath. "We could have spent the evening doing anything, and I would have loved it. Because I got to do it with you."

Those words are a balm that soothes my frayed nerves. Then, the rest of me relaxes when I see two pairs of headlights cresting a hill. The vehicles move towards us from a couple of miles down the road.

We cheer when the Revved Up tow truck pulls off the highway, and the driver, Mal, jumps out. Beckham pulls to a stop behind it, and Ellery rockets out of the passenger side door. Beckham joins me while I explain the situation to Mal, and Ellery rushes over to Piper, throwing her arms around her.

"Are you okay?" Ellery asks with concern.

Piper meets my gaze over Ellery's shoulder. She smiles brightly and says, "Definitely. It was a night to remember."

Based on the intense heat in her gaze, I know the exact moment she is thinking of.

"A night to remember," I echo, grinning back.

Yeah. I will remember this one for years to come.

∗∗∗

Beckham offers to stop at the closest fast-food restaurant on our way home. I am so grateful I may consider giving him my firstborn—or at least letting him name them.

But that could just be my stomach talking.

When the familiar red sign signaling Wendy's comes into view off one of the exits, Beckham turns off the highway. Piper claps excitedly, and I might honestly weep from relief.

I spot maybe two or three late-night people milling about along the edges of the dining area. They seem harmless. One is reading a book while dipping their fries into a Frosty. The other has headphones on and is bobbing their head while taking a massive bite from a burger.

Otherwise, the place is empty.

Now that my cop instincts are sated, I turn toward the front counter to satisfy my hunger. One very bored-looking teenager operates the register. His black hair hangs over his eyes, pushed further down by the Wendy's hat on his head. He is hunched over the counter, staring at nothing in particular. When our group reaches him, he slowly lifts his gaze and blinks.

"Welcome to Wendy's," is his unhurried, monotone greeting. In my head, I call him Sloth—even though his name tag clearly states *Michael*. "May I take your order?"

Sloth looks like he would rather have a root canal, but he dutifully enters everything into the register as we toss it his way. Since they actually ate dinner, Ellery and Beckham each get a Frosty while Piper contemplates the menu. Finally, she orders spicy chicken nuggets.

"Would you like to make that a combo?"

"God, yes."

He stares blankly at her. "Drink?"

With a twinkle in her eye, she leans forward and asks, "Any chance you have a gigantic bottle of hard liquor? Any will do. Vodka, tequila, bourbon. Hell, some wine will work in a pinch. It has been a *day*, let me tell you."

Sloth sighs and lifts an eyebrow. I think. The thick hair covering the upper half of his face makes it difficult to see much.

Still, that eyebrow raise shows more emotion than I have seen on the kid since we walked in.

"Ma'am, this is a Wendy's," he says. He motions vaguely toward the menu behind him. "We don't sell alcohol."

"Well, shoot." She pouts, and I have to smother a laugh with my hand. "Bottled water, then."

My turn. Famished, I order the biggest burger they have and an upsized meal. Piper reaches into her purse for her wallet, but I clamp my hand down on her wrist and glare at her.

"Nu-uh, little bird," I scold, "this is still a date."

Behind me, Ellery quietly gushes to Beckham, and I have to force myself not to roll my eyes. In front of me, Sloth looks back and forth between us, showing the first bit of emotion all night. Disbelief. Then, his attention shifts entirely to me.

"Dude," he says. "Wendy's? You need to work on your game."

Beckham chokes on a laugh behind me, and I flip him the middle finger over my shoulder. Like hell am I going to take dating advice from a kid with more hair on his head than his junk. He looks barely old enough to drive.

"Thanks, *dude*," I say, grabbing our empty drink cups from the counter. "I'll keep that in mind."

We opt to eat in the car. Everyone is exhausted, Piper and I especially. As soon as she finishes scarfing down her food, she nestles against my side and promptly falls asleep. I lift my arm so I can gather her close. Then I shift in my seat so my chest becomes her pillow.

Ellery falls asleep soon after. Her wild red curls peek out from the passenger seat headrest. I hear her quiet snores.

Beckham looks fondly over at her, chuckling and shaking his head before turning his eyes back to the road.

After a minute or two of silence, he clears his throat. When I tear my attention from Piper—watching the gentle rise and fall of her chest—my gaze meets his icy-blue one in the rearview mirror.

"Happiness looks good on you," he says quietly.

"What do you mean?" I ask.

"You faked it well over the years—but c'mon man, I know you. You weren't happy. Not really." He shifts his glance to Piper briefly before looking back at me. "Not like you are with her."

"Yeah," I say, watching the peaceful smile on her face. "Guess maybe I was a little lost before."

Beckham hums in agreement. "You deserve to be happy. I'm glad you found it again."

"Me, too."

"Just don't run her off this time, yeah?" Beckham's voice is teasing, but when I look back up at him—despite the smile on my face—my promise is as serious as they come.

"Not a chance in hell, buddy."

Now that I have Piper back in my arms, I am never letting her go.

"Ma'am, this is a Wendy's."

INTERLUDE 5

Five

- Friday at 12:45 am -

Unknown number: I made you

Unknown number: You owe me

Missed call.

Missed call.

- Friday at 1:15 am -

Unknown number: PICK UP THE DAMN PHONE

- Friday at 4:35 am -

Unknown number: You've obviously fucking forgotten who's in charge here

Unknown number: Time for a reminder

This number has been blocked.

Chapter 24
Possession

Piper

***You know better**, Piper.*
Why did you let your guard down?

Because the last several weeks have been so wonderful that I let myself get complacent. False feelings of comfort and peace wrapped me up in a safe little bubble, and I let myself be consumed by the love of my family, friends, and *Simon*.

Simon especially.

I should have realized that a storm was brewing and the outside world would soon come crashing in. But, no. I stayed willfully oblivious.

No chance of that anymore.

"How bad is it?" I ask.

On the other side of the phone, Rue sighs. "Well, it's not good. But I think I can do damage control. At the very least, get the magazine to post a retraction and start pulling the article."

"Yeah." I rub my fingers along my forehead, where a headache is starting to form. "Not going to help with people who already saw it, but better than nothing." Tears prick at my eyes. I blink them back, refusing to let that bastard get the better of me. "I should have expected Cedric to do something. I *did* expect him to. Just, maybe not so soon."

Panic threatens to drown me. I am just barely treading water. Suddenly needing to move, to bring air back into my lungs, I pace back and forth across the living room rug.

"Cedric must have been stockpiling anything he could get his hands on," Rue says absently, looking over the article again. "Some of this stuff goes back years. Taken out of context…"

Taken out of context, *indie rock's sparkling princess has fallen from grace*. It's just the type of salacious story trash rags would devour. I can only imagine how far and fast this fire will spread, with Cedric pouring accelerant onto the flames.

"Send me the link."

At the end of the line, Ruth falls silent. After a particularly long pause, she asks, "Are you sure?"

"No, I'm not." I sigh, then add, "But I need to know."

"Okay. Sending now."

I hear the quiet ping of a text message. Putting Rue on speaker, I stare at the link she sent while my thumb hovers over the screen. But every tendon and ligament is locked in place, and no matter how hard my brain tries to send a signal to my hand, I cannot make myself press the link. Instead, the weight of my situation presses down until I sink back against the wall and slip to the floor.

"No more pretending," I say. My voice is bitter and drips with sarcasm. "I thought if I ran and hid, Cedric would leave me be. Stupid. The text messages should have been evidence enough."

"You aren't stupid," Rue argues. "You needed out, and you got out. You needed time, so you took it. We will get through this, Piper. Okay? You've got me in your corner, and you know how tenacious I am. I'll get you through this through sheer willpower if need be."

I laugh, then. "Yeah, yeah. My very own pit-bull."

"That's better." She chuckles. "Look, I'm going to do my best to fix this. You focus on your music. The faster you can put something out, the quicker this will all blow over."

I'm not so sure about that, but I know better than to voice the concern. Instead, I say, "Thanks, Rue. Truly."

"Anytime, babe."

After we hang up, the facade I had been holding up crashes to the ground as every feeling I have pushed back rushes to the surface. I thought I had time. I've only just begun to find my voice again. The thought of losing that has my pulse thundering in my ears.

Sensing my distress, Ozzy and Cooper hovered nearby throughout the phone conversation. Now that I am on the ground, they rush over and nuzzle against me. I bury my hands and my face into their fur and fight back a wave of sobs.

I will not cry.

I refuse.

The time for tears is over.

Lifting my phone again, I select Daisy's number and hit the button to connect. She answers after a few rings.

"Hey, sis!" she says brightly.

"Hey, Daisy." I hesitate momentarily, the muffled background noise making me realize she's not home. I ask, "Are you busy right now?"

"Just taking some photos for the Quill's website." I hear a door opening in the background when Daisy steps outside.

"Sorry." I cringe when I realize today is Thursday, and regular people work on weekdays. "You're working. Of course, you're working. I can call back later."

But as I pull the phone away from my ear, Daisy says, "Wait! You sound upset. Is everything okay?"

The concern in her voice wraps around me, and I take a shuddery breath. "No. Not really. I didn't mean to bother you, though, and—"

"No, stop right there," she scolds. "You're my sister, Pip. If you're upset, if something happened, I want to help."

"But—"

"No buts. Now, what do you need?"

With a sigh, I relent. "Would you mind coming over? Just for a few minutes."

"I'll be there in ten."

After a shaky goodbye, I hang up the phone and snuggle up with Ozzy and Cooper on the floor, too tired to move. Daisy finds me like that after she arrives. I hear the doorbell ring and groan, still unable and unwilling to do anything more than lift my phone.

- 3:10 pm -

Piper: Door is unlocked. I'm in the living room

Daisy: OK

A second later, the front door creaks open and closes.

"I brought lunch!" Daisy calls out. Her footsteps click on the hardwood, muffling when she hits the living room carpet. As soon as she sees me, Daisy gasps and rushes over.

"Piper, oh my god," she cries, "what happened?"

"I'm fine, I'm fine." I sit up and wince when I see the disbelief on her face. "Okay, maybe not *fine*. But I'm not hurt or anything."

"Maybe not physically. Your face is telling me a different story." Daisy sighs, shakes her head, and then holds her hands to help me to my feet. "Let's sit on the couch like humans, and you can explain what's happening."

After we settle on the cushions, it takes me a full minute to speak. But once the floodgates open, the words pour out of me until I have laid everything Rue told me at Daisy's feet.

When I finish, she rocks back and flushes with anger. "That son of a bitch," she hisses. "Let me see the article."

After a brief hesitation, I hand her my phone. "I was hoping you would, maybe, read it out loud. The article. I can't bring myself to look at it, but…" I swallow thickly. "I also can't fight this blind."

"Alright," she says slowly, clicking the screen link pointing to the article Rue sent me. Then, she begins to read:

> **Songbyrd has Flown the Coop:**
> *Indie rock's prolific nightingale and her meteoric fall from grace*
>
> Sources close to the singer/songwriter have revealed that the performer disappeared after her last show in early October, forcing the record label to cancel several interviews and other prearranged engagements. While they have kept the nature of her disappearance hidden from the public, new information has leaked that shows what Songbyrd has been doing on her impromptu sabbatical.
>
> And things look bleak.
>
> Evidence shows that Songbyrd has fallen prey to the rock god's triple threat: sex, drugs, and alcohol. Sources have confirmed that Songbyrd was placed in immediate protective custody and is currently undergoing rehabilitation therapy in an undisclosed location to protect her privacy at this time. Officials at the rehab facility have declined to comment.

"Sissy. These photos..." Daisy breathes out shakily, her face turning ashen while she scrolls through photos attached to the article. "This is sick, what this bastard did. Whatever these photos are, they look 100% real."

"Rue thinks Cedric stockpiled any potential blackmail material over the years." I wave my hand toward the phone. "Exhibit A."

"Holy—is that Simon?" Daisy pulls the phone closer to her face, squinting. "Wow, that's hot…"

"Daisy!" I leap to my feet and snatch the phone from her hands.

Then I almost drop it.

She has a photo pulled up that I immediately recognize as Simon and me, cropped to show only his neck down. His hand grips my chin while I kneel on the floor at his feet.

"How did they get a photo of that?" I ask, voice breaking.

Unease skates down my spine while I scroll through the photos.

How can this be happening?

My stomach turns at each recent photo I come across. Several sexual scenes—each one more explicit than the last—have been cropped to show a faceless man and framed to appear in a different place. With a little bit of photo magic, anyone will think that I have numerous sexual partners.

Worse still are the photos that show me with Simon and his fellow on-duty officers dressed in full uniform. The photographer also cropped these below the necks. Between the expressions on my face—all carefully taken to make me look angry, petulant, or sad—and the altered context of each picture, people will assume the worst, especially with captions that depict me getting arrested for drunk and disorderly conduct or charged with possession of illegal goods.

This "anonymous source" laid out my whole life in brilliant, high-definition color and then twisted it into something dark.

Another disturbing thought weasels into my mind and takes hold: whoever took these photos knows that I am in Sweetbriar.

Someone figured out where I live and the house I am renting.

Someone knows where Simon lives and works, and they know he and I have started a relationship.

Someone has been *watching* me.

My shaking hand hovers over the current photo as I swipe again. The following image appears very different from the others. An open lingerie drawer takes up the entirety of the frame, along with several bottles of prescription medications—some opened so that pills scatter throughout the fabrics.

More drugs.

Of course.

I almost swipe past until my eye catches on the image's background.

This time, I *do* drop the phone.

Daisy curses, grabbing for it before it smashes against the floor. When she looks up and sees my frozen, wide-eyed stare, Daisy jolts forward and grips me by the shoulders.

I barely feel her. My mind focuses firmly on the image burned into my mind.

"What is it?" Daisy demands. "What did you see? Piper?"

Based on the frantic tone in her voice, I must be as pale as a ghost. I feel lightheaded, and dark spots dance along the edges of my vision.

Daisy gently leads me back to the couch and helps me sit. Then she perches on the edge of the coffee table across from me and takes my ice-cold hands.

"Hey." Her voice, small and worried, calls my name and says, "Say something. You're starting to freak me out."

My mouth opens and closes while I gasp for air. When the adrenaline rush starts to recede, I feel like I just went ten rounds with a grizzly bear, and I slump back against the couch cushions while Ozzy and Cooper rest their heads on my lap.

"That photo," I rasp, barely able to form the words. "That's my bedroom, Daisy. Somebody is stalking me and taking pictures, and they've been *inside my house.*"

Daisy's ashen face slowly fills with a red flush of fury. "You need to tell Simon."

"What?" I bolt to my feet. "No! No."

Daisy sits back, an incredulous look on her face. "What do you mean, no?"

"I mean, absolutely not." I press my hands against my ears and rush out into the middle of the living room. Maybe I can block out Daisy's words by sheer, stubborn willpower. When I whirl back to face her, she stares at me, trying to puzzle me out.

Good luck with that, sis.

"Daisy, I can't tell Simon. I-I'm not ready." Wringing my hands together, I begin to pace. "What will he think of me when he finds out?"

Tears I have been holding at bay come perilously close to spilling over. Deep inside of me, fear that has been festering like cancer starts to take over, spreading and infecting everything in its path. I am too far into my panic to notice what I say next.

Not until I speak the words into being.

"I'll lose him again, don't you see?" I wrap my arms around my torso, trying and failing to hold myself together. "He'll realize that I'm not worth the trouble, and I'll lose him."

Everything shifts at my confession. Every bit of my composure that I struggle to hold onto fractures. All of my insecurities are bubbling to the surface. Because this relationship with Simon—and this rekindling of our feelings—has barely started. It is new. Fragile. I am scared it cannot survive the fallout.

As horrible as Cedric is and as much damage as he inflicted, Simon is the one who broke me first.

I will never survive if Simon learns the truth and leaves.

My confession hangs heavy between Daisy and me like thick, billowy smoke. It sucks up all the air from the space and leaves a hazy sort of disbelief behind when it dissipates. Our eyes flare in sudden realization.

Daisy's eyes flare in disbelief at the words I said.

My eyes flare in disbelief that I spoke them.

I cover my face and the sob that escapes. A moment later, Daisy gently wraps her hands around my wrists. Instead of using them to tug my hands away from my face, they provide comfort and remind me that I am not alone.

"Piper," Daisy says gently—but with a steely undercurrent. "You will never lose Simon. *Ever*. Do you know why?"

Slowly, I shake my head.

She tugs my wrists, and I reluctantly let my hands fall. However, I am unable to make myself look up. My gaze remains firmly trained on my fingers as they nervously fidget with the fabric of my shirt.

"You will never lose Simon, not now or in the future," she continues, "because you never lost him to begin with."

I do look up, then. Surprise colors my features. "How can you say that?" I demand. "You know what happened."

"Yeah, I do." Daisy sighs heavily. "I know that Simon made a stupid, reckless, monumental mistake. One that he regretted almost immediately. By the time he got his head out of his ass, unfortunately, you were gone, and it was too late."

Daisy rolls her eyes to the ceiling, likely praying for patience. Then she continues. "Do you know that he hounded Mom and Pop for months after you left? He begged them for any news they could share, for your new number when you changed it, and to relay message after message when they held firm and honored your wish to be left alone. You know how much Mom has always loved him. It *killed* her to see him so wrecked.

"They bonded even more after you left because they both felt it was the only way to keep you alive here," she says with a poke to my sternum. "Grace calls it trauma bonding. Why do you think Mom guilted him into continuing to join our family dinners? Why do you think we stayed so close over the years, even after you were gone?"

Hurt flares behind my ribcage, but that burn quickly spreads into shame. I have no one but myself to blame. No one forced me to leave. No one forced me to stay away for so long.

I did all that myself.

Daisy lobbies one final truth bomb at me. "Simon broke *both* your hearts when he ended things. Then you left and broke all of ours."

"I'm sorry," I breathe. "So sorry. I wish I could go back and change how I reacted to everything."

"Stop," Daisy replies, waving my apology away. "I already forgave you. Besides, why should you keep paying for a mistake you made over a decade ago? No one should have to do that." Daisy wraps me in her arms. I sigh into her shoulder, slowly letting go of my guilt.

When she finally releases me, Daisy gives me an earnest look. "Don't you think Simon should get that same consideration?"

I blink in surprise.

Daisy is right.

For all these weeks, I have kept Simon safely at a distance. My fear prevented me from letting him get too close because I would never recover if he shattered me like he did before. I barely recovered the first time.

But I need to stop letting past hurts dictate my present and future happiness.

Moving slowly toward the front window, I take a moment to look out at the world beyond. Outside, life ticks away second by second, never stopping—always moving forward, never turning back, no matter how much we may wish it.

"I'm scared." My admission is quiet. Timid.

But I gave my fear a name, taking away some of its power.

"I know." Daisy comes up beside me, leaning her head on my shoulder. After a moment, she asks, "But what does Pop always say about fear?"

Words I know by heart. "Don't let fear keep you from living," I recite. Something I forgot until recently.

I feel the truth of Pop's words soaking in. Then, a smile slowly stretches across my face—my first genuine smile in hours.

"Pop is right, you know," Daisy says.

"I know." I take a deep breath, then add, "You're right, too."

"Oh?"

"Yeah," I reply. "I need to tell Simon."

No more will I let fear keep me from fully living.

Chapter 25
Fix You

Simon

- 4:00 pm -

Piper: Hey. Can we talk? Once you're off work, I mean

Simon: Sure

Simon: Your place or mine?

Piper: Yours

Nate and I are finishing our patrol when Piper sends me that cryptic text.

"What do you make of this?" I ask, holding my phone up to his face after he parks in front of the station.

Nate frowns, reading the text thread. "Not sure." His gaze flits up to me. "But nothing good ever follows the words, 'Can we talk'?"

"Yeah," I mumble. "That's what I thought."

After a brief and absent hello to Elaine, we head into the building and I make a beeline straight to my desk to grab my things. Amidst a chorus of greetings and gossip-mongering, I toss a cursory wave over one shoulder on my way back out. Let Nate fill the busybodies in. I swear they can be worse than a bunch of old ladies at a book club.

I am on my way as soon as I get behind the wheel. On a good day, it usually takes me ten to fifteen minutes to get home.

Today takes me eight.

When I turn onto the driveway, Piper's SUV sits beside my truck, so I pull the police car up on the other side and shut off the ignition. Instead of moving, I sit there staring at the front door for an indeterminate amount of time, trying to anticipate what will greet me when I open it.

My mind comes up with any number of scenarios.

None are good.

Either way, I know I can no longer put off heading inside. Piper is sure to have heard the engine when I parked. With an audible groan, I lean against the headrest and look at the roof, praying for strength. I then force myself out of the vehicle and up the front steps.

At first, nothing but silence greets me. Piper's bag and shoes are by the front door—I notice them when I remove my boots—but where is she? Frowning, I peek into the living room and find it completely undisturbed.

Maybe Piper went upstairs?

When my foot hits the first step, Ozzy and Cooper appear at the stairs landing. They peer down at me with their massive heads, tongues lolling out, and tails wagging and thwapping each other from behind.

"Hey, boys," I say with a grin. "Guess Mama's in my room, huh?"

Cooper huffs quietly at me, turns, and disappears down the hallway. Ozzy waits to move until I reach the top. I follow behind their massive loping bodies, noting with some confusion that my bedroom looks dark.

In the doorway, I finally notice the pale light of my nightstand lamp. My eyes follow it to where it faintly illuminates the figure curled into a fetal position. Piper has burrowed her head into my pillow, completely covering her face from view. Duchess lay on the bed with her. Piper's arm curls around the spoiled dog, snuggled tightly against her front. Duchess sees me first, and she acknowledges my presence with a twitch of her large, pointed ears and a single thump of her tail. Then her eyes promptly closed, my presence forgotten. I start to chuckle—but then Piper lifts her head, and the laugh dies on my lips.

Piper looks wretched. Her puffy, swollen eyes, red nose, and blotchy face betray her tears. My earlier insecurities fall away in the face of her distress.

"Who?" I grit out, stepping further into the room.

Piper pulls herself to a seated position and gently shifts Duchess out of the way. Then, she wipes under her eyes and, sniffling, asks, "Who, what?"

My chest burns with molten fury, seconds away from erupting. I stride across the room until I loom over Piper.

Reaching up, I catch a stray tear with my thumb before cradling her face with my palm.

"Who do I need to kill?"

Piper spills out a watery laugh at my words. Then she says, "I wish you could."

"Not a joke, baby." My other hand joins the first, cradling the other side of her face and wiping away another droplet.

Since returning to Sweetbriar, Piper shed tears around me only one other time: the night she played her song in my father's study. I can count on one hand the number of times I have ever seen Piper Easton cry. She never used to be prone to tears.

That makes me want to go to war.

"What's all this, then?" I ask, gently prodding.

"I..." Her voice fades away. She reaches up to clasp my hands, and her grip is firm, like she fears I will leave.

Not a fucking chance.

When she opens her mouth to try again, no sound comes out. Frustrated, Piper shakes her head. She tries to block me out by pinching her eyes closed—but that only causes more tears to spill over and down her cheeks. Her hands tremble over mine. Each breath grows increasingly turbulent.

Piper fights hard to keep her composure and tries to hide the rising agitation. None of that will work. I know an anxiety attack when I see one. Ellery used to get them, once upon a time. I recognize the signs.

"Piper." Her name is a soft command—kindly given but still meant to be obeyed.

When her eyes snap open, they have turned glassy and unseeing. An unnatural flush spreads across her cheeks. The skin beneath my hands feels hot.

Fuck.

Carefully, I pry one of my wrists from Piper's rigid fingers. I have no desire to sever the connection completely, but I need to lose the firearm strapped to me if I want to help her. As soon as I have freedom of movement, I unholster the pistol and release the magazine. It drops into the top drawer, where I deposit the rest of the gun to get it out of the way.

I can store the thing properly later.

Right now, Piper needs me.

Gently, I scoop her up out of the bed and into my arms. Her whole body has started to shake—faintly, but enough to worry me. Small hands fist around the fabric of my uniform shirt, and she instinctively curls into my chest. Despite her flushed face, the rest of Piper's body feels cold and clammy.

At my movement, all three dogs clamor to follow me into the bathroom. I have to nudge the door closed with my foot before they can converge.

"Sorry, guys, but I need to take care of your mama. You'll get your turn later." To Piper, I ask, "Think you can stand?"

There is a beat of silence before I hear a muffled "yes."

Good. Her mind is at least somewhat lucid. I sigh in relief and carefully let her slide down and out of my arms, holding her steady until her feet finally touch the floor. Then I press a quick kiss on her forehead. After I turn toward the bathtub, I focus on filling the basin with warm water and checking the temperature every so often.

After adding some bubble bath, I peek at Piper to check-in. She silently watches me work, and her eyes are no longer glassy. However, her face still holds a feverish flush, and her breathing is more ragged than I like. Tremors continue to wrack her body.

While the bath fills up, I stand and step in front of Piper. "Arms up," I instruct.

Slowly, she lifts them into the air. I grip the hem of her shirt and tug it over her head. Then I toss it somewhere in the corner and slowly move around to Piper's back. Unable to help myself, I let my fingers drift along the slope between her neck and shoulder before lightly grazing down her back. There, I reach for the clasp of her bra. A slight shiver runs down her spine at the touch.

Once I discard the bra, I face Piper and crouch at her feet. Then I grip the waistband of her leggings and panties before gently tugging them down to her ankles. I tap her left leg. She lifts it free of the bunched-up fabric. I tap her right leg. She does the same. Over onto the growing pile of discarded clothes they go.

After checking the water, I turn off the tap and stand. I motion for Piper to step close. Then, lifting her into my arms, I help Piper over the lip of the tub until—using my hand for leverage—she lowers herself into the bath.

Once she has settled, I sit on the tile next to the tub.

Other than a one-word command here or there, I say very little. I have no intention of breaking the silence with superfluous chatter, and my focus never strays from Piper and helping her to relax. I start with washing her hair. Since I only have my shampoo (for now), I grab it from the shower and squeeze some into my palm. I lather up my hands while I walk back to the tub.

When I am close enough, I run the shampoo through her thick tresses and then massage her scalp. Piper moans lightly. Her neck arches back to give me better access. I watch the liquid lather in her hair while the suds bubble up and spill over and down her back.

Minute by minute, inch by inch, the panic starts to loosen its hold on her. Meanwhile, I bring a washcloth to her skin and massage some sweet-smelling soap wherever possible. Piper takes a deep breath, lips curling up at the corners. "Peaches," she murmurs.

I shrug. "Your fault that I have an obsession with that scent."

Piper only hums in response. But her expression has relaxed into contentment, which does the talking for her.

Once Piper's body is entirely pliant, her head draped over the back of the clawfoot tub, I move to gather the towels I will soon need. But before I can step back, I feel a hand on my leg. Piper's eyes open, and she holds her bottom lip between her teeth. I bend over and tug it back into place.

I run my thumb gently across the soft skin and ask, "What do you need little bird?"

"You."

So much heat compresses into that one tiny word. I fight back my baser instincts and shake my head. Piper needs comfort. I am not about to take advantage of her in this state.

"Baby..." I trail off.

"Sorry." Her cheeks flush, but this time, they heat from embarrassment. "It's just that your touch is soothing. We don't have to do anything, but I need you to hold me." Her expression turns pleading. "Please?"

This time, I groan. How the hell do I say no to that?

Keeping our gazes locked, I reach up and unbutton my shirt. Piper follows the motion with her eyes. Once it falls, I toss the garment onto the growing pile of clothes in the corner, quickly followed by the rest. I motion for Piper to scoot forward. Then I climb into the warm water behind her. We fit snugly even for a two-person tub, though I like the closeness.

It takes me a moment to situate myself behind her—but after I do, Piper settles against me and lets her head fall back against the slope of my shoulder. Her hair tickles my nose when she turns her head into my neck. My shampoo's sandalwood and bourbon scent blends with the peach bubble bath. I breathe deeply. The unique aroma settles into my lungs.

After a moment to adjust, I let my hands slide around to the front of her body, one arm slipping under her breasts, the other resting above to hold her to me. Her chest rises and then falls in a deep sigh. With one hand directly over her heart, I can feel how its previously erratic heartbeat has settled into a calm cadence.

Mine soon matches its slow pace. Together, we drift in a kind of dreamy haze. It feels good to enjoy each other's bodies like this. Piper has always been able to ground and center me like no one else. I know she will be okay if I can give her even a fraction of that back.

"How are you feeling?" I murmur in her ear.

She hums. "Wonderful."

"Good." Then I smirk. "Brat."

Her pulse jumps, but I can hear the smile in Piper's voice when she asks, "What did I do now?"

"You derailed my plans," I said, pulling her close enough to rest my chin on her shoulder. "I had noble intentions bringing you in here. Get you out of your head, soothe whatever had flipped on your fight-or-flight response. But there you went, biting that pouty lip and flashing me those pretty green eyes, and now I'm naked in the bathtub with you."

"Because I needed you."

Pressing a kiss to her neck, I reply, "Exactly why I'm here."

After a beat of silence, Piper says, "You did do all that, you know. You got me out of my head and caught the anxiety attack before it got much worse." She pauses briefly. "How did you know that I was having an attack?"

Piper shifts and turns in my arms so she can look at me. The feel of her fingers playing with my chest hair while she speaks is distracting. I cover her hand with my own to still them.

"Ellery started getting them after Mom and Dad died," I say. "It took months of therapy for her to get a handle on them. In the meantime, I read everything I could to know the signs and what to do."

"Wow. I didn't know that." I catch a hint of hurt in Piper's voice.

Shit. I lift my hands to her face in an attempt to stave off a relapse. Then I say, "We didn't know what it was at first, and Ellery—she didn't want anyone to know. I had to honor that."

Piper nods. Slowly, her expression clears. Her gaze dips down to my lips before flickering back up. I shake my head and chuckle.

"What am I going to do with you?" I ask, but the question is rhetorical.

She answers, anyway, with a slight shrug. "You could kiss me."

Good idea. I hold Piper's head still and cover her mouth with mine. Just a gentle press of my lips, though, lingering for a moment before I pull back. Piper whimpers.

"None of that," I admonish. "Anyway, bath-time is over."

Gripping Piper by the shoulders and moving her away, I brace my arms on either side of the tub and stand. Then, I help her up. She continues to pout while I step out onto the plush rug before reaching out to bring her with me.

Once Piper stands steady on solid ground, I grab the closest warm towel. With gentle strokes, I wipe her down from head to toe until every drop of water is gone. Then, taking the towel from my hands, she proceeds to soak up the excess moisture clinging to her hair. I quickly dry off with another towel.

After tossing them off into the corner with the rest of the laundry, I scoop Piper up and into my arms again, bridal style. Then I head back into the bedroom. Her quiet laugh settles in my chest like a balm.

"I can walk, you know," she says.

"Maybe." I stop at the bedside before setting her down. "But I like holding you."

She watches me with curiosity shining in her eyes while I turn away and head toward my dresser. I rummage for a few things, quickly slipping into flannel pants and a plain white t-shirt. The second shirt stays in my hand until I return to Piper and hold it out expectantly, motioning for Piper to lift her arms into the air.

With a deep sigh that contrasts with the happy little smile on her face, Piper does as I instruct. I slip the soft cotton over her head, arms, and down. Once it is free of its confines, I let go and watch the hemline drop down to rest against her upper thighs. It dwarfs her slight frame and makes her look young—and fragile, even though I know she is nothing of the sort.

Reaching behind her, I drag the comforter and sheets down to make an opening. "Get in, little bird."

Piper's gaze flickers to the bed and back. She crawls onto the mattress, moves to the headboard, and settles back against the pillows. Her eyes track me while I tuck her in. When I slip under the covers, I move into the middle of the bed and pull Piper against me. With her back to my front, the little spoon to my big spoon, I relish how her body feels against mine. Even after all this time, we are a perfect fit.

"Not that I'm complaining," she says, "but is there a reason you're putting us to bed this early?"

Tugging her closer, I say, "Because I have had a long-ass day, and you need rest after putting your body through all that strain."

"I thought you wanted to talk." Even though she says the words, they sound like the very last thing she wants to do.

"It can wait." I kiss the side of her head. "Now, rest."

"Okay," she mumbles, sleep already pulling her under. The poor thing had no clue how exhausted she would be after that ordeal.

But she has me to take care of her from now on.

I will never again take that role for granted.

"Who?

"Who, what?

"Who do I need to kill?"

Chapter 26
Bad Dream

Piper

His name is Cedric Thomas.

We met in Nashville when I was twenty-five years old. I lived there then and stayed after college to focus on building experience and, hopefully, a fan base. It worked well. I was making decent money—I even got to do a couple of tours with more prominent names in the area—but the pay was inconsistent. I had to supplement with odd jobs in between my singing gigs.

The first time I saw him was at Bootleggers Inn, one of my regular haunts. I had just finished my set and sat at the bar to grab a drink to celebrate a good night's work.

A stranger was sitting at the other end of the bar, someone I had never seen before in this place. Out of the corner of my eye, I saw him stand and move closer, settling into a bar stool two down from mine. He caught me watching and smiled. "That was something," he said, nodding toward the stage. "You're very talented."

Flushing with pleasure and embarrassment, I stared at the bourbon in my glass. I never even drank the stuff, but I felt nostalgic every time I played. My songs always made me think of Simon.

Clearing my throat, I replied, "Thanks," and then inwardly cringed at my lack of social skills.

He didn't seem to mind. "I'm Cedric. Cedric Thomas."

"Piper Easton. Though, uh, when I'm up there"—I waved a hand awkwardly at the stage—"I go by Songbyrd."

"That fits. You have a beautiful voice, like a nightingale." His smile grew with the blush on my cheeks. He motioned at the seat in between us. "Do you mind...?"

After I shook my head, he shifted over. Then his hand slipped into his shirt pocket. Pulling out a business card, he silently handed it to me and then waited.

When I looked down at the words, my eyes flared.

Cedric E. Thomas
A&R Manager
Evermore Records, Inc.

"Evermore Records," I read out loud. Then, I returned the business card to the counter, pretending to look unaffected.

"That's right. The label I work for is part of Evermore Media. Are you familiar?"

He had to be joking. Everyone knew who Evermore Media was. It was a juggernaut in the music scene—honestly, in every part of the entertainment industry, including music, film, and television.

Then I realized he was name-dropping, letting me know what a big deal this chance meeting was. Of course, I was impressed. Why wouldn't I be? But I didn't let any of that come through in my expression or voice. I needed to play it cool.

"So you're, what, a talent scout?"

Cedric smiled. It was a nice smile attached to an appealing face. He also looked older, maybe in his early to mid-thirties. Knowing he worked in this industry longer than I had comforted me somewhat.

"Not quite. Yes, I'm here scouting the local talent, but I'm a talent manager. I work closely with my clients and manage their careers." I nodded without comment. After a few breaths, Cedric leaned closer, his dark eyes gleaming. "Look. I'm going to skip straight to the point, Ms. Easton. You would be a perfect fit with our record label. Your voice, lyrics, captivating stage presence, and unique sound all recommend you. Based on tonight's packed house, I can already see what a sound investment signing you would be."

With those words, Cedric lounged back in his chair, studying me for a moment before continuing. "What would you say to a trip to New York City to talk more? We can take a tour of the facilities. Maybe spend some time in the on-site recording studio."

What would I say? I would say that this whole conversation was a dream come true. I bit my lip, carefully considering his words. Soon enough, curiosity and excitement got the better of me, and I could not stop the giddy smile that stretched across my face.

"I would say, Mr. Thomas," I replied, "that I'm ready whenever you are."

***

Our chance meeting happened in the spring. Within a few weeks, I signed with Evermore Records, was provided an expensive condo in New York, and completed the last song on Songbyrd's debut album, *Midnight Serenade*.

By the time I hit this milestone in my career, I could choose each song from an impressive catalog of lyrics, music, and complete songs that I had written and composed over the years. Ones I had spent a lot of time perfecting. That album was my catharsis. It was the first step of letting go of the past and moving into the future.

Cedric was there the whole time, just waiting in the wings for his chance to swoop in. He helped curate the tracks to appeal to a broader audience. With a few tweaks to the music here and a few musical adjustments, my debut turned out better than I ever could have dreamed.

And he was right in making those adjustments. Seemingly overnight, my social media following doubled—almost tripled. My fan base grew, and so did my trust in him.

When I started my first tour that summer, Cedric was there every step of the way. He guided and mentored me, making me a "better version" of myself. And while I was traveling, he was my anchor. We talked often. He gave me advice and listened to my troubles. He told me about the other artists he was working with.

We grew close in that first year. Our relationship felt more like good friends than manager and client—I needed close friends then. I had lost the ability to trust easily. The relationship I had with my family, save Grace, was tenuous. Having someone in my corner became as necessary as breathing, and Cedric cared about me. He was looking out for my best interests.

Things were good.

Great even—until they weren't.

Everything in my life fell apart gradually. So gradually, in fact, that when my therapist asked me when I think it started, I failed to pinpoint an exact moment in time. She explained that, in cases of gaslighting, sometimes it takes years before abuse starts. Early in the relationship, the primary focus is to build trust and make yourself invaluable to the victim until they trust you implicitly in knowing and doing what is best for them.

At first, the lies and manipulations Cedric fed me were few and far between. They also started small. Most people would completely overlook these types of deception, and I never caught onto them until it was too late.

First, he added a well-placed comment on my word choice: *Piper, this chorus is perfect, but I'm concerned with the bridge. Why don't we try something a little different?*

Second, he remarked off-handedly about how much I would fidget when anxious: *You can't let them see you nervous, sweetheart. Sharks in suits rule this world. If they smell even the tiniest drop of blood in the water, they will swarm you, and they will tear you apart.*

Third, he worried about my health: *You aren't sleeping well. Is your insomnia getting worse? Maybe you need a sleep aid. I know a few different ones you could try.*

He strategically placed his words each time, speaking them lovingly and concerned. They were things a friend would say to another friend when they wanted to help. So I listened. I made the changes. Then, he would reward me for my efforts in some way to reinforce that he cared. And, in the rare instances when I questioned him, he would turn things around on me.

You're too sensitive. To survive in this industry, you need to grow thicker skin.

I never said that, Piper. You're imagining things. See, this is why you need to take better care of yourself.

Once, Cedric called me his little songbird, knowing how that nickname was a special one from my dad—who died when I was young. He had to know I wouldn't take it well. But when I told Cedric never to call me that again, do you know what he said?

Lighten up, sweetheart. It was just a joke.

Then he got angry with me.

You let that, what's his name—your ex—call you little bird. That's pretty damn close to songbird. Cedric scoffed. *So what, that man is the exception? Where is he now? Is he the one here, helping you chase your dreams? Oh, wait, no. That's me. See, this is why nobody likes you. You're selfish. You have no appreciation, and it's why you don't have any friends. They've all left because you're too much to handle.*

Cedric never called me his little songbird again. I got what I wanted. But somehow, I was the one who apologized in the end instead of him. I was the one who left the argument feeling like I had done something wrong.

As horrible as he had been, as cruel as his words were, Cedric lashed out because of me. It was my fault.

✳✳✳

Just after my twenty-sixth birthday, things started to escalate. Cedric had been working with other artists throughout our relationship. I knew that was how the business worked. But I failed to notice that, around that time, Cedric began focusing much more of his time and energy on me.

My contract was ending in just a few weeks. Before it did, Cedric approached me with a proposition: *I think the time is right for me to branch out independently. I want to build a smaller, more intimate label. I want to provide a way to help more independent artists like you by giving them that foot in the door.*

Cedric never kept a secret from me that he wanted to start a label eventually. We bonded over our shared dreams in the early days, so that news was no surprise to me. What surprised me was the timeline and his desire for me to join him.

Sign with me. You can be my star client, the shining example everyone wants to emulate. He made it sound so easy and perfect, adding, *Together, we can take the world by storm. You and me, we'll be unstoppable.*

Evermore Media had already discussed extending my contract for at least three more albums. The best part of the new deal was that I would have non-exclusive rights, and the label would grant me ownership of the music I created. I had a guaranteed spot within a reputable company to continue growing my brand.

How could I turn that down?

Cedric used every trick in the book to ensure that I did. He planted doubt about the contract, Evermore Media, and my ability to manage my career. Those seeds quickly took root. Cedric fed and watered them until they wrapped around every inch of me and started to choke. By the time my contract ended, I feared that everything would crash down around me if I didn't sign with his label.

He said that he knew what was best for me.

He said that he wanted me to succeed.

Stupidly, I believed him.

After Cedric registered the label, and once Dreamscape Music was officially under the Evermore Media umbrella, the very first thing Cedric did was have me sign on the dotted line. He sat with me to review a new Exclusive Recording Contract with the label. He explained all the details it would entail, completely disregarded my concerns about the nature of the agreement, and twisted my words and emotions until I had no idea which way was up.

I finally signed the thing to get it over with.

Besides, I had good reason. After all, Cedric led me this far. He knew what was best. He had been doing this a lot longer than me. More than that, I trusted him.

Didn't I?

Maybe not as much as I thought. My twenty-seventh birthday came and went while Cedric was busy getting the rest of Dreamscape Music off the ground. During that time, I had a little breathing room and wrote a ton of music. I completed my second album, *Migratory*, and even planned a good bit of my third album.

In that brief moment, I felt invincible. I was on top of the world, riding high on the success I had worked hard for, and I was finally beginning to see the fruits of my labor.

But Cedric continued to dig his claws into me. He had a much easier time inserting himself into every facet of my life now that my name was beside his on the contract. I had unwittingly signed away my soul to the devil.

There was no more reason to hide behind false accolades and fake concerns. At last, Cedric had me where he wanted me. He began to critique my clothing choices, style, hair and makeup, and piercings. At first, Cedric only mentioned little things: I needed to tone down the grunge a little, or ripped jeans didn't look professional.

Then, the criticisms started to become more significant. More personal.

Piper, he would say, *you're going to a charity event at one of the most prestigious venues in the city.* Then, he would wave a hand in my direction. *Don't you think you should wear something a little less thrift-store vintage? We want to ensure you catch the right people's attention tonight.*

So I changed from my vintage cocktail dress and leather jacket into a little black dress he had picked out of my closet.

Sweetheart, I love that messy rocker-chic hair on you—very sexy—but I worry it's too much for today's interviews. Cedric would take my hands and look down at me, eyes alight with tenderness and concern. *This show is on a very conservative station. How about we try something else? Tone down that vibrant purple and give it a more timeless style so we don't offend anyone.*

I entered that salon as a completely different person than the one who had walked out again. Of course, Cedric was there, watching the stylist work. He quickly gave suggestions and vetoed stylistic choices that went against his vision of my brand. I did nothing. I just stewed in silence, watching a transformation I had no say in and never asked for.

The stylist dyed my hair back to its original white-blonde color, with highlights and lowlights that made me look like I belonged in a teeny bopper's music video, not an indie rock album. She then smoothed the edges of my choppy, asymmetrical bob and evened out both sides until they were perfectly symmetrical—and *boring*.

By the time the appointment was over, I felt like a stranger in my skin.

Cedric's driver took us straight to the interview after my appointment. Then, the makeup artist lathered me in clown paint meant to cover up the real me. But I went onto that show and used every ounce of my Southern charm. By the end of the episode, I had the audience eating out of the palm of my hand, the hosts were begging for another interview, and Cedric had such a proud look on his face that I faltered for just a moment and thought, *It was just a little hair dye and styling cream—nothing to get worked up over.*

But I knew, deep down, that wasn't the issue.

Cedric could sense that I was upset. As soon as we were in the back of the car, I turned to stare pointedly out the window. That was when he invaded my personal space. He got into my face and snipped, "You need to stop this little tantrum. Right now."

"Excuse me?"

"You heard me."

I turned slowly in my seat, feeling a sliver of unease run down my spine. Cedric's voice was stern, and his words vibrated with barely restrained anger. I had never heard that particular emotion come out of his mouth before. At least, he had never directed it at me before.

As soon as I fully faced him, I asked, "Why?"

"Why, what?"

"Why all these changes, Cedric?" I motioned toward myself. "When we first met, that person caught your attention. She was the

one with the songs you praised. She was the one you wanted to sign. What's so different now? Why am I no longer enough?"

"Stop making this all about you," he scoffed. "This is business, Piper. You knew when you signed up that you would have to make sacrifices for your career."

"Well, yeah," I argued, "but I thought that meant changing around some lyrics or shifting my wardrobe slightly. Not a complete overhaul of my personality and everything that makes me who I am."

"And look at how far you've come, huh?" His eyes flashed dangerously. "After all I've done for you, this is how you repay me? By questioning my motives?"

I felt a twinge of guilt at that. Cedric had done a lot for me these past couple of years: more than I ever expected and more than I ever could have dreamed. But I was afraid that if I let him get away with this much now, what did that mean for the future?

"I'm only asking you to help me understand." I shake my head. "I thought—"

"See, that's the problem." He leaned forward, jabbing a finger in my direction. "You overthink. You also think you know better than me. I've been doing this for over a decade, and it's my job to ensure you're always the best version of yourself."

Another pang of guilt invaded my chest cavity—more brutal this time. Maybe I was overreacting. Perhaps I needed to step back and look at everything surrounding me.

Maybe this was how things needed to be.

My face flushed in embarrassment. "I'm sorry. You're right." I deflated, looking down at my lap. "You know this industry best, and I need to remember that."

I felt Cedric's fingers under my chin and fought a flinch. He gently tugged my face in his direction so I could look at him. The smile on his face soothed some of my anxiety.

"That's better," he said.

His gaze flitted down to my lips and held. My breath stuttered, and every muscle in my body locked up. As though he could read the confusion and discomfort flooding my system, Cedric dropped his hand and leaned back in his seat.

Once his attention was off me, I shoved back as far as possible. Then, angling my body toward the window, I pressed my fevered forehead to the cool glass. I spent the rest of the ride in silence, watching the world pass by outside while I tried to calm the turmoil brewing on the inside.

✳✳✳

Before Cedric, Rue was the only constant in my life (other than Grace, who lived on the outskirts of Nashville). She and I met in college. We started as roommates during the first year and became best friends. When she learned I was a music major and an aspiring singer/songwriter, she quickly offered her services as a budding entrepreneur who wanted to work as a virtual assistant.

There was no one I trusted more than her.

But whenever she tried to tell me her concerns about Cedric, I looked the other way, made excuses, and told her she didn't know what she was talking about.

After all, she didn't know him like I did.

Grace tried, too. She was the only member of my family who stubbornly refused to let me rip them from my life. As a child psychiatrist, I'm sure Grace saw all the signs I had willfully ignored. So, despite all the poison Cedric fed me, despite my anger when she would continually try to get me to see reason, she stayed.

She and Rue continued to blast me with the truth. I continued to pretend I couldn't see it.

But I could.

I think that was the worst part. Some part of me knew what was happening. I had fallen so deep into the hole by then that I couldn't see any glimmer of hope in the perpetual darkness. Despite their cries and their pleas for me to open my eyes, I couldn't.

Because what if he was right? What if I was genuinely worthless and unlovable and lost my one chance for happiness by breaking free of those bindings? I was scared and felt so completely alone. Cedric was the only thing I had to hold onto.

He had made sure of it.

Bit by bit, Cedric tore apart my identity and refashioned me into a doll—dainty, fragile, vapid—something to pose, look at, and admire.

He turned me into something with no mind of its own.

I think you need to work on dropping the Southern accent. It's cute but a tiny country bumpkin to appeal to a broad audience.

This music is good, but it's a little too rock-and-roll. That was okay when you were starting, but if you want to launch yourself into the next level, you will think more mainstream.

Do you want to hang out with people of that caliber?

I don't think your parents have your best interests at heart.

Your sisters are just trying to manipulate you. They've always been jealous of your talent. I see the real you, and I'm the one you should put your trust in.

These lyrics are fantastic, but...

You look beautiful, but...

But...

But...

But...

Cedric repeatedly drilled those words into my head until I eventually believed them. Until his voice melded into mine, and I couldn't tell the two of them apart.

Until his lies became my truth.

Even from the beginning, the lines between professional and personal blurred. What started as a professional friendship—at least in my eyes—quickly turned into a profoundly personal one. Whenever I began creeping up to a boundary I didn't want to cross, Cedric found a way to manipulate me. It was a slippery slope that I unwittingly stepped onto, and I was halfway down the mountain before I even realized I had fallen.

I was exhausted—physically, mentally, and emotionally—from trying to live up to his expectations. I was tired of constantly feeling on edge, waiting for the other shoe to drop or for Cedric to find fault with something I did.

There was no point in holding onto what little bits of myself Cedric would dangle in front of me like a carrot. He used them as bait to continually get me to fall in line. Somewhere along the way, even those stopped mattering. What was one tiny piece of my autonomy compared to an ocean of conformity that had swallowed me whole?

So I gave up trying to keep my identity, and he gave up all pretenses. Day by day, he revealed more and more of the monster hidden behind the mask. As time went on, our relationship twisted and changed, becoming increasingly abusive. Verbally, physically, emotionally, and sexually. And none of it was a power grab. It was all just a sick game to Cedric. He didn't have to break me to get me to do what he wanted by then.

I was already broken.

He was just a predator that liked to play with his meal.

As soon as the door to the recording studio clicked closed behind me, something shifted in the air, and I felt a chill that had nothing to do with the weather. Unease started to creep under my skin. As I walked toward my car, my steps hastened, and I held my keys between my knuckles. Thankfully, the street was well-lit, and I parked directly under a street lamp. I knew it would be dark when I finished recording, and I didn't want to take any chances.

When the car came into view under the dim yellow light, I noticed a prominent figure leaning against the passenger door. I faltered until I realized it was Cedric. It did nothing to ease my fear but only heightened it. Cedric looked down at his phone, his legs crossed at the ankle. When he heard my footsteps, he lifted his head, and I shivered at the predatory smile he gave me.

"Cedric," I said, voice holding a note of resignation. There was no point in asking why he was here. He never gave a reason; he just expected me to fall in line.

"You sang well tonight," he said, "albeit a bit lifeless. Are you sleeping well?"

I fought the urge to roll my eyes. Cedric knew very well that I wasn't. "I'm fine," I gritted out. "Just anxious to finish these songs."

Cedric stood and closed the space between us. When his hand reached up to rest on my cheek, I closed my eyes, forcing myself not to flinch.

He hummed quietly, gripping my chin, forcing my eyes open when he yanked me closer. His other hand slid down my back to the curve of my ass. "Get in the car, Piper," he growled. "I'll drive you home."

Which meant he was staying the night.

All the fight drained out of me. Feeling weighed down and near tears, I slipped into the front seat and buckled myself in. Then, I spent the ride home with my forehead pressed against the frosty glass, pretending I was far from here.

✳✳✳

My third album, *Gilded Cage*, released just a few months before I turned twenty-nine and was my most successful to date. It was also the album that sounded the least like me. Everything about it, including the lyrics and the music, was handpicked and approved by Cedric and his team. Despite Dreamscape Music having grown quite a bit over the past two years, I was still his giant cash cow. Because of that, I received the lion's share of his obsessive focus.

Lucky me.

It was a hard pill to swallow, knowing Cedric had never really cared about me or my music, even though some of me had long suspected. He only wanted to turn me into whatever would make him the most money: another cookie-cutter pop princess.

So, when *Gilded Cage* went Platinum in its first week, Cedric started planning a rigorous schedule for my next tour. I was on the road beginning in April and would travel around the country for six months. Just in time for the holidays, he expected me to spend every waking hour in the recording studio for album number four.

To say I was burnt out would be an understatement, but what I thought or felt held no importance to Cedric and would not change what he would force me to do. Our contract was binding. Cedric treated me like a commodity meant to be used and thrown away. Every ounce of creativity he drained from me only strengthened his success.

Cedric Thomas was powerful, well-connected, and charming.

I had no chance of winning this fight.

But for once, I was going to try.

His *lies* became my *truth.*

Chapter 27
Feral

Simon

When I took my oath to become an officer, I made the same vows as my fellow officers. I vowed to serve and protect my community, always uphold the law, and never betray my badge, character, integrity, or trust this town and its people bestowed upon me.

This is the first moment in my career when I want to throw everything out the window. I always knew that someday I might need to take a human life—an unfortunate truth for this line of work. But I also believed it would only occur in self-defense or in defense of others.

Yet here I am, contemplating murder.

Cold-blooded, premeditated murder.

No half-assed gunshot wound to the head or knife across the carotid artery will satisfy me. I want it to hurt. I want Cedric Thomas to scream in agony for hours, plead and beg for his life. I want to toy with him, make him believe I might let him go, only to turn around and inflict more pain. Every time he thinks, *this is the end*, I will drag the torture out even longer.

Cedric needs to feel every ounce of pain and terror that I heard in Piper's voice while she recounted the events of the past several years.

And he needs to feel it tenfold.

I am downstairs in the kitchen, systematically plotting that motherfucker's demise down to the second while I pull out the ingredients to make my mom's special tea—as she liked to call it, Sereni-Tea.

Quite the paradox, this tangled web of healing and destruction taking up space in my mind. Then again, the whole damn situation is messy.

With a sigh, I move to fill the kettle with water. The act of preparation is itself a calming bit of meditation. Mom likely planned it as such.

After I set the kettle on the stove and turned on the burner, I think about how often Mom prepared this tea over the years. Whenever one of us needed some extra-soothing bit of comfort, she would pull out these same ingredients. When we got sick, hurt, heartbroken, or had a bad day, out came ingredients. And whenever I needed it, Piper always helped Mom in the kitchen.

To make it extra special, she would say.

The top of the kettle starts to whistle as steam escapes. Acting quickly, I pull it off the burner and move it over the teacup. The boiling water pours out, submerging the mixture of herbs. I make one for myself, too. Then, once enough time has passed, I strain the tea, set the mugs on a tray, and head back toward my room.

Cooper is lying at the top of the stairs, head on his paws while he waits for me. I scratch between his ears and then tap my leg for him to follow. When I reenter my bedroom, my gaze immediately searches out my girl.

Piper sits in bed, propped against the pillows, with her knees to her chest. The skin of her face is pale but freshly washed and still covered with faint blotches of pink. Her nose is red and puffy, and her eyes are bloodshot.

Battle scars. Every one of her tears. In my mind, I start to kill Cedric Thomas all over again.

Setting the tray onto my nightstand, I lift one of the cups and hand it to her, but I have to ensure her hands are wrapped firmly around the mug before I let go. Because Piper barely acknowledges it. Barely notices at all. Even when the mattress shifts from my weight as I perch on the edge. Even when I lean forward, kiss her forehead, and then run my fingers through her hair to push it away from her face.

She has fully detached herself from the moment. Her eyes are vacant, staring off into space like she is trapped deep in her mind. Somewhere I have no reach.

The thought of it kills me.

I want to fix this for her, burn everything to the ground, and help her rebuild from the ashes. I want to slay dragons. But no matter how much I *want* to, I have no way to defeat the monster in her mind.

Piper has to do that one on her own.

Lifting my cup to my lips, I let it linger there after I take a fortifying sip. The steam is soothing. With each inhale, my nose and lungs fill with the comforting scents of chamomile, lavender, and other herbs and fruits from Mom's blend. With each exhale, I release a little more tension.

Some part of Piper's subconscious eventually picks up on the teacup in her hands. She lifts it to her lips and takes a sip. The steam coaxes blood to the surface, bringing color back into her cheeks.

Whether she can taste the blend or smell it through her nose, I'm not sure, but a bit of life comes back into her eyes and loosens some of the worry behind my ribcage.

With a small smile, she whispers, "You made Sereni-Tea."

"You remembered."

"Of course, I remembered." She looks up at me, eyes glistening. "I never forgot a single moment. Not one."

"Baby…" I lean forward and press my lips to hers in a soft kiss. When I pull back, I kiss away the tear that has escaped and is trickling down one chin. "Neither did I."

I take another sip, waiting for her to do the same and watching the tension dissipate. No more anxiety attacks hit tonight, for which I am equal parts grateful and stunned. But her body still went through the trauma of reliving her abuse, even if only through memory.

Her body—her *mind*—needs rest.

"Drink," I tell her.

When I speak, Piper recognizes the steel tone in my voice, and her green eyes flit to mine. She quickly does as I instruct.

"Bossy," she huffs, hiding a grin.

I smirk, relief coursing through me that she is starting to feel well enough to tease. "You haven't seen bossy yet, little bird." The green in her eyes darkens at the insinuation. I shake my head and motion to her tea. "Every drop."

"Hmph."

Once all the tea is gone, I finally see its effects starting to work. Piper's eyelids droop and her body relaxes fully against the pillows. I take the empty teacup from her loose grip and set it beside mine.

When I go cover her, I realize Piper is laying fully on top of the comforter and sheets. I slide one arm under her knees and lift her bottom half so that the other hand can grip the top edge of the blanket and carefully tug it down. She giggles at my—albeit gentle—manhandling. A smile tugs at my lips while I set her gently back onto the mattress. Then I pull the linens back up over her and tuck her in.

Piper curls onto her side, looking up at me with a sleepy smile. Relief courses through me at the sight of it, and at hearing her laugh after everything she admitted to me tonight. Both things are a balm to the swirling darkness in my head, fighting to overtake me. I lightly brush my fingers through her hair before letting them trail down along her hairline and jaw. Her smile widens at the gesture. Then her eyelids flutter closed.

I continue to stay strong for her, pushing aside my inner turmoil to focus on her care. But as soon as her breathing evens, and I know she is asleep, that darkness threatens again.

Ozzy and Cooper surround Piper with their furry bodies. Ozzy stretches out behind her where I would usually lay, resting his head on the dip in her waist so he can watch the door. Cooper stretches along her front and focuses on the same spot.

"Good boys," I whisper.

Now that I know they will keep Piper safe in my stead, I have something I need to do.

***

Hawk's cabin is dark when I pull into the driveway. But I know the man sleeps lightly and often suffers from insomnia. I have a strong suspicion he is awake in there.

I pull out my phone and start to type.

- 1:25 am -

Simon: H, you up?

Then I wait. It only takes a minute until three little dots start flashing on the screen.

Hawk: No. Apparently, I'm stuck in a nightmare. One where you text me in the middle of the night.

I snort out loud. Sarcastic motherfucker.

Simon: Would I bother you this late for something insignificant?

Hawk: Fuck you and your logic after midnight.

Hawk: *sighing emoji*

Hawk: Fine. You can come in.

As soon as I slip out of my truck, Hawk stands at the front door, leaning against the frame with his arms crossed. He has pulled his long blond hair back at the nape, and *thank god* he decided that the occasion warrants pants *and* a shirt.

The number of times that man has answered his door in boxer briefs…

I shudder and then shove that thought away, striding up the sidewalk until I reach him.

Hawk raises an eyebrow at me in question, taking in my own haphazard attire, but motions me inside without asking what the hell I want. Yet. And I am oddly grateful. I need a minute to gather my thoughts.

"Based on the expression on your face, I'm going to need coffee," he declares, heading into the kitchen and turning on his coffee machine. "You want some?"

It seems counterproductive since I just drank something to relax, but I need all my focus. "Yeah, please."

"You got it."

He grabs two mugs out of a random cabinet and starts to brew the first cup. While he works, I sigh loudly and rub my palms down my face. My body feels haggard. The night is beginning to catch up to me.

"Oof," Hawk says, setting one of the mugs before me. "That sounds like the sigh of a man with a lot of shit on his plate."

I peek through my fingers at him. "Yeah, you could say that."

"Does this have something to do with that sweet little thing you've been keeping close?"

Pulling my hands away from my face, I glare at him. "That 'sweet little thing' has a name, you know."

Hawk barks out a laugh. "Ooh, sensitive. You've got it bad, Brooks." He takes a large swig of his coffee. "Yeah, I know all about Piper Easton. Songbyrd. Quite the catch. You should be proud."

"It's not like that." I roll my eyes. "We have history. I knew her long before she was Songbyrd."

"Mm-hmm." Another sip. "I knew that, too."

"What did you do, you nosy bastard?"

Hawk grins. "Same thing you're here to ask me to. I looked into Piper. And when I failed to find anything, I had Toby the Tiger take over. Just to be on the safe side."

My chest burns at the mention of Hawk's brother—an insanely gifted hacker. "You had Tobias dig into Piper's past?" I say accusingly.

"Just high-level stuff. Background check. Looking for any red flags. No deep dives, I promise." Hawk's face grows uncharacteristically severe. "But yeah. Anyone I don't know starts hanging around the people I care about, then I look into them." He shrugs. "She's clean, by the way. Spotless, which is pretty unusual in the music world. I mean, other than the occasional joint. But who hasn't done that?"

"For fuck's—Look, I know her history. I know she's clean." I groan in frustration. I guess I get to jump right in, then. "That's not the reason I came. Well," I add, cringing slightly. "Not in the way you think."

He rests his hip against the counter and crosses his arms. "Explain."

"I need Tobias to look into a record label, Dreamscape Music, and the owner, Cedric Thomas. He lives in New York City. I can get him anything else he needs—address, phone number, etc."

Hawk waves away my words. "No need, that's plenty of information. Anything specific you're looking for?"

"Yes." My expression darkens as the banked fire of fury rekindles. "Tell him to dig up all the dirt he can—extortion, coercion, illegal contracts, tax evasion, *anything*. Hell, if Cedric even looked at anyone wrong, let me know. I want all the skeletons in his closet unearthed along with his label's shady dealings."

My pulse thunders through my ears, and I pause to breathe. Then I hold the hot coffee mug in my hands, trying to focus on something other than the hatred coursing through my body.

"Dude." I glance up to see Hawk staring at me. "You alright there? You're about ready to crack my mug in two."

I see my white-knuckled grip around the mug and the steaming liquid shaking inside. I quickly set it back onto the granite countertop. "Sorry."

"Just a mug."

Hawk squints at me in the way he does, like he is trying to ferret out all the things you are unwilling to admit or maybe have no recollection of. The first time he did it to Beckham, I laughed my ass off. Unfortunately, the situation feels a lot less funny when he directs all that intuition at you.

"Is there something I need to know?" Hawk finally asks, silver-grey eyes clear again.

Too damn perceptive.

"Not my story to tell, man." I sigh and drop my head forward between my shoulders. "All I can say is that Piper is locked into a contract from hell with that asshole and—wait. The contract." My head snaps up, my gaze boring into his. "I need a copy of that, too, if Tobias can swing it. No." I clench a fist and pound it onto the counter. "No ifs. The contract is non-negotiable."

"Non-negotiable. Got it." He cocks his head to one side, studying me. "What are you planning to do with all this, if you don't mind me asking?"

"I'm going to take the contract to Priya's law practice. If anyone can find a loophole, she can. As for the rest..." My nostrils flare as I take a deep breath, shoving back the burn of acid in my throat when I think of the shit that monster is capable of—letting it instead fuel the conviction in my voice and my thirst for vengeance. "The rest I'm going to use to annihilate him."

Hawk blinks. "Metaphorically, or...?"

I train my blazing gaze on him. But I say nothing, letting my expression do all the talking. Hawk straightens—and, based on the way his chin dips slightly in deference, I gather he got the message.

Then, a wicked smile weaves its way across his face. "Remind me to never get on your bad side."

I chuckle, feeling some of the tension lift. "Didn't Beckham warn you? We gingers are dangerous."

"Yeah, beginning to see that."

After the strain of the past several minutes, I can feel bone-deep exhaustion biting at the heels of my anger. I have no desire to fall asleep behind the wheel, so I stand up. "When do you think Tobias can have something for me?"

"Not sure," he admits, walking with me toward the door. "T-bone is a miracle worker, but Thanksgiving is this week."

"Yeah." My shoulders slump. Part of me hoped he might have something in the next few days despite knowing how unrealistic that request is. "Just as soon as he can, yeah?"

Hawk claps me lightly on the shoulder. "I'll make sure he knows this is his top priority."

"Whatever his going rate is," I add. "Plus rush fee."

He nods, and we fall into silence until we come up to the front door. When I cross onto the small porch, I turn back, feeling a sudden burning curiosity. "Exactly how many nicknames do you have for your brother anyway?"

Hawk's grin is infectious. "At least one for every mood. And holiday. Every day of the week…"

"Okay, okay, I get it."

I step down onto the sidewalk but, again, turn back. "Hey, you coming to Thanksgiving?"

Ellery and Beckham have taken over hosting. I know that they invited all our closest friends, including Hawk. Ellery even invited Piper's family to join us this year.

He shakes his head. "Not this year. I'm flying to spend the holidays with my moms. Toblerone will be there, too, so I can pass anything along between you two."

Last Thanksgiving, he flew his moms down for the holiday, and they quickly charmed everyone in the vicinity. Tobias even showed up, a recluse that he was. This year will be lacking some hilarity without them, that's for sure.

"Well, we'll miss you," I say. "Tell Bonnie and Claire hi from me."

"I will." He scoffs. "Pretty sure they like you better than me now, anyway."

I grin and reply, "That's because they have amazing taste."

We lapse into silence again. But before I head home, I have one more question eating away at me. "I've been meaning to ask, how is your search going?"

A shadow crosses Hawk's face for a moment before the expression clears. "It's going. Tobias is working his ass off but still no real leads."

"Shit, man. I'm sorry."

He waves me off. "You have enough on your plate. You don't need my troubles, too."

"Hm." I squint up at him. "Well, I don't know how much help a small-town police officer could be, but if there is anything I can do…"

"I'll let you know." With that, he turns to head back inside. But not without one last parting shot. "Now get your ass back to your woman."

My woman.

Fuck, it sounds even better when someone else says it.

But Hawk is right. I need to get home. Tomorrow, I intend to start implementing my plans.

Tonight, I need to get home to my woman.

Right where I belong.

Chapter 28
Be Your Love

Piper

True to her word, Rue suppressed my unfortunate run-in with the music industry news outlets. While that fails to erase the hours that the article was floating out in the aether, at least I can take comfort in the fact that no one else will be able to see it.

But something needs to give. Now that Cedric has gone rogue, I have no idea what will happen next or when. I need to stop hiding away and find a way to end this.

Somehow.

These thoughts run rampant through my head when my eyes open on Thanksgiving morning. I am unsure what woke me at first. But then I hear my phone buzzing loudly on the nightstand and blaring an alarm through its speakers.

Beside me, Simon stirs. I have basically been living at his place since the whole magazine incident. He knows nothing about that particular issue, but he insisted I stay with him after the drama I laid at his feet. I had been half-scared he would toss me out after that, but I should know better. Simon would never do that—not to a stranger in need, let alone someone he cares about.

So, when Simon told me to stay, I chose not to fight him on it. Why would I? I have no desire to live in a place where Cedric so thoroughly violated my sense of safety.

I feel safe in this house.

And I feel safe with Simon.

Except maybe when he acts all growly like a grizzly bear. Then, he makes me feel all sorts of amused.

"Turn that demon phone off," he grumbles, grabbing the nearest pillow and shoving it over his head.

I giggle and roll my eyes. "Sorry, sleeping beauty."

Shifting to the side, I reach for my phone and tap the screen to shut off the alarm. Then I stretch my limbs like a cat, arching my back and curling my toes. Simon's arm snakes out and curls around my waist, catching me by surprise as he tugs me into his side. Once the shock wears off, I smile and snuggle into his warmth. I can afford to sleep a little bit longer.

Unfortunately, fate has other plans. Simon's alarm decides to go off just a few minutes later. While it blares a particularly aggressive rock anthem, he groans loudly, followed by a fake sob into his pillow and then a blind reach for his phone on the other nightstand.

Once he has it in hand, Simon rolls onto his back. Then he blinks blearily up at the screen before punching something with his forefinger. The sound cuts off, leaving us in blissful silence.

"Fucking finally," he says with a beleaguered sigh.

Laughter bubbles up and out of my throat at the supremely disgruntled tone in his voice. Before I can even blink, Simon has me on my back and is between my legs. He looms over me, hands bracketing my head, expression stern except for the twinkle in his eyes.

"What's so funny, little bird?" He lifts an eyebrow, daring me to answer.

I blink up at him with an innocent expression. "You are."

"Fucking brat."

One lip turns up at the corner. Simon's hips give a lazy thrust against mine. I am suddenly thoroughly distracted by the delicious pressure of him between my thighs. I gasp quietly at the motion. Then he does it again.

"What about this?" he asks with another thrust. "Is this funny to you?"

His movements are slow and deliberate, and I whimper at the throbbing ache deep inside from every torturous slide of his length over my clit and between the slick walls of my labia.

"N-no," I answer. "That"—I punctuate the word with a roll of my hips, trying to create more friction—"is serious business."

"That's what I thought."

I try to slide one of my hands along his chest, but Simon captures it and lifts it above my head. He does the same with the other. Held captive, I can do nothing but drown in the sensation of his body pressing me into the mattress, his hips moving languidly against mine, and the feel of him kissing, licking, and biting at all the sensitive parts of my neck. The ones he knows drive me wild.

He nips me hard when I struggle to break my hands out of his firm grip. "Uh-uh. Don't make me get the handcuffs." I growl in frustration, which only earns me a deep chuckle.

His teasing movements stimulate as much as they torture. My breathing turns ragged. Pleasure coils deep in my core, tightening as the tension slowly mounts. Even dragging out his movements, Simon works me up enough that I get right up on the edge, and unable to get any further, I beg him for release.

Then Simon's weight is gone. I lay there, frustrated and unsatisfied, as I hover over the precipice, stretching toward a climax just out of reach. The bathroom door clicks shut. The water turns on a moment later.

Picturing Simon in there and taking a shower turns my frustration into petty annoyance. I am half-tempted to let my hand finish what he started.

But then I hear the bathroom door reopen. I lift onto an elbow. Simon stands there, peeking out, and as soon as my gaze meets his, he winks.

"Hurry up," Simon orders me, "or I'm showering without you."

Yes, Sir.

✳✳✳

Thanksgiving is one of my favorite holidays. Not because of the food, although that is a definite bonus, but because of the sense of belonging, the community, and the bonding. It has been years since I last celebrated a holiday like this with my friends and family in one place. I'm already overwhelmed—in the best possible way, of course—but I am still overloaded with emotions I will have no time to sort through.

Today is *not* the day to try and figure out my mess.

Simon and I walk up the drive to Beckham and Ellery's home. Ozzy and Cooper flank us. Simon carries the food we prepared while I carry Duchess. Halfway through our walk here, she flopped onto the ground and refused to move. Ozzy hovered. I picked her up, and then the tiny dictator settled happily in the crook of my elbow.

"What are you smiling about over there?" Simon asks, glancing over at me.

I chuckle. "Just the little drama queen's antics from before."

"Damn spoiled dog," he mutters. Then he shakes his head with a smile when she yawns at him, gape-mouthed, before nuzzling her head against my breasts. He quirks an eyebrow. "Is it sad that I'm jealous of an animal right now?"

"Yes." I snort and move up the stairs ahead of him.

Glancing back, I catch Simon openly staring at my behind. I roll my eyes. Before he can make whatever crude joke is on the tip of his tongue, the front door opens. Ellery rushes out and throws her arms around me.

"You made it!" she cries out.

In between us, Duchess squeaks in alarm. Then she barks, scrambling to remove herself from her sudden cage of death. I laugh while trying to keep her from tumbling to the ground.

Simon swoops right in. He somehow balances the food under one arm while simultaneously scooping Duchess into the other. He presses a kiss to the top of my head as he does.

"Did you think we wouldn't show, pipsqueak?" he says, breezing past us. He pauses at the doorway to lower a wiggling Duchess to the ground. Then, over his shoulder, he adds, "Like I would miss a meal I didn't have to cook."

Ellery looks pointedly at the food in his grip.

"The joke's on you." He smirks. "Piper made most of this."

Then he disappears inside.

"You know that's a lie." I shake my head, grinning at Ellery. "He barely let me help."

"My brother, the gourmet chef," she quips.

"Dominates the kitchen as much as the bed"—I cut myself off quickly, cheeks reddening.

Ellery shudders. "Nope. No. We're going to pretend I didn't just hear what I think I heard."

"Have any of my brood arrived?" I ask, quickly changing the subject.

Ellery looks relieved and motions toward the open door. As we move inside, she explains, "Yeah, your parents got here a little while ago. Stella has already taken over in the kitchen. She kicked Beckham out to go out back with Pop."

Relief courses through me at knowing Beckham has been in the kitchen, not Ellery. Bless her heart; she could barely boil water at thirteen, and Simon warned me earlier that nothing has changed.

True to Ellery's word, I find Mom in the kitchen, looking quite at home. Most of the food seems already prepared. Mom scrubs a pot in a sink full of sudsy water. Beside her towers a pile of already clean pots and pans.

"Hi, Mom," I say with a kiss on her cheek.

She sets the pot on the dish rack and then turns to hug me, careful not to get me wet with her soapy gloves. "Hi, sweetheart. Happy Thanksgiving."

"Happy Thanksgiving." Those two words taste bittersweet on my tongue. Grabbing a clean towel, I pivot the conversation into safer territory. "I'll dry?"

"Okay."

Mom smiles happily at me while I come up beside her. Then we get to work, silently moving in sync until all the dishes are clean, dry, and put away to the best of our ability. I head to the backyard to say hi to Pop when we finish.

Pop sits with Beckham and Simon in Adirondack chairs along the back porch. They watch the dogs romp around with Daisy in the yard. Daisy sees me first and waves. Then, not waiting for a response, she returns to playing with the dogs.

Pop stands as soon as he sees me. When I get close enough, he engulfs me in a bear hug.

I laugh. "Hey, Pop."

"Hey, Pip."

Pop's laughter mixes with mine. He lets me go, but not before ruffling my hair. Next in line, Beckham hugs me—much less aggressively. By the time I reach Simon, I am grinning ear-to-ear. He reaches up from his seat to tug me onto his lap. I fall into him with a surprised squeak.

Pop and Beckham resume their conversation, but Simon tugs me close and rests his chin on my shoulder. "You look happy, little bird."

"I am happy," I say. Then I melt against Simon with a contented sigh, although I feel a slight pang in my chest as I look out over the yard.

"But...?"

Sometimes, I forget how easily Simon can read me. "But," I admit, "it would be even better if Grace could be here."

Simon hums and tightens his hold on me. From the corner of my eye, I see Pop look in our direction, and for a few moments, the two of them silently converse. Eventually, Pop nods and stands before walking inside.

"What was all that?" I ask.

"What was what?"

I turn in his hold. "Don't play coy. You and my dad, acting all cloak and dagger just now."

Simon shrugs. "Oh, that? He just wanted to know if I need another beer."

"What, did he ask you with his eyes?"

"Are you mad that he didn't ask you for one?" Simon wiggles his eyebrows.

Even though I am trying to look mad, I snort. Then I shove Simon's shoulder for good measure. "Now, who's being the brat?"

He presses his lips to mine to avoid the question.

Just then, the door opens. Ellery calls out Beckham's name when she steps onto the porch and looks around. When she sees us kissing, she gasps loudly and whisper-shouts, "Beck, look!" followed by a soft, girlish squeal of excitement.

I pull back, giggling.

Simon turns and glowers at Ellery. "Don't even start."

"Not a word, I promise." But then her eyes dart back and forth between us, and she bursts out, "Okay, but like, I know this was happening, still—seeing it just makes me so freaking happy!" She slaps her hands over her mouth, muffling her following words. "Sorry! I'm sorry."

Beckham is laughing as he reaches out to pull her onto his lap. "Alright, shortcake, I think you embarrassed them enough."

"He should be used to it by now." Ellery rolls her eyes, but she still snuggles against him. "I've embarrassed him all his life."

"My therapist thanks you," Simon deadpans.

Ellery responds by sticking her tongue out. Simon does the same thing back. I shake my head, grinning goofily. I failed to realize how much I needed that patented Brooks' good-natured family teasing.

"Okay, children," Beckham says. "That's enough."

Simon huffs before looking down at his watch. "Hey, Pop is taking an awful long time." He glances at me. "Mind checking on him?"

"Sure, handsome." I untangle myself from him and head inside.

More than likely, Pop was forced to do more manual labor for Mom. She can be a real taskmaster, especially around the holidays. Unfortunately, when I enter through the back doors, I hear nothing resembling commotion from the upstairs kitchen. I head up the steps, and as I get closer, I hear distant, lively conversation from the front of the house, along with—

—is that *children's* laughter? Filled with curiosity, I rush the rest of the way. Beckham created a beautiful open floor plan, and as soon as I enter the kitchen, I can see straight through to the front of the house. My older sister and her family stand inside the front door, talking with Mom and Pop.

"Grace?" I ask, gasping.

"Hey, little sis." She turns toward me with a smile.

"Oh my gosh, Grace!" I dart into the living room and launch myself at her. "I can't believe you're here."

"Blame that man of yours," she says, laughing and holding me tight. "Simon insisted on keeping it a secret."

I look over her shoulder at Mom and Pop. "He arranged this?"

Mom grins. "Grace and Jake had already planned on coming down for Christmas, but Simon convinced them that you might appreciate having everyone home for Thanksgiving, too."

When I pull back to look at Grace, she watches me with concern. "How are you doing?" she asks quietly.

"Getting better." I pull away and turn to Jake, wrapping my arms around his tall runner's frame. "Thanks for bringing her home."

"You think I had any say in the matter?" He snorts loudly. "That's rich. I'm not the one in charge of this marriage, you know that."

Giggling, I say, "That's what you get for marrying an Easton."

"Yeah, well. You guys are pretty okay." He ruffles my hair in typical brotherly fashion. I smack his hand away and step back as two small figures come rushing at me.

"Auntie Piper!" They screech, flinging themselves at my legs.

"Hi, Sebastian," I say—hugging him first, then his sister. "Hi, Bella Bean."

The six-year-old twins look up at me with matching gap-toothed grins and large grey-blue eyes that they inherited from Grace. The rest comes from Jake, from their dark brown corkscrew curls to their skinny bodies and almond skin tone.

"Where are Ozzy and Cooper?" Bella asks, jumping excitedly.

"They're out back with Aunt Daisy," Grace interjects. "Why don't y'all head downstairs and say hi?"

"Yay!" They shriek in unison before shooting like a bullet toward the back of the house.

"Do they know where they're going?" I ask, wide-eyed.

Jake shrugs. "I'll go make sure they don't break anything."

"Come on." I tug Grace to follow, adding, "I need to go thank a certain sneaky cop for my surprise."

Mom tells us everything is ready and to meet them in the dining room, which we do as soon as I give Simon a very enthusiastic hug and kiss. Then I whisper my promise to thank him more enthusiastically (and much more privately) later.

When we finally gather around the table, lively chatter fills the room along with the comforting aroma from our bounty of food. My heart feels full to bursting. Once again, Simon knew what I needed even before I did.

The man in question peeks over at me as though he can hear my thoughts. His eyes crinkle at the corners, and his gaze roams over my face. "Still happy, little bird?" he asks quietly.

I squeeze his hand underneath the table. "Over the moon."

"Good." He presses a kiss to the top of my head.

The rest of the meal passes in a flurry of conversation, reminiscing, and dreams of the future. I join in when the occasion calls for it, but mostly, I am content to listen and observe. Near the end of the meal, Mom asks everyone to say what they are most thankful for. When my turn comes, I say without hesitation:

"Family."

***

Gravel crunches underfoot while I descend the backyard path. My destination lies just beyond, by the water on the edge of Beckham and Ellery's property. By November, South Carolina days are generally mild. But the warmth disappears with the sun, and the temperatures at night have dropped significantly. Before I stepped outside, I had to swipe one of those chunky knitted blankets from the back of Ellery's couch and don it like a cloak.

As I close in on the fire pit, I spot Simon. He sits hunched over on a cushioned bench near the flames. A long poker with a marshmallow skewered on the tip is in his hands, hovering over the fire while he slowly turns it like the spit of a rotisserie. Hidden in the shadows, I watch him, able to look my fill without risk of discovery. He looks younger here, unfettered by the weight of his responsibilities. The firelight dances over his face, and for just a moment, he reminds me of the Simon I remember: carefree, full of dreams, and ready to conquer the world.

Back before the world conquered him.

But that vision disappears like smoke. Suddenly, I am staring at Simon as he is now. *This* Simon is different but no less striking. He is steadfast and strong, shouldering his burdens yet making room for mine, willing to burn the world down without remorse if someone hurts me—or even if I ask him to.

Simon is arrogant and stubborn, and his savior complex gets him into trouble. But he is also caring, intuitive, patient, and protective of his friends and family. And Simon will never hesitate to give the shirt off his back to a stranger in need.

Every facet of him, past and present, has made it impossible for me not to fall because he is impossible not to love.

With that thought comes a jolt of surprise—for just a moment—before surprise shifts to clarity and something in me settles. I silently speak the words again, testing them out. They are rusty from disuse, like a familiar childhood toy abandoned on a shelf.

Love.

I *love* him.

I love Simon Brooks.

Simon has owned my heart for over half of our lives. If I am honest with myself, I never took it back. My love for him may have gone into hibernation—hiding beneath thick layers of ice and snow encasing my heart—but it has always been there, caught in a delicate stasis.

Now the ice has thawed. My heart fills to the brim, warming me from the inside until the cold air barely registers while I continue down the path. Soon, I reach Simon. He glances my way. Smiling, I sit quietly next to him and tug the blanket tighter.

Comforting silence surrounds us for the first few moments. The fire crackles gently, tiny sparks dancing in front of my face before they break apart and float into the night sky. Beyond that is the pond, dark except for the rippling reflection of the fire and the moonlit sky.

After a moment, Simon turns his attention from the fire to me. I feel the heat of his gaze warming my cold skin. Here on this oversized bench, there is only a scan amount of room between us—everywhere we touch, I feel his heat like a brand.

Simon clears his throat. "Toasted marshmallow?"

I blink in confusion and look over at him. He holds up the poker and the brightly burning marshmallow, then blows out the flame. It smolders in charred perfection. The bottom of it has already started to drip down his fingers.

For some reason, that strikes me as funny. I shake my head, a light laugh bubbling before I say, "No, thanks."

Simon carefully pries the marshmallow off the poker, grimacing when it sticks to his fingers like glue. Then he shoves it into his mouth, setting off another burst of giggles while I watch him struggle to chew and swallow.

"How can you still be hungry?" I wince when I think of all the food I just consumed a few hours ago. I'll be in a food coma for at least a week.

He grins at me and shrugs. "I'm a growing boy."

"Mm-hmm." I shake my head at him, still grinning like a fool, while I look down at his fingers, bits of marshmallow still clinging to the skin. "You're certainly messy like one."

"Shit." He looks around for something to wipe his hand on. I roll my eyes and take hold of his wrist.

"Allow me," I say, grin turning wicked. Then, I lower my head and take the first digit into my mouth. My eyes are locked with his, so I see the way the flames flicker in their depths, and I catch the desire written on his face while I lick him clean. I do the same to the second digit, then the third.

Simon's breathing has gone ragged as the last finger slips from my mouth. He whispers my name. Then, his other hand is in my hair, holding me hostage by the back of my head as he seizes my lips in a bruising kiss. I need to taste him more than my next breath. My tongue invades his mouth, and the roasted marshmallow's sweet buttery flavor teases my tastebuds.

Simon gives as good as he gets. Of course, he does. He devours my mouth so skillfully that he wrenches a tortured groan from my throat. His other hand rests on the small of my back. Then Simon tugs me to him, dragging me onto his lap until I straddle his thighs.

The cold air hits me like a shot to the veins when the chunky blanket slides off my shoulders and pools down around my waist, but that slight bite of pain feeds the passion between us. Simon replaces some of the warmth with his strong arms. The rest of me flickers with a different heat that threatens to ignite.

Before the blaze can consume us both, however, Simon douses the flames. He stills the motion of my hips with a forearm along my lower back. Gentles the kiss. He slows down before stopping entirely. Then he nips at my lower lip once before he pulls back.

"Such a tease," Simon scolds, kissing my forehead despite his words.

My eyes flutter open, and I catch his lips twitching like he is fighting off a smile. That makes me smile wider. "Worth it."

We settle into a comfortable silence after a beat or two. My head nuzzles under his chin, and his arms band tighter around me, further anchoring me to him. Behind me, the fire crackles.

"Simon?" I speak quietly, not wanting to disturb the peace but needing to talk.

He rests his chin on my head. "Hm?"

"When we went around the room earlier, each saying what we're thankful for, I left off something important."

"Oh?"

His large palm glides along my hair in soothing strokes but stills at what I say next. "You." Using my hands on his chest as leverage, I lift my upper half until we are face to face. So I can look at him when I say, "I'm thankful for you."

His expression softens, melting into something warm that looks a lot like hope. But there's vulnerability, too. I break a little, knowing that I'm the cause of it. Because I have been holding myself back, focused all this time on protecting myself, I failed to see how my actions might affect him.

He has given so much of himself to me. What have I offered him in return? Only the tiniest pieces of me I felt I could spare.

Daisy is right. I need to stop punishing Simon for his mistake when we were kids. I need to throw away the caution I have been clinging to. With that thought, I cup his face with my hands, running my thumbs gently back and forth across his cheekbones.

His eyes are trained on me, and there is a question in them.

So I answer. Reaching deep for strength, I tell this remarkable man the truth I have been terrified to admit.

"I love you, Simon Brooks." My words are soft but unwavering. I watch and wait with bated breath for them to penetrate.

When they do, he inhales shakily and then presses his lips to mine. I feel every ounce of emotion he pours into the kiss. Even after we break apart, he gathers me close, nuzzles his face to mine, and fills me with an overwhelming sense of completion.

This, I think. *This is home.*

"You have owned my heart since I first saw you." Simon's voice is raspy and rough. I can feel the vibration of each word against my skin. "Every day, every second since, I have loved you. That never changed, little bird, and it never will."

Tears prick at my eyes. The happiness and relief I feel rush over me like a tidal wave. It sweeps away the last of my armor. But, instead of feeling naked and vulnerable, I feel free. Simon is my anchor. He will keep me from getting swept away, and now that I know he is mine forever and always, I can spread my wings without fear of having them clipped ever again.

"Want to know what I'm thankful for?" He asks after a brief interlude.

"Sure, handsome." I smile against his chest. "What are you thankful for?"

"That you finally came home."

I close my eyes and whisper, "So am I."

Love.

I *love* him.

I love Simon Brooks

Chapter 29
Old Days

Piper

Sweetbriar celebrates tradition. Every December first, seemingly overnight, the entire downtown area transforms into a winter wonderland. Holiday-themed decorations and merchandise fill the store windows, and on almost every corner, Santa Claus or one of his many helpers rings his bell for donations.

The town holds its annual Winter Festival over the month's first weekend. Ellery and I choose the first day to have lunch and go Christmas shopping—since Beckham has gone to the city, and Simon is on duty. We head to Jelly Beans to eat and greet the owners before we enter. Anna and Faith wear matching Mrs.

Claus costumes and have elaborately decorated a booth out front to resemble a gingerbread house where they sell hot cocoa and Christmas cookies. I smile at what a cute couple they make in their holiday getups.

After we eat, Ellery and I stroll along the main strip—sipping hot chocolate, looking in all the stores, and checking out the arts and crafts booths. Although much larger and more crowded than I remember, the festival still makes a pretty picture. Nostalgia settles deep into my bones while I take in the scenery around me, and it warms me from the inside out. Red ribbon and colorful string lights wrap the street lamps like gifts—while the lights continue up and out, crisscrossing overhead—and handcrafted wreaths hang from them. I envision the scene at night, twinkling overhead, and smile at the romantic picture it makes.

Maybe Simon and I can come back here one of these nights.

"You seem to be enjoying yourself," Ellery comments, gently nudging me and pulling me from my reverie.

"What's not to enjoy?" My lungs breathe in the crisp air and scent of evergreen. After a moment, I admit, "For me, celebrating holidays like this stopped a long time ago. I want to soak everything in, you know?"

"Oh, Piper, I'm sorry." Ellery cringes into her paper cup. "I do love to put my foot in my mouth."

Smiling, I say, "Don't apologize. My past is getting easier to talk about—bit by bit." Then I sigh. "I just wish this whole mess was finally over."

"Any luck about your contract?"

"No." I want to groan in frustration. "I'll have a battle if I can't get out of it by the new year. Also, I don't want to let down my fans. It isn't their fault I signed my soul away."

"Hey." Ellery gives me a fierce look and says, "It's not your fault, either. Okay? So get that out of your head."

"So bossy," I say, smirking. "You sound like your brother."

"God, I hope not." Ellery looks so horrified that I start laughing.

"Good lord, Elle," I giggle, "Simon isn't that bad."

"Pfft, that's because you love him."

I stumble a little at her words.

"Come on, Piper." Ellery glances at me, eyes twinkling. "It's written all over your face. Tell me I'm wrong."

"No," I say slowly, blushing profusely. "You're not wrong."

"I knew it!" She claps her hands in excitement. "I told Beckham, but then he told me to mind my business and let you two figure things out without my meddling."

Bless Beckham and his keen intuition. I love Ellery to pieces. I do. But that woman is like a dog with a bone when something catches her interest.

"Anyway," she continues, "does Simon know?"

My face flames brighter. "We, uh, we had a moment at Thanksgiving. So, yeah. He knows. And before you ask, yes, he said it back," I blurt out.

Ellery squeals, causing a few people ahead to peek back at us. I smile awkwardly and wave. Then I say to Ellery, "Come on. Let's finish shopping before all the good stuff is gone."

We spend the next few hours browsing the different booths for the perfect presents. We also eat our weight in homemade baked goods and drink way too much hot chocolate and egg nog. Taking advantage of my sugar high, I manage to check off almost everyone on my list.

That fact alone is worth the impending sugar crash.

Near the end of the day, Simon and Nate appear, still in uniform. We greet them both with a friendly smile—or Ellery does. Nate gets a friendly smile from me, but Simon gets a kiss.

"What are you guys doing out here?" I ask, grinning.

Simon tucks me under his arm. I snuggle further into his warmth while he replies. "Chief's making us all take turns at the festival doing rounds."

"Oh no," Ellery deadpans. She looks at the cup of hot chocolate in both men's grips. "How dare Chief *make* you two wander around the Winter Festival so there's a police presence? You poor things, that must have been so difficult."

Simon releases me during Ellery's little speech. He hands me his cup, and I watch in amusement while he stealthily shifts closer. Then, when Ellery falls silent, Simon wraps his arm around her neck and aggressively ruffles her hair. She shrieks and pinches him hard in the side to get away.

"Ooh!" Ellery huffs, trying to smooth down her curls. "No Christmas present for you, big brother."

"Does that mean I can have it?" Nate asks hopefully. Simon glowers at him. "What? She gets you the coolest gifts. I'm jealous."

"Sure, Nate." Ellery gives him a sideways hug and a cheeky grin. "You can be my new big brother."

"Sweet." Nate winks at Simon. "Sorry, man, you've been usurped."

Rolling his eyes, Simon turns to me while Nate and Ellery banter in the background. He notices the bags on my arm. "Get all your Christmas shopping done?"

"Yeah, mostly."

"Anything in there for me?" he asks, eyes lighting up in boyish excitement. Before I fully register the question, he leans forward and tries to peek.

"Simon!" Gasping in outrage, I slap his hands away. "No peeking, nosy."

He pulls back in mild surprise. But only for a moment. I watch his shock give way to mischief as a wicked grin weaves its way across his face, and the promise that burns in his eyes threatens to consume me.

With Nate and Ellery otherwise occupied, Simon leans forward and whispers a delicious threat in my ear: "Just wait till I get home tonight, little bird. You'll be paying for that one. Be on the bed, naked, waiting for me, and I'll consider going easy on you."

He smirks at the hitch in my breath. Then, after a quick kiss on the lips, a discreet ass grab, and a cheeky "later, baby," he leads Nate back into the crowd.

Ellery and I slowly make our way back toward the entrance. I quietly try to regain my composure while she chatters away. However, before we make it to my car, we hit the brick-and-mortar shops again, and Ellery gasps when she sees something in one of the windows.

"Oh, that would be perfect for Beckham!" Ellery cries. Then she looks at me, hooking a finger over her shoulder at the store. "Do you mind if I…?"

I smile and wave her off. "Go on. I'll wait here."

"Thanks!" She hugs me and darts into the building.

After a moment, I look around for a place to sit, noticing several already occupied benches and tables. But on my second pass, I see a small bistro table and chairs between two stores and tucked partially in the shadows of an alleyway—private and perfect for me to hide away.

Once I have settled into the chair facing the street, the gift bag pile gets placed on the table in front of me. Then I pull out my phone. I am just a few minutes into managing my unread emails when three women pass by me. One of them looks familiar, and after wracking my brain, I remember why. The third woman is Nate's wife, Britagne. I only know her through photos on social media—well, that plus all the stories of how terribly she treats poor Nate and how bitchy she acts with everyone else.

Usually, I ignore those types of people. Having dealt with my fair share of gossip and mean girls over the years, I am *not* a fan. But Cedric and his article have me feeling overly paranoid, so when they stop just a few feet away and my name floats in the air between them, I immediately go on alert.

Britagne is the first to speak. "Don't you think it's strange that Songbyrd came back here, of all places? She's a celebrity! If I had that glamorous life of hers, I'd be jet-setting all over the world, not spending my time in this podunk little town."

Oh, sweetie. If only you knew. Part of me wants to call out that she is more than welcome to that part of my life if she wants it, but I am too invested in the conversation to speak.

Next to Britagne, the brunette huffs and says, "God, Brit. Don't call her Songbyrd like she's somebody important. *Piper* is a passable musician at best." Then she shakes her head and scoffs. "No, what I find strange is Simon actually dating her again. Especially after all the trouble he went through to get rid of her last time."

The blonde on the other side of Britagne rolls her eyes. "Come on, Lilian. You're just jealous because he never took you on a date."

Britagne perks up. I admit, so do I.

"Amber, Lilian!" Britagne looks affronted. "You have juicy gossip about Sexy Cop that you haven't shared? Spill."

Amber starts her story with a gleeful grin. "Simon and Piper dated all through high school. All the girls hated her."

"Of course, they did," Britagne cuts in, fanning herself. "Have you seen him? Simon Brooks can arrest me any day."

"Ooh, don't let Nate hear you say that," Lilian quips. Britagne glowers until Lilian blushes and awkwardly clears her throat. "Sorry, Brit."

"Anyway," Amber continues, "Simon's parents were killed in a car accident during his first year of college. He got saddled with raising his little sister. Everyone could see the strain on his and Piper's relationship. Piper was still in her senior year, so how could she possibly help him? Anyway, he dumped her just after her senior graduation. Then he went wild."

"Wild?" Britagne asks, intrigued.

Confusion coils in my stomach at their words, but I keep listening.

"Majorly wild," Lilian says, determined to have her say. "But he never actually did anything during all the dates he went on—and he went on a lot, each with a different girl."

Britagne wrinkles her nose. "Why not? Seems stupid."

Lilian shrugs. "He did it to piss Piper off. I guess he finally got tired of her clingy desperation. But he didn't seem interested in any of the girls he dated."

Amber adds, "He treated each date like a transaction. I spent time with him and posted a few photos on our socials, and in return he owed me a favor. No questions asked." She leans forward with a wicked grin. "Honestly, it was worth it. I got to make my ex supremely jealous, and I was the only girl Simon kissed. Right in front of Piper, too."

Amber's words slice through me. I close my eyes, trying to block them out while the confusion in my stomach swirls and shifts until I feel sick. I have no desire to hear more, but I need to.

Lilian leans in toward Britagne. "Amber saw the huge blowup between them at some college party."

Amber nods. "It was brutal."

Every word that comes out of their mouths twists my confusion into anger. When they all start tittering, I decide that enough is enough. Gathering all my bags together, I carefully slip past them and go in search of Ellery.

Once I find her, I need to go home and figure out what the hell just happened.

***

Downstairs, the door opens. All three dogs perk up at the sound, but only Duchess jumps to her feet and races out of the bedroom, yapping excitedly. Ozzy and Cooper seem content to stay here with their heads in my lap. I am leaning against the headboard, sitting cross-legged.

After a minute or two, Simon starts up toward the bedroom. My anxiety ratchets up with each creak of the steps. I love Simon, but I am still new to his dominant side and never before blatantly challenged him on anything.

But I have to know the truth.

When Simon finally enters the room, Duchess is curled up in his arms, belly up and ready for rubs, but his attention has already shifted to me. I gaze steadily at him despite my inner turmoil.

"Now, that won't do." Simon shakes his head in disappointment, and I feel a nervous flutter in my belly when he motions to my fully clothed body. "You only followed half of my instructions."

After setting Duchess back on the ground, he stands back to full height and studies me with an unreadable expression. As a professional performer, I consider myself pretty adept at hiding things—but never with Simon. Somehow he can cut through the bullshit every time.

"What's wrong?" he asks, frowning.

His gaze is so intense that I immediately break eye contact and fidget, picking at my fingernail polish. "I, um, heard something interesting at the market earlier."

"Oh?" He crosses his arms, waiting.

Tension starts to clog my throat, and I try to swallow. Then I say, "It was about that week—the one after you texted me and broke things off." I lift my gaze to his. "Do you remember?"

Of course he remembers. How could either of us forget?

Simon's silence stretches for so long that I am seconds away from doing something drastic. I think of crying, yelling, even throwing something—but just before my agitation ratchets up to that irrational degree, he speaks.

Never taking his eyes off me, Simon clips out a terse, "Ozzy. Cooper. Downstairs."

Those two traitors immediately jump off the bed, meandering through the door without a backward glance. I guess his dominant voice works on dogs, too. Not to be outdone, Duchess scrambles out of her bed and prances after them before Simon can even utter the command. Then he starts to move around the room, and I turn my attention back to my hands. The bedroom door closes. I hear him remove his boots and toss them lightly into the closet. Shifting to the nightstand to my right, he removes his gun and badge before safely storing them. Then I feel a hand slide underneath my chin, lifting my face so I have no choice but to look up at him.

"Explain."

The steel undercurrent in Simon's voice never fails to strip away all my barriers. It also soothes something in me that craves someone to take control. That might be a sick result of all those years under Cedric's thumb—but sometimes, I need a hand to guide me and tell me where to go. What to do.

Taking a deep breath, I say, "Britagne and two women were at the festival, and I overheard them gossiping about you and me in high school. They said you lied about all those girls you went out on dates with—that it was some quid pro quo thing for one favor of their choosing."

After that, the story spills out of me. Frustration, anger, and humiliation fuel my words. Simon drops his hand from my chin, his expression unreadable, and goes quiet while he listens.

Afterward, he lowers onto the mattress beside me and expels a heavy sigh.

All the while, I watch him. I wait for him to say something. I wait for him to dispute their words.

Tell me not to listen to silly gossip.

Tell me they lied.

Tell me I hallucinated the whole thing.

Tell me anything except for what my heart already knows.

But Simon tells me the truth, and it *hurts*.

"Fuck, Piper," he says in a resigned tone that stabs me right through the chest. Then he grabs the knife and twists. "I never wanted you to find out this way."

My breath stutters. Old wounds tear open at Simon's words, and I feel like I am eighteen again, having my heart broken for the second time.

"Hey." Simon's hands reach up and cup me, turning me to face him. "You're panicking again. You need to breathe, Piper."

My lungs automatically suck in breath at his command. I feel dizzy and disoriented—like I am coming up for air after spending minutes underwater. When my vision clears, Simon's face comes into view, and I jerk back out of his reach.

I hold up two hands when he moves to come closer. "Don't. Please. I can't—It was true?" My voice wavers at the end.

Simon watches me, sadness in his eyes, regret written all over his face. He nods in affirmation. I want to laugh, cry, and do everything in between. I want to scream at him.

Only one raspy word leaves my lips. "Why?"

"You need to understand something first," he says.

Standing, Simon starts to pace across the room slowly. When he stops in front of me again, he steps in between my legs. This time, I let him. Then his hands press into the mattress on either side of me, placing us at eye level and caging me in.

"You have to know that it killed me to hurt you like that. I hated every second." The truth shines in his red-rimmed eyes, in the pinch of his brows. But I steel myself against the desire to bend. "I hoped you would hear me out, eventually," he continues, "but you changed your number. No matter how often I begged your parents to let me talk to you, they had to respect your wishes."

Simon closes his eyes and hangs his head, hiding his pain from me. I have a thousand words lodged in my throat, but they refuse to budge. Not that it matters. He has more to say—so I keep my mouth closed, and I wait.

"You never came back. You were supposed to come back," Simon whispers, almost to himself. "I hurt you, and you had every right to be angry. But I hoped that given time, you would understand why I did what I did. That you would let me explain."

"Explain what, Simon?" I cross my arms over my chest, trying to build some armor. "You broke me. You tossed me aside, and then I had to watch you parade all these different girls around like I never meant a damn thing to you. Every photo posted on your socials or theirs was another reminder, another cut that would never heal right. I felt dead inside. That was bad enough, but this? This is worse. You wanted to get rid of me so badly that you faked all that shit?" My voice breaks. "Why was I not enough for you?"

Simon stands to his full height at my words. His jaw clenches tightly. "You were—*are*—more than enough. You are everything to me, Piper Easton. Never question that."

"Then why did you push me away?"

"So you would leave! You're so goddamned stubborn that you would have stayed, given up everything for me, and eventually, all that love would have twisted into resentment."

"You don't know that, Simon," I argue.

"Yes, I do know."

"How?"

"Because that was exactly how I felt," he roars, snapping. "I resented my parents. They fucking left me, and my whole life went up in smoke—and I was *angry with them*. What kind of person does that make me?"

Simon leans back against the nightstand, bracing himself like the weight of his confession is too much for his body. I watch him run a sleeve across his eyes to wipe away the gathering moisture. His chest rises with a deep inhale. He lets his breath out slowly, prolonging the silence and gathering his thoughts. And when his gaze finally meets mine, I see pain. I see sadness, and regret, and so many other emotions. They shred through me like shrapnel from the bomb he just laid at my feet.

My heart breaks for the boy he was—for the pain he shouldered all on his own. I know I need to say something, but how do I respond? Every time I try, all the right words disappear.

Simon watches me for a moment before coming up to me. He grips me gently around the neck and rests his forehead on mine. Part of me wants to pull away, still raw, but the other part wants to melt into him and forget.

"Little bird," he murmurs, and my heart clenches. "I love you too much to hold you back the way I got held back." He pulls away so he can look me in the eyes. "I lost out on the chance to chase my dreams, but I'd be damned if I did the same to you."

"That was my decision to make," I argue. "My choice. Do you have any idea how lonely I was? How lost?" Tears gather in the corner of my eyes, but I blink them back. "All because you decided you knew better."

That's what this all boils down to.

Trust.

"Do you want to know what made those dreams so special?" I ask. "Not the dream itself. *What* we chased had no bearing at all. It was that we chased those dreams together."

My words end in a broken whisper. The tears I have been keeping at bay finally spill over. They sting, carving a burning path down both cheeks.

"You didn't trust that I would happily find new dreams with you." I pull away, shaking my head, unable to lift my gaze. Afraid of what I might see. "You had no faith in me then, and you have no trust in me now. Otherwise, you would have told me all this before."

"Piper. Look at me."

I shiver at the heavy tone of his voice, just daring me to resist. Sniffling, I lift my eyes to his. Their hazel color is darker and more subdued, marked by the determination on his face. Arms crossed, Simon considers me in silence. The air around us grows heavy with anticipation.

"You're right."

I blink in surprise at Simon's words.

"I didn't trust you then—not really, and I should have," he continues. "But now? The only reason I held back on telling you all this was timing. When you first got home, you barely wanted to talk to me. I needed to rebuild your trust. Then everything with that asshole came to light, and I hated the thought of piling this on top. You had enough to deal with."

I open my mouth, but before I can say anything, Simon lifts a palm to stop me. "I know. You could handle it, and it was your choice to make. I'm sorry I took that choice away," he adds. My heart warms at the sincerity in those words.

"So, what now?" I ask.

His answer is decisive. "You think I don't trust you now. Baby, I trust you implicitly. And I'm going to prove it."

> "You are *everything* to me, Piper Easton."

Chapter 30
Take Me To Church

Piper

Simon uncrosses his arms and slowly reaches for my hands. I let him slide his palms against mine, threading our fingers together before he tugs me to my feet. Then we stay like this for a few breaths, hand in hand, eye to eye—each waiting for the other to decide what to do next.

"How do you intend to prove that you trust me?" I finally ask, taking the first step.

"Simple. By giving you the reins."

I blink at that. "What?"

His lips quirk up in amusement. "Control. For tonight, you call all the shots in this bedroom. If you want to tie me up, you can tie me up. If you want to blindfold me, then blindfold me. If you want me to eat you out until you see stars, then"—I slap a hand over his mouth, stopping his dirty mouth before I self-combust.

Then I contemplate his meaning, my heart fluttering at the precious gift I have just received.

For someone like Simon, control is integral to who they are. Even in high school, he knew exactly what he wanted and how to get it. Looking back, I see little bits of the dominant personality inside of him now. Only I had no frame of reference, no name for that trait.

Neither did he.

Simon has since learned what true dominance means, though. In all the years since then, he has taken the time to hone his craft. The fact that he will willingly give me that control he craves—me, a complete and utter novice—goes a long way to strengthening my wavering faith.

But am I truly up for this?

What if I only mess everything up?

Simon must sense my uncertainty because he takes our joined hands and lightly pulls me toward the bed. "Stop overthinking," he chides. "Here, let's start slow."

Dropping my hands, Simon settles back against the mattress, resting on his palms while he watches me. Then he tilts his head, a contemplative look stealing over his face. "What would you like me to call you?"

"I, uh..." I blink at him, my mind coming up completely blank.

He chuckles. "Okay. Let's see... We could use Mistress. Or my lady, if you feel fancy. Queen. Goddess."

My mouth stretches into a smile. "Goddess, really?" I step closer, reaching out to play with one of his shirt buttons. "Do I look like a goddess?"

"Sweetheart, you *are* a goddess." His fingers twitch underneath him like he wants to touch me but refrains. I realize that we have already started the game. "Is that what you'd like me to call you?"

I hum slightly, still smiling. "I think I like the idea of being worshipped."

"I'll worship you any way you want."

"Okay, then. Goddess or my lady."

"As you wish, my lady." He looks at me expectantly.

Wracking my brain, I think about what would typically come next. But too many possibilities come racing at me, and I freeze. My eyes widen, and I must look like a deer in headlights.

Simon senses my struggle, thankfully, and once again offers himself up. "Would you like me to help, Goddess?"

My shoulders relax a fraction. "Yes"—I almost say *please*, but catch the word before it lifts off my tongue.

A goddess would never say please.

"What was the very first thing I asked you?" His hazel eyes twinkle at the memory.

"To kneel?" I bat my eyelashes. "That might be fun."

"If that's what you want me to do," he says earnestly, then shakes his head. "But, no. That part was a command, if you remember."

I blush. Of course I do. Every single second—every detail—of that first encounter etched itself onto my mind.

"Alright, then." I think for a moment. "You asked me if I had a safe word."

"Good girl."

I shiver in pleasure at the nickname. Even playing the sub, this man is a Dom through and through. Knowing that makes this interaction feel more meaningful, and my chest warms.

"Would you like to know mine?" Simon gently prods, raising an eyebrow.

"Yes." I straighten and pull my shoulders back in (what I hope is) a majestic pose, taking on a slightly haughty demeanor. "Well, then? Tell me your safe word, pet."

A smile teases at his lips. "Pet, huh?"

My eyes go wide. "Was that too much?"

He throws his head back and laughs. After he quiets, he looks back down at me with open affection, the laughter still twinkling in his eyes. "Baby, if you want to call me pet, you can. You don't have to explain yourself. You're in control here, not me."

"Why am I so bad at this?" I groan, hiding my face in my hands. A mortified giggle bubbles out of me. Then I feel Simon's heat when he sits up, gently grasps my wrists, and pries my hands away.

"Hey," he says, suddenly serious. He lifts my chin so I can't hide from him. "Is this too much? Do you want to stop?"

"No, it's just…" Frustration seeps in when I feel tears welling up in my eyes. "I keep thinking I'm going to do or say the wrong thing."

I am so tired of feeling helpless and weak. Why did I think distancing myself from Cedric would be enough? I will never get rid of him. He is always here, the devil on my shoulder that tells me I am nothing—not good, pretty, capable, intelligent, or strong enough.

I am *never* enough.

But now, I look at Simon, Cedric's opposite in every way. Because Simon always makes me feel like enough. No. He makes me feel like I am *everything*. Especially when he pulls me in by the back of the neck and kisses my forehead as he does now. I close my eyes, focusing on the rich timbre of his voice while Simon tells me precisely what I need to hear.

"When we are in these four walls," he declares, "there is no such thing as wrong. Nothing is taboo or forbidden. And nothing is off-limits unless we agree it is. Understand?" I nod. He lightly squeezes my neck. "Words, Piper."

"I understand." My eyes flutter open, and I smile at him a little.

"Such a good girl when you're not being a brat."

I flush with pleasure, and my smile turns teasing. "Being a brat is so much fun, though."

Simon chuckles. He tugs me forward again, this time landing a smacking kiss on my lips. Then, when he pulls back, Simon checks in one last time.

"You sure you want to keep going?" he asks. "This thing is for you, not me. I want you to know that I trust you so that you can feel safe to trust me." His hands cup my cheeks. "Without trust, none of this works."

"I do trust you, Simon." Weaving my arms around his neck and staring deeply into his eyes, I let that truth settle over me. Then I say, "That you would be willing to do this for me means more than I can put into words."

Simon smiles tenderly. "I would do anything for you, little bird."

"Yeah, I'm starting to see that." I smile back up at him, tightening my hold. "I love you. No mistake will ever change that."

"I love you, too."

We stay there momentarily, enjoying our physical connection before Simon finally breaks it. He sits back on his elbows, hooking his leg around mine and tugging me so that I tumble on top of him. Laughing, I lift until I straddle him with my hands resting on his abs.

"What would you have me do, Goddess?" His eyes devour me, the tip of his tongue peeking out to wet his lips. "Shall I worship you as you deserve?"

With a hum, I pretend to think while rolling my hips lazily over his. I bite back a moan when I feel him grow hard between my thighs. He has no such scruples, growling low in the back of his throat while he fights the desire to grab my hips and control the movement. That knowledge sends a jolt of pleasure right through me.

This sense of power, of control over another person, is a heady sensation.

I am beginning to see the appeal.

Something pricks at my memory. After a moment, I lean over him, and my hair settles around us like a curtain. "What is your safe word, my pet?"

His lips curve into a sinful smile. "Peaches."

"What?" I shake my head in disbelief. "You cannot be serious."

"One hundred percent." He winks.

I feel a rush of pleasure and say, "Okay then. Peaches it is."

Taking a slow, deep breath, I try to settle back into the mindset of my Domme persona. The transition gets a little easier each time.

"Well," I say, biting my lip, "you can hardly worship me with all these clothes on. So I want you to strip me." When he sits up to reach for me, I stop him with a hand to his chest. "Slowly. Make it last."

"As you wish, my lady."

Then Simon's hands are on my body. He carefully peels the clothes away, piece by tantalizing piece. I feel each brush of his knuckles along my skin, how his fingers tease and torture with each bit of fabric removed. By the time he reaches my panties, I am breathless and burning up with sensation—melting into a puddle in the middle of the mattress. But when he goes for the tiny scrap of lace, I lay my hand in front of it.

Simon pauses, eyes lifting to mine, one eyebrow lifting.

"Uh-uh," I admonish. "Now, using only your mouth."

His gaze grows heated. "With pleasure, Goddess."

I lift my hand away when Simon descends, jolting slightly when his lips caress my hip bone. He licks and nips his way toward the panty line, taking his time to be thorough until his teeth finally clench around the fabric. Then Simon slowly tugs them down, one side before the other, until they pass over my hips. They come off much more steadily after that, sliding down my legs until they have been completely removed.

Simon pops up, triumphantly holding the lace between his teeth. I giggle when he turns his head and spits them out onto the bed. Then I crook a finger at him.

"Come here, you," I say.

Grinning, Simon crawls up my body, sitting back on his haunches when he reaches my hips. He is careful only to touch those places I have given my permission.

But I want him to touch.

So I command him, "Strip down while you kiss me here"—I tap my fingers playfully along the length of my neck—"and then kiss me here."

Simon watches, transfixed, while the fingers of my other hand drift down my body, slide between my legs, and start to play with the slickness gathering there. A helpless whimper slips out when I dip two fingers inside. It takes me a moment to notice that Simon has yet to move a muscle.

I stop and cluck my tongue in admonishment. "You still have way too many clothes on." My foot makes its way up his pant leg, stopping to rub along his length. "Am I going to have to punish you?"

He jerks against me with a hiss, and his hands quickly start to unbutton his shirt. "No, ma'am," he says, slightly breathless.

I tilt slightly to the side and tap my neck, silently reminding Simon of his second task. He grins and eases himself down beside me. His tongue licks a path up from my collarbone to just under my ear, and I gasp. My fingers slip back inside, and I start to move them languidly, timing their thrusts with his licks and bites.

"I don't know..." My voice is breathless, punctuated by needy sounds as the pleasure starts to build. "I think I may still need to punish you. Maybe I should take care of myself and make you watch."

Simon sucks on the sensitive skin on the underside of my jaw. My hips jerk in response. "Would you truly be so cruel to your humble servant, Goddess?"

Out of the corner of my eye, I notice that Simon is gloriously naked. *Finally*. One large hand is wrapped around the base of his cock as he pumps it once, twice, and then a third time when he catches me looking.

I narrow my eyes. "I didn't say you could touch yourself."

His hand stills. "No, you didn't," he admits.

There is a flash of heat in his eyes when I suddenly sit up and press my palm against his sternum, guiding him to his back. I straddle him and capture his lips with mine. I tease him for just a second before pulling away.

"I changed my mind. You do need punishment." I dig my fingernails into the tops of his thighs and crawl backward.

"What do you—ah, *fuck*!" His hips bow off the bed in shock when I swallow his cock down almost to the back of my throat in one go.

I grip the base and, sucking in my cheeks, I slowly lift my head until he is almost out. Then, I lavish the sensitive underside of his tip with attention from my tongue. His guttural groan has me smiling so big that I have to come up for air.

"Fucking hell, woman, your mouth is lethal."

"What was that, pet?" I lean down and lick him from base to tip without waiting for an answer. Then I take him in my mouth again.

My movements fall into a steady rhythm, taking my cues from Simon. I make up for whatever technique I lack in enthusiasm. Based on his reaction, Simon approves. Each tortured sound that I drag out of him hits me like a drug, and I hum with pleasure.

Just when I start to feel Simon losing control, I back off, sitting back on my heels so that no part of me is touching him. He stares at the ceiling, chest heaving, and part of me wants to laugh at the image. Instead, I crawl up to the headboard, leaning forward to kiss Simon and coaxing him open with my tongue. I spend a few moments leisurely exploring and teasing in equal measure. When I pull back, he tries to follow. Laughing out loud this time, I press him back down with my hand.

But then I soften my rejection. "I think that's enough punishment."

Moving into the middle of the mattress, I settle down and drape my body like royalty against the pillows. Turning so that I face slightly toward Simon, my lips turn up in a sensual smile. I keep my gaze on him while I trace a finger down the middle of my torso, between my breasts, up along the dip in my waist before I let my hand rest on the swell of my hip.

"Time to worship," I say. Then I spread my legs in invitation.

Simon shifts over to my side. He looks down at me like a starving man in front of a buffet but otherwise stays put. When he lifts his gaze to mine, his eyes hold so much promise that I shiver.

"Where would you like me to touch, my lady?" Simon asks.

"Anywhere," I breathe, arching my back to bring my chest closer to his mouth. "Everywhere. Make me see stars."

He gives me a deliciously wicked smile in answer. "Your wish is my command."

His hands finally rest on my skin, cupping and palming my breasts, and the sudden warmth shocks my system. I jolt in surprise, gasping from the intensity—then again when Simon pinches both nipples. He rolls them between a thumb and forefinger until they are painfully hard.

Abruptly, he releases one.

I hiss at the sudden release of pressure.

But it lasts only seconds.

Quickly lowering his head, Simon sucks the rigid tip into his mouth. I cry out, arching my back. He bites down gently on the nub while his hand continues to massage my other breast. Then he switches sides.

Soon, Simon has reduced me to nothing but sensation. He uses his hands, mouth, tongue, and teeth to slowly and methodically map every inch of my body. A strategic kiss here, at a small birthmark just under my ribcage. A bite there, at my hipbone. His tongue dips into my navel. His hands spread, massage, and pinch.

He marks me and makes me his.

Simon is also a master at the art of torture. He plays my body like I play the guitar, with a skill that only comes from years of practice. My sounds might have embarrassed me without his enthusiastic response to each one.

And when he finally, *finally* runs the flat of his tongue up my slit, capturing the arousal pooling there, I am strung so tightly that I weep in relief.

Dom or not, Simon follows instructions beautifully, taking direction from my bodily cues with enthusiasm. He tongues my clit until I cry out his name. Then he sucks it into his mouth, nipping lightly. I curse, bowing off the bed. Afraid that I may float away, my hands seek purchase on the sheets and fist tightly in the jersey-knit fabric.

Then, as Simon sets a steady rhythm, I follow with a sobbing refrain: "More, right there, yes, don't stop!" Bit by bit, the restraint holding him in check erodes with each demand. He hoists my thighs over his shoulders, grabs my hips for purchase, and devours me.

My orgasm hits me like a freight train.

And I do, indeed, see stars.

Once my legs stop shaking uncontrollably and my mind floats back down from the aether, Simon carefully disengages himself. He presses gentle kisses to the insides of each thigh before sitting back on his heels. We both breathe in heavy pants. The smell of sex and arousal hovers around us, thick and potent, while we stare at each other in weighted silence.

Then, with a deep exhale, Simon opens his mouth and utters a single word:

"Amen."

My lips wobble until I collapse against the mattress, giggling so hard that I worry I might choke. In response, Simon's lips stretch into a Cheshire cat grin. He looks inordinately pleased with himself.

"Was my worship satisfactory, Goddess?" Simon asks.

I peek down at his lap. His dick stands proudly at attention, jutting out from a nest of ruddy gold curls. I lick my lips and then shake my head in response.

"Not quite," I say, voice raspy from use. I reach out to Simon with one hand. When he takes it, I pull him up toward me. "Why don't you try worshipping me with that holy grail between your legs? Take me higher than the stars this time."

I press a kiss to his lips, tasting myself on his tongue. It sends a shiver down my spine, quickly chased away by the warm weight of his body over mine. He quickly rolls on a condom and lines himself at my entrance. Then, bracketing my head with his forearms, he thrusts deep.

And he sends us both to heaven.

> "Shall I *worship* you as *you deserve?*"

Chapter 31
Panic Room

Piper

Something shifts between Simon and me after the intensity of the other night. That night, Simon instructs me on the importance of aftercare while we take a soothing bath together. Then, we lay tangled up in bed for hours, sharing little pieces of ourselves we have kept locked away—things we may even have hidden from ourselves. Things that, once spoken, become the missing threads needed to finish this wonderful tapestry we have been weaving over the past several weeks.

The tapestry that connects our pasts to our present—and us to each other.

One thing I have still not shared, however, is Cedric's article or the potential stalker situation. At first, I just wanted to bury my head in the sand and feign blissful ignorance. Now, I wonder what the point would be in causing Simon to worry about something in the past—especially since Cedric has been silent since his article got buried. I am not so naive to think the bastard has given up, but I believe Rue got him back in his box for now.

I hate the thought of that mess tainting all the good in my life with Simon.

One thing—I just need one tiny thing that Cedric cannot touch.

After wandering aimlessly in the dark for years, I finally found the path Simon and I had deviated from. Now that we are on it again, my heart is whole. My life feels like one of those intricate puzzles, and I have just slotted the final piece into place.

When Simon returns to work on his next shift, I write and compose the final songs to round out my newest album. Now, I need to find a decent recording studio nearby to record and release the title song to my fans.

I have also been working with Ellery on my idea for the album art. I want to involve the community because my musical rebirth comes from them as much as anything. We are holding a contest with the children's art classes, where I have asked them to draw or paint a phoenix in their style. Ellery and I will collage our favorites into a single phoenix design for the front cover.

While excited, I also feel nervous. Nothing can happen until I figure out how to get out of this contract—and so far, none of the lawyers I hired have found a single loophole, so I still have no chance to exit gracefully and without risk of legal ramifications.

January speeds toward me faster than I'm ready for. Anything can happen. If I break the terms of my contract, I have no doubt Cedric will rip me to shreds to make an example out of me—if only because he loves to watch me bleed.

Now more than ever, since I have my fight back.

I *will* fight Cedric for my freedom.

And I *will* win.

Until that happens, I plan to bide my time and focus on the things I can control—like surprising Simon tonight by cooking one of his favorite meals.

A few days ago, he mentioned how much he missed his dad's Beaufort stew. Simon often cooks dishes from the old recipe cards his mom kept in a large tin in the kitchen. Unfortunately, he was never able to locate that particular recipe.

So, I decide to recreate it to the best of my ability.

Early this morning, after Simon leaves for work, I search the internet for recipes that most closely resemble what I remember of the Brooks family staple. If the recipe gets close enough, I can taste-test the rest of it because the stew John Brooks made is one I could never forget. The man's cooking rivaled that of a classically trained chef, and he passed that particular talent on to his son.

Lucky me.

During my search, I remember that John always served the stew with hush puppies. I quickly add the ingredients for that to my growing list.

Once finished, I decide that the rest of the Brooks clan should enjoy this surprise, too. Grabbing my phone, I quickly text Ellery.

Piper: Hey! Are you and Beck up for dinner tonight at Simon's?

Ellery: Always! And B has an early day today, so we're free anytime after 5

Piper: Great! How about 7:00? Give Simon a chance to de-cop

Ellery: *laughing emoji* de-cop, I love that

Ellery: What are you cooking?

Piper: It's a surprise *wink emoji*

Ellery: Oooh *eyes emoji* We'll be there! Can't wait *heart-eyes emoji*

Piper: See you then! *heart emoji*

Now that I have a head count, I enlist Mom's help grabbing supplies. If I try to do the shopping myself, Simon may see me around town and wonder what I am up to. He and Nate are on patrol duty today, so the chances of running into each other are pretty high.

Mom says yes, of course. She will do anything for that man—not that I can blame her.

I mean, I would do anything for him, too.

Sometime just before noon, I hear the doorbell. Racing out of the study, where I have been tweaking song lyrics, I greet Mom at the door with a wide smile.

"Holy cow!" I cry out, looking at all the food she purchased. "Did you buy enough for an entire army?"

She chuckles from behind the paper bags in her arms. "Oh, stop. Help me with these, will you?"

I quickly grab half of her haul and lead her to the kitchen. On the way, all three dogs bark their hellos and follow close behind. They must sense something good is coming.

"None of this is for you, sillies," I scold.

"You mean to tell me that you're going to make *hush puppies*, and you would deprive these sweet angels from having some?" Mom looks mockingly affronted on their behalf.

I roll my eyes and respond, "Yes, Mom, because hush puppies have onions in them, and dogs can't eat onions." Pausing to look down at the three wildly hopeful faces staring up at me, I groan. "But I guess I could make a doggy-safe batch just for them…"

"See? And you wonder why I brought so much." She titters while we begin to pull everything out of the bags. "And, anyway, you can make extra and give some to Beckham and Ellery to take home. I'm sure they would appreciate that."

My heart melts, and I wrap her in a sudden hug. "Oh gosh, I didn't even think of that. Thank you for being so wonderful."

"Oh, come now. You know I love doting on my family."

A smile stretches across my face. "I know."

We separate and start to wash and prepare the ingredients. Mom husks and quarters the corn while I peel the shrimp and cut up the andouille sausage. I remember that specific ingredient from John's version of the stew and his unique seasoning blend. Unfortunately, I cannot create my own, and since I am not entirely sure what John used in his, I just had Mom buy ready-made seasoning from the store. I can tweak it if needed.

Together, we make quick work of everything and put it into the slow cooker to start simmering. Then, I begin preparing the hush puppies. As promised, I set aside some of the ingredients for the dogs, leaving out any unsafe ones. We can serve them as a treat at dinner.

While we combine the ingredients, we work side-by-side in comfortable silence. But then, after a while, Mom breaks the silence to ask a question—albeit in a roundabout way.

"So," she says slowly, studiously avoiding my gaze, "you and Simon seem to be doing well."

Ahh. It's time for the patented Stella Easton interrogation, I see. Luckily, I have been preparing for this. And honestly, this is one bit of news I am happy to share.

"We are." My lips curve up, and I shoot her a sideways glance. "*Extremely* well."

She beams at me. "I'm so happy for you, sweat pea."

"Thanks, Mom." I go quiet for a few moments. Then I add, "I love him."

"I know."

"How, though?" I ask with a breezy laugh. "I mean, even I had no clue until Thanksgiving."

"Because," she replies, "you have loved Simon since high school, my dear. That kind of love can't be willed away. It sticks with a person. And Simon"—Mom gets a wistful smile—"well, that boy has been head over heels for you since he first saw you. He was horrible at hiding his feelings, and I noticed it every time you came into his orbit."

"Really?" I ask.

"Mm-hmm. You took a little longer, of course," she continues. "You feared Simon's looks and popularity, thinking he was looking for a good time every time he asked you out—worried he would eventually get bored and move on."

"God." I hide my face in my hands. "Did I tell you that?"

She chuckles before reaching up to tug my hands down. "I'm your mother. You didn't have to tell me. Besides," she adds with a wink, "teenage girls are hardly discreet."

"Okay, fair."

All the hush puppies have been rolled out and are on trays by then. I move to put them in the fridge, planning to air-fry them closer to dinner time so they're fresh. Once I close the refrigerator door, I lean back on it and sigh.

"We missed out on so much time," I whisper, looking down at my hands.

"Hey." Mom leans against the door beside me and nudges my shoulder with hers. "Sometimes life gets in the way. That's just how the world works. But the kind of love you two have is a once-in-a-lifetime kind of love. You were always going to find your way back to each other."

"Hmm." I lean my head against her shoulder. "You've given me and my therapist a lot to talk. about."

I hear her chuckle above the top of my head. "Better that than something to complain about."

"Oh, there's plenty of that, too."

Mom shoves me away, laughing. "On that note, don't you have your therapy appointment soon?"

I look down at my watch. "At four. I'm meeting Daisy for coffee first, so I need to leave in an hour. No rush."

"Well, let me get out of your hair so you can finish getting ready for tonight," she says, standing up and brushing off her pants.

The smells starting to waft out of the slow cooker are mouthwatering, and I take a moment to take a deep breath before leading Mom across the house. When we reach the front door, I give her one last hug. "Thanks again for your help."

"Anytime. You know that." She winks and steps out onto the porch. As she is walking down the steps, she adds, "Next time, I expect an invite to dinner, though!"

"Promise!" I call out. "And I'll bring you and Pop leftovers from this one, too."

I wait for her car to pull away before closing the door. Something makes me pause—a feeling of unease at the base of my skull—but nothing looks out of place when I look around.

It's just more paranoia.

With a sigh, I shut the door, all the while thinking, *I can't wait for this mess to end.*

Maybe then I can stop looking over my shoulder.

***

Coffee with Daisy is, as usual, just what I need to get my mind off more serious matters—a bit ironic, I suppose, since I spend an entire hour talking about those serious matters during my therapy appointment. At least we focus less on Cedric today. What I told my Mom earlier is true. She gave me a lot to think about, and I end up talking about Simon for most of today's session.

I leave the appointment with a huge smile and a little less weight pressing down on me from all sides.

It is just after five when I step out onto the sidewalk. By now, the sun has dipped below the horizon. The sky is in that in-between state of dusky gray—and rapidly darkening. A crisp wind blows around me, cutting through layers of clothing and sending a shiver down my spine.

Zipping my jacket and wrapping the heavy scarf more securely around my shoulders, I tug on my gloves and head south. The parking spot where I left my car is in front of Jelly Beans, two blocks south of my therapist's office. But I only take a handful of steps before realizing I forgot drinks. I also want to pick up something for dessert.

Luckily, there is a convenience store a few blocks away, at the other end of the downtown district. They should have whatever I need. It will mean cutting it close if I want to get home before Simon, but I should still make it with enough time to change.

That decided, I slip my keys back into my bag. Then, I turn in the opposite direction. While I walk, I pull my phone out and absently scroll through checking emails and messages. I have one from Rue, who is giving me a status update from the lawyers—more of the same, I sadly realize, although they think it would be beneficial to meet with Cedric's lawyers again. I don't know the point, but I don't pretend to understand half of the legal jargon they throw my way. I quickly reply that we can schedule something and I'll call her tomorrow. Then I hit send.

When I close out of the mail app, I receive a new text notification. I smile when I see Simon's name pop up on the screen. Pausing to cross the street, I open his text thread once I safely reach the other side. Then, I reread today's entire thread, starting from the first text he sent me this morning.

- 7:00 am -

Simon: Miss you already

Piper: *heart-eyes emoji* It's only been like 90 min

Simon: Too long

Piper: Poor baby

Simon: Are you giving me sass, brat?

Piper: *smirk emoji*

Simon: *smiling imp emoji* *paddle emoji*

- 11:30 am -

Simon: Did you know I gave Miss Betty four citations this week? She's racking up parking tickets like the damn lottery

Piper: Miss Betty—didn't she used to teach astronomy?

Simon: Yep.

Piper: Dang, how old is she now?

Simon: Ancient.

Simon: But not old enough to know it's inappropriate to grab my ass every time she sees me

Piper: I mean... I get the temptation

Simon: YOU may grab my ass any time you like

Piper: Noted *heart eyes* Anyway, I thought you were supposed to be working

Simon: Nate and I are on patrol duty *yawn emoji*

Piper: I think Nate needs a new partner. His current one thinks it's okay to sleep on the job.

Simon: Watch it, brat.

Piper: *halo emoji*

Simon: The spanking you're getting when I get home...

- 1:15 pm -

Simon: Bored...

Simon: Buried under paperwork

Piper: Aww, poor baby

Piper: Are the SCANKs causing trouble again?

Simon: The what now?

Piper: *laughing emoji* members of the Sexy Cop Addict & Naughty Kook club. SCANK.

Simon: Dear god, y'all named those crazy women always trying to get arrested by me?

Piper: I mean, technically they named themselves...

Simon: Don't care. They do NOT need more power; they're organized as fuck as it is

Piper: *lmao emoji*

Simon: I'm serious. I think Miss Betty is the ringleader

-2:10 pm-

Simon: Do you know anything about B&E coming over for dinner tonight?

Piper: Yep. I invited them. Is that okay?

Simon: Of course, but what's the occasion?

Piper: It's a surprise *kiss emoji*

Simon: *eyes emoji*

Simon: Is it a naked surprise?

Piper: *laughing emoji* With your sister and Beckham in the house?

Simon: I mean, there are a lot of rooms we could hide in

Piper: *shocked scream face*

Simon: If not a naked surprise, what is it?

Piper: You have to wait and see

Simon: Meanie

I reach the end of the thread, see his newest text, and quickly reply.

- 5:00 pm -

Simon: See you soon

Piper: Can't wait *sparkling heart emoji*

Giggling quietly, I start to close the app when I notice an unread text thread from an unknown number—recent, too. Feeling uneasy, my thumb hovers over the number. Then, twin sparks of fury and fear ignite in my gut when I read the alert. Smashing the name on my screen, I stare at the texts in growing horror.

Unknown number: This game has gone on long enough, you cunt

Unknown number: The clock is ticking

Unknown number: You better have your ass back in NYC in time for the New Year

Unknown number: And if you think of trying anything shifty, just remember that I know every fucking move you make

Unknown number: Where you eat and sleep

Unknown number: Who you're with at all times

Unknown number: Who you're whoring yourself out to

When I get to the last text, a series of photos blow up my screen, and my pulse thunders in my ears. I see photos of me. Pictures of Simon, Ellery, and Beckham. Group shots from Thanksgiving, taken from a telescopic lens. Photos of Easton family dinners. Pictures of me at the Christmas Market, sipping hot chocolate, and walking with Ellery. One from over the weekend reveals me standing on the back porch of Simon's house, drinking coffee.

Photos from today show up, too: one of me greeting my mom at Simon's house earlier and one of Daisy and I sitting in a booth at Jelly Beans, drinking our coffee and laughing.

Then I get to the last photo. Hand shaking, I scroll down until the image fills the screen. Fear fists around my throat and tightens until I can barely breathe. In the picture, I stand in front of my therapist's office not even ten minutes ago.

And now—another photo pops into the thread directly under the last one. I see the back of me, standing right where I am now. My head snaps up. Frantically, I look around, expecting to see someone with a camera out in the open and blatantly staring. But, other than one or two stragglers here and there, the streets are almost empty.

Shit. Shit. Shit.

My feet dislodge from their frozen state, and I propel forward before my brain even catches up. Even as I race toward some unknown destination, my thumbs fly across the screen, pulling up my list of favorite contacts. The phone starts to ring, and Simon picks up before I even register that I clicked on his name.

"Piper?" he asks.

"Someone is following me," I hiss into the mouthpiece.

My breaths are shallow and shuddering while my footsteps pound on the pavement. I am not running yet but still walking as fast as possible. My face feels cold and wet—from rain, I think at first. But the sky is clear, and the droplets are my own tears. Panic tries to claw its way out of me, but I shove it back while my focus stays firmly on getting away.

Simon immediately goes on red alert. His voice hardens, and he barks out, "Where are you?"

"Uh," I say, frantically looking around. "Halfway between 11th Street and Holland Avenue. Headed in the direction of the Speedy Mart. I"—my voice breaks into a sob—"needed to pick up some drinks, and"—I gasp for breath, trying not to hyperventilate—"I left my car blocks in the other direction, and I don't know what to do—"

"Piper. Calm, baby. I need you to stay calm." His voice hardens into cold steel that tightens around me. But it doesn't suffocate. It gives me something to hold onto. His muffled voice in the background repeats the address to Nate. Then Simon gets back on the earpiece to say, "I need you to get inside the nearest store you can, okay? Anywhere you see other people around."

I want to. God, I do. But I am half-running and looking at each door; they are all tightly locked up. I even yank on one, hoping that maybe it will magically open. When it fails to, I sob and kick the frame.

"Everything is c-closed," I stammer, "and locked tight."

My teeth start to chatter from cold and nerves. Dim street lamps light very little, and I can see nothing around me but darkness. I wish I could see the person following me, at least. Every faint movement attacks my sanity, thinking they are about to jump out at me from the shadows.

I need to move now—only my feet refuse to cooperate. It takes every bit of willpower to force them to arch and lift off the ground. But somehow, they inch forward, picking up speed until I look up and see the bright lights of the convenience store parking lot in the distance. Street lamps and interior lights flare like a beacon, calling me to it. Saying, *here is safety.*

"Speedy Mart. I can see it."

"Okay, baby, that's good. Head that way. Just keep moving, okay? We're almost to you."

My heart rate starts to calm along with the steady cadence of Simon's baritone voice.

Safety is up ahead. Simon, too.

I am going to be okay.

Then, two strong arms grab me from behind.

My phone clatters to the ground. I open my mouth to scream, but a large, gloved hand covers it before a sound can pass my lips. My breaths come in frantic bursts. The scent of male sweat and familiar cologne chokes me.

"Miss me, darling girl?" Cedric's voice is acidic and vile, burning me from the inside out.

Adrenaline jerks my body fully into its fight-or-flight response. I start to struggle in Cedric's iron grip. He squeezes tighter. Bile burns in the back of my throat while I am dragged away from the street and into a dark alley.

"Uh-uh-uh," he grits out while I struggle again in his arms. "No more running. No more hiding. I didn't want to get my hands dirty, but when you want something done right..."

Panic starts to overtake me. I know I only have a slim window to escape, so I thrash and claw at anything I can reach. My elbow connects sharply with the soft spot just under his rib cage. The heel of my boot slams down on his foot. He grunts and loosens his grip.

I have one shot.

So I take it.

Breaking free, I jolt forward. But I only get a couple of steps away before I am wrenched in the opposite direction by my hair. I shriek in pain, flying backward, and my back hits the ground hard, pain blooming in my head when it slams against the unforgiving cement. I feel a heavy weight press me down.

Then that gloved hand is back over my mouth.

Cedric is the man I hoped and prayed to never see again in my lifetime—and one I wish I could forget. But my eyes flutter open to the blurry image of a man. When that image blinks into focus, Cedric looms over me, face only inches from mine.

My nightmare, come back to life.

"I was only planning to scare you," he says cryptically. His lips move to my ear. "But, now? Think I'll have some fun, too."

Chapter 32
Burn It All Down

Simon

- 4:00 pm -

Simon: Still no luck on the Tobias front?

Hawk: I haven't heard anything new. Let me check in again.

Shit.

I groan and let my head fall back against the passenger seat headrest.

Nate looks over from his seat in the police cruiser. "No luck?"

"Nope," I reply tersely.

Thankfully, Nate takes no offense. He knows how much this whole situation has been eating away at me. The longer I go without hearing any good news—or hell, *any* news—the more I feel Cedric slipping through my fingers, the slimy bastard.

Tobias did locate Piper's contract early on, at least. I sent it to Priya immediately after getting my hands on the file, but so far, every word of it seems above board. She also found zero loopholes. Part of me wants to slam my fist into something—Cedric, preferably.

How can one man be this squeaky clean? No way does someone like him have no skeletons in his closet. I need to find them.

Tobias can hack better than anyone I have ever known.

If he is unable to find anything, no one will.

"I'm sorry, man. This can't be easy," I hear from the man beside me.

Nate knows a little about the situation. Not enough to betray Piper's trust, but as my partner and a good friend, I value his opinion. He is also levelheaded.

Beckham would have hopped on the first plane to New York City to put his special ops training to good use by making Cedric hurt. I have only revealed the smallest amount to him for just that reason.

Not that he seem too surprised, though—which means Ellery knows as much as me if not more. That chafes a little, to be honest.

Hell, Ellery probably knew before I did.

Christ, Brooks. Not the time to act all butt hurt.

With a quick shake of my head, I add, "Sorry, man. I should be paying more attention."

Nate looks at me sideways. "Dude. We're in the middle of a small town on a Monday afternoon in December. There ain't shit happening that requires two sets of eyes."

I snort a laugh. "That's fair."

Just then, a new text comes through.

- 4:25 pm -

Hawk: T-diddy hit the mother load!

Hawk: Asshole is using an alias

Jolting up in my seat, I frantically punch at the screen with my thumbs.

Simon: Send it to me

Hawk: Already done. Check your email. He sent it encrypted from a secure account, so you'll need the key to open it

Simon: Thanks, man

He pastes a long, intricate series of letters, numbers, and symbols into the chat window. I copy it and open my mail app. It takes a couple tries to get the damn thing to open, but once I do, I see a single compressed folder as an attachment. After successfully unzipping the files, I focus on Tobias's endless records, photos, and notes.

The most recent dates catch my eye, spanning the weeks leading up to Thanksgiving. With a frown, I select the single text note and scan it.

An anonymous source submitted the article. Once I discovered C's real name, I also located several fake IP addresses. The article came from one of those. The photo source is unknown.

T.

My anger erupts when I open the article in question. Cedric, the bastard, tried to paint Piper as an unhinged, out-of-control party girl addicted to sex and drugs. Every word I read turns my stomach.

But the photos send me through the roof.

"Son of a bitch," I hiss, clicking on the first one and beginning to swipe through the gallery.

Photos taken include Piper and me in erotic poses, with my face cut out of the frame. I see pictures of her with our police force, framed to look like arrests. Several times, shots of her place and mine show up.

When I reach the last photo, *taken inside her bedroom*, I snap. "I'll fucking kill him."

"I'm going to pretend I didn't hear that. Plausible deniability." Nate peeks over at me. "I take it you found something?"

As much as it sickens me, I continue sifting through the other evidence Tobias found. Rage boils my blood. I close my eyes and take a deep, cleansing breath—even though I would much rather punch my first through the window.

Once my blood pressure lowers, I answer Nate. "Enough to lock this deranged motherfucker up until the end of time, if we can figure out a way to get this evidence into the right hands"— *using proper legal channels*. Otherwise, any decent defense lawyer would chew the evidence up and spit it out in seconds. It will never hold up in court.

But I am a determined motherfucker, and I have a lot of resources.

Cedric Thomas is going down, one way or another.

But right now, I have more pressing concerns:

What the hell am I going to do about Piper?

She could have been unaware of the article, but my instincts tell me she knew. Why else would she have broken down like she did on the same day as its publication? And if that is the case, not only did she conveniently forget to tell me about the article, but she blatantly ignored the fact that some fucker is *stalking* her.

No. Scratch that. Some fucker has been stalking *our entire family.*

Piper shared enough the evening I learned her history with Cedric. She gets a pass for that night. But the article came to light over two weeks ago. Piper could have told me on any number of different occasions. Hell, she should have said something after I revealed the true nature of our breakup. We spent that entire night rebuilding our trust. That would have been the perfect moment.

But she failed to take advantage of it.

Piper needs to learn—I need to teach her—just how many people care about her. An army of people stands in her corner, ready to battle in her honor—and *I. Fucking. Lead. It.*

Whatever her lesson, I will make sure it sinks in and she never, ever forgets.

My mounting irritation makes me twitchy. Once it reaches DEFCON 1 levels, I open my phone to check the time. I bite back a groan when I see the numbers lit up to read five-fifteen.

I am due to head home at six.

Fuck. I will be walking straight into a surprise dinner that includes Ellery and Beckham. I'm in no frame of mind to pretend.

I should tell Piper to reschedule.

The blinking cursor taunts me when I open our text thread and start a new message. I type one message after another, shaking my head each time, then delete the whole thing and start again. Nothing sounds right. Every time I go to hit send, I picture Piper's excitement about her surprise. My hand hovers over the phone, but I cannot force my fingers to press the send button.

Am I pissed? Hell yes.

But when it comes to Piper, I am also a fucking fool.

So, of course I refuse to hurt her feelings. I can suck it up, put on a smile, and do the thing. Maybe dinner will give me enough time to cool down. I need to figure out a suitable punishment before I broach the subject of her disobedience.

And I will *never* discipline her in anger.

With a sigh, I shoot off a message. Something short and sweet that does not indicate my mood, happy or otherwise.

- 5:20 pm -

Simon: See you soon

Piper: Can't wait! *heart emoji*

My lips twitch.

Such a fool.

"Ready to head back to the station?" Nate looks at me and adds, "Paperwork awaits us, my friend."

Yet another annoyance I have to deal with. Fuck. Sometimes, I hate being an adult.

"Sure," I sigh. "Let's head out."

Nate nods and starts the ignition. We get within five minutes of the station when my phone starts blaring its ringtone. As soon as I see the name, I pick up.

"Piper?" I ask, exchanging a confused glance with Nate.

"Someone is following me." Her voice, a broken and scared whisper, goes off in my ears like a trumpet blast.

Immediately shifting into cop mode, I jolt straight in my seat and ask, "Where are you?"

Nate goes on alert at the tone of my voice. He pulls to a stop on the side of the road. Together, we stare at the phone and wait for her answer.

"Um…" For a moment, I hear only her panicked breaths. "I'm between 11th Street and Holland Avenue. Headed in the direction of the Speedy Mart. I"—her voice breaks on a gasping sob—"needed to pick up some drinks, and—I left my car blocks in the other direction, and I don't know what to do—"

Shit. Piper sounds seconds away from a panic attack. I bark her name and then say a gentler but no less commanding, "Calm, baby. I need you to stay calm."

Covering the mouthpiece, I look over at Nate. "11th and Holland. Step on it." My attention shifts back to Piper so I can give her clear instructions. "I need you to get inside the nearest store you can, okay? Anywhere you see other people around."

My voice is stern and assertive while I speak to her. She needs something to focus on other than her fear. Hopefully, it works.

After a handful of seconds, she sobs and kicks at something. "Everything is c-closed," she stammers, "and locked tight."

SWEET OBSESSION

Damn it. My chest clenches at the fear in Piper's voice, but I quickly shove my responding panic deep down. Action and decisions now. I can sort out my emotions later.

Suddenly, I hear Piper gasp. "Speedy Mart," she says excitedly. "I can see it."

Thank god. "That's great, baby. Head that way. Just keep moving, okay? We're almost to you."

We speed south on Main Street. I can see the building in the distance, getting closer, and the tiny figure walking fast toward it. Piper's blonde hair dances in the wind, and she curls into herself with each frantic step. Nate sees her, too, and speeds up.

Her figure inches closer.

But we are still too fucking far away.

I watch in horror as a figure in dark clothing lunges out of the darkness and grabs Piper. They cover her mouth with a gloved hand. Seconds later, shadows swallow her whole.

"Fuck!" I roar, tossing my useless phone to the side.

We both jolt back when Nate slams hard on the gas to erase the last hundred yards.

"You focus on Piper," he barks. "I'll take the perp."

Nate pulls up to the sidewalk with a screech. Before the car stops, I grab the handle and wrench the door open. My feet hit the ground at a dead run. Nate follows right behind me.

I hear a shriek in the darkness that turns my blood to ice.

We both barrel into the alleyway. Nate switches his flashlight on and shines it straight toward the back, sweeping left to right. He stops on two figures. Piper lays on the ground, struggling, while the stalker—a male, based on the size—covers her body with his. He leaps up when the light hits his eyes—wearing a ski mask, the fucking coward—and takes off down another alleyway.

Nate curses. "I got him!" he shouts, racing ahead of me.

When I yank my flashlight from my utility belt, I flip it onto the highest setting, and the light flares out in all directions. My knees hit the ground as soon as I reach Piper's side. Already sitting, she holds her head with her hands. Her limbs shake with adrenaline and fear.

"Shit. Piper," I say, my voice breaking from the relief of seeing her in one piece.

Lowering her hands when she hears my voice, Piper searches me out through eyes blurred with tears. "S-Simon?"

"Yeah, baby. I'm here." I gently grip her face with my hands. My gaze holds hers intently while she fights to focus. "Are you hurt anywhere?"

"The back of my head." She lifts her right hand, wincing, and motions to that side.

"I'm going to take a look. Stay still for me, okay?"

"Okay."

Holding Piper steady, I carefully pry the beanie from her head. Then, I lean over to check for damage—not easy in this low lighting, but I still manage to find the injury. No blood, thank god, but a giant goose egg has already started to form.

When I pull back, Piper's eyes follow me. I smile gently, trying to smooth the hard edges of worry from my face. "Anywhere else hurt?"

She frowns in thought. "Hip. Same side."

I expected as much since I found her on the ground. Bile burns the back of my throat. I have to pinch my eyes closed until the sudden mental image disappears. Then, taking a steadying breath, I return to my examination. No blood paints her skin or stains her clothing, but I see a bruise peeking up over the hemline of her jeans. I am sure she has more. She is going to hurt something fierce tomorrow.

Just then, Nate reappears—but with no perpetrator in tow. He bends over, hands on his knees, and tries to catch his breath. After a moment, he straightens and clenches his hands into fists. Gritting his teeth, he says, "Bastard got away."

In a sudden burst of rage, Nate rears back and slams the heel of his boot into the brick wall beside him. "Fuck!" he shouts. Then, after taking a moment to gather himself, he sends a look of wretched apology my way. "I'm sorry. I thought I had him, but he vanished into thin air."

I stare at him in shock. A stoic, steady man like Nathaniel Walker never falls apart. When he speaks again, his voice is quieter, focused inward. "He has to be a local who knows these back alleys well. Which probably means he's close by."

Piper's head starts to shake back and forth. "No. N-no, he…" Her breathing picks up, and tears of frustration leak out. She stares at me like she needs to tell me something but the words are lodged in her throat.

Either way, I need to stop it before the panic takes over.

"Nate," I bark.

His head snaps up in confusion. I quickly cut my eyes toward Piper, curled up and shaking in my arms. He gets the message loud and clear: *Now is not the time.*

"You did your best," I add. In no way do I blame Nate, and he needs to know that.

With a terse nod, Nate starts walking our way. "I called the paramedics on my way back. They should be here any second."

"Good."

I turn my focus back on my girl. "Hear that?" I said. "We're going to get you all patched up. Then you can go to bed and snuggle up with the dogs and me. I won't even complain about having no room."

Her face warms with the ghost of a smile at my attempt to lighten the mood a little.

"Does that sound okay?"

She nods, but her chin starts wobbling, and tears again spill down her cheeks. "I want to go home."

"We will, baby. Soon."

***

"Soon" turns into an hour, give or take. As soon as the paramedics arrive, they check Piper over and determine that she has a concussion in addition to the goose egg. Luckily, it seems mild. They give her some Tylenol for the pain before sending her home with me under strict instructions to wake her up every three hours for the first twelve to check on her.

I get situated in the back seat with Piper, gathering her to my side while Nate drives us back to my house and helps me get her inside. After I promise to keep him updated, I scoop a sleepy Piper into my arms and head upstairs while Nate locks up for me.

After sitting her down on the edge of the mattress, Ozzy and Cooper quickly snuggle to each side, sensing their mama needs them. Even Duchess comforts her, although she first stands on the floor at her feet and looks up at me with a disdainful expression that surely means, *Pick me up, peasant. I, too, require the snuggles.*

So, I lift her and settle her on Piper's lap.

Then I kneel in between Piper's legs, resting my hands on her thighs while I look up at her. After the night from hell that we both just experienced, all I want to do is gather her up and hold her close all night. But this time, she gets to make the decision.

"Bath or bed?" I ask.

"Bed." She says it with so little hesitation that I almost smile. Almost.

Instead, I nod and then head over to my dresser. I quickly change out of my uniform and into something to sleep in. Piper's clothes now occupy the top drawer of my dresser, but I continue to rummage through my own. I want her in my shirt tonight. Then, before I head back to her side, I stop in the bathroom to run a washcloth under warm water.

First, I help her out of her layers of clothing, and then I methodically use the washcloth to wipe away whatever remains of the encounter, like the dirt on her face and her smudged makeup. Even covered with winter gloves, her hands have tiny bits of gravel embedded in the skin while tiny red scraps mar the skin. When the gloves lay on the growing pile of her clothes, I wipe the skin there, too. Then I kiss each palm. I press a feather-light kiss to her hip next. Finally, I stand, toss the washcloth in the hamper, and slip my t-shirt over her head.

All three dogs watch the entire scenario in fascination. I turn to them and say, "Bedtime."

Ozzy and Cooper immediately jump off my bed and go to the shiny new dog beds I bought. Duchess stands at the edge of the mattress, wagging her tail and whining at me. But when I carry her to her bed, she bypasses it and prances over to Ozzy. He watches, enraptured, while Duchess searches for the most comfortable spot. Once she settles into his side, Ozzy curls his massive body around her tiny one.

God save the men in this family. We are all hopelessly obsessed with our females. I shake my head with a tiny smile and round the bed. Once under the covers, I curl around my lady exactly like Ozzy did with his. Then, mindful of Piper's injuries, I carefully slip a hand under her t-shirt and slide my palm to rest along her ribcage.

I need to feel her skin-to-skin.

I need to know, without a doubt, that she is truly here.

Tonight took about ten years off my life. All evening, the weight of my fear threatened to crush me. Even now, different scenarios keep racing through my head: what if something worse happened? If we had been just a few minutes later—

No. I refuse to think like that. Piper *is* here, breathing, alive, and warm in my arms. To hell with everything else.

But then, before sleep claims me, Piper murmurs my name.

"What do you need, little bird?" I whisper into her ear.

Piper turns to face me, a silent request, and shudders in relief when I gather her into my arms. She burrows into my chest. I carefully rest my cheek against the crown of her head.

"It wasn't someone local," she says, her voice hoarse from overuse and nearing its limit.

My brain seizes. While I hear what Piper says and feel the words vibrate against my skin, I fail to understand their meaning. How can she possibly know that? The alley was pitch black, and her assailant wore dark layers and a mask. I want to demand answers but clench my teeth against all my questions. Piper needs to do this in her own time.

"Cedric," she says. "It was Cedric." As close as we are, I still must strain to hear her whispered words. "Shadows made him impossible to see, but I could hear his voice. And the cologne he wore—I would recognize it anywhere."

Piper's admission triggers something in me. Every muscle locks up even as my mind rebels against the truth of her words. She starts to sniffle, her shaking worsens, and right now, all I can do is hold her until it passes.

I hate feeling so fucking weak.

"He called me 'darling girl.' I always hated that pet name." Then her voice splinters when she says, "He wanted to scare me. But he wanted it to hurt."

"Baby." I can barely talk through the lump of fear in my throat. "That man is never going to touch you, not ever again. Not while I still have breath left in my body."

"Everything is my fault."

"Don't even think that," I reply, anger sparking. "None of this is your fault."

"This *is*." She sounds disgusted with herself. "After I told you about Cedric, I should have told you about the texts, the harassment.... Then, he published an article. He hired someone to watch me, to take pictures and—"

"Piper, I know." I have no desire to broach the subject tonight, but I also need her to not work herself into a frenzy.

"You know?" After a beat of silence, she asks, "Are you—?" Piper cuts off, swallowing thickly, and tries again. "Are you angry at me?"

"No, I'm not—" Shit. I will not lie to her. Trust and honesty are what we promised each other. Always. I will not break that vow. So I sigh heavily and amend my response. "Yes, Piper. I'm goddamned furious."

"I'm sorry, Simon…" She sounds so very timid. It breaks me up inside.

"Just—don't," I say, knowing how tired I must sound. I *am* tired. Every bone in my body feels several hundred years old. "Now isn't the time. We both had a horrible night. We both need rest. This can wait."

We do need to talk, but not with our emotions running high. We can have this conversation tomorrow after our bodies and minds have rested. Once the deluge of information settles in my brain, I can process it and figure out what to do next.

We can talk then.

For now, I just feel thankful nothing worse happened.

After Piper finally falls asleep, I can stop being strong. Everything I forced down—all the fear, anger, worry, and panic strangling me on the inside—rushes to the surface. With no other outlet, the emotions bleed out of me, tears of relief gathering in my eyes and spilling over. Before long, my depleted mind and body join Piper in sleep.

That night, I dream of a phoenix rising from the wreckage and setting the world on fire.

Trust and *honesty* are what we *promised* each other.

Always.

Chapter 33
Raise the Red Flag

Simon

My eyes blink open to an empty bed and cold sheets the following morning. *Fuck. Where is Piper?* With that thought I jolt upright, pulse racing while my gaze frantically ping-pongs around the room. My brain is a bit slower to awaken fully. When it does, I force the panic down. No way did Piper leave the house, especially not after last night—that would just be foolish—and she has the dogs to protect her. That final thought does nothing to soothe me, however.

As thrilled as I am that she has Ozzy and Cooper to keep her safe, we are in my house. Under this roof, I do the protecting.

Sunlight filters in through the curtains, and a quick peek at my phone confirms the time as just after seven. Strange to admit, but I feel off-kilter without Piper next to me. Having her in my space and part of my life has become an unquenchable craving.

Some people might say this all happened too fast. But I waited twelve years for a second chance with Piper Easton. Though I would wait an eternity more, there is no need—I am not wasting another minute. I love her.

Even when she acts like an incorrigible brat.

No, *especially* when she acts like a brat.

Because Piper feels comfortable enough with me to push my buttons and test my limits, she trusts me enough to know that I will never give her more than she can handle. I will never *take* more than she can provide. That trust is more precious than gold for someone who had so much stolen from her.

I will guard that trust—and her—with my life.

But first, I have to break her down and strip away all the self-doubt, anxiety, and fear that Cedric bred in her over the years.

That starts today.

When I slip out of bed, I notice all three dogs are gone, too. I quickly throw on some sweats and a shirt before heading toward the door. I pause halfway and return to my nightstand, grabbing my phone and opening a text to Nate. Thank goodness I have the day off, but Nate will be at the office and needs to write an official report of last night's events.

- 7:10 am -

Simon: The perp is Cedric Thomas

Nate: Her asshole ex?

Simon: The very same

Nate: How could she tell?

Simon: Recognized his cologne, voice, and a pet name

Simon: I want him found, and I want an address

Nate: *salute emoji*

I pocket my phone before padding down the stairs. Then I head toward the kitchen, the tantalizing scents of food and coffee growing stronger with every step.

Piper gracefully moves around the space, mixing a small batch of something in a glass measuring cup. I pause in the entryway, mesmerized, watching her every move. Our dogs also watch from their spot on the floor, piled together, ever hopeful for a stray morsel of food.

The oven timer beeps and breaks the spell.

Piper rushes over while tugging on an oven mitt. However, when she goes to grab the door handle, her body sways slightly to and fro, and she grabs her head. Then her eyes pinch shut, and her face grows pale and drawn.

I am at Piper's side before I even register that I moved, a quiet command on the tip of my tongue. "Alright, little bird. That's enough."

Opening my arms, I pull her in and anchor her to me until her dizziness fades. Even after Piper grows still, I keep my hold and eye on her until the color returns to her cheeks and her eyes open.

"You should be resting," I say in gentle chastisement.

Piper rests her forehead against my chest. "I know. I'm sorry."

We stay like that for a minute, sharing comfort. Then I kiss Piper on the head, turn her around, and lead her to the kitchen island. Once she safely rests on one of the high-back bar stools, I announce, "I'll take it from here."

When I reach the oven, I notice that Piper has everything laid out already. I only need to pull the casserole from the middle rack and set it on the waiting trivet. Curious, I peek under the lid. The dish inside smells like French toast, with cinnamon, sugar, and warm, buttery scents that make my stomach growl. The white mixture from earlier sits on the counter. I pick the glass up, recognize the mixture as a glaze, and drizzle it on the casserole.

Typically, I would crack a joke or chat about random topics, but I am still too worried about Piper's injuries, too stressed from last night—too much of everything, to be honest—to do much other than what's in front of me.

So, I grab two plates from the cabinet overhead and add a heaping helping to each. Stepping up to the island, I place one of the plates in front of Piper before pausing for a quick check-in.

"How are you feeling?" I ask. "Any headaches?"

"Yeah. Not a bad one, but…" She shrugs.

I nod and set my plate next to her. Then, I move toward the coffee machine and start it up, needing caffeine more than my next breath. While my cup brews, I grab a water bottle, uncap it, and set it in front of Piper.

"You need to stay hydrated," I say.

That small smile appears again. "I know. Thanks."

My shoulders relax a little. Piper would know since I had my fair share of concussions in high school. Despite rigorous safety protocols, football injuries were all too common.

"No thanks necessary." I nod to the bottle. "Drink."

"Yes, Sir."

I finish preparing my coffee and ignore the zing of pleasure that I get every time she calls me Sir. Fucking biology, I swear. *Now is not the time, dick.*

Piper silently watches me walk to the kitchen island and settle into my seat. When I dig into the food, she attempts the same. We skipped dinner last night, and my stomach is letting me know this morning. I am fucking starving. But when I shovel a third forkful into my mouth, I notice that Piper has only taken a few bites. Now, she pushes the food around the plate with her fork.

"Not good?" I ask.

"Hmm?" Piper glances at me. "No, it's fine. I'm just not that hungry."

We lapse into silence again. Once my plate is empty, I sip my coffee and say, "The casserole was delicious."

"Thanks." Her cheeks flush with pleasure.

"If you weren't hungry, why go through all that trouble? I could have made something."

Piper looks down at her plate. She slowly traces the edge with her fingertip. I notice how she curls into herself, trying to make herself small and insignificant, and I want to wreck that bloodsucking leech all over again.

"I wanted to do something nice for you," she murmurs. "To apologize."

"You didn't have to do that."

"I know. But I thought maybe it would help—and maybe you would be less angry." Her voice splinters as she fights back tears and says, "I don't want you to be mad at me. I hate it."

"Baby." I grip her chin and gently turn her face toward me. "Look at me."

Piper takes a few seconds to comply. When her pale green eyes finally meet mine, I see so much sadness in them that a little of my simmering anger boils away. I sigh heavily.

"You're right," I admit. "I am angry. And, full disclosure, I will probably be angry for a while."

My words hit Piper like a slap. She flinches, trying to pull away, but I still have more to say. Both hands reach up, fingers slipping into her hair while I hold her in place by the back of her head.

"I'm going to get mad sometimes," I continue. "That's life, little bird. I'm going to piss you off plenty, too. But do you know what I'm never going to do?"

Piper slowly shakes her head once. "What?"

"I am never going to take my anger out on you." Doubt clouds her eyes until I add, "That's a promise. Even when I'm so furious, I could spit fire. I will take the time to cool off before coming to you. And when I do, I will be calm and level-headed, and we will discuss things together."

"Together," Piper echoes. Then, she inhales shakily. "On a scale of 'inconvenienced' to 'furious enough to spit fire,' how angry are you with me?"

"Piper..."

"I need to know." She reaches up and squeezes my wrists. "Please."

"Furious enough to spit fire." I hold her in place when she tries to shrink back. "But that's not all for you," I clarify. "Most of it is for that insecure, inbred son-of-a-bitch who thinks he can come to *my* town, mess with *my* family, and try to hurt *my* woman."

Relief fills the expression on Piper's face.

"But make no mistake," I add, a hard edge slipping into my voice. "I am not happy about you keeping things from me. And soon—once this whole mess is behind us—there will be consequences."

Her breath hitches. "What sort of consequences?"

"Baby, you aren't ready for that conversation."

Piper looks at me with equal parts apprehension, curiosity, and intrigue. I feel her shiver, and when she bites her lip, I have to bite back a groan. One hand releases her head so I can tug that bottom lip between her teeth.

"What did I say about biting your lip?"

She flushes, completely unaware she had even been doing it. "Sorry."

Reluctantly, I let Piper go and lean back in my chair. Crossing my arms, I let my gaze wander over her face. I take in her still-too-pale complexion and the dark circles under her eyes. She needs rest.

But first:

"We need to talk about Cedric."

She closes her eyes against his name, shaking her head like it will dislodge the sound. Her arms slip around her middle when she curls into herself—always trying to make herself smaller.

No more.

"Hey," I bark. Not to frighten Piper but to startle her out of whatever dark place she is slipping into. I grab her hands. "Come on."

Confused, Piper lets me help her off the chair and lead her by the hand into the living room. I sit on one edge of the couch, place a throw pillow on my lap, and motion for her to lie beside me. We may as well get comfortable while we have this supremely *uncomfortable* conversation. Plus, I be doing most of the talking. Piper can rest for a bit.

Once she settles in, I tell her everything from when I went to Hawk's place to ask for his help until I received those files from Tobias. I also explain why I kept what I was doing from her until now. Simply put, I wanted to avoid prematurely raising Piper's hopes. Even someone as talented as Tobias has days where he discovers nothing. Either the perp has no prior convictions or shady dealings, or else they are much better at covering their tracks than anyone anticipated.

Thankfully, Cedric made mistakes.

Afterward, I fall silent and give Piper time to process the sudden avalanche of information. A little while later, she tilts her head up at me. In her face, I see hope—a tiny spark, but still there. "What does that mean for me, exactly?"

At her question, I feel a genuine smile spread across my face. Because, finally, I have something to smile about.

"It means that we're coming for that motherfucker," I say, "and his days are numbered."

***

The night of the attack, Piper fell right to sleep, but I was far too wired. After staring at the ceiling for an hour, I got out of bed and spent the rest of the night awake, scouring the documents Tobias sent. Slowly, a plan of action began stitching together in my head.

Proof in hand, I just needed to figure out how to put the information to good use. I refused to pull the trigger on anything without a clear path forward. I have way too much to lose for me to get cocky or make assumptions.

Failure is not an option.

Today, I have that plan—and a path forward. Once I get Piper back into bed after my big revelation, I give her acetaminophen and water to take. I leave her with strict instructions not to move from that spot until her headache is gone.

Then, I call Foster and Stella to see if they can stop by and keep an eye on her. Usually, I would just ask Stella, but with Cedric in town and after the stunt he pulled, I have a feeling he may try something again if given the opportunity. Foster will ensure that both women stay safe while I have to be away.

Thirty minutes later, I am waiting on the front porch for Foster's truck to pull onto the drive when my phone buzzes with a text message. I pull it out of my pocket. When I see Nate's name, my heart starts to pound.

- 9:00 am -

Nate: It didn't take long to find the bastard

Simon: Where?

Nate: In that roach motel

Nate: The one over on Dogwood

Simon: Uncle Buck's?

Nate: The very same

Simon: Fuck. I didn't have that on my bingo card

Nate: The owner takes cash, looks the other way, and never asks questions

Nate: Makes sense to me

Simon: Yeah, but your mind is way more twisted than mine

Nate: Sorry, I forgot about your innocence and naivety

Simon: Damn straight. I'm an angel

I am grinning when I hear tires on gravel, but it fades when I look up from my phone. I watch Foster pull up by my police cruiser. Stella wastes no time getting out and racing to meet me by the front door. The poor man has barely stopped the ignition.

"How is Piper?" she asks, worried.

I am distracted, my mind running in at least three directions already, but I pause a moment to reassure her. "Much better than last night. She still has a headache and feels a bit dizzy."

"Has she eaten?"

"A little."

"Drank anything?"

My lips quirk in amusement. "I made sure of it. And before you ask," I say, holding up a palm, "Piper just took pain meds and is resting in bed."

Stella's eyes water. She grips my hands tightly in her own. Foster meets us at the top of the steps to hear her say, "Thank you for taking such good care of our baby."

"Stella, I love Piper," is my earnest reply. "I will always take the very best care of her. You never have to thank me for that."

"We know, son," Foster adds, gripping my shoulder in a gesture of thanks. "But you still have it."

"Sweet boy." Stella reaches up to pat my cheek.

My chest warms and knots up whenever she does anything motherly—a hug, a kiss, or a pat on the cheek, even silly pet names. I love her and Foster for taking me on as their own. Even when it seemed like Piper and I had no chance for a future, every Easton treated me like family. But that love also reminds me of everything ripped from my life on the day my parents died.

They always seem to sense when my thoughts turn dark, like now. Stella quickly pivots and does something disarming to pull me back into the present.

"Well," she says, clapping her hands together. "You go do whatever it is you need to. We'll take it from here."

"Thanks." I give her a small peck on the cheek before turning to Foster. "You have my number if anything happens."

"Yes," he says, smiling in understanding. "Now go."

With a nod, I start down the stairs.

Stella stops me. "Oh, and Simon?"

I turn back and ask, "Yes?"

"Tonight, I'll finish that dinner Piper never got to surprise you with. We can have family dinner here this week."

I learned about the big surprise when I called Ellery last night to tell her to stay home. Then she offered to store the food so it would keep.

"Thanks, Stella, that sounds wonderful," I say, and I sincerely mean it. Piper needs something to take her mind off the attack. Hell, we both do.

After a quick wave, I turn away from them and head to the truck. Once inside, I pull out my phone and send Nate a quick question.

- 9:15 am -

Simon: Room number?

Nate: 116

Cedric can no longer hide in the shadows like a damn coward. He and I need to have a little chat. But first, I have some things to take care of.

Unity Art Co-op is my first stop. When I step through the entrance, the woman I came to see leans against the front desk, pouring over documents with their assistant. I wait for her to look up.

"Lena," I say in greeting.

Her face breaks into a friendly smile. "Hey, Simon. Ellery didn't mention you were stopping by. I'm afraid you just missed her."

"I came to see you, actually." I peek behind her shoulder. "Is there somewhere private we could talk? It will only take a minute."

She squints, trying to get a read on me, then nods. "Come on, we can use my office."

I follow her behind the reception desk and down a hallway to the left. When we pass by, I smile at the assistant—their name is Shay—and they blush, smiling shyly back at me.

Lena leads me into her office, where she rounds her desk and sits, arms folded across her chest. She takes a second to consider me. "So, what can I do for you?"

I shut the door behind me and sit. "Something for Piper. And it involves your father."

Lena sits up straighter and shoots me a shrewd gaze. "Is this about her... past situation?"

"You know?" Her eyebrow arches. "Of course, you know. Did the whole town hear about this before me?" I pinch the bridge of my nose. "No. Don't answer that."

"Simon, girls confide in other girls first. Nothing against you." She shrugs. "And the whole thing just sort of... happened. My affiliation with Evermore Media triggered her."

Her words remind me why I came. "Speaking of Evermore Media…" I start, then proceed to explain what I need from her.

Lena agrees to do everything she can to help. I had no doubt that she would. With that, we quickly part ways, and I head toward the next destination: a meeting with Priya Kumari's law practice.

Priya is not an easy woman to pin down. Thankfully, Ellery can reach her directly. Having that in with my sister helped this morning, and knowing Ellery's friends have taken such a liking to my girl, helps even more.

Especially when—once Priya hears my plan—she is determined to help in any way she can.

Now, for my last stop—and the most important.

In the time it takes me to get from downtown Sweetbriar over to Uncle Buck's, the anger I kept to a banked fire all morning threatens to engulf me. I park around the corner and out of sight of the beach-style motel. The hotel may look the other way on most things, but the owner will recognize me even without my uniform.

Before I leave the vehicle, I take a few calming breaths. After securing my gun, I pull up my collar, tug down my cap, and brace myself against the cold air. Then I start a brisk walk up the sidewalk toward the—honestly, "motel" is much too nice a word for this run-down, flea-ridden, drug-laden building.

Unfortunately, as long as money keeps shifting hands in this part of town, everyone's willing to look the other way. I pass none of the regular prostitutes that like to hang out on the corner here. Small mercies. They would recognize me, too.

The first door I reach on this side of the building is 100. I check the numbers on every door I count until I finally reach 116. Luckily, the asshole is staying on the lower level.

Time to see if Cedric is home or already ran off like a coward. Taking a deep, cleansing breath, I raise my fist and pound on the door three times. Then I wait.

I never had a clear vision of what Cedric Thomas would look like, but the man who answers the door is nothing like I pictured. He looks surprisingly normal. Handsome, I suppose, if you like the tall, dark, studious type. He seems more suited to office work at an accounting firm than a cutthroat industry like entertainment.

Then again, I know what lies underneath. There's an undercurrent of something dark behind the glasses and the warm, friendly countenance. When you get into the kind of stuff I'm into, you meet a rather eclectic assortment of individuals—not all of them good. And, in that world, you have to develop a sixth sense about what lurks behind the masks people wear. If not, you can quickly get taken advantage of.

Like Piper did because of this piece of work.

"Can I help you?" he asks with an impatient expression on his face.

He has a lot of nerve acting superior while he stays in this shit hole. I clench my jaw, biting back all the colorful things I would love to say to him. Instead, I settle on just one.

"Yeah," I say tersely. "You can get the fuck out of my town and go back to whatever corner of hell you crawled out of."

"Excuse me?" His chest puffs like a peacock, and he takes a menacing step forward. I almost bark out a laugh. *Ridiculous.* "Who the hell do you think you are coming here to harass me?"

My arms cross over my chest. Then I tilt my head slightly to one side, narrowing my eyes at him.

"Wait a minute." His eyes flare in recognition and I catch a spark of uncertainty before his unassuming mask slams back down. He laughs darkly. "Ahh, yes. The boyfriend. Did you come to try and scare me off? Please. I'm here to check on my star client during her little sabbatical. Nothing nefarious."

The audacity of this fucker. Cedric plays a dangerous game with me and has no idea, even as the end draws near.

"You expect me to believe a word that comes from your mouth? You're much stupider than I thought." I lean forward. "And, news flash, I never thought you were that smart."

His mouth twists in an ugly sneer. "We're done here."

As soon as he starts closing the door, I wedge my boot between it and the frame. My open palm slams on the door and shoves it back, almost slamming Cedric in the nose.

What a pity it fails to connect.

"Not even close," I bark at him, throwing the door back open. "I have more to say, asshole." The sharpness in my tone is enough to make him think twice. He takes two steps back but still holds tightly to his veneer of disdain and boredom.

At least Cedric is smart enough not to try to shut the door on me again.

Once I know for sure that I have his undivided attention, I continue. "I'm not sure how things work up in the Big Apple, buddy. But here in Sweetbriar, we never touch a woman without her permission. And even then, *never* in anger."

"That's cute," he says dryly. "But I'm not sure what you're implying, officer."

"Let me make myself crystal clear, then." My hands clench into tight fists to staunch the fury building in my veins. Cedric tests every ounce of my composure, held on by a quickly fraying thread. But as much as I want to throat-punch him right now, I refrain.

Instead, I bow up and snarl, "I know the truth. You followed Piper last night. You attacked her. You hired someone to stalk her. You also published that little article online a few weeks ago, citing an anonymous source."

"Yeah?" He crosses his arms, puffing out his chest as a smug smile steals over his expression. "Prove it."

Cedric jolts when I lunge. I get right up in his smarmy face, close enough to see the fear in his eyes when they flare. He takes an involuntary step back. Good. That pencil dick *should* be fucking wary. I have him by an inch or two in height, and I am *much* broader.

I also have raw, unfiltered rage on my side.

"Listen, you narcissistic, tyrannical piece of garbage." My voice has a dangerous edge to it. "Only my badge could keep me from disassembling you slowly, piece-by-piece, from the inside out while I force you to watch. And even *that* becomes less of a deterrent by the second."

Cedric's earlier smirk falters slightly, but only his eyebrow arches in response. "Is that a threat, officer?"

My fists twitch. They itch to wipe that smirk right off. I clench and unclench them while I try to get a handle on my fury.

It doesn't work.

I decide to lean into it.

"No." The corners of my mouth turn up in a savage smile that feels more than a little unhinged. "That's a fucking promise." Then, unable to resist, I shove my finger roughly into his sternum and add, "Leave town. Now. This my only warning: leave, and you might get out with your balls still attached to your body."

Cedric sneers to hide the fear, so thick that I can fucking smell it all over him. "Why should I?"

"Because, asshole, I'm about to burn your world to the mother-fucking ground. Trust me when I say that you'll beg for death by the time I finish with you."

I finally hit my limit with this conversation. Turning on my heel, I storm out the front door. But I only make a few steps before Cedric's oily voice reaches my ears.

"Piper does bring out that possessive streak, doesn't she?" he calls out. "I get it. Such an accommodating little whore. And so sweet, too, once a healthy dose of fear courses through her. Don't you think? I heard you like that sort of thing, too."

Cedric is nowhere near ready for how fast I turn on him. My fist slams into his stomach. He doubles over with a pained groan. Good—it means he fails to see my boot until it lands right between his thighs. My heel grinds into his balls, and he lets out a satisfying shriek of pain. Then he collapses onto the ground. There, Cedric writhes around like a worm and clutches at his junk.

"I'm nothing like you," I snarl.

"Fuck you! I'm pressing charges," he wails. "You fucking assaulted me!"

"Yeah?" Just before I turn away, I crouch over this pathetic excuse for a human being. Then, I look him right in the eyes and say, "Prove it."

That trust is *more precious* than *gold* for *someone* who had so much *stolen* from her.

Chapter 34
Six Feet Deep

Piper

Today, I reach a crossroads.

After several days of implementing the different pieces of Simon's plan, the culmination of our efforts has finally arrived. Simon insisted that we wait until I fully recovered. Thankfully, I talked him down to wait until I showed no more concussive symptoms.

Until then, I helped. Simon—naturally taking the lead—recruited Beckham, Nate, Hawk, and even Tobias to help him. Then, he asked Ellery and Daisy to babysit me.

Simon called it hanging out.

But I knew better.

Lucky for him, I love spending time with my girls.

Besides, I have had one important thing to keep me busy when not on forced house arrest under Warden Brooks. (I tried calling Simon that the other day. He was not amused.)

In addition to annoying my boyfriend, I have been playing the guitar and writing a lot. Lyrics flow more and more every day. My song journal already has half its pages filled—more bits of poetry and prose went into that book over the last several weeks than I have written in almost a decade. At this rate, I'll have enough song fodder for almost two albums before the new year.

Finally—now that my life is on the path meant for it—I can see a light at the end of this long, dark tunnel.

Only one thing remains in my way.

And he won't be there for much longer.

"You ready?"

My head lifts from the journal in my lap at Simon's voice. I sit on my favorite chair in his dad's study. A few minutes ago, some new lyrics came to my head, and I wanted to jot them down before I forgot them.

"Hey." I close the book and set it next to me.

Simon moves to my side, reaching a hand out to pull me to my feet. I slip my arms around his neck to look directly into his beautiful hazel eyes. They are full of tenderness and concern.

"Yeah, handsome. I'm ready."

My heart rate calms when he presses his lips to mine. "Good. Then let's go get your life back."

Part of me wants to tell him that I already have my life back, and that he gave me that precious gift. Instead, I smile and take his hand. "Let's do it."

While Simon drives us to Priya's small office building, we review the plan again. Simon put all the most important parts into play. The only thing left is for me to play my part.

I'm the bait dangling in front of Cedric to reel him in.

Priya already cast the lure.

Now we wait.

Cedric arrives with his scumbag lawyers in tow, waltzing into the conference room a full fifteen minutes past the scheduled start time. Well past what qualifies as fashionably late. Thankfully, I warned Priya of his propensity for theatrics, so the actual start time is fifteen after the hour, so none of us have been waiting very long.

"What the hell is he doing here?" He asks Priya, ignoring me entirely while he points a finger at Simon.

In a deceptively casual pose with his arms crossed, Simon arches an eyebrow. "I'm Ms. Easton's bodyguard," is his glib reply.

Cedric opens his mouth but shuts it again when one lawyer rests his hand on his bicep and shakes his head almost imperceptibly. His expression reads, *Pick your battles.*

Cedric folds his arms with a sigh and falls back against the chair like a petulant child. "Fine, let's get this over with." He finally turns his attention to me. I force a bored expression, even when he says, "I'm glad you finally came to your senses, darling girl." Then the bastard winks.

I grit my teeth. No way will he see an ounce of reaction on my face. "You don't get to call me that. Call me Ms. Easton if you must, though I'd prefer if you kept my name completely out of your mouth."

"I agree," Simon adds, nostrils flaring in restrained anger.

Cedric rolls his eyes. "Kind of hard not to call you anything when we work so closely, my dear." Then he gets a glint in his eye. "I suppose I could just think of a new pet name, hmm? How does that sound?"

He dares to smile at me. How did I ever think that smile was charming? All I see now is the gaping smile of a snake before it strikes.

"I'll pass, thanks. Now, like you said, we should get this over with."

"Fine." Cedric and his lawyers look expectantly at Priya. "Well? Where are the papers I need to sign for the renegotiation? My lawyers already looked everything over and are pleased with the terms."

"See, that's the thing, Cedric." Simon leans forward on his forearms, his intense gaze landing across the table. It flits to each person until they all squirm uncomfortably in their seats. "You may be pleased with the terms, but we need a few amendments to the original agreement."

"Namely, what?" one lawyer asks.

Simon turns his attention to the little slime-ball, who immediately flinches and falls silent. I get it. He intimidates the hell out of folks. If that lawyer had been a turtle, his head would already be hiding inside his shell. (Even now, he makes an admirable impression.)

My man also oozes sex appeal when he goes into cop mode. His work persona stays separate from his personal life, but when I see him in action, I feel all sorts of turned on.

I may need a new pair of panties soon.

Though for Simon, I could remove them...

Cedric swiftly yanks me from my inappropriate daydreams when he asks, "And what makes you think you have any say in the matter?" He leans forward to mimic Simon, refusing to be upstaged or show any reaction other than haughty disdain. "I thought you were the bodyguard."

"Bodyguard, courier, boyfriend… I wear a lot of hats." Simon's voice goes hard. "Right now, I'm your worst nightmare."

With that cryptic statement, Simon slides the folder across the table. At first, Cedric frowns deeply and stares at it. Then he looks up at Priya, then Simon, and then me.

"What the hell is this?"

Simon meets his demand with a caustic chuckle and shakes his head. "Just look inside the damn thing."

When Cedric makes no move to do so, the slim—ball turtle lawyer shoots him a look and drags the folder closer to himself. Then he opens and starts to leaf through. Pages and pages of documents fill the folder. The more the lawyer reads, the whiter his face turns until I'm sure he may pass out from lack of oxygen to the brain. Finally, he closes the folder with a snap and pinches his eyes closed.

"Cedric," he whispers loudly. "You need to look at these." Then, he slowly slides the folder over to his client.

Cedric huffs and flips the top over, scanning the first page. He slowly and methodically goes through each document, his face betraying none of the emotions brewing beneath the skin. While we wait, the wall clock keeps time. With no other sound in the room, every tick of the second hand hits like a gunshot.

Everyone sits here, stuck in a holding pattern, and the air grows heavy with anticipation. Hope lingers on one side, dread on the other. Not even Cedric is immune, though he does better at hiding it than most.

Cedric meets our gaze as he closes the back of the folder. Then he folds his hands on the table, leans back, and asks, "What do you want?"

"I'm glad you asked," Priya interjects, taking over. She pulls a stack of papers out of her briefcase. "The terms are simple. Piper's previous contract is, now and in perpetuity, null and void. All of it. Which means the old contract gets shredded—assuming you brought it, as instructed?" She looks at the first lawyer, the one who, up until now, has been dead silent.

He nods, opting to keep his mouth shut yet again. By far, I think he is the smartest in the group.

"Good." Priya taps her fingertips on the papers in front of her. "All parties involved will sign this new contract today, which gives my client absolute control of her musical assets. Dreamscape Music will transfer the following to my client by the end of the week: masters of all songs, all brand copyrights and trademarks, and all company files concerning my client. Finally, Dreamscape Music will immediately cease and desist all communications with or regarding my client."

After a dramatic pause, she adds, "In short, gentleman, after this meeting, you will part ways with Piper Easton, and she will cease to exist." Her eyes land on Cedric. She holds his gaze in a game of chicken, her expression as hard as stone while his remains unreadable.

Cedric swerves first.

Staring down at the folder holding his downfall, he clenches and unclenches his hand while his temper mounts and nears its limit. I recognize the action.

"Every one of you has gone insane," Cedric scoffs. "This so-called information?" He waves his hand over the folder. "How did you stitch this together? Not by any legal means. None of these lies will hold up in court."

Simon's voice drops into a menacing rumble. "You want to take that bet?" He nods toward the folder. "From what I've read, you're a shit gambler. Loan sharks hold an awful lot of your debts."

Peeking up at Cedric's face, I notice sign number two that his temper has reached its boiling point: the muscle in his jaw starts to clench and pop.

Cedric turns his flinty gaze to me. "Do you think you can just walk away after all the time and money I put into you over the years? After all the sacrifices I made for you?"

Simon goes tense beside me. I reach under the table for his hand, squeezing once gently, showing him I'm okay.

I know he would slay this dragon for me if I let him.

But I need to slay this dragon on my own. Knowing that Simon will be by my side, supporting and cheering me on? That gives me all the strength I need.

"Sacrifices?" I ask calmly. "What sacrifices would those be, Cedric? Do you mean the sacrifices you made when you took control of my music? What about when you made me change my clothes, hair, look, and accent? How about when I got sent on tour nine months out of the year, only for you to shove me in a recording studio for the other three? Are you talking about *those* sacrifices?"

Cedric's eye starts to twitch. When that happens, I know I've hit a nerve. And when I hit a nerve, he hits back.

I brace for the explosion.

"You ungrateful bitch! I MADE YOU!" Cedric is on his feet in seconds, his clenched fists slamming onto the conference table as he looms over me. His face is mottled red. In his fury, the force of his words sends spittle flying from his mouth. "You are nothing without me."

Before, that fury would have choked the air out of my lungs. I would have flinched at the force of his words and prayed for the anger to stay out of his hands. Cedric's anger would have paralyzed me with fear.

Not this time.

Not anymore.

Simon tenses, muscles coiled and ready to spring, prepared to jump in if I need him. But I hold up a hand at my side so only he can see, silently asking him to wait. He inclines his head in a subtle nod and settles back in his chair. Beneath the table, he threads his fingers through mine and squeezes, and the love in that gesture lends me strength.

Instead of cowering as Cedric expects, like he *wants*, I shove that flare of fear deep down until it disappears, square my shoulders, and stand. I press my palms into the laminate top of the conference table and lean forward. Then, I meet the face of my nightmares head-on.

"No, Cedric, you didn't," I say.

My voice has taken on that hard edge that Simon wields so well. Hot, molten steel runs through my veins, bolstering me. I feel stronger than ever. Unyielding where once I would have been bendable. Moldable.

"You didn't make me." With every word, I loosen his hold on me. "You broke me, tore me down, and then twisted me into some lifeless plaything you could control behind the scenes. But guess what? You don't have that power anymore. You wouldn't cut the damn strings, so I learned how to cut my own, and I will *never* be your puppet again."

The last word rings out in the stark silence that remains. My heart is racing with adrenaline. When I peek over at Simon, he watches me with such an intense expression of pride and love that my face heats with a blush. But then Cedric's mask falls away, and he shows the world his true self.

"Please." He sneers down at me. "You'll come back. They always come back. You won't be able to hack it on your own. I'll be there waiting when you fail, when you crawl on your hands and knees and beg for my help, when you suck m—"

"Alright, that's enough." Simon launches to his feet, slamming his hands onto the table. Everyone in the room flinches. "We're done here. Sign the damn papers and go back to New York before I come up with a reason to lock your ass away."

"Oh, we are far from done," Cedric shoots back. "If you think you're going to get away with this, this extortion—"

"Extortion?" Simon barks out a snide laugh. "You are a fucking piece of work."

"Alright, gentlemen," Priya interjects. "If you've finished…?"

We all turn to look in her direction. She appears calm and collected, seated at the head of the table, having quietly observed the entire interaction. Despite her stern expression, I see her dark eyes twinkling with amusement. I almost smile when both men reluctantly sit.

As with most contracts, it takes work to get everything signed—especially with Cedric dragging his feet and acting like a petulant child. I watch his already boiling temper ratchet up with every signature on every page. He turns red when Priya's assistant takes the old contract from the room to shred it. And when Priya hands her assistant the newly signed agreement, he looks ready to pop a blood vessel.

Pity that all his blood vessels stay intact.

"Pleasure doing business with you, gentlemen," Priya says, opening the door and coming to stand by me. "You'll forgive me if I don't shake your hands."

Cedric shoves back his chair, almost crashing it into the wall behind him. Then he storms through the door. The rest of us slowly trickle out of the room, with Simon and me behind. He takes my hand in his and squeezes it. I smile, feeling my pulse settle a little at the warmth in his gaze.

"You did good, little bird," he whispers.

"Thanks, handsome." I smile. "But it's not over yet."

He grins back at me. Then we both look toward the front of the building and Cedric, who is stomping off toward the elevators. He only gets about halfway when someone steps directly into his path.

Helena Morgan, heiress to the Evermore Media empire and someone I now consider a close friend, swoops in like an avenging angel. She cuts a formidable figure, arms resting on her hips, a vulpine smile stretching across her beautiful face.

My smile grows when I catch her gaze. She shoots me a quick wink before turning back to Cedric. He stands across from her, looking confused, while the lawyers move past us to get to the elevators.

Just before she passes me, Priya rests a hand on my shoulder. She smiles, and her face glows with triumph. In contrast, the two lawyers employed by Cedric seem to have washed their hands of him. They step onto the elevators and press the button for the ground floor without so much as a glance in his direction.

Simon and I follow the three of them—Cedric's lawyers and Priya—just far enough to pivot and flank Lena. Between the three of us, Cedric has nowhere to escape. *Good.* I want front-row seats for this show.

"You look familiar," Cedric says with a frown. "Do I know you?"

"Hmm." She tilts her head slightly to the side, pretending to think. "Maybe, maybe not. But I know all about you, Cedric Thomas."

"What the hell do you mean?"

Instead of answering him directly, she starts to count using her fingers. One. "You're the owner and CEO of Dreamscape Music, an Evermore Media subsidiary." Two. "You, up until today, represented our dear Piper." Three. "You're also an abusive, gaslighting asshole."

"So you say." He rolls his eyes. "And who the hell are you?"

"My name is Helena." Lena looks down at her nails, pausing for dramatic effect. Then she drops the bomb. "Helena Morgan, that is. Though you may be more familiar with my father, Rhys."

Cedric pales in recognition of the name. But he recovers quickly, eyes narrowing. "Okay, so you're Rhys Morgan's little brat. Not seeing what the hell that has to do with me."

"Don't you?" Lena asks.

Her eyes twinkle with merriment when she takes a menacing step forward. Cedric stumbles back a step to keep the distance between them. Probably smart. Those heels look killer.

Simon and I sit back and watch, impressed and amused in equal measure. Lena loves to perform. Right now, she shines at having a worm like him at her mercy. Knowing that she's about to crush him like the bug that he is.

"You see, Cedric, I know all about what you did to Piper. About the other women *and* men contracted under your label. I know the victims you paid off and the civil suits you somehow managed to sweep under the rug."

She takes a step with each word, and he retreats until his back physically hits a wall. Then she pokes him in the chest with a manicured nail. "I know about the gambling debts." Poke. "The prostitutes." Poke. "And how you've been embezzling money from your label—from *my father's* label—to keep your head above water."

Cedric swats her hand away. "That may be true, but you're too late." The anger on his face melts like candle wax, shifting into a smug smirk. "We already settled, little girl. The contract is signed, and that information will never see the light of day. So go back to your daddy. What proof do you have?"

"Proof? Proof." She taps her finger to her lower lip in thought. "Oh! Do you mean the gigantic digital file an anonymous source emailed me or the gigantic paper file that came in the mail?"

"What the—?" He turns his head toward me, eyes flashing. "You signed an NDA, you lying cunt."

Simon starts forward, but I grab his bicep. Lena's got this.

"Correct, Sir." Lena's grin widens, taking on an almost sinister quality. "But all your dirty laundry got put on the clothesline long before now, emailed over an encrypted line to my father and brother the moment I received the package. He's had all that juicy information in his hand for days now. And my father is nothing if not a man of action."

Cedric's face goes pasty white. This time, it stays that way, all of the red from before shifting down to his neck and chest. Splotchy, bright red spots from the anxiety of knowing that he's well and truly fucked.

"I see you understand where I'm going with this. Your little empire is no more, Cedric Thomas. Being dismantled as we speak." She puts on a fake pout. "All that hard work down the drain."

He looks between the three of us with wide, crazy eyes. When he laughs, there's a hysterical tinge to it. I never thought I would see the day, but Lena officially broke him.

"It doesn't matter!" he says, still laughing. "You think I didn't plan for something like this? Do you think I haven't done this before? I already had one alias. What's another?"

Lena watches him with one perfectly trimmed eyebrow lifted. "It's so cute that you think you're going anywhere besides prison. Isn't that cute, Piper?"

"Adorable," I deadpan.

Cedric sneers and sidesteps the both of us. "I'm done with this conversation."

We turn to watch him stomp down the large hallway toward the elevators on the opposite end. Halfway there, he whirls around, taking backward steps while he glares in our direction.

"You think you can stop me?" he scoffs, pointing at Simon and me. "You and your beefed-up boyfriend over there?"

Simon looks down at himself and then back at Cedric. "Off duty but still a cop, idiot." His gaze meets Cedric's again, and he smirks. "But I'm not the one you need to worry about."

Cedric has been so busy dealing with us that he missed the two hallways off the side of the elevator wall. Those walls hide more uniformed officers. Nate appears while Cedric continues making a scene, blocking his path to the elevators. It only takes one more step for Cedric to slam his back against the formidable officer's front. The force of the impact jolts Cedric forward.

"What the—?" He whirls around and, seeing Nate, curses loudly. "Not another podunk pig."

Nate crosses his arms and looks bored. "Yep, another one." Then his face splits in a grin, lighting up his onyx eyes. "But guess what? I have several friends dying to meet you. Come on out, boys."

Three more officers stroll into view. But they wear very different uniforms—ones with F.B.I. letters on their chests. With five armed officers surrounding him, Cedric doesn't have a prayer.

And he knows it.

Cedric, for once, looks thoroughly defeated. His shoulders slump when the fight leaves his body. While the agents get him cuffed and onto the elevator, I take my time and watch every second. This moment is one I have dreamed of for so many years. I intend to make the most of it now that it's here.

That includes watching him disappear behind the elevator doors, knowing that it will be the last time I ever have to look at or think of Cedric Thomas after this.

He is my nightmare no longer.

When the elevator opens again, Nate and Lena both get on at the same time. I notice that they stay as far away from each other as humanly possible, looking for all the world to want to be anywhere but next to the other. Having never seen them in the same room together, I wonder what their story is.

I'm so preoccupied with that question that I don't notice Simon sidle beside me. I jump when he slips an arm around my waist and presses a kiss on my head. He chuckles warmly, the sound quickly relaxing me. I melt back against him, feeling a little silly.

"Did I scare you?"

I turn my head and smile up at him. "Only a little."

"How are you feeling?" he asks, his gaze caressing my face while he looks for signs of strain and fatigue.

"Simon, I'm fine." My smile grows wide and bright. "*Better* than fine. I promised to tell you if my head bothers me, but it hasn't. Truly."

"Good," he murmurs. "And what about your heart?"

"Never better."

Simon smiles gently. Then, after he tucks me under his arm, we move together down the hall. We are the last people around, and it seems like a fitting way to end this chapter of my life: Simon and me, side-by-side, together like we always should have been.

We enter the elevator, and I watch the doors close on my past. We start to descend. Simon turns toward me and, reaching out, pulls me against his chest.

When he envelops me in his arms, I can take my first full, cleansing breath, letting go of all the doubts, worries, and stress I have been carrying.

When he kisses my forehead, I feel it down to my toes.

And when he asks me, "So, Ms. Easton, what do you plan on doing with this newfound freedom?" my answer is simple.

"I'm going to fly."

"You wouldn't cut the damn *strings,* so I *learned* how to cut *my own,* and I will *never* be your *puppet* again.

Chapter 35

Nervous

Piper

Simon is avoiding me.

After we watched the FBI haul Cedric away in handcuffs, Simon took me home. I hoped we could talk after—about us, the future, and the fact that I hid something crucial and dangerous from him. But the threat of it stays in the back of my mind where there has been no resolution.

It feels like our whole relationship waits in limbo.

Unfortunately, we never got the chance to talk that day. When we returned to Simon's house, our family and closest friends were waiting to celebrate. That evening rivaled the raw emotions of Thanksgiving. (Spoiler alert: there were a lot of tears involved.)

Since then, Simon has found countless reasons—like work—to make himself scarce. While not his fault, work is still a convenient excuse. He had to return to the office the day after, which didn't help. It also didn't help that he had to work late all four nights because of paperwork and bureaucratic red tape. While necessary, the FBI's involvement with Cedric's arrest brought a lot of extra hoops Simon, Nate, and the station had to jump through.

By the time he got home each night, he had about enough energy to eat the food I had waiting for him in the refrigerator, peel off his uniform, and drag himself to bed, where I was already asleep.

That ends today.

I miss Simon.

He is a million miles away even when he is here with me. When he gets home tonight, I intend to force the issue—to hash things out so that we can move forward. Together.

I enlist help from Nate to ensure my plan goes off without a hitch. He has offered to take over any lingering paperwork that would keep Simon longer, and he promises to make sure Simon leaves when his shift is over. I have no clue how to repay him, especially since this will take him away from his wife.

(Then again, Britagne would make any man want to work overtime. Knowing that, I feel a little bit better about the circumstance.)

Today, Nate keeps his end of the bargain. A little after six o'clock, I hear Simon's truck pulling down the drive. When the engine cuts off, I slip away from the window where I have been spying and head into the bedroom. Ozzy, Cooper, and Duchess have all been instructed to stay downstairs until released. Downstairs in the kitchen, I have set the table—providing romantic ambience like my mom often did for my dad—with lit candles and a fully laden plate of food under a fancy silver warming dome. Soft music plays in the background, and a note rests on the table before his chair.

Handsome,
When you finish your meal, please meet me upstairs in the bedroom. I think it's time for my punishment. Don't you?
XOXO
Little Bird

Meanwhile, I lounge in bed and reread some of the things I have researched all day. I want to make sure I have everything correct—or as close as I can get, being a complete novice. It also gives me something to do other than sit and wait for Simon to finish. Wanting him to hurry up and come upstairs has my whole body twitching like a live wire.

But then, just when I think I can't take anymore, I hear Simon's heavy footsteps on the stairwell.

Showtime.

Right then, a switch flips inside my head. Every bit of nervous energy disappears, replaced with a calm confidence.

I know I can do this.

Moving quickly, I scramble off the bed and slip on a pair of stiletto heels. Then I step carefully into the center of the bedroom, facing the closed door. I pause for a second to adjust my lingerie before kneeling. Finally, I shift my body into the proper position: spine straight, shoulders back, and hands resting on the tops of my thighs. Then, my head tilts up. I watch the entrance, waiting.

Only moments later, Simon stops just on the other side of the door. I hear his muffled voice ask, "Piper?"

The knob turns. Simon steps into the room, and I instinctively lower my gaze. Only his heavy black work boots are visible. They halt just inside the doorway. His sharp intake of breath may as well be a shout of pleasure for the way it floods my system and makes my heart race.

"What are you doing?" he asks slowly, as though his mind cannot fully grasp the scene before him.

He steps closer until I feel his heat. If I wanted—if I was allowed—I could reach out and touch his thigh. Even this late in the evening, a hint of cologne still clings to him, tickling my nose with every inhale. Both the sweet tobacco and bourbon notes have faded, leaving sandalwood. His breaths are slow and even, giving me no indication of his current state. I desperately want to see his expression. Instead, I fight the urge, remain still, and respond to his question.

"Whatever pleases you, Sir," is my solemn vow.

This time, Simon groans low in his throat. The sound sends a bolt of pleasure to my core. My face flushes with pleasure.

Other than that one sign of acknowledgment, Simon completely ignores me. He hovers on the edge of my peripheral vision and shuffles around the room until I can no longer see him. With my other senses heightened, I hear him move behind me. He proceeds to perform the same nightly ritual as always, removing his badge and handcuffs and setting them down in the drop drawer of his nightstand. Then he removes his gun and places it in the mounted safe beside the bed. Finally, he walks toward the bathroom.

No that I have a decent view out of the corner of my eye, I can watch Simon remove his uniform piece by piece. He drops each article of clothing into the hamper as he goes and then pauses by the bathroom door to hang his utility belt on a hook. The action gives me a clear view of his incredible ass. I want to bite my lip—but, even without Simon watching, I know not to.

He moves farther away, then, stepping inside the bathroom and shutting the door. Moments later, I hear the shower turn on. My flush of pleasure slowly bleeds into a flush of embarrassment.

Okay. Okay, this is fine.

I guess the punishment has already started.

Based on my limited research, I know that I stay in this position until my Dom releases me. So, I wait. Thankfully, Simon chose a shower. He could have picked a bath and really tortured me. Even so, I wait several very long minutes until the water finally cuts off.

Simon moves around behind the closed door, toweling himself off. I can barely hear him, but my imagination fills in the blanks. I suddenly have the uncontrollable urge to squirm in place, needing to create some friction between my thighs. The ache there has become distracting.

Just then, the door opens. Simon steps out. The steam from the shower follows him, heating my already flushed skin and sticking there like sweat. It is just uncomfortable enough to dampen a bit of my arousal.

Somewhere behind me and to the right, a drawer opens. Fabric rustles. Then, a pair of bare feet steps into view.

"You did well waiting for me like this," Simon murmurs.

His thumb and forefinger grip my chin and gently lift my face for inspection. Like this, I can finally look my fill without consequence. Simon watches me, too, his handsome face stern. His hazel eyes glint with something dark and dangerous, but his gentle smile softens some of the hard lines in his expression.

"Normally, I wouldn't make a new sub wait like that." Simon's smile broadens slightly. "But you caught me the hell off guard, little bird. Believe it or not—I needed a minute to collect myself."

Pleasure surges at Simon's words, and allow myself a small smile. I admit that I like knowing how off-kilter I make him.

I like it a lot.

Simon's thumb traces the curve of my upturned lips. "Beautiful," he breathes.

He lightly brushes his fingertips along my jaw and then down my neck. They slip under the front strap of my corset bra and then move down, down, down beneath the lace edge of the décolletage.

"Nice choice of lingerie, too." Simon traces along the silky fabric's edge until he reaches the little bow in between my breasts. "I approve." Without warning, he leans forward for a better view. He traces the openwork pattern of the lace cups. "Are those...?"

"Peaches?" I finish. Simon's eyes meet mine. I nod, unable to stop a cheeky grin from peeking out. "Yes, Sir. I thought you might like them."

"Naughty girl." Simon's gaze, if possible, grows even more heated.

He gently pinches the hard bud of my nipple before leaning down farther to suck it into his mouth. I gasp in surprise. He nips the swollen flesh with his teeth, and I just barely manage to bite back a moan before it escapes. Unfortunately, I end up making a slightly choked squeak instead. He chuckles. Those vibrations send shockwaves straight through to my core.

After another sharp tug, Simon lets my breast go. His hand also drops away, and he steps back. I worry I did something wrong until I see the warmth of his gaze.

I keep my head up, watching Simon walk over to the armchair in the corner of the room closest to the window. He lounges back, looking to all the world like a king. Then he considers me for a moment.

"You've done your homework, I'll give you that," he says, finally breaking the silence. "But I wonder how ready you are. Because this is just the beginning, little bird."

Afraid that Simon will turn me away if I say nothing, I open my mouth and beg. "Please, Sir," I say, voice a hoarse whisper. "I'm ready. I swear I am."

Please give me the chance to prove it.

Simon's eyes sweep over my face one more time. Whatever he sees on my face, shining in my eyes, is enough. He gives me an almost imperceptible incline of his head, and I swear, I feel this heavy weight fall right off my shoulders.

"Remember: *meatloaf*. You feel uncomfortable, like it's too much—if anything at all doesn't feel right—use your safe word, and I stop. No questions asked. Okay?"

I nod eagerly and wait.

There is a shift in the air, a slight change in Simon's demeanor as he slips into his role. Some of the darkness swirling in his eyes unfurls and seeps into his blood. Then, he leans forward after a moment, resting his forearms on his thighs.

"Crawl to me."

His words cause something in me to catch fire. My knee-jerk reaction is utter humiliation, yet my entire body flushes with pleasure, and the deep ache in my core pulses in answer.

Focusing on his gaze, I lean forward and drop my hands to the carpet. Then, I begin to crawl. I place one hand in front of the other and one knee in front of the other, advancing slowly across the room until I reach Simon. Then, I kneel between his legs.

"Good girl," he says. "Take my cock out."

This command I am eager to obey. My fingers fumble a little on the drawstring of Simon's lounge pants because of my excitement. When I feel his rigid shaft, hot and heavy in my hand, I wrap my fingers around the thick base. Then, I gently tug him free of his clothing. My lips have already parted, and I am leaning forward to wrap them around his tip when I realize he never gave permission.

I pause, looking tentatively up at him.

"By all means, baby." He leans back, spreading his legs more, and shoots me a sinful smile. "I'm always happy to fuck that pretty mouth of yours."

Oh, god.

This man could *talk* me to an orgasm with that dirty mouth of his.

As soon as my mouth envelops Simon's length, I take it as deep as it will go. Then, sucking my cheeks in, I slowly slide back up. Simon seems to forget all sense of language for a moment, though I thoroughly enjoy his guttural groans.

Suddenly, I feel a fist in my hair. Simon lifts my head off of him and then uses his free hand to tuck his dick back into his pants. I look up with a pout. He shakes his head with a quiet laugh.

"Your fucking mouth," Simon mutters. Then, louder: "Stand up."

I rest my hands on his knees, pushing myself to stand but first taking advantage of my position to give him a charming view of my cleavage while I do. He looks unaffected and bored, but I catch how his eyes track my every move.

"Now," he commands, "strip for me."

Happily. Taking a few steps back so I can maneuver, I slowly slide my palms along my hips and the dip of my waist. My fingertips graze the undersides of my breasts while they travel up and over. When I reach the peach-colored ribbon straps, I playfully toy with them. Then, I continue on my path, reaching around the back. I hear the quiet snap of the hook and eye disengaging before the pressure of the band releases. I let the bra inch down my arms until the cups catch on my breasts, hooking a finger into the center, pulling it down, and then tossing it to the side.

Finally, I hook my thumbs beneath the thin ribbon that holds my panties in place. I silently perform to a song in my head, seductively rotating my hips, sliding the fabric over the swell of them until the panties slip down to the floor. I lift them with my foot and playfully toss them next to the bra.

Simon takes his time inspecting me. My only acknowledgment is a hand motion to turn in a circle, telling me to do a slow turn. Once face forward again, he stands and slowly strolls over to me.

"Do you remember why I need to punish you?" he asks.

I blink up at him and slowly nod.

"Tell me."

"Because I hid that article from you," I whisper, shifting uncomfortably.

"And?"

"I also didn't tell you that someone was stalking me." I pause then and shake my head. "That someone was stalking *us*. Sir."

"That's right." He tilts my head up and glares down at me. "And after tonight, you will never hide things from me again. Is that clear?"

"Yes, Sir."

He nods to himself, seemingly satisfied with my answer. Taking one step back, he nods over my shoulder. "Get on the bed. Keep the heels on."

A delighted shiver runs through me as I turn to start toward Simon's bed. Before I even take a step, a sharp smack stings the curve of my ass. I jump slightly but otherwise don't react.

I think I may be getting the hang of this.

Once I reach the bed, I crawl up on the mattress, up to the headboard, and settle back against the pillows. Simon is close behind me. He opens the top drawer of his nightstand and reaches for something. My pulse ratchets up when he pulls out a pair of leather cuffs—at least, I think that's what they are—in one hand and a blindfold in the other.

I lick my lips, mouth suddenly dry.

"Hands up," he barks.

Since I already rest against the headboard, I scoot a little lower before lifting my arms. Then I watch while Simon binds me. Despite the harsh tone of his command, his grip is gentle while he cuffs both wrists. He then takes the chain that links them together and hooks them to the wall over the headboard.

I had been wondering what those were for.

As the final piece to my costume, he secures the silk blindfold over my eyes, leaving me in complete darkness. It feels odd to be without sight. Everything else seems heightened, somehow. Like I am more in tune with my other senses. Even though he has yet to touch me, I know Simon is close by from the heat coming off his skin. I can smell the sweet tobacco soap that lingers from his shower. The salty, musky taste of his skin still lingers on my tongue. I hear the rustling of fabric as Simon shifts closer, and his breath tickles my ear just before I hear his rich baritone.

"Just checking in," he says. "All good, baby?"

"Mm-hmm."

Anticipation winds my body so tightly that any capability for speech fails. I need Simon to touch me. He chuckles at my distress and then does the exact opposite.

Simon disappears.

More rustling fabric. The sound of him getting down off the bed. Footsteps. The bedroom door opens and closes. And then all I hear is silence.

Silence and the rapid beat of my heart.

Is he going to leave me here?

But, no. I hear the door open again not too long after Simon leaves. At least, I think so. Time seems to have no meaning now, though it appears to have started moving again. I hear Simon's footsteps in the distance, growing closer, and the tick of my internal clock matches his cadence.

"The thing about sensory deprivation," he begins, his voice coming from the bedside table at my right, "is that the loss of one sense heightens the others. I'm sure you have figured that out. Sniff this."

Something clinks lightly against the glass close to my nose. As Simon demands, I smell a sharp combination of caramel, chocolate, and toasted oak. My lips curve slightly. Bourbon, of course. Simon's drink of choice.

"Now taste," he instructs.

The edge of the cool glass rests against my lips. Obediently, I open them, letting the liquid coat my tongue. When Simon pulls the glass back, I close my mouth and hold the drink there momentarily, tasting notes of vanilla, dark caramel, and hazelnut. I swallow, the bourbon sliding down my throat with a slight burn, leaving behind a faint, spicy, fruity aftertaste. I open my mouth expectantly, but Simon clicks his tongue in admonishment.

"No more, little bird," he admonishes. "I need you fully present for this. We can finish it later." He pauses, and I swear I can *hear* him arching an eyebrow. "If you're good."

At that, Simon moves away from me, taking the bourbon. After a second of silence, I hear a thud when he sets the glass tumbler on the nightstand. "Touch, in my experience, is the sense that most people gravitate toward when sight is impaired." I hear more faint clinking, then silence, until he says, "For good reason."

Frigid cold zaps my collarbone. I shriek and bow off the bed. Or, try to. The cuffs keep me from moving too far. The ice cube—or what I assume is one—already starts to melt from the heat of my skin, and cold water dribbles down toward my cleavage.

Held hostage, I can do nothing but endure while Simon begins sliding the ice cube down the center of my chest. He slowly traces the underside of each breast. My nipples have hardened almost to the point of pain, and my breathing turns ragged. Simon drags the ice around and around my breast, tightening the circle each time until he traces the edge of my areola. He moves closer still.

Bracing for the shock of ice on the hardened tip, I am still wholly unprepared for the sharp mix of pleasure-pain that hits my system. Gasping in shock, I arch my back, trying to get away—or maybe to get closer. Simon's mouth quickly replaces the ice, and my gasp morphs into a loud moan of pleasure. The sudden change in temperature shocks me. That jolts shoots straight down between my legs, where the ache deep in my core throbs unbearably.

I want Simon to touch me. I *need* him to touch me.

As though he can hear my thoughts, I feel a large hand sliding up my inner thigh, a warm palm spreading me open, and rough fingers sliding through my already drenched folds.

Simon groans and, under his breath, says, "Fuck. Me."

No, Sir, I want you to do that to me.

That thought stays firmly in my head, as much as I want to beg.

"Here's the deal," says Simon after a moment. His fingers continue to stroke me lightly. "You withheld something important that I needed to know. So, I think withholding something from you is a perfectly fair punishment. Don't you think?"

Words fail me. I can barely think, let alone speak—not with every bit of my concentration locked on the movement of

Simon's fingers teasing me, staying just outside where I need him most.

Did he ask me something?

Simon traces my vaginal opening. Whimpering, I tilt my hips and try to get closer. Simon clicks his tongue in admonishment and removes his hand.

"Piper," he barks. "I asked you a question."

Okay, he said your name that time, Piper. Focus!

But then one of Simon's fingers slips inside, then two, and I feel my brain short-circuit.

Suddenly, he pulls out and lands a sharp slap right on my clit. I cry out, hips jerking at the sting, and my traitorous core pulses and aches in the places only Simon can reach.

In between ragged breaths, I say, "I'm sorry, Sir." I sift through splintered memories of what he just said and piece together enough to respond. "Um, yes, Sir. Very fair."

"Much better. Next time, pay attention. Now"—Simon slides his warm palms up my inner thighs—"be a good girl and open wide. I want my dessert."

I have no other option, not that I would be insane enough to want one. Because as soon as I feel Simon's mouth on me, I am a slave to sensation. He alternates running the flat of his tongue up my slit, dipping inside my channel, and sucking my clit into his mouth and biting it.

Wearing this blindfold makes it impossible for me to anticipate his next move. I have no warning when his fingers join his mouth and plunge into my heat. My hands itch to bury into his curls, but they are trapped and immobile. I need to move my hips, but Simon has them firmly in his grip, and I am unable to do anything other than take what he gives me. So I do. I ache, tremble, and moan. His name falls from my lips like a prayer, a plea that goes unheeded.

Just as the pleasure starts to crest—when I feel like I'm about to launch into the heavens—Simon pulls away. He leaves me there, teetering on the edge, suspended with no way to take that last leap. Something between a desperate sob and a shriek of frustration bursts out of me.

After a moment, I feel Simon's lips slowly caressing a path up my body. Each kiss feels like a tiny shock of electricity straight to my core. Each touch torments and teases me because they are still not enough.

None of it is enough.

Simon reaches my collarbone, and his body drapes over me. Often a comfort, now the weight of him holds me immobile and heightens my discomfort because I am unable touch him back. My thighs clamp tightly on either side of his hips. I am so desperate for friction that I could scream.

Simon's open palm lands hard on my ass.

"Don't move," he growls, the lobe of my ear pressed between his teeth. He bites down just enough to feel a pinch, and I respond with a tiny mewl of protest.

Simon continues to lavish my neck with attention while his hands have free reign to roam my body. His touch skillfully avoids the places I need it most. The attention he gives is far from the attention I crave.

And he knows.

"This is your punishment, little bird," he says next to my ear. "I'm going to take you right up to the edge, let you hover over the precipice, and then I'm going to pull you back."

And he does.

Simon works me over, taking me to the edge, letting me dangle over the side, and then yanking me back so many times and in so many different ways that I lose count. My mind starts to fracture, separating from my body. I end up hovering in a hazy, in-between state of consciousness.

When that happens, Simon unhooks me from the wall and removes the blindfold. He drapes the chain over his neck so my arms can loop around him. So I can finally touch while he lines himself up at my entrance, pushes through my tight channel, and seats himself to the hilt. Looking for purchase, I dig my fingernails into his skin, curling into and away from him.

My mind and body are conflicted and moving in different directions.

Simon slowly, gently begins to move his hips with short, languid thrusts. "You've been such a good girl." He presses his lips to my temple. "You took your punishment well and deserve a reward."

I want that more than anything.

But I also have no clue if I can anymore.

"Too much," I whimper.

He chuckles and says, "You can take it."

Simon proves his words with a slow, gentle assault. He brackets my head with his forearms and leans down to kiss me. That starts gently, too. His tongue tangles with mine and moves in time with his hips. Simon surrounds me and fills all my senses as I breathe him into my lungs, listen to his deep groans of pleasure, and taste him each time our tongues tangle together.

My lust-drunk haze sharpens, causing my senses to unfurl like flower petals in the spring.

Then, it happens.

I feel that first spark of desire flare from the friction caused by Simon filling me, loving me, and owning my body. A sudden hunger for more heats my blood and spirals outward. My whimpers turn to moans. The flames spread. Simon tenses, his thrusts speeding up and growing more erratic the higher we climb.

With a sudden growl, he wraps his arms around the small of my back, anchoring me to him while he flips us over.

"Ride me, Piper. Finish yourself off," he says, gritting his teeth and digging his fingers into the fleshy part of my hips. "You earned it, baby."

My core pulses at his words. I carefully slip the chain of my handcuffs out from behind his head, pressing my palms to his chest for purchase. Then, I move my hips slowly, testing until I find the right rhythm. Soon, I gain confidence, and the banked fire of pleasure erupts, sending me speeding toward an explosive end.

Simon grows tense beneath me. He is close, too. My hips start to lose their rhythm as the orgasm builds, and I panic when I feel it backing off. "Need more," I gasp out. "Simon, please."

He sits up, pressing his back against the headboard, and wraps his arms tightly around my waist to take control. Within seconds, I throw my head back and scream when my climax blasts through me. A moment later, Simon follows, slamming our hips together one final time before we both shatter into a million pieces.

When the dust finally settles, I am thoroughly depleted, covering Simon with my prone, limp body. My limbs are spaghetti noodles. My brain cannot form a single coherent thought.

I think I may be dead.

But what a way to go.

After a few long, drowsy moments, Simon stretches beneath me. I crack open my bleary eyes when he gently lifts me off of him, tucks me into his side, and wraps his strong arms around my waist. Then my eyes flutter closed again as I sink into his warmth. I hum in contentment, floating happily along in my dreamscape, knowing his strength anchors me.

"Lesson learned?" Simon asks with a hint of amusement.

I am too tired to speak, not even sure I can at the moment. So I answer Simon with an enthusiastic sigh.

He chuckles. "You did wonderful, little bird. I'm proud of you."

Warmth blooms in my chest at his words. Unbidden yet unable to help myself, I lift my head and press my lips to his. We stay like that—savoring each other like a fine wine—until I need to break for air.

Simon smiles down at me while his thumb gently traces along my cheekbone. "Such a brat." He shakes his head, adding, "I didn't give you permission to kiss me."

An impish grin steals over my face. "So punish me."

Chapter 36
Playground

Piper

Simon and I enjoy the quiet aftermath of the most intense sexual encounter I have *ever* had. We lay tangled together, not quite awake but not sleeping, just floating along on a fluffy cloud in the aether.

Sometime during my euphoria, the mattress shifts, and I feel a loss of warmth when Simon disappears from bed. I open one bleary eye to watch him pad into the bathroom. It drifts closed again. I make a happy little sound in my throat and burrow deeper into my self-made cocoon of blankets and pillows. The faint sound of running water reaches my ears. A few moments later, Simon is back and gathering me into his arms, and I snuggle against his warm skin with a sleepy smile.

He momentarily tightens his hold, kissing my head and lingering to breathe me in.

"Okay, little bird," Simon speaks against my hair, starting to move. "Time for a little TLC."

Water splashes beneath me when Simon steps into the tub. He sets me down, chuckling when I pout at the disturbance. I blearily squint my eyes to watch him sink into the water. He reaches up, gently tugs my hands, and directs me to sit before him.

We stay like this through my aftercare, with Simon holding me close until the bath turns cold. During that time, I enjoy the sweet scent of bath oil on his skin, listen to the gentle ripples in the water, and feel steam from the bath, along with heat from the water, seep into my pores and aching muscles. I melt back against Simon, reveling in the sense of security only he can provide.

Six months ago, I never would have envisioned a life where I lounge against Simon Brooks like a queen while he pampers me. Yet here I am. He gives me cues with his body whenever I need to shift. Otherwise, Simon never says a word. He washes my hair with a gentle scalp massage and cleans my body with my peaches-and-cream soap. Finally, when the bath has used up all its magic, he guides me out of the tub, towels us off, and then carries me back to bed.

In the wake of our intimacy, Simon and I once again curl around each other, neither ready to leave our safe little bubble. But eventually, all good things come to an end. A little while later, Simon breaks the silence.

"Are you awake?" he murmurs.

I nod slowly.

"I have something I'd like to show you downstairs." He clears his throat. "It's sort of a surprise."

Blinking away the sleep hovering over me, I stupidly echo, "A surprise?"

"Yeah. Something I've been planning for a while." He pauses briefly before asking, "Do you want to see it?"

The way Simon asks, sounding both eager and timid, melts my heart. Tilting my head back, I look up at him and smile. How could I say no to him when he looks down at me with that boyish expression of anticipation?

My sweet, handsome, sexy, dominating man.

"Yes. Please show me," I reply.

"Yeah?" Simon's gaze sharpens as he looks at me, and his smile brightens. "Okay, yeah. Come on."

Before I can react, Simon hauls himself out of bed and pulls on his discarded sweats. Then he grabs my hands, hauls *me* out of bed, and slips a t-shirt over my head before I even realize my feet have touched the ground.

I laugh while he takes my hand and drags me into the hallway, down the stairs, and through the living room to the back of the house. We finally come to a stop in front of his childhood bedroom. I notice a fancy digital lock above the doorknob that was never there before and watch in fascination as Simon steps forward and types in a four-digit code. The lock beeps, then disengages. He pushes the door open before stepping aside. Then he motions for me to walk through first.

Because Simon's old room is an interior bedroom, no windows let in light. I hesitate in the doorframe, looking into the darkness beyond. Curiosity wins over doubt, and I cautiously make my way inside.

I have no idea what to expect.

I have no idea what I will find or what has changed.

Either way, Simon is about to show me.

Behind me, Simon follows. He stops inside the door and moves his hand along the wall until he reaches the light. A soft, warm glow bathes the entire room when Simon flips the switch.

Now I can see the difference.

And oh, what a difference.

There is much less stuff in here than before. The small space was once occupied mainly by Simon's bed, a large dresser, a desk and chair, and a set of bookshelves—not to mention all the random junk that teenage boys collect and leave lying around.

All of that is gone.

Gone are the posters of famous NFL players and framed photos of us, family, and friends he used to have lining the walls. In their place are several large prints of erotic art, each displayed in an ornate, vintage frame. Also gone is his old bed. Instead, one of those overstuffed modular sofas lines the back wall where the headboard used to be. It is the kind of sofa that can be just a sofa, a set of chaise lounges, or a bed—and almost anything in between.

Unbidden, I start to move about the room. There is also an antique armoire—I pause briefly to wonder what he has stored inside—on the wall opposite the couch. My fingertips absently brush the various items as I walk by them. My gaze is too busy looking around to focus on any one thing. That is until I get to the last piece of furniture left. It stops me and demands my full attention because this is something I have never seen before. At first glance, it looks like a saw horse, which would be more at home in a wood shop than a bedroom. But the gadget is much more than just a few pieces of wood. Two padded bits, one on either side, remind me of mini benches. They run parallel to the larger, middle saw-horse piece. The padding is a sumptuous dark brown leather over wood-stained chestnut.

I want to ask Simon what it is, but I feel silly being this naïve. I feel like I should know.

"Curious?" he asks, startling me out of my thoughts.

When I peek at him, Simon watches me intently with his back against the wall. His arms and ankles are crossed in a casual pose, but his expression is guarded.

I hate that. I open my mouth to ask Simon what is the matter, but he doesn't give me the chance. He pushes off the wall and stalks across the room toward me, moving with the grace of a natural-born predator. Everything about this side of him puts me on edge, but only in the best ways.

"Very. I think." I laugh quietly and then admit, "Maybe a little nervous, too."

He stops in front of me and spends a moment studying the details of my face. But he doesn't touch me like I expect—like he so often does. Instead, he breaks our connection to look down while he runs the palm of one hand along the leather padding of the top beam.

"It's okay to be nervous," he says. "It's also okay to ask whatever question is rattling around in your head."

As usual, Simon can read me like a book. His eyebrow arches when he glances back at me, and he wears a slight smirk. The guarded expression is still there, but also something hopeful.

That gives me the strength I need. "What is this stuff, exactly?" I look around the room. "Some of it looks like normal, regular bedroom furniture, but then you have"—I wave my hand at the saw-horse contraption—"and"—I wave my hand at the erotic art on the walls.

Simon fails to answer. He simply locks his gaze on mine and waits for me to have my epiphany. So I look back around the room, paying closer attention.

Then, I realize what it is that Simon is sharing with me.

"Oh my god!" I lean forward and whisper excitedly, "Is this a sex dungeon? Do you have a sex dungeon?"

Simon is startled for a second. Then he throws his head back and laughs until tears threaten to spill down his cheeks.

"Yeesh," I mutter, huffing. "It wasn't that funny."

With only us here, whispering is unnecessary. I probably could have toned down the enthusiasm, too. So sue me. I have never seen one of these before outside of the movies.

"Sorry." Simon gasps for breath. "I'm sorry, baby. That just wasn't at all the reaction I was expecting."

"What were you expecting?"

He shrugs, lighthearted expression melting away like it had never been there. "I'm not sure. Curiosity probably. But, more so, hesitance and—I don't know—anxiety. Skepticism. Suspicion." He runs a hand nervously over the back of his neck. "The way most people would react."

"Simon," I breathe, my heart breaking at how unsure he looks. "I'm not most people."

I quickly close the distance between us. My hands slide up to rest on Simon's chest, and I feel the slight elevation in his heart rate. Then, I continue their upward path until I reach his neck.

Wrapping my arms around him, I tug his head down to look him directly in the eyes. So he has no choice but to listen.

My voice gently scolds him when I ask, "In all these weeks, during all our times together, have I ever been anything less than enthusiastic?"

"Well, no."

"That's because I trust you. Even when I thought I didn't, even when I was guarding my heart because I was scared, some intrinsic part of me still trusted you. I will always trust you because you're kindhearted, trustworthy, protective, and loving. You are the best man I know." I smile big, tacking on one last thing. "And because I love you."

His expression softens. "I love you too, little bird."

"I know. No more uncertainty, though. Okay? From either of us. I think we're past all that now." I slip my hands back down his torso to thread my fingers through his. Then I tug him forward while I take a step back. "Now. About your sex dungeon."

He chuckles, shaking his head.

"I have to admit," I say, turning and walking toward the center of the room, "for a sex dungeon, it doesn't look very dungeon-y."

Simon looks skeptically at me and asks, "Do you *want* it to look dungeon-y?"

"Honestly?" I look around. "No. That would only creep me out."

"Okay." He looks relieved, which makes me want to laugh. Then he says, "I've never liked the idea of a dungeon. I prefer calling it a playroom."

"Playroom, huh?" I try it out, rolling around the word in my head. "Playroom. Yeah, that sounds way more fun."

"Some people like to lean into the pain. Sadism and masochism are very much a part of the scene. But"—Simon looks around, shrugs, and then looks down at me—"it's not something I've explored too deeply."

"Hm." I tilt my head, considering him. "Is it something you want to try?"

"Haven't really thought about it, to be honest." He narrows his eyes. "Why? Do you?"

My immediate answer wants to be 'no,' but I force myself to take a mental step back and give it serious consideration. "I'm not sure," is my eventual answer. "Given my past…" I shake my head. "With you, I think I'd be willing to try. Someday."

He kisses me. "And that's all I would ever ask. But that's a problem for our future selves."

I giggle at his lopsided grin. Then, slipping out of his grasp, I wander back over to the contraption I noticed before. "So, what is this thing for, now that I know the room's purpose?"

Simon's expression heats when he says, "That is a spanking bench." He follows me over and then quickly explains the different parts. Then he falls silent. When I peek up at him, I notice that his intense gaze is now focused entirely on the piece of furniture.

Simon looks like he is imagining me on it.

Suddenly, I imagine myself on it, too. A shiver of anticipation runs down my spine. But I have more questions, so I table that thought.

"How long have you had all this?" I spin in a slow circle before facing him again. Simon shakes his head, dislodging the daydream that had him so enthralled. Then I continue, "I guess I assumed you would have more. You've been doing this for a long time."

Simon clears his throat. "Yeah, I have. But this is all sort of new."

"Like the furniture?" I ask.

He nods. "The furniture, the lock on the door... all of it. Before October, this was just a junk room. I sold my furniture years ago, painted the walls, and planned on turning it into something. But life got in the way."

"So you put this together, what, since I got back?"

I try to wrap my head around everything he has just told me—and everything hidden between the lines. Simon can sense my confusion because his answering smile is gentle. He takes my hands again and tugs me back against him, unable to help himself—something I completely understand. I am just as obsessed with this man as he always says he is with me.

"I told you," he says, "I've just been waiting for you to come home. And when it looked like I had a real shot at winning you back? Well, I might have gone a little bit overboard."

"Just the right amount, I'd say." I kiss the sweet, bashful look right off Simon's handsome face. "And you always had a real shot at winning me back, you know."

"Yeah?"

I nod. "Looking back, you never really lost me to begin with. Once I got rid of the anger and the hurt, I realized my feelings were still there."

"You and me, Piper," he murmurs. "I want to continue this journey together. If that's something you want, too."

Simon looks up and around the room. At this moment, I realize his question is different than before, separate from when we spoke our feelings out loud for the first time in twelve years. This is a different sort of journey Simon wants to embark on.

Because I can say no. If I want to have a typical vanilla relationship with him, Simon will do it. He would shut this door, lock it tight, and never bring it up again. That is how much he loves me.

But I crave every facet of Simon Brooks. I want all of him, every single piece he will give me: his light, his dark, and everything in between.

That is how much I love *him*.

"Hmm," I say, stepping back out of his hold.

Simon stays put, watching me with that intense gaze of his that never fails to send shivers down my spine. I wander over to the large armoire and do what I wanted to do earlier. I open it.

Unlike the rest of the room, this is chock full of goodies. My hand reaches out, and I let my fingers run along the contraptions hanging on the back of the doors. Some of them I recognize: cuffs like the ones upstairs, one of those fancy feather dusters, a—flogger, I think?—a paddle, and—

Oh, god.

Is that a pair of nipple clamps?

My pulse steadily increases with each item I study, envisioning Simon using each one on me. I am slightly surprised when, rather than trepidation, the thought of using those clamps sends a wave of arousal shooting through me.

When I peek over my shoulder, I catch Simon watching me with amusement. He has a sly little smirk on his face. One that I am suddenly itching to wipe off. I look back at the assortment, carefully considering each one. Then I make my pick.

Strolling back over to the spanking bench, I keep the object carefully hidden from view. Exactly as I hope, Simon's smile is gone, replaced by curiosity and a heat in his gaze that could melt stone. I run my fingers again over the bench's supple leather. Then, after a long pause, I turn to face Simon and lean back against it, my butt hitting one of the knee rests.

"So," I say cheekily, holding up the flogger, "what do you say we break this thing in?"

I want *all* of *him,*
every single piece
he will give me:
his *light,*
his *dark,* and
everything in
between.

Chapter 37
In Love with a Girl

Simon

Christmas morning dawns bright, and I have been awake since well before sunrise. My eyes open, and my body floods with the same joyful excitement children feel when they realize Santa has come and presents wait for them under the tree.

Piper lays curled up next to me, her limbs and mine intertwined. I tighten my arm around her, tucking her tighter against my side. Her head lies on my chest, and she sighs happily.

My Christmas present is already here in my bed.

I want and need nothing else.

If I could stay in bed with Piper all day, I would. We could even curl up in front of the fireplace downstairs. But since we have family obligations, neither of those are an option.

Carefully, making sure not to disturb Piper, I disengage myself from her body and slip out of bed. The dogs perk up when I walk past them and head into the bathroom. I do my business and throw on lounge pants and a T-shirt. When I step back into the middle of the bedroom, I notice Cooper stealing my spot. I chuckle and shake my head. Then I head toward the door. Ozzy and Duchess quickly follow me into the hallway and down the stairs.

We head into the kitchen, where I start the coffee machine. I let Ozzy and Duchess outside to do their business and then rummage through the fridge, pulling things out until they are ready to return. When I have three dog breakfasts ready, two are already being devoured on the floor when Cooper trots in.

"About time, usurper," I mutter. Then, I lovingly ruffle the fur on his large head and set his bowl in front of him.

Piper wanders in next, just about when our food is ready. A hot mug of coffee is already waiting for her.

"I love you," she says, pulling the mug toward her with a deep sigh of pleasure.

Lifting an eyebrow, I ask, "Who? Me, or the coffee?"

"Yes."

That gets a chuckle out of me. Piper shoots me a sleepy smirk and hops up onto the bar stool, tracking me as I place a plate of food in front of her and a kiss onto her upturned lips. We proceed to eat our breakfast in comfortable silence. She finishes first, rinsing her dish and setting it in the dishwasher before letting Cooper outside since he wasn't downstairs for the first round.

All three dogs rush out to run around, and I hear her giggling. When she returns, I've finished, and she quickly swipes the plate with a quick peck on the cheek.

"I got this, handsome," she says, sashaying to the sink and giving me a delectable view of her backside.

When she peeks over her shoulder to see if I'm watching, I lift my eyes from her ass to her face and wink. She grins, face flushing. Then she returns to her task while I wander over to let the dogs back out of the cold.

Everything about this morning feels seamless, and I can't help but envision what it would be like ten, twenty, or even thirty years down the road. I wonder how it will feel after we have built up decades of patterns and routines. I wonder how we will act, knowing what the other thinks before they even say a word.

Fuck, I want that life.

I look over at Piper and catch her eye. She makes a silly face, and I shake my head, laughing. But when she thinks I can't see her, I catch the way she looks at me.

My parents used to look at each other that way. Piper looks at me the same way Stella looks at Foster and Ellery looks at Beckham.

Maybe, just maybe, she wants that life, too.

As soon as I finish the last drop of coffee, I turn to Piper and motion toward the living room. "Presents?" I ask.

Piper has an on-switch this morning, and I just triggered it. With an excited squeak, she races past me and out of the room, shouting, "Yay, presents!"

It reminds me so damn much of the way Ellery was growing up that I nearly end up doubling over from laughing so hard.

Once I finally compose myself and make it into the living room, Piper already sits on the floor cross-legged with the dogs sprawled around her. She has her stocking in her lap and is passing out the stockings we put together for the dogs. When she sees me, she hands mine out to me.

Then she starts to dig through hers like a raccoon looking for trash in a dumpster.

"Eager, are we?" I ask, pulling things out of mine at a much slower pace.

Piper freezes. "Sorry." She immediately sets the stocking down, looking up from her growing pile of treats to glance around the room. Her face flushes in embarrassment, and she quietly states, "It's just been a long time since…"

Even though she trails off, my mind finishes the sentence for her: *since I got to experience this.*

"Baby, don't you dare apologize for being excited about something." I get down on the ground beside her to look at her directly. My voice turns hard. "Ever. Got it?"

She nods quickly.

Picking up her discarded stocking, I hand it back to her before picking up my own. "Now," I say with a competitive glint in my eye, "the first one to empty these gets to open their gifts first."

Her eyes flash, and she smirks. "You're on, officer."

I let her win, of course. Anyway, the game does what I intend: it puts a smile back on her face and reignites her childlike excitement for the holiday.

After that, I pull her gifts out from under the tree one by one. There are several, all from our friends and family, and with each gift she opens, her mood improves until she has forgotten ever getting upset. Meanwhile, I make a silent vow to spend the rest of my days continuing to rewrite every lousy thing that happened to her until all she can see when she looks inside is good.

The next thing I pull out from under the tree is a square box, large in surface area, thin in height, and wrapped in bright paper and ribbon.

"Oh!" Piper hops a little in place. "That one is mine. I mean yours. To you, from me."

I chuckle. Piper is so damn cute when she gets flustered. But she grabs my bicep when I put it back down to get her something else. "No! Open it now."

"You sure?"

"Yeah, I'm sure. Open it now, please."

She looks up at me with those doe eyes, and I say, "Okay."

Clapping in excitement, she jumps up and reaches for the box. Slightly bewildered, I hand it over. Then she takes my hand and tugs. Getting the hint, I stand and let her lead me over to the couch. She settles onto one cushion and pats the spot directly next to her. I sit and then press a kiss to her lips.

"Thank you," I say with a smile.

She blushes. "You haven't even opened it yet."

"Don't care. It's from you, so I'll love it."

Piper watches on when I unwrap the box, biting her lip nervously. She has no clue, of course, but she picks up on how my hands pause their action. She glances up at me in confusion.

I arch an eyebrow at her and wait.

As soon as she realizes what she is doing, Piper gasps. Then, she immediately releases her lower lip from between her teeth. I shake my head at her, an amused smile weaving its way across my face.

"There's a good girl," I say. "One of these days, you'll remember that your lips are mine."

Her blush from before darkens, but she grins cheekily. "What lips are yours again?" she asks. Her fingers trace the outline of her mouth. "These lips?" Her other hand snakes down between her legs. "Or, these lips?"

Growling, I capture the lips on her face in a bruising kiss. My hand shoves hers to the side, and I cup her mound over her clothes. She moans into my mouth and helplessly bucks her hips up into my hand.

I pull back enough to declare, "Both." Before releasing her, I nip at her lower lip to drive the point home.

Piper sits back, dazed and panting slightly. I wink when she meets my gaze before returning to the task at hand. Once the wrapping paper has been removed, all that remains is a plain white box. I lift the lid. Then my chest warms at the single item inside.

"You finished it." I carefully lift out Piper's newest album.

Taking a moment to stare at the vinyl record sleeve, my awed gaze traces every detail of the unique art that illustrates her cover. Ellery and Piper put on a wildly successful contest with Ellery's child art classes. The end result blows me away.

Each chosen artwork is cropped to a different part of a phoenix—wings, tail, head, and body—and stitched together into a collage of the mythical bird. The collage serves as a backdrop do the phoenix depicted in Piper's tattoo. That phoenix rises—not just from the ashes of the smoldering fire between the pieces of art but also from the art itself—as though coming back to life.

From the Ashes appears in bold, intricate hand lettering. I trace the words with my finger. "This title," I murmur, "is it the same song you wrote that first night together?"

She nods.

Piper has come a long way since I first saw her. Every obstacle thrown her way, she meets head on, surpassing expectations with each personal victory. And I am so fucking thankful that I get to be a part of her journey.

"I was right, by the way," I say.

Her eyebrows raise. "How so?"

"I love it."

The expression on her face softens and she leans up to kiss me. "I'm glad."

"Thank you. For real this time."

"Wait!" She says, then takes the album from me and turns it over. "You almost missed the most important part."

When she hands it back to me, I look down and read the back. At first, all I see is the discography and the typical legal jargon until I skim past it and see a short paragraph centered at the bottom, printed in Piper's handwriting.

To Simon, the only man I've ever loved.
You are my always and forever.
Here's to chasing new dreams together.

My eyes lift to Piper. Warmth flares in my chest at her expression—a mixture of expectation, uncertainty, hope, and love. I carefully set the album back into the box she wrapped it in.

"Do you like it?" she asks, hands fidgeting in her lap.

I still them with my own. Then I tug Piper toward me until she straddles my lap, reaching up to frame her face with my hands. Every ounce of love coursing through me flows into the kiss we share. She fists her hands into my T-shirt, mewling when I part her lips, seeking entry, and again when our tongues twine together. At the risk of losing myself completely, I let things go on longer than I should.

But dammit, Piper makes it hard to maintain control.

With my hands in her hair, I hold Piper's head still to break away. Our eyes are closed, and our foreheads touch. For a moment, I simply breathe her in.

"Does that answer your question?" I ask.

She hums. When I open my eyes, she is already looking at me. Her green eyes twinkle in the morning light, and she is smiling.

"Not sure," she says. "I think maybe I need you to tell me again."

Piper squeals when I launch forward and attack her sides with my fingers. She laughs hysterically and wiggles in a half-hearted attempt to get free, but I am relentless in my onslaught until she cries out, "I'm sorry. I'm sorry! Yes, Sir, you answered my question!"

I stop, then, and lean over her with a wicked smile. "Always the fucking brat."

Lifting her head to nuzzle our noses together, she replies, "You love it."

"I love *you*."

She melts under me. "I love you too, handsome."

"Now, behave," I scold after helping her back to a seated position. "You still have two presents left."

"Two?" Her eyes light up, and she claps her hands together, jumping giddily. "Gimme, gimme!" I roll my eyes to the ceiling, but I'm grinning. Then, after getting up, I hold out a hand. She looks at it in confusion and asks, "What's this? Where are we going?"

"Always with the questions," I say in mock exasperation.

She huffs quietly, slips her tiny hand into mine, and lets me lead her out of the living room toward my dad's study. I open up the door. Then I take Piper by the shoulders, turn her around, and gently push her through the door in front of me.

"Hey, handsome?" Piper asks once we are standing in the middle of the cozy room. "Wouldn't it have made more sense to put the gift under the tree?"

"So much sass." I shake my head. "Wouldn't fit under the tree, little bird. Not really."

If anything, she looks even more confused after my cryptic statement. Sighing, I start to speak while I round Dad's old desk and tug open the top drawer. "This gift is still in progress, but I thought maybe I could bring you in and let you picture it in your head. Maybe add some input of your own."

I pull several sheets of drafting paper from the open drawer. Piper leans forward, curiosity getting the better of her. "What are those?" she asks.

"Come over here, and I'll show you."

While I lay them out on the desk, Piper walks across the room and stops beside me. She stares at the paper, trying to make sense of the architectural plans I've revealed.

"You're looking at plans for this study," I explain, pointing to the first technical drawing. "I've contracted Beckham and Hawk's company to soundproof this room and turn it into a music studio for you. I want you to have somewhere you can play my dad's guitar whenever you want, sit at the desk, and write your music. Fill up the shelves with whatever books or trinkets inspire you."

Piper is silent throughout my description of the plans. When I look over to check on her, I see tears in her eyes and feel a sudden, sharp pang of concern. Shit. "It's okay if you would rather not. They still have some plans to finish. I wanted to get your input, and—"

Her hand on my arm stops me. She shakes her head, wiping away the tears, and laughs. "No, Simon, I love it," she says between hiccups. "It's the best gift anyone's ever gotten for me. But it's too much."

I shake my head and slide my arms around her. She tucks her head beneath my chin. We stay like that for several moments until her tears turn to sniffles, and then her sniffles turn silent.

"Nothing is too much for you, baby," I murmur. Then I grip her shoulders and bend my head to glare at her. "Besides, I decide when something is too much. Understand?"

She nods and gives me a slightly shaky smile. "Yes, Sir."

"Alright, no more tears." I brush away the remaining strays that have leaked out. "We have a little time before we need to get ready to leave." We are due at her parents' house to have Christmas brunch in over an hour. "How would you like to spend them?" My voice has turned husky with all the naughty ideas I have running through my head.

Piper doesn't hesitate. "However you want. Sir."

When I slide one hand around the curve of her neck, Piper's eyes flutter shut, and she immediately tilts her head up, expecting a kiss. *Fuck*. Piper's blind obedience is almost as much of a turn-on as her bratty side.

So I reward her—thoroughly—until my lungs scream for air and my hands are on the small of her back. They drift down to cup the soft globes of her ass. When I squeeze, she hops up and wraps her legs around my hips. I cradle her with one arm under her thighs and one around her upper body. Then I carry her toward the bedroom while she presses little open-mouthed kisses all over whatever skin she can reach. I groan out loud and hasten my steps.

"Think your parents will mind if we're late?"

She pauses to look me in the eyes. Her own are twinkling and full of mischief. "Maybe. But who cares?"

Good enough for me.

✳✳✳

Later (but not too much later because I'm not a complete asshole), Piper is in the bathroom putting the finishing touches on her makeup and outfit. Not that she needs it. She would look beautiful no matter what, but I have been firmly schooled and instructed "that is beside the point."

So I sit on the edge of my bed while I wait, fully dressed and playing with a small wrapped box in my hands. When Piper finally exits the bathroom, she stands in the middle of the room and rotates slowly from my inspection.

"Well," she asks, "how do I look?"

"Perfect." And I mean it. Piper has gathered her hair into a low ponytail. All her sparkling piercings are on display, and she is wearing a small amount of makeup. Honestly, I think my girl is gorgeous with or without it. I can also admit that, done right, makeup does enhance all that natural beauty.

Covering Piper's sinful curves is a simple pair of denim jeans and a deep red, slouchy sweatshirt—the kind that droops off one shoulder and gives just a peek at the lingerie underneath. I smile when I see her bra strap is red and green plaid.

"I am seriously tempted to see what else those clothes hide," I admit.

"You're insatiable." She saunters up to me, hips swaying side-to-side, and stops when she is standing in between my splayed legs.

When she presses her glossy lips to mine, I groan. Fucking peach-flavored lip gloss. *Damn. Fucking. Tease.* I snake my arm around her, trying to pull her onto my lap, but she dodges me with a laugh.

Once safely out of reach, Piper shakes her head. "We have to go, Casanova. We're late enough as it is."

"Are you trying to give me orders, little bird?" I ask, raising an eyebrow.

Her face flushes, and Piper quickly lowers her gaze, folding her hands in front of her. "Only an observation, Sir." She looks contrite, but a wicked grin tugs at the corners of her mouth.

Then she notices the box in my hand, the one I have been waiting for her to see.

"Simon," Piper whispers, taking a small step closer. Hesitating while she puzzles things out. "You said you had two presents for me."

"Caught that, did you?" Outside, I am smirking. Inside, my pulse has started to thunder in my ears.

"Is that… is that the second?"

Swallowing thickly, I nod.

Now or never, Simon.

Before I lose my nerve, I hold the box out in the palm of my hand. Then, I lift it so it sits directly in front of Piper. Questions are in her eyes that want to form on her lips. But then she shakes her head, dislodges the questions, and reaches for the gift.

She hesitates until I say, "Open it."

Her hands tremble, I notice, while she slowly lifts the lid. Piper breathes my name, her voice breaking on the first syllable when she sees the ring nestled in white satin. After the shock starts to fade, she runs her forefinger along the top grooves of the design.

I look down, trying to see the ring through her eyes. The center stone is a teardrop-shaped ruby flanked by a smaller black diamond on each side. The ring itself is a white-gold vine and leaf pattern. A few smaller black gemstones rest within the vines like little rosebuds.

Call me sentimental or crazy. No ring I chose would be anything short of perfect. It has to be so much more than just pretty. It has to have a personality that complements hers.

Her ring is unique—one of a kind.

Because Piper Easton is one of a kind.

Looking back at the woman in question, I find her expression hard to read—stuck on neutral, undecided between disbelief and hope.

Cleaning my throat, I say, "This requires a bit of backstory."

Slowly, Piper nods for me to continue.

"I bought this ring a month or so before your graduation—" her quiet gasp rings out like a gunshot and cuts me off. I look up sharply, worried I said something wrong.

Tears shimmer in her eyes. "Twelve years?" she croaks. "You've had this for twelve years?"

My free hand runs over my hair, and I blow out a breath before I nod. Then I admit, "I had no set plan, no idea when I would give it to you… maybe as a graduation present. Maybe on your eighteenth birthday or Christmas. But the day I saw it in a store window downtown, I just knew."

"How?" she whispers. "We were so young…"

For me, the answer is as easy as breathing. "Because it has *always* been you, little bird. I knew from the moment I laid eyes on you that you were my future. My forever."

Her chin wobbles, but she manages to keep her composure. I turn the box toward me and take the ring between my thumb and forefinger. Lifting it out of its holder, I contemplate it for a moment.

Then I say, "My feelings for you never changed. Not once."

My gaze lifts to hers, and I let her see it all. All my love. Every dream I have for the future. That deep-seated fear that Piper won't want me. The recent, burgeoning hope that she will.

"I'm not asking for anything. Nor am I expecting an answer. But it felt wrong for this not to be on your finger now that you're mine."

"You don't think it's too soon?" The expression on her face finally settles on hope—and something in me settles, as well.

"Baby." I use my free hand to tilt her chin back up so she's looking at me. "For me, we're running about twelve years behind." I run my thumb lightly over her lower lip. "My heart has been yours since I was sixteen. It will still be yours long after we are gone from this earth."

The tears in her eyes spill over even as Piper laughs with pure joy. "Then, ask me," she says.

I blink in surprise. "Ask you?"

Piper's mouth curves into a faint smile. "If you're going to put a ring on my finger, Simon Brooks, then you should ask the question that goes along with it." She peeks up at me and timidly adds, "Please."

"Piper Easton." The expression on my face is earnest, and my voice is solemn as I say, "I want to live here in this house with you. I want to get married, have lots of babies, and grow old and gray together." I cradle her head with both hands, gently rubbing my thumbs along the cheekbones. "Be my wife."

This time, when she smiles, it wraps around me like an embrace and warms me from the inside out. Happiness infuses her beautiful skin with a soft glow. Piper lifts her hands to my wrists and holds me in place. Then she says, "Isn't it more traditional to *ask* the other person?"

"Cheeky minx." My eyes narrow. "I never ask. And, as you well know, I'm also not accustomed to repeating myself."

"Hm," she replies, holding her left hand out to me with the palm facing down. She playfully wiggles her fingers. "Then I guess I have no choice."

"Damn right, you don't." My face relaxes into a grin. I slide the ring on her finger, where it should have been all this time. Then I pat my thigh. "Come here."

We can celebrate with all our friends and family soon. But this moment is for us only. Right now, I need to feel her.

After Piper straddles my lap, I slip my arms around her waist and anchor her to my chest. With a hum of contentment, she melts into the embrace. I tighten my hold, breathing in her addicting scent and feeling like she can never be close enough.

My lips hover next to her ear as I whisper, "I love you, Piper Easton."

"I love you, too, Simon Brooks," she echoes back. "Always have. Always will."

Her lips tell me just how much when she turns her head and kisses me. A few breaths later, she pulls back. Her forehead presses against mine just as her eyes flutter closed.

"Good," I say. Then, a brilliant smile stretches across my face. "Ready to chase those new dreams together?"

She answers me without hesitation.

"Yes, Sir."

Epilogue

Hawk

Four months later

Beckham and Ellery get married on a pleasant spring day in their front yard. They stand with the officiant along the waterfront beneath a flowering arch covered in ivy and apple blossoms. Rows of rustic wooden chairs transform their front yard into the perfect space for a ceremony. That poof-y, gauze-y fabric decorates each chair—the kind that weddings always use. A spacious aisle cuts the section in half, but a hand-painted wooden sign sits just before the seating area and instructs people to pick a seat, not a side.

Trés cute.

The first time they kiss as man and wife, an impressive sunset paints the sky behind them, which is fucking magical.

For their reception, the backyard becomes a fairy tale wonderland with hanging candle votives, strands of fairy lights crisscrossing overhead, and round tables surrounding a large dance floor. That same gauze covers the tables, and fancy centerpieces of ivy and apple blossoms decorate them.

Seriously. Five out of five stars. Ellery's closest friend, Lena, knows how to throw an event to remember. Then again, she grew up in that world. Fancy champagne parties, balls (are balls even a thing anymore, or am I thinking of some period drama Jane Austen shit?), brunches with socially acceptable alcoholic beverages.

Whatever.

My point is that the ceremony kicked fancy-pants ass.

Beautiful wedding. Beautiful bride. Beckham—with permanent stars in his eyes—follows Ellery around like a puppy. I will be giving him a significant ration of shit about that until the end of forever. Mainly to mask how incredibly jealous I am.

Of all the weddings I could envision myself having, tonight comes closest to my dream. I want a wedding precisely like this.

Or, I used to.

Did I think about getting married a lot growing up? No. What teenage boy does?

Do I still want it to be the best goddamn wedding on the face of the planet when I did think about it? Damn fucking straight. I wanted a wedding with all the bells and whistles.

Unfortunately, my wedding didn't pan out that way.

Tale as old as time: Navy boy meets girl in between deployments. Boy thinks girl is fucking sexy. Boy has fun, no-strings sex with her. Girl gets knocked up. Boy does the right thing, and they marry at the courthouse. Nine months later, and here comes Baby in the baby carriage:

My precious daughter, Maisie.

Light of her father's life.

Our start to married life went pretty well, all things considered—until I had to leave on a six-month deployment. Some serious shit went down a few months in, the Navy medically discharged me, and then I went home to an empty fucking house.

I lost my career and my family in one fell swoop.

Wherever my wife disappeared to, taking my child with her, I haven't seen or heard a thing from them in over two years.

That makes my baby girl three years old now.

Not a day goes by that I don't think of Maisie and wonder where she is. I pray that she's okay. Is Violet taking good care of her? Where did they go? Why did Violet disappear in the first place? Did she run? Were they taken? See, that's the problem with a shotgun wedding. Often, the couple knows very little about their spouse and their spouse's past.

I certainly know nothing about mine.

My brother is a world-class hacker, and even his luck has run out in trying to locate any information that would help me track them down. I find it difficult not to resent the fuck out of the woman I married. We may not have been a love match, but I cared about her. Enough that I wanted to spend my life with her and raise our daughter together. I believed that, given time, we could grow to love each other.

I *thought* Violet cared about me, too.

"You look way too pensive for a wedding reception, mister."

A feminine voice filters through my thoughts, yanking me back into the present. I look around, slightly dazed, and notice Lena and Simon standing by the table where the bride and groom are seated. Lena has a microphone in hand while she gives her maid of honor speech.

Well, then. I guess I'm more distracted than I realized.

When I peek at who spoke, I catch Piper Brooks slipping into the empty chair beside mine. Yes, you saw that right. After Simon proposed on Christmas Day, the couple went to New Orleans over the New Year. They also thought it would be fun to elope during their trip.

With Ellery and Beckham's blessing, of course.

I have to say, calling Piper by her married name has taken some getting used to—that and thinking of her as Simon's wife.

It amuses me to imagine the number of hopeful fans who will weep when the news about Songbyrd breaks.

Piper looks just like a songbird in her bridesmaid attire. Her white-blonde hair has bright red, gold, and orange streaks that get brighter nearer the ends. She wears the strands in one of those fancy, super-girly styles, and the colors go perfectly with her pastel-yellow bridesmaid's dress. Ellery wanted them to each pick something themselves, as long as the dress had thin straps and the length hit around mid-calf.

Ask me how the hell I know this.

Being a groomsman means I have to "be involved."

But, even I—the king of I-don't-give-a-fuck-about-fashion—can admit that the mini-rainbow effect is fetching. Perfect for whatever fairy-tale-ish celebration Lena brought to life.

"Hey, Piperoni," I say in greeting.

"Hi there, Teddy Bear."

"Ooh, good one."

She replies, "I thought so," with a wink. Then she tilts her head to the side, squinting at me like I'm a puzzle she's trying to figure out. Circling the air around my face with a finger, she asks, "So what is it that has you looking like this, huh?"

"Like what?" I ask. "Sexy as sin? Dashingly handsome?"

"Try sad."

"Ah." I look away when the room titters at something Lena said. Then I sigh and shrug. Without looking at Piper, I say, "Everything, I guess. Just thinking about weddings. Family."

Her expression softens. "Oh. I see."

Piper and I are kindred spirits. She had a rough go of things for quite a few years, so she understands that sometimes you have to wear masks to hide the pain festering inside. I have never wanted to burden my family with my issues, and I also have no desire to broadcast my past to the world.

However, since moving to Sweetbriar, my family has grown quite a bit. Beckham is my brother-in-arms, of course. Then Simon—as Beckham's closest childhood friend—has become a good friend of mine, as well. Ellery, for apparent reasons. Now, Piper.

Eventually, my past will come to the surface, so I decided beforehand to control the narrative. I shared the bare minimum, just enough to keep curiosity at bay.

My brother, Tobias, and Beckham were the only ones present for the entire sordid affair—from the point when Violet got pregnant all the way to this moment. Ellery is familiar with the story in broad strokes because I like her better than Beck. (I mean, I don't tell *him* that, but she knows the truth.) Simon knows a bit, as well, from those times I thought insight from a cop might be useful and drunkenly asked him for help.

And now I have Piper. She knows about as much as Ellery—but she has never asked for more and never needs to fill in the blanks. Piper has become the person I turn to on an off day. We sit in silence, watching the world go by. Or I will listen to Piper strum on the guitar.

Piper never asks for reasons or details. She never feels the need to fill the silence with meaningless chatter. And when I say shit like I just said, she gets it, and she never presses for more.

I love her for that.

Still, I refuse to be *that* guy, the one who brings down the mood, so I shoot Piper a lopsided grin. "Aw, don't worry about me, Pippin."

Piper makes a face. "Are you calling me a hobbit now?"

"I mean, if the height fits…"

"Excuse me," she huffs. "I am five-foot-six."

"Sweetheart, to me, anything under five-foot-eight is short."

That's not strictly true. I'm just under six feet myself. But I love giving Piper shit any chance I can.

Like now, when I toss a smile in her direction and sling an arm over Piper's shoulders. Moving fast, I loop around her neck and then squeeze her into a light headlock.

"Ugh! Don't mess up my hair, jerk," she complains, struggling in my grip. "Why are you like the older brother I never wanted?"

Then she pinches my side. Hard. I yelp in surprise more than pain, but my hold stays steady. A few people peek over at us in varying shades of annoyance.

Whoops.

Heaving a dramatic sigh, I let Piper go. "You know you love me, Pipsie Girl."

"Against my better judgment." She rests her head on my shoulder in direct contradiction to her words. Her gaze is on Simon, who is watching Lena finish her speech. The hearts in her eyes may as well be a neon arrow pointing from her to him.

Their love for each other is palpable, a living, breathing thing. As though he can sense her watching, Simon's eyes seek her out, and his expression morphs from politely pleasant to pure devotion.

I'm not jealous of them. I'm not. But I know that kind of relationship is no longer in the cards for me. After what Violet did, I could never trust another woman like that.

But Piper deserves all the love and happiness in the world after the nightmare she lived through. Hell, so does Simon. Both of them have had their fair share of pain and heartache. The two have been in love since high school. Their relationship would have had the natural progression of many other high school sweethearts, but then the tragedy of Simon's parents during his first year of college hugely derailed them.

Luckily, they found their way back to each other. I would be hard-pressed to find two individuals more perfect for each other.

And I know our friendship is still new, but Piper has this way of burrowing under your skin and making a place in your heart. Using her earlier sentiment, Piper is like the little sister I never wanted. But she is also one hundred percent the family I need.

"Simon's up!" Piper whispers loudly in my ear. She grips my arm in excitement. "Aww, look how cute he is when he's nervous."

I roll my eyes. "Only you would think a man is cute doing something supremely uncomfortable."

Once Lena hands off the mic to Simon, she steps to the side so he can take her place closest to the table. "Well," he says, testing his voice through the speakers. "For those who may not know me, I'm Simon, Ellery's brother."

Someone in the crowd yells, "Woohoo! Sexy cop!" A wave of enthusiastic giggles washes over the women in attendance tonight. Simon flushes and clears his throat.

Piper snickers and says in my ear, "He seriously hates that nickname."

"Well, shit. Guess I'd better stop spreading it around, then."

Piper squeaks when she tries to suppress a surprised laugh at my comment. She then proceeds to slap my stomach with the back of her hand. "Behave, Theodoraus."

"Rawr."

I smile as I turn my attention back to the main event.

"Beckham here has been my best friend since we were ten years old," Simon continues, "so of course I was going to be best man at his wedding. But had you told me a few years ago that I would walk my sister down the aisle, and this guy would be on

536

the other end? I would have laughed in your face before I slammed it with my fist."

When the crowd laughs, Simon's shoulders start to relax. "Kidding, of course. I'm a cop. I'd never do something like that." He pauses, adding, "I would have enough smarts not to leave physical evidence."

Louder laughter—including mine—sweeps through the crowd for that one. Beckham looks impressed. Ellery looks mortified.

"You being a cop hardly mattered when you clocked me in the jaw," Beckham quips, grinning.

Simon glares at him. "That's because you dated my baby sister behind my back, asshole. I had a right to be pissed." He looks between them and says, "Thankfully, it didn't take me long to realize you two are the real deal. You act just like Mom and Dad did, Ellery. That's the biggest reason I came around so fast. Because Beckham looks at you like Dad looked at Mom, which is my gold standard for true love."

Ellery's smile is watery as she looks up at her big brother and says, "Thank you."

Simon returns her smile with a slight nod. He shifts his focus back to Beckham. "Thank you for being the best friend a man could ask for. And thank you for being the only man to whom I would ever entrust my sister." Simon raises his champagne glass and concludes, "To Beckham and Ellery."

The room erupts in cheers and booming echoes of "To Beckham and Ellery!"

Simon hands the microphone to the wedding coordinator just as someone clinks their glass. Everyone starts chanting, "Kiss! Kiss! Kiss!"

Taking advantage of everyone's distraction, Simon stalks back to our table. He collapses into the chair next to Piper and says, "Fuck, that was excruciating."

"Aw, you did amazing, handsome." Piper lifts her head for a kiss—and I have to look away.

Simon mutters, "I'll happily deal with Mrs. Ryder's demon cat over that any day."

I snort quietly. From what I've heard, that cat is a menace, so Simon must really hate public speaking to entertain the idea of dealing with the furball on any given day.

Lena and the coordinator are discussing the reception schedule or some such nonsense with Beckham and Ellery while the servers clear the tables of the remnants of dinner. Piper shifts so that she is leaning against Simon instead of me, starting a hushed conversation of their own. I sip my beer and people-watch for a few minutes.

When the DJ announces the "pseudo-father-slash-older-brother pseudo-daughter-slash-younger-sister dance," Simon groans in mock annoyance, and Piper laughingly shoves him out of his chair. The familiar strains of some pop ballad or other start to play, and Simon twirls Ellery into his arms with an exaggerated flourish. Everyone laughs, the two of them included.

They take a typically dull part of the evening and at least make it entertaining. But I am near my limit on feel-good romance and family ties. As soon as I start to feel twitchy, the dance floor opens to everyone. Beckham steals Ellery from Simon, and then Simon promptly comes to collect Piper for a dance.

I take this as a perfect excuse to stand and stretch my legs.

Someone grips my arm as I walk away from the commotion, trying to find somewhere quiet to breathe. I turn, feeling frustrated, until I see that the woman in question is Melanie, one of my on-again, off-again casual flings.

This situation may be on-again based on the smile stretched across her face. I feel my mouth quirk up in a smirk. Some horizontal acrobatics may be just what I need to get out of this funk.

"Evening," I say, voice oozing charm.

As usual, she eats it right up. Her cheeks flush a pretty pink, and her tongue peeks out to lick her lips. "I was hoping I'd get a chance to say hi. You seemed busy with your groomsman duties today, so I didn't want to bother you."

"Mel, Mel, Mel," I admonish, moving a step closer, "you can bother me anytime you want." Then I tilt my head to the side, considering her. "Are you staying for the whole reception? If so, maybe we could"—my words get drowned out by my phone, which starts to blare with whatever ridiculous song Tobias changed his ringtone to the last time we were together.

I send a silent curse up to the heavens before grabbing the offending contraption to put it on silent. "Sorry about that, doll. Now, what was I saying?"

Mel reaches up to toy with my necktie. "I think you were about to invite me to your place for a nightcap."

"That's right. So, how about—?" My phone starts to vibrate in my pocket. This time, I curse out loud. "Fuck me." Yanking my phone back out, I decide to shut the damn thing off when I see Tobias on the screen yet again.

He hates phone calls with every fiber of his being, so the fact that he's called me twice in a row, even when I put him on read, tells me this isn't some social call.

"Sorry again, gorgeous, but I gotta take this. I'll come find you in a bit, okay?"

"Sure thing, Hawk. I'll be around." With a wink, she saunters away.

I quickly move to the outer edges of the yard, where the thick line of trees muffle the reception sound. The vibrations of my phone have stopped, but now his texts spam my app, telling me to *pick up the damn phone.*

I immediately call him back.

He picks up on the first ring.

"I found them!" His voice explodes in my ear.

"Are you fucking kidding me right now?" My heart starts pounding in my chest. I start to pace, needing an outlet for the sudden rush of nervous energy. "When? How? Where?!"

"I've been putting feelers out like always, but just a little while ago, one of them came back. I tracked the data, and there she fucking is in black and white."

"Violet?"

"No, Maisie. Some recent medical records." My chest clenches painfully. As though Tobias can hear it from across the line, he quickly adds, "Nothing bad. Just routine checkup shit."

"Why the hell would that pop up now of all times?" I pinch my eyes closed. "Never mind. Not important. You haven't answered the most important question, man."

"Which is…?"

"Where the hell is she?"

A long pause stretches out between us, and I start to feel a sinking sensation in my stomach.

"Tobias."

"Yeah?"

"You know where to *find* Maisie, right?"

He lets out a deep breath, and when he finally answers, I feel like the world has dropped out from under me. "Yes. I do. But you aren't going to like it…"

The End.

Author's Note

I could honestly write an entire novel about what went on behind the scenes of Sweet Obsession. Instead, I'm going to keep this note as short and sweet as possible, and focus on the two most prominent themes in the story—and why I chose to write what I did.

1. Abuse

This story was difficult at times. I have personal experience with emotional abuse, and I know people who have experienced grooming, gaslighting, and abuse by men in positions of power. Because of that experience—and because I always want to treat tough subjects with the utmost care and sensitivity toward my readers—I was like Santa. I checked everything twice. Three times. As many times as needed. I researched all aspects of Piper's abuse extensively. Then I consulted with a licensed therapist and abuse victims to validate my facts, timeline of events, even the characters' emotions and reactions.

2. BDSM

Simon completely blindsided me on this one. I had no grand scheme of making this book about BDSM until Simon—as the Dom he is—completely took control. I had no other option than to say, "Yes, Sir."

Now, because BDSM is an area that I enjoy on a conceptual level but have no actual experience in, I also did copious amounts of research. I was lucky enough to have the help of both an ex-professional Dominatrix and a brat submissive to answer questions and give me invaluable insight into that world.

This allowed me to write as accurate a depiction as possible of Piper's introduction into that lifestyle—and, I hope, serve as a guide to safe and proper practices.

For anyone who may be curious… *wink, wink*

3. Music

Since music plays such a prominent role in Piper's life, each chapter title within Sweet Obsession corresponds to a song. You can view the list of songs that inspired the titles on Amazon Music or Spotify:

Amazon Music

Spotify

With each story I write, this town—and all of its residents—take up more and more space in my heart. I hope that they find a home in yours, as well. After all, I have more characters for you to fall in love with—and quite a few more stories left to tell in Sweetbriar!

xo, Danika

Content Warnings

Please review the list below for potentially sensitive topics that some readers may wish to avoid.

Explicit Language - If you are not a fan of strong language, then this book may not be for you. There is a lot of !@#$%& throughout.

Mental Health - Mental health (esp. anxiety) is an important theme Sweet Obsession and will be found throughout. However, I have listed more extreme situations below.

BDSM - While the plot does not revolve around BDSM, it is a prominent theme in all sexually explicit scenes and in several interactions between the two main characters.

References to:

Car accident
- Chapter 1
- Chapter 29

Emotional abuse & gaslighting
- Chapter 1
- Chapter 14

Parental death
- Prologue
- Chapter 20

Physical abuse
- Interlude 4

Sexual abuse/assault
- Chapter 1
- Interlude 4
- Chapter 26

Stalking
- Interlude 5
- Chapter 24

Violence
- Chapter 17
- Chapter 27

Depictions of:

Anxiety/panic attacks
- Chapter 1
- Chapter 9
- Chapter 13
- Chapter 14
- Chapter 25
- Chapter 31

Emotional abuse/gaslighting
- All Interludes
- Chapter 1
- Chapter 32

Harassment
- All Interludes

Hospitalization
- Prologue

Stalking
- Chapter 31

Violence
- Chapter 31
- Chapter 32
- Chapter 33

What comes next?
Not ready to let Sweetbriar go?

Stay in touch with the town and its residents.

Grab a coffee at Jelly Beans. Check out Unity Art Co-op and say hi to Ellery and Lena! Hire Beckham, Hawk, and their crew for some renovations or new construction. You can also keep in touch with Ellery, Beckham, Simon, and the rest. You'll be able to ask them questions, read exclusive bonus content, view character art, and so much more. I'm constantly adding more, so you don't want to miss it!

Visit Sweetbriar now at **danikalynnbooks.com**.

The Sweetbriar Romance Series

Book 1: Sweet Temptation
- Small town, brother's best friend romance

Book 2: Sweet Obsession (Fall 2024)
- Small town, first love, second chance romance

Book 3: Sweet Redemption (Spring 2025)
- Small town, single parent, age gap romance

Book 4: Sweet Deception (Summer 2025)
- Small town, single parent, age gap romance

About the Author
Danika Rose Lynn

Sugar, spice, and words that entice

Danika does more than write: she creates magic through words, imagery, and total reader immersion. She is an author, an artist, a software developer, a neurodivergent with ADHD, an autoimmune warrior, a wife, a dreamer, a brat, and a total geek. When not dreaming up new stories, Danika can be found either painting, curled up with a good book–or her hubby and her dogs–or having spirited debates with make-believe characters.